PINOCCHIO'S NOSE

Books by Jerome Charyn

ONCE UPON A DROSHKY
ON THE DARKENING GREEN
THE MAN WHO GREW YOUNGER
GOING TO JERUSALEM
AMERICAN SCRAPBOOK
EISENHOWER, MY EISENHOWER
THE TAR BABY
BLUE EYES
MARILYN THE WILD
THE EDUCATION OF PATRICK SILVER
THE FRANKLIN SCARE
SECRET ISAAC
THE SEVENTH BABE
THE CATFISH MAN
DARLIN' BILL
PANNA MARIA
PINOCCHIO'S NOSE

PINOC-CHIO'S NOSE

by
JEROME CHARYN

ARBOR HOUSE

New York

Library of Congress Catalogue Card Number: 80-70214

ISBN: 0-87795-438-0

Manufactured in the United States of America

10 9 8 7 6 5 4 3 2 1

This book is printed on acid free paper. The paper in this book meets the guidelines for permanence and durability of the Committee on Production Guidelines for Book Longevity of the Council on Library Resources.

Portions of this book first appeared in *Le Monde* and *Le Nouvel Observateur*.

THIS BOOK IS FOR LIONEL AND BATHSHEBA

I would like to thank the John Simon Guggenheim Memorial Foundation for its generous support during the writing of <u>Pinocchio's Nose</u>.

AUTHOR'S AFFIDAVIT

I, Jerome Copernicus Charyn, solemnly swear that I am sound in the head. I reside in the country of Texas. I have no children. This is the story of how I became a wooden boy. It's no trip through the Looking Glass. I'm not shrinking Alice, and I have no mad hatters on my list. If you're expecting a keeper to appear on these pages, forget about it. I can't provide you with pictures from an institution. There is no institution. I am who I am. Full grown, with a VISA card in my pocket and an account at the Pecos National Bank.

Like you, I had mother and father, but they've been lost to me. Bathsheba was a jailbird who loved to cook chicken Kiev. My father Bruno left her for another woman. Bathsheba's baby brother, Lionel the millionaire, became like a dad to me, a vengeful dad. But I wouldn't have had a scribbler's career without him. He read all the classics while he sold protection in the Bronx. Uncle Lionel perished of sadness in a psychiatric wing, but I walked away from his own jagged time to become Pinocchio. Pinocchio was my survival kit. He was also the accident of authorship. There would have been no Pinocchio for me if I hadn't stumbled upon Kafka, Melville, Proust in the public library and declared myself a writer around the age of ten.

—Copernicus Charyn

ONE

BRUNY THE RAG

BATHSHEBA'S face.

Red under ropes of black hair.

Her nostrils suck in and out.

Lionel's purple hands peek from her dress.

My uncle and my mother getting smothered by a man.

It's the first memory I have. I was in that scratchy forest between three and four. I took giant steps wherever I went. Somebody stole Bathsheba. The man who'd been smothering her touched his forehead with a handkerchief. My father Bruno arrived. He argued with the man and made a trick. He could reach in and pull money out of himself.

It took me years to unravel that afternoon when Bathsheba vanished and my father was a money tree. I had to hunt out the witch that's behind every story. The witch sits and laughs, while you slave your ass off.

My father was a junkman who mocked the fixtures of his trade. He

11

would have nothing to do with horses, mules, and motor engines. He carted rags in a broken truck. He'd begin in the truck's steep heart and layer rags up to the roofs. No one but my father could have kept the rags from falling. He'd lash himself to the truck and pull.

Families would hunker on a stoop and watch for that vertical caravan. Bruno was better than a movie ticket. He'd drift deep into the Bronx, disappear, until everybody believed the rags had swallowed him, and then a dirty red mountain would bump along the roofs of the next block. Children would shout, "Bruny the rag."

My mother wouldn't follow the traces of his caravan. Bathsheba had her own business. She was a purveyor of stolen merchandise when she wasn't preparing chicken Kiev and cleaning the house. Her career had blossomed with my baby carriage. She could hide swag under the blankets and in the hull. That hull warehoused her baby brother whenever Lionel was wanted by the police. Bathsheba would roam Southern Boulevard with me in the bow and Lionel in the belly of the carriage.

She would have sentenced me to that carriage for life if shopkeepers hadn't told her I was big enough to walk. But Lionel remained in the hull. That's why his hands were purple. He had poor circulation from his time as a submarine.

Once she wheeled the carriage into a shop, Bathsheba could chat with her hands on the counter and give Lionel a chance to drop down from the bottom of the hull. "Hey look at my Jerome . . . smart as a professor. Would you believe that he comes from a junkman? His papa goes around the world with a fleet of rags."

A milliner on Southern Boulevard, Percival Newgarden, saw around her constant chatter. My mother had been shielding Lionel with her rump, directing him into the milliner's blind spots, so uncle could stuff silky things under his shirt. And where was I? A puppet at three and a half, dancing for a milliner on my mother's string.

Percival broke that string. He lifted the counter shelf, called me a little worm, and went for Lionel's throat. And that's when uncle climbed inside Bathsheba. He burrowed up her dress while my mother wrestled with Percival Newgarden.

Men and women marched in and out of the shop, begging the milliner not to strangle my mother. But none of them thought to take

Percival by the coat and pull him off Bathsheba. And so my memory begins. I woke up out of whatever sleep I was in and fell onto the junkpile of human history. It was terror that got me going. Bathsheba's red face trying to suck air while the milliner held her down. And uncle reversed my historical process: he abandoned that moment in the milliner's shop, crawled out of time and into my mother's dress.

The rest is humdrum.

Cops arrive. They appeal to Newgarden, drag Lionel out of Bathsheba. Her dress tears with the strain of so much pulling. Bathsheba has to cover her tits.

The cops keep shaking silks out of Lionel. They gather up this evidence, handcuff Lionel to the milliner's sink, and start their interviews. They scribble in black notebooks as the store fills with merchants who condemn Bathsheba. My mother closes her bodice with a safety pin. The cops loosen Lionel from the sink and walk him and my mother out of the store.

I'm forgotten in that hubbub. No one interviewed me. I could have screamed and made demands on my mother and the cops. But I held to the dark side of the store, around the fitting closets. I hug myself in the shadows and hear Southern Boulevard congratulate Newgarden and call my mother the ragman's wife. I move to the deepest part of the dark.

Newgarden takes a cup of Holland gin. He does a victory dance, and then he sniffs the dark and discovers me.

"Carriage boy, where's your tongue?"

His face is in a swollen fury.

"Does your mamma give out licenses to steal?"

He stoops over me, a balding furnace with suspenders that can breathe, sits me on his counter, and offers me a drink.

I bite his paper cup and I'm rewarded with a moustache of Holland gin. I can't remember Bathsheba, Lionel, or the baby carriage. I belong to Percival Newgarden. I was conceived in a millinery shop.

And just when I'm getting comfortable, a face appears in the window. Bruny the rag. My father sends the gin out of my hand with one digging knuckle. He talks to Newgarden and changes into a money tree . . . he was wearing a junkman's vest, which had to serve as a cash register while he was on the road. He reached into his line of pockets and pulled out dollar bills.

"Does that pay for the damages," he said, "and the time you lost on Bathsheba?"

Newgarden wouldn't touch the bills in my father's hand. Bruno went deeper into his pockets.

"No, no," Newgarden said. "It's not a question of money. The Bible says, forgive a mother, lest you make an orphan of her son. And I would forgive. She's learned her lesson. She won't rampage on Southern Boulevard. But what would stop her from going into a second neighborhood?"

"I will," Bruno said.

"You should have stopped her before."

Newgarden wanted to give me a piece of silk. Bruno hurled it back at him and shoved me into the street. His wagon stood in the gutter with its harness hanging out. My father was at the beginning of a hunt. The rags were only two stories high. He sat me down on the truck's wooden lip, a pint of whiskey in his back pocket, harnessed himself, and heaved me out across the trolley tracks and over Southern Boulevard, Bruny the rag and his boy.

Uncle had become a boarder at the children's jail on Valentine Avenue. It wasn't a scummy old barn sitting in the street. The jail had its own hill. The steps were too high for a pisser of three and a half, and Bruno carried me on his neck up to the jailhouse.

My father had to empty his pockets while a matron explored his cuffs. She was the countess of sucking candy, with dozens of dirty, cracked jars behind her desk.

The matron brought Lionel to us. His shirt and pants were prison green, his suspenders made of skipping rope. He must have been

Valentine Avenue's oldest pupil. His pants came to an end inches below the knee, like unwanted knickers.

The matron returned to her jars of sucking candy and left us alone with Lionel. My father didn't mention Percival's silks. He kissed Lionel on the nose.

"Newgarden is a tough customer. He swears you and Bathsheba assaulted him. He has witnesses on his side. And the courts prefer him to a junkman who doesn't have a store. But I'm not a charity case. A store with a fixed address is no advantage in my line. A junkman gets to see the world. I know how to grease a judge. You have to go under the table."

"Will you go under the table this week?" Lionel asked him and started to cry. "I want my bed."

He didn't have a bed. He shared a mattress with me. It was only later that Bruno added sideboards and a spring, so the mattress wouldn't have to live on the floor and provide a fancy pocket for mice.

Uncle was fourteen, but that didn't stop my father from clutching Lionel's calves and lifting him up to the ceiling in a Russian embrace. Lionel pretended to walk on the ceiling with his hands. He didn't seem so disappointed up there.

Bruno held him until the cords in his throat began to jump with vicious red worms. And when Lionel landed, it was as if he'd come from a different weather zone.

My father knocked on the door, and the countess of candy arrived. He had the cunning of a man who could build rag mountains. He softened the countess with his stock of dollar bills so she wouldn't confuse my uncle with other children. Then he dragged me down the hill of steps and we got on the trolley that went to Bathsheba. Her jail didn't have sucking candy. The matrons wore men's shirts. Rings of keys sat like skulls around their middles. Bruno couldn't have softened such women. They were outside the pale of his money tree.

Bathsheba wore the ripped bodice she'd been arrested in. The jail wouldn't give us a private room. My mother stood behind a special screen with other lady prisoners. My father hunkered over Bathsheba on his side of that long wire box.

"Will you give up that unbearable occupation and be my wife?"

My mother's eyes were at the screen. Her face had a golden shiver between the wires. "I am your wife."

"Not when you steal."

"But darling Bruno," she said with her teeth. "We were so poor. I had to depend on my income."

I felt the heat at the back of my father's head. No one could enrage him like Bathsheba.

"Don't mingle your history and mine. I never failed you. I'm the junkman. I provide for my wife."

"Yes, shoes and hats from China, medieval underwear."

"I could buy new," my father said. "But the old styles are more classical, Bathsheba. They won't begin to stink in a year, like a sad kettle of fish."

"That's a fine philosophy, Bruno, but I'm not your museum that you can cloak with rags out of the corner."

She pointed to the safety pin in her bodice. "The old styles don't have buttons where they ought to."

They'd been arguing that way since they'd met at a Hunter College dance. Bruno was a dropout from C.C.N.Y. He'd studied Spinoza, Hume, Descartes, and he could provide discourses on matter, spirit, and the mind's mechanical laws. But he couldn't turn matter and spirit into bread.

Bathsheba worked fifteen hours a day at a fruit stand to support her baby brother. Her father, Leo Copernicus, was an M.D. out of Odessa whose practice had failed. Her mother took to bed on account of a doctor husband who hated to collect fees. Both of them died on Bathsheba. And she'd gone dancing to meet a college boy with good sense, someone she could marry. Bachelors of arts and sciences proposed to her on the waxed floor. Masters in accounting couldn't live without her black hair. But the only boy that appealed to Bathsheba was the philosopher prince. He was like Leo Copernicus, with his contempt for marketplaces. Bruno's dad was also from Odessa. My father-to-be was famous in his section of the Bronx. He could carry a horse on his shoulders, rip a telephone book while reciting from Descartes. Bathsheba danced with him once and ran out of the Hunter

College gym. She didn't want a philosopher without clean pants. She'd had enough poverty with Leo Copernicus.

Bathsheba tumbled from job to job. Salesmen bought her flowers. She wouldn't sleep with them. She had this wayward dream of love: she'd give herself to the first philosopher with clean pants. She lost her apartment on Attorney Street waiting for such a man. She whored with a married grocer to help feed Lionel. Bathsheba asked herself: why not become a whore with a marriage license? More men proposed. She moved uptown to the Bronx.

Bathsheba considered drowning Lionel and herself. But the tub she had was too small. It was in this condition that she met my father again. He happened to knock her down with his caravan. Bruno had risen in the world, graduated from carrying horses to being a horse himself. And he was dreaming while he played the horse and forgot to squeeze the bulb of his horn. He recognized Bathsheba from the ground. My mother saw it as the worst of fates: discovering a junkman in the streets. She picked herself up and proposed to him. I got born out of that junket and had to watch my mother through a wicked screen at the women's jail.

"Darling Bruno, aren't we both dealers in rags?"

"My rags are legitimate. They don't come from behind somebody's counter."

"Of course not. You pull them out of old men's estates. I rob the living, and you rob the dead."

My father's throat began to quiver. Standing at the screen he did look like a powerful horse doing an angry waltz on his hind legs. "Quiet. You'll poison the boy. I slave, and you call me thief."

"He can't understand our subtle charm, Bruno. He's up from the cradle. Only three."

"He understands," my father said. "I'll take him from you, Bathsheba, if you invite him on one more safari."

"My lord Moses, you'll take nothing but your junkcart, and I'll put a lien on that if you try to bully me out of my son. I'll tell them at criminal court how you abandoned us for weeks at a time."

Bruno knocked on his chest. "Abandoned? I was out buying job lots of rags. I couldn't pick the hours to buy. A junkman has to suffer."

"And where did you sleep, my sufferer?"

"In the truck."

"Under a rag carpet, I suppose. With or without your hussies?"

"Why do you manufacture filth in front of the boy?"

"Because I'm a manufacturer at heart. You're so righteous, Bruno. You pull your monster wagon and scorn the world. One day your rags will reach to paradise and you'll scream at God, I'm Bruno the philosopher, hullo, hullo."

"You're the philosopher, Bathsheba."

"No. I occupied my brother and my son, took them on safaris while my husband was away."

"To the casbah, where you sold your rotten goods."

The casbah was Charlotte Street, the South Bronx's own black market, two and a half blocks long. At the northern end, near Crotona Park, lived Russian lawyers and doctors, the aristocrats of South Bronx society. This end produced physicists and brokers and tennis stars, like Minna Mongolov, who would have gone into the quarter-finals at Wimbledon one year if she hadn't broken her ankle out on the turf.

But it was the area below the Russian doctors that defined the real Charlotte Street, home of the peddler and the pickpocket, land of stolen goods. Wares were hawked from the fire escapes. Vacuum cleaners, tents, frying pans, live or dead chickens, lovely girls. If you stopped in the shadow of these goods, a barker would leap out at you and recite from a list of merchandise on his cuff, jacking his prices if he smelled a hungry man. That was Charlotte Street's agenda, buy and sell, sell and buy.

"Swear on your brother's life," Bruno said, his shoulders rocking at the borders of the screen, "that you'll quit the casbah."

"Don't dictate to me, darling Bruno. Junkmen have their casbahs too."

"Hold your tongue, or I'll leave you to rot in jail."

"It won't be the worst home I've had," my mother said.

Bruno clutched my hand. "Say goodbye to your mother . . . we're going."

He dragged me from the vicinity of the screen. I kept looking at Bathsheba.

"Bruno . . ."

My father shoved me back into my mother's territories.

"What about Lionel?" she asked.

"He'll rot, same as you."

Bathsheba's body shivered. I heard a brutal sound, as if she had a whip somewhere in her bodice that ordered her not to sigh.

"Bruno, please don't take your vengeance out on my brother."

"Vengeance, Bathsheba? He's a truant and a thief."

"And if I give up all my safaris?"

Bruno stared into the screen. "You'd lie to save your brother's skin."

"Bruno, I haven't lied."

The whip seemed to plunge in her bodice. Her shoulders dropped. Her black hair fell onto her face like an eyepatch. She was beyond the art of crying.

"I'll be your wife," she said.

"No casbahs and no baby carriages?"

"Dear Bruno, I'll write it in blood."

"I believe you," my father said. And for the second time I was dragged from Bathsheba. I had to peek at my mother from the neighborhood of my father's thighs. She'd grown enormous, like a smiling balloon pocked by a prison screen.

The jail returned her to us in a week, and my mother took on all the obligations of a junkman's wife. She wore the old clothes my father loved to buy, with velvet bodices that didn't button right. She kept her promise to Bruno and shunned Charlotte Street. She shopped at Newgarden's, learned to pay with my father's cash. She cooked chicken

Kiev, taught me to sew and spell. She wouldn't reminisce about our time with the baby carriage. She led me to Pinocchio, sang about him in abbreviated form, since my vocabulary was small.

Long ago there lived a piece of wood that knew how to talk; this piece of wood was dying to have arms and legs, so he crept along as quietly as a piece of wood can creep and shouted into the window of an old baker, "Geppetto, my dear, will you put me in your oven and make a nice pie out of me?"

—*No pies, my darling dears.*
That was Lionel. He liked to interrupt Bathsheba in the middle of a story. He had little else to do. He'd spent six months in children's jail. Bathsheba blamed my father, insisting that a junkman should have had more pull, but Lionel never spoke about that boardinghouse on the hill. He would sneak off to the casbah and visit the girls.

And my father? He left our family after a few years. Kasha on the table didn't make a marriage. He must have wanted something beyond civility and chicken Kiev. Bathsheba wouldn't fight with him after Lionel got out of jail. He'd provoke her, drink from his whiskey bottle, yell at Lionel, yell at me, and she'd offer him that prison smile, big enough to eat a baby carriage.

He hit her once or twice. She'd wipe the blood with a finger, without giving up the smile. He went to live with a furrier's widow on Crotona Park East. He'd leave packets of money on our doorstep, and then he died. We didn't starve. Lionel went out into the street and became a millionaire.

I grew up, graduated from Pinocchio to James Joyce, and taught at the Bronx High School of Science. I talked to Herman Melville's ghost. He begged me to write a novel. I did. I left Bronx Science and began to lecture on the art of writing novels.

I was eight the last time I saw Bruno. He'd been gone a year. Broke with us, divorced his family. I wasn't allowed to mention him by name at home. He'd become the man who went to live on Crotona Park East. But he was always Bruny the rag to me.

I was coming from school in a yellow forage cap when he appeared with his harness and his truck. Bruno must have fallen out of grace with himself. His eyes were tiny and red. The jersey he wore, his summer and winter uniform, was broken at the sleeves. His elbows were full of a rough, peeling bark. He had his whiskey bottle, but he didn't linger in the harness.

Bruno reached out and tossed me onto the rags without breaking the motion of his truck. I settled in half a story over his head.

"How's Bathsheba?"

"She wants to go to college, dad, and become a medical person, like her father."

"She has ambition, your mother, I'll say that."

It's hard talking to the back of your father's head. I had to imagine the look he had from the way he wiggled his ears.

"Dad, can I meet your new wife?"

His ears wiggled a long time. "I don't have a new wife. What I have is an understanding with a widow who prefers my company to other men."

"Mamma says you gave up the rag trade."

"I did."

"Then why are you pulling, dad? The widow is rich."

He stopped the caravan for just about a second, and it was like being caught in some crazy syntax. I was suspended there, alone, inside a different clock from Bruno's, until he started up the caravan.

"Rich, rich, rich," I heard from the smoke in his head. I put a mouth in the middle of his skull, and I felt better, thinking I could talk to that mouth, but it was more like a piece of merchandise. I squeezed it out of my eyes and went on listening to the back of his head.

"The widow's rich is her rich. I live with her for other reasons. We both like Chopin. Your mother's a savage. She wouldn't let music into the house."

My father was running wild in the street. He chased his own caravan, like a dog at its tail. I heaved from side to side, bundling up with my father's rags. He wouldn't hold back his caravan for trolley cars, children, or pregnant wives. Everything had to make way for Bruny the rag.

Then the storm was over. We clopped along the pavement with the stutter of my father's boots. The bark on his elbows seemed black. His head wheezed.

"You in the haystack," he said, without looking back. "Want to come and live with Bruno for a week?"

My tongue traveled into the hollow of my mouth and started to say yes. But it stopped in the middle, while I calculated in my yellow hat. If I went with my father, I might lose my place with Lionel and Bathsheba. And suppose the widow didn't take to me? I wasn't Chopin.

"I'll have to ask Bathsheba."

The horse's ears wiggled once. The harness curled behind him. I lay in the rags.

Bruno stopped the caravan on Charlotte Street. Women with blue bandannas on their chests clucked at us from the fire escapes.

"Darlings, honey boys, come upstairs to mamma . . . ragman, bring the little toad."

Bruno swerved in the harness and stood over me. He'd grown younger on his ride. The red eyes were gone. They were clear as bandanna blue.

He signaled to me, and I dropped from the rags into Bruno's arms. He held me there, like a big cradle child, and his elbows seemed softer than bark.

He put me down, rubbed my ears, tightened the harness at his hips, and pulled the caravan into Charlotte Street. The casbah turned dark from sidewalk to roof as the caravan passed each station of the street. Peddlers, pickpockets, chickens, ducks, bandannas went into eclipse.

Bruno arrived at the doctors and lawyers' domain, near Crotona Park, and I stroked the yellow hat, wondering why he'd brought me into the casbah when he'd made my mother promise to renounce all of Charlotte Street.

One of the women from the fire escapes spilled out of her bandanna and I saw the two eyes on her chest. They were round and rosy red. She cupped the eyes in her hands and pretended they could talk.

"Come up and have a conference, little toad."

The women around her laughed, but I could feel that croaking out of her chest.

It was a wiser voice than my mother's or father's.

The junkman wasn't trying to convince me of his power over Charlotte Street. Stopping here was a signal of regret. He liked my mother better with the baby carriage.

The woman on the fire escape began to grind her hips.

"Oh sweet little toad, come to mamma."

Her bandanna moved upstairs when the woman saw she couldn't have me. My father crossed the street with his caravan. I fiddled with my cap and walked home to Bathsheba.

TWO

PINOCCHIO'S NOSE

CHARYN, JEROME COPERNICUS, author, educator, magician; b. Bronx, N.Y., May 13, 1937; son of Bruno and Bathsheba Charyn; educated at public schools of Manhattan and the Bronx, Columbia University, and Magicians College of Long Island. Author: *Blue Eyes over Miami.* Former shill in a baby carriage, night watchman, English teacher, Bronx High School of Science. Has lectured at Bowling Green, Marquette, University of Wisconsin at Whitewater, Old Dominion, Agnes Scott, Kutztown State, and ten other institutions.

Once you ride in a caravan, you can't sit still.

I'm the warrior teacher who's gone from university to university, chasing Herman Melville's tail and demanding works of genius from my students. Moby Dick in New Haven. Corpus Christi and the Confidence Man. The San Diego Chargers meet Billy Budd.

27

Wouldn't allow exercises in my class. We went for the whale. My students had to strike under the belly fat, harpoon the bowels of pure form.

The San Diego Chargers lost and won without Billy Budd, and I'd drag my carcass home to Jane Street in the little country of Manhattan, with Moby Dick in my pocket and the Portable James Joyce. There's no market for aging Herman Melvilles. Publishers didn't want novels about harpooning in the Bronx. They hardly wanted novels at all.

Went to my Syrian grocer, whom I hadn't paid in a month. Have to soften Harold, remind him of our love for sea novels: *Treasure Island, Anna Karenina, Peter Pan.* Harold has an Oxford education. There was nothing for him to do in the British Isles. He sold pita bread near the London docks and scribbled poetry on slices of cardboard ripped from an egg crate until he was knocked in the head by a gang of wogs who resented his poetry, his college neckties, and the white man's tobacco he chewed with his nose. Harold reached America and borrowed enough coin to open his store. Now he sells pita behind a window grille.

"Harold, I'm a late bloomer. Cervantes didn't get started until he was fifty-five."

"Your uncle paid the bill."

"Lionel was here? You told uncle about my debts?"

"Your mother sent him. She was worried about you. I couldn't lie."

"Harold, did you have to count my tuna fish in public?"

"Come off it," he said. "We all work for Lionel."

He handed me an envelope marked *Copernicus.* The envelope had a hundred dollars.

Harold wouldn't take it back. "He'll kill me, your bloody uncle will."

I marched down past Sixth Avenue with a boiling hunger near my heart. Had to put Lionel straight. Spent thirty-five years with Copernicus in one room. He used my fucking toothbrush. Even when he got his millions, he brushed his teeth in my debris.

Lionel has his own dominion on Washington Square. He occupies the tower of a giant marshmallow made of red brick. You can't approach Lionel through a common elevator. You have to get off the building's elevator bank, hike around a bending window, and negotiate the rest of your trip on uncle's private elevator, for which I had the key.

Lionel's our Louis Quatorze. He has sunbursts painted on the ceiling of his elevator car to remind you where the sun king lives. I rode up to Louis Quatorze's tower. The landing was crowded with poor relations, distant cousins from my mother's side of the house who'd come to eat chicken Kiev and caviar. I had to knife my way through their bodies. I grabbed a charlotte russe off a chiffonier, nibbled under the crown of whipped cream, and pinched the cardboard battlement that held the cake in one piece.

But I didn't have time to finish. Uncle grabbed me by the arm.

"Shakespeare, why don't you visit mamma? You wouldn't be alive without Bathsheba."

He led me down a flight to his playroom, where my little cousins had been put so they couldn't disturb the grown-ups in uncle's family circus. It was a crib with rocking horses, tunnels, and dry moats. The girls had seized the rocking horses, and the whole giant crib swayed under their influence.

"Kiddies, come and meet the storyteller, Jerome."

My little cousins looked upon me as less than human. I was their servant, the storyteller. The girls left the rocking horses, and Lionel abandoned me. I had to produce.

I began the story of a Bronx Pinocchio, sprung from the ribs of a baby carriage. No puppet could have thrived on Crotona Park, so I went into flesh right away. Pinocchio's human name was Copernicus Charyn. I left Bruno out of the picture. Why complicate things with a dad who didn't participate in Pinocchio's birth?

My little cousins, Pinocchio belonged to your uncle Lionel and aunt Bathsheba. Bathsheba was mother *and* godmother to him. When he lied to her, his nose would thicken until he couldn't carry it through the door. It became a camping spot for pigeons. Peddlers stood under Pinocchio's window with the idea of turning his nose into firewood.

He begged Bathsheba to spare him.

"Pinocchio, will you ever lie again?"

"Bathsheba, I'll never lie."
His nose stretched to accommodate five more pigeons.
"I'll do my best," he squeaked.

The children's eyes were closing, and I had to dice up the story.

Housewives admired Pinocchio's nose. A group of them plotted to capture him and waltz his nose under a pillow. Pinocchio had to dodge these housewives and pray that his nose would shrink.

My little cousins laughed at the smut I had introduced. They weren't interested in character or plot. "Tell us about Pinocchio's nose."
"Hold your horses," I said. But I changed my mind and moved from the extravagance of a children's story to the gray wonderland of my own life. It was 1944. My father was with his widow on Crotona Park East. Lionel was a bushy boy, mingling with traffic in the casbah. My mother was something of a caterer, fixing the kasha and pies of Copernicus for invalids and lonely men. And this Pinocchio was in the second grade. A new girl arrived. She wasn't like any of us, the children of janitors and junkmen. Her name was Belinda Hogg. The kids in my class made fun of Belinda. Her dresses weren't ironed, she had a hole in her shoe, and she wore string in her hair instead of the ribbons that were popular among junkmen's daughters.
Belinda was from Texas, and she could sing arias about something called the Panhandle. It was a piece of country that you could fry potatoes in.
She lived on Charlotte Street.
I followed her home from school. She escaped behind a storefront with the words NOTIONS & NICKNACKS in the window.
"What's a nicknack?" my male cousins asked.
"Stupid," the girls said. "It's your mamma's stomach. Nicknack's where a baby grows."

Madam Andrusov, the nicknack lady, had a bunch of foster children in her care. Belinda was one of them. How did a girl from Texas get to

Charlotte Street? The other brats were orphans with rabbity eyes. They had spindlenecks, terrible dandruff, they sucked their fingers and were gone after a week.

I shut my eyes and knocked on Madam's door. Her Italian bodyguard, known as Morris the Bitter, opened the top lock and stared down at me.

"I'm Copernicus Charyn from Boston Road and I'm looking for a job."

"Shove off, Copernicus Charyn."

But I had a friend in the shadows behind the door. Andrusov had been listening to me and Bitter Morris. She pushed her bodyguard to the side and swooped me off the ground. She was an enormous woman, with the shoulders of a butcher and deep cuts in her face. "Why do you discourage the boy?" she shouted at Morris.

"Sylvia, he could be working for Jennings Street . . . they've sent spies to us before. It won't be the first time."

Andrusov cuffed Bitter Morris on the cheek. His eyes turned black with rage. But he swallowed the blood that was lying in his cheek. And I was caught somewhere in Andrusov's bosom. She smelled of soap and sardine cans. She brushed me off her chest to scold Bitter Morris.

"I don't like my employees to call me anything but Andrusov. And you shouldn't slander the boy. Jennings Street wouldn't shove a dwarf at us. When they come, they'll come with ice picks . . . hey you, Copernicus Charyn, what kind of job do you want?"

"Andrusov, I can sweep."

"I have enough brooms," she said. "Can you take care of an octopus?"

"There are no octopuses in the Bronx."

"He's fresh," she told Bitter Morris. "He thinks the world is between his armpits." She dragged me into the store. We were in some foul, dark place that could have been a home for onions, potatoes, and unwashed flesh. No one bathed in the casbah. That was the truth of Charlotte Street. The soap I'd smelled on Andrusov was probably a charm to warn her when the Jennings Street mob was near.

Soon we were outside again, in Madam's back yard. Andrusov was raising a farm behind the walls of Charlotte Street. She had whole families of hens, turnips, green tomatoes, and an octopus in a barrel. It was Tatiana, a big-eyed girl and Madam's pet. I was hired at twenty cents an hour to groom Tatiana and attend the farm. I combed her body with a streetcleaner's brush and fed her green tomatoes and buckwheat groats. This was a Russian octopus, and she ate what Andrusov ate.

Tatiana had sixteen arms, and if she didn't like you, she'd squirt black ink and hug herself until all of her was arms.

Boys and girls, I had to sneak around my mother to labor for Andrusov. From three to six I was with Tatiana in the yard (Bathsheba thought I was at the library). Then I'd rush to Boston Road and gulp my dinner down.

"Romey, you have feathers on your sleeve."

"It's the pigeons . . . they come into the library and sit on the shelves. What can the librarians do?"

"That library looks to me like a stable," my mother said.

I was back at Andrusov's from eight to nine. I'd sit in the parlor with Madam's gang, shell some peas, and go searching for Belinda. She was in the common room, where all the orphans lived. They had minestrone for their evening meal. Morris was their cook. He'd crush green tomatoes under his toes and prepare a broth for thirty children. Andrusov's brats had pathetic white mouths from the dust they ate with their soup.

I listened hard and learned the ways of Andrusov. She acquired children at bargain rates from kidnappers who worked on commission. Some of the children were feebleminded. Others were simply out of luck. They didn't remain long in the casbah. Andrusov sold them to couples who were desperate for a child, older husbands and wives who'd been turned down by adoption agencies or were put on some horrible waiting list. So they went to Andrusov.

I'd catch Belinda sitting in the dark, soothing the children around her. "Leonard, you behave now . . . Myron, Andrusov will get you the best mother she can . . . shame on you, Rhoda. Did you pee in your pants?"

A woman crept out at us. Andrusov. She was more secretive than an octopus. And she would glide from corner to corner, her heavy body in shadow most of the time.

"Back to the parlor, Copernicus Charyn. Leave my family alone." She was drunk. Her eyes were the color of Tatiana's barrel: dirty green. She had her own distillery. Madam pickled potatoes in underground tubs. She was a vodka merchant as well as a dealer in secondhand boys and girls.

I'd have grown old in Andrusov's parlor, waiting on Tatiana, mingling with each new crop of brats, but Jennings Street bribed one of Madam's lookouts, scrambled down from the roof and murdered Tatiana with their ice picks, leaving her buried in her own black juice.

Nobody would tell me what the killing was about. Andrusov mined potatoes and Jennings Street had a monopoly on all the sour pickles in the Bronx. Why should potatoes and pickles be at war?

Madam sat two nights near her dead octopus in the barrel.

"Tati," she said. "Why did they butcher such a helpless girl?"

She blew her nose with a handkerchief that was an old bath towel and walked to Jennings Street at the bottom of the hill. She turned over twenty-five pickle barrels, shoving heads into the brine, she tore out the scalps of pickle men, she smashed their gold teeth.

"Tatiana," she said.

"Andrusov," the pickle men screamed. "We'll get you another octopus."

She overturned ten more barrels.

"My Tati can't be replaced."

"We'll build her the finest monument . . . in the borough of Queens."

"Croak with your monuments. I put her to bed in Charlotte Street."

The news began to circulate, even while she stood around the pickle men in her summer shawl. "Hah," the wisest crones said, "Andrusov broke the pickle monopoly. Andrusov's our queen."

The queen trudged up the hill and consoled herself with a charlottka, the Bronx charlotte russe, a tower of sponge cake with almond windows and whipped cream tiers. Andrusov swallowed the tower in her grief, windows and all. You could tell how unhappy she was. She talked politics with Bitter Morris, who was a follower of Mussolini and his Blackshirts.

These Blackshirts were the bad boys of Italy. They forced communists and socialists to live on castor oil, which was a good thing in Morris' eyes, because if communism took over the world, there would never be a Charlotte Street. You'd have casbahs with government inspectors, pickpockets who worked for the United States . . . Andrusov was a Bolshevik. The storing up of money made your soul stink in her opinion.

"She's no hero," the children said. "Didn't she buy and sell boys and girls?"

"Andrusov had to provide for her old age."

There must have been some rum in her charlottka. She had a fight with Bitter Morris, calling him the tool of Jennings Street.

"Madam, why do you wound me? I hate the pickle men."

"But you're part of their crowd," she said. "Those swine are friends of Mussolini."

"How can you say that? The Duce wouldn't have murdered an octopus. They're gangsters, the pickle men."

"And so is Mussolini."

She went off to her vodka tubs, queen and pirate lady, fierce, independent, and alone.

The ice-pick men visited with her while we were at school. I returned with Belinda and the brats to a storefront that was much too quiet. I realized something was afoot after I opened the door. There was an absence in that blue air, palpable as a cockroach. I couldn't smell Morris' soup.

We put the children out to play in the yard. Then we walked into Madam's bedroom. She was lying with Bitter Morris. Both had ice picks dug into that hill between their eyes. Jennings Street had killed them without the least bit of struggle. There was nothing but a slight plunge at the corners of Morris' mouth, like the start of a cry that was never allowed to finish itself.

We waited for Madam's allies to come. Somehow her henchmen were scarce. Queen and pirate lady. All she had was us.

We wrapped Morris and the dead queen in blankets and dragged them out to the yard. We picked a grave next to where Tatiana was lying. We couldn't find a shovel. We had to dig with spoons and forks. Thirty of us scratched in the yard around Andrusov's chickens and the corpses we had.

We were spotted from the roof.

No one mourned Bitter Morris and the pirate lady. Charlotte Street was much too practical for that. The dead can't protect the living. The casbah surrendered to Jennings Street. Pickles and potatoes were in the same pocket.

Andrusov didn't get to sleep with Tatiana. The pickle men buried her and Morris in another borough. And the casbah assumed the business of selling off Madam's brats. They were gone in a few hours. Pinocchio went with them. I had no choice. I looked like a secondhand boy. That was enough.

A truck hauled us away. Charlotte Street hired a moving man and pirates to be our guides. It was a short haul to the edge of Crotona Park: a rendezvous point for buyers to come into the truck and handpick their merchandise. These were only middlemen. They had moms and dads in mind who would take the best of Andrusov's crop. There weren't a lot of babies around in 1944. Soldiers were fighting, and women were in the factories. That's why Andrusov had reigned with the children she had.

I pleaded with the buyers. "Take all of us . . . we're one family."

The pirates told me to shut up.

Belinda was the first to go. Every middleman wanted her. They bickered at the rear of the truck. They shoved and had their own nasty little war.

A bigger commotion started outside the moving van. The pirates were slapped on the head. The middlemen hid behind the children they were going to peddle. A face I knew appeared in the truck. It was your uncle Lionel. A hurly-burly guy, drinking and whoring, he was in and out of the casbah as often as Pinocchio.

"Lionel, we're hungry . . . Bitter Morris didn't leave us any minestrone."

He slapped me on the mouth. Then he threw me off the van. I lay on the ground until Lionel gathered me up.

"What about Belinda? What about the secondhand boys and girls?"

He tipped me higher on his shoulder and let the kidnappers have their auction in the van.

My cousins didn't seem to care about Andrusov's brats. They were only interested in Lionel. "How did uncle know where you was?"

He learned from Bathsheba. She had the sense to worry when I didn't come home for dinner. She had a throbbing in her calf that told her I'd been swiped somewhere. She took her throbbing calf to her own baby brother, who was about to visit some prostitutes and was taking a bath.

Lionel put on his darkest suit and ran to the casbah on an errand for mom. He purred to one or two girls and discovered there was going to be a children's sale at Crotona Park North. He assembled an army of louts, snatched me from the pirates, and got back into the tub.

"Don't cry," Bathsheba said. "Aren't you glad uncle Lionel found you?"

I told her about the children's sale.

"That's an awful thing," she said, and she pleaded with Lionel to rescue the brats.

"Where will we put them? In Romey's pocket?"

My mother wouldn't allow practical matters to get in her way. "Lionel, bring me those poor children. Then we'll argue where to put."

Her baby brother rose out of his tub a second time and galloped to Crotona Park North. But the pirates had fled in their van. There wasn't a trace of Belinda.

Did I expect an ensemble of handkerchiefs, tears in my cousins' eyes? No. Not a word for the storyteller and those Bronx streets he'd pressed into their ears. They preferred dry moats to war with the pickle men. My cousins had no place in their brittle hearts for Andrusov. Lionel was their pirate. He plundered without an ice pick and gave them rocking horses under his own roof. But I found a pair of eyes among them that wasn't so obscured. The eyes belonged to Edgar, Lionel's boy. He was my single convert to Pinocchio. The story must have rebounded somewhere inside Edgar. He didn't smirk the way his cousins did. He was a withdrawn child who hadn't learned to grab onto Lionel's coat and bully people. He was the only one who cared about the texture of my story. Edgar was wordblind. He couldn't figure out the clutter of ink on a page. A disaster at school, he existed in his own private holocaust of nonreaders. But Edgar had an ear for details.

"Cousin Jerome, what did it feel like to comb Tatiana with a streetcleaner's brush?"

I started to angle out an answer and create a little compendium of lies. I'd never combed Andrusov's octopus. You can't reach into a barrel with a streetcleaner's brush. The blade is too long. Tatiana cleaned herself. It would have been an imbecile's job to lay unbending bristles on an octopus' soft wet hide. But I had no chance to insert a new brush into the story and manufacture bristles that might adhere to Tati's back.

Lionel interrupted me. He'd been beside the rocking horses all this time. "There was no octopus. Andrusov was a pathetic witch with a millinery shop. She sold buttons out on the street. And her boyfriend, Morris, was an old piss-in-the-pants. They kept their merchandise in a stinking alley between a pickle stand and a kosher bakery. The fat witch stole charlottkas from the baker and helped herself to so many free pickles, the pickle man complained to his brothers down on Jennings Street. That's how the witch got into trouble. It had nothing to do with monopolies and vodka rights. She'd pose as a married couple with Bitter Morris, get her hands on a retarded kid, bribing the commandants of reform schools, churches, shelters, and synagogues in the deep south, where children go for cheap, and she'd peddle them off to widowers and old maids who were hungry to have a child and didn't stop to think that the kid couldn't pronounce his own name."

"Belinda could say Belinda," I yelled into the teeth of Lionel's counterstory.

"There was no Belinda Hogg."

"Go on, sweep away the Panhandle and Pinocchio's nose."

"I don't have to," Lionel said, and my little cousins considered that a great triumph.

"I suppose you didn't rescue me from the moving van?"

"I rescued you, but your moving van was a glorified dump truck."

"And mom didn't send you back for Belinda and those other children?"

"I never went. We had no room for retarded children. You can ask your mother. She didn't really expect me to fetch the brats. It was a way of soothing her Pinocchio . . ."

I dug Lionel's hundred dollars into his fist.

"What's that?"

"Blood," I said. "And the money you've been giving the grocer for my tuna fish. Lionel, keep out of my life."

I loped around the rocking horses, but I wasn't quick enough. Lionel tossed the hundred into the back of my neck. The children grabbed at the money that rained off me. It wasn't so easy to exit from the land of rocking horses. I climbed out of Lionel's crib and recognized my mother's blue hair. What happened to her own strong color, Odessa gray? I wouldn't chat with Bathsheba. The blue hair made her look like a peahen in Louis Quatorze's circus. But that's not why I avoided Bathsheba. She's been Lionel's helpmate all these years, and I'm the left-handed fool that keeps searching for mothers and fathers inside Melville and James Joyce.

Couldn't seem to arrive at the front door. Blame it on Edgar's mamma, my aunt Marie-Pierre. Her eyes could hang on you like an insane web of light. Uncle married the tallest beauty in the Southwest. Marie-Pierre was a Canuck whose daddy had migrated to the Panhandle state. But she was no Belinda, bred in a nicknack shop, around bowls of minestrone.

"Hullo, auntie Pierre," I said. She wore the thinnest crepe, and she was like a breathing skeleton under her gown. The cusp of her belly seemed to shatter with the skin of that material.

"Romey, don't run away. I'd like to hire you."

"Can't," I told her. "Remember what happened the last time I was your teacher?" I whispered, ready to eat the crepe off Marie-Pierre. It's an embarrassment to have an aunt like that.

"Imbecile, I was the baby in your class."

"Some baby. Your father had to put detectives at the gates, or you'd have disappeared with carpenters and insurance salesmen. You concoct bordellos wherever you go."

"Tell me about bordellos. I had enough trouble with you leering at me in the halls."

"Didn't leer. I couldn't let you fall down in grammar and speech. That was my filthy, stinking job."

"Then go on with it . . . help Edgar to read."

"How can I cure Edgar when I'm as blind to words as he is? I have nightmares about printed matter. I'm only good at scanning a blank page. White is my lucky color."

"Keep it that way. Teach him Pinocchio and the octopus. Tatiana will carry him into books."

Had Marie-Pierre stood behind the rocking horses taking notes? I didn't want her hooks in me. I'd end up a nanny to Edgar and Marie's indentured servant, no better than a wooden boy.

I was Moby Dick in shiny pants, octopus and city whale, sixteen arms searching for stories and a ride out of uncle's tower sanctuary. I summoned his private elevator with my key, but it wouldn't come. I tried the fire exit. The luxuries of a brick marshmallow on Washington Square didn't include lightbulbs in the back hall. I had to feel my way down the rough steps like a whore whose services were done. Madam Pinocchia.

I've gone through the casbah, survived ice picks, charlottkas, and pickle diplomacy. I could survive the tower stairs. But I should have kept away from auntie. I was in love with that tall bitch.

She'd been my protégée at Bronx Science. I was the ancient English teacher at thirty-five, living with Lionel and Bathsheba because the Bronx James Joyce couldn't risk his own apartment, and Marie-Pierre was sixteen when she stepped into my class, an exchange student from Austin, Texas.

She'd sit next to teacher Jerome in a cashmere sweater that revealed the imprint of her lungs, and I'd forget the dangling modifiers on the board and jabber about the monkish existence of high art. *Kafka earned seven cents in royalties all his life. Joyce was the biggest leech in Trieste. Proust had to bribe his publisher to keep himself in print.*

"And where would you put yourself, Mr. Jerome Copernicus Charyn?"

That was Marie-Pierre in the front row.

"Me?" I said, trying to manufacture poverty with a squint. "I'm next to Kafka, or I wouldn't be at Bronx Science."

"Then your students are just the rags of your writing career."

Sixteen, and she had her knuckles in my throat.

She'd never met a monk like me, a monk in baggy pants. We didn't exist in Austin, Texas. We were a breed apart, wild folk who'd danced out of the Black Sea, where my grandfather, Leo Copernicus, was born, and traveled to Cleveland, Quebec, Chicago, or the Bronx, in search of something stranger than cold cash. Even my uncle Lionel, who continued to live at home with us after his first, second, and fifth million, was more than a moneygrub. He was a gangster who underlined his Karl Marx. And like an idiot I introduced Marie-Pierre to Lionel and my mom, brought her to a family dinner of kasha and charlotte russes. Lionel was nearing fifty, but he had a camel's-hair coat. That coat was familiar to Marie. It had all the extravagance of central Texas. And my uncle, who was frightened to death of airplanes and swore he'd never fly, got on a plane to Texas and pleaded his case to Marie's dad.

He must have been eloquent in his mad desire. He's my uncle, after all, and the baby of the house. Lionel declared his love and then listed his assets. Factories, warehouses, distilleries, pickle plants. And he meant to have her dad murdered if that man had refused him, because in his own cunning Black Sea heart, uncle decided that an orphan might be simpler to marry. But her dad returned to New York with Lionel and persuaded Marie-Pierre that high school was a foolish business. She must have realized that she couldn't crawl out from under Lionel's passion. Besides, she adored the camel's-hair coat . . .

Lionel captures Marie, and I have to plunge in the dark. Couldn't locate the fire door to the building's own stairwell, under the tower. There were no knobs in the wall, nothing to pull me out of that well. It was as if I'd entered some ancillary world, between Lionel and the street. I couldn't touch ground. I was beyond the range of other human beings. My only purpose was to climb down stairs. It was better than writing novels. I developed a swagger, a musical jerking of the hips. I had all the rhythm I'd ever need. Goodbye Melville, goodbye Moby Dick.

I started to blubber after a mile of walking like that. I wasn't lonely for Lionel and the rest of that rag-tail clan in the tower. I'll have no more uncles or mothers in my dominion. I'll have slugs and snails that inhabit dark wet walls. I'll have titmice and baby crocodiles. All the lesser creatures, beasties that can't harm you with a corrosive sound or the lack of a smile. But it was humans that I missed, their silly, leering faces and pudgy fists.

"Romey."

A fist wormed out of the dark, clutching a pocket torch with a blinking yellow eye. I hadn't lost my powers. I could smell my mother's moisturizer and skin cream.

"Bathsheba, did I ask you to come into my well?"

"If I waited for an invitation from you, we'd both be dead."

"Mamma, I can ferry myself to the ground floor."

"That's what you say. The staircase is defunct. Lionel uses it as a storage bin."

She took me out of the well with her electric torch. And I had dreams of stuffing Bathsheba's mouth with strands of blue hair. Because I'm sure my mother used to bribe me with her milk. When I was bad, she took me off the tit. Bathsheba didn't have time for me. She was plotting her brother's career. And if I was good and didn't cry, she'd shove me into her blouse and let me suck a little. But I got more than my father ever did. Bruno was third in line.

Bathsheba loved to complain. "I'm surrounded by Pinocchios," she'd say when I was a boy. But she couldn't have borne the competition of another female in the house. One queen to a family. And my father wasn't much of a king. He could tear out the heart of a telephone book and be his own horse. But he never got his way with Bathsheba. And if he couldn't have Bathsheba's milk, he'd suck on a whiskey bottle, mutter at me with hate in his eye. That was the sound I went to sleep with. He promised to murder me, Lionel, and my mother, and then he went to his widow on Crotona Park East. But he couldn't prosper there. He had a terrific view of the park, and he didn't have to share the widow's nipple with anyone else. My father grew thin. He died in his junk wagon, with whiskey bottles at his feet and a hundred years of rags tucked behind him.

"Romey," my mother says. We've reached the top of the well. She kisses me on the eyebrow, a deep, biting kiss, and opens Lionel's elevator with her key.

I ride to the bottom of the tower and climb aboard the public elevator, free of Lionel and Bathsheba.

I prance into the street without a penny to my name. A cricket is grinding in somebody's windowsill. Fireflies snap against the trees. I think of a dead junkman, my father trapped in a small sea of rags and whiskey bottles. I'd swear he died with the image of my mother's tit somewhere in his head. He couldn't have loved that furrier's widow. Once he'd tasted Bathsheba's milk, he was finished as a man.

THREE

MIZ ALABAM

P

ENNIES for the kid?

I wouldn't sponge off the Syrian, who'd swear his devotion to me and send the bill to Copernicus. Didn't want to be listed in uncle's little black book: Pinocchio's pot cheese, $106.81. So I got in line outside the Dominick Street mission, a souphouse for artists and other bums of lower Manhattan.

Lemuel Rice, the superintendent of Dominick Street, had discovered Jesus while scribbling in a furnished room, and that's why he had an investment in poets, painters, sculptors, and novelists. Lemuel knew we'd never get to paradise without him.

He was a big, brawling character who could go from Jesus to James Joyce, identify every ounce of Scripture in *Finnegans Wake*. We were fools next to Superintendent Rice. He ran Dominick Street like the politburo, cuffing you on the ear if you entered another man's trouser pockets.

45

He had his psalm of the day in the window:

Whosoever lieth with a beast shall surely be put to death.

Was Lemuel going to preach about buggery this afternoon? He sat behind his desk, handing out meal tickets and stopping to interview every second or third sinner. Lemuel wasn't the surly kind. He'd ask about this man's mother, or that man's cat. And if you were a newcomer, he'd ticket you at his own table, so you wouldn't feel alone.

I had to dance a little for Superintendent Rice.

"How's Lionel? Up or down a million?"

What had Dominick Street to do with my uncle? Copernicus wasn't involved with rescue missions.

"Lionel's up this year," I told the Super. "He prospers in the worst of times."

Went with my fellow sinners into the commissary and sat as far from the Super's table as I could. We maundered with our soup spoons. We couldn't even nibble on our fingers until the Super arrived. He came with his microphone, the cord traveling between his legs. His servers, artists who'd given up their craft to sleep at the mission, brought us white wine in a pitcher, soup, and wedges of sponge cake. We had minestrone on Dominick Street. I looked into the bowl and smelled Bitter Morris. Touching that soup would have been like feeding on a corpse. Minestrone meant Tatiana the octopus and other secondhand girls.

Lemuel said grace into the microphone and the sinners sucked their soup. I dug my mouth into the bowl like all the yeggs at my table and swallowed bits of Tati and Belinda. I was hungry, and I couldn't help myself. I had three bowls of soup. I asked the Super's Jesus to punish me, hurl my soul into the devil's sink. Nothing happened. Stuffed myself with sponge cake and asked again. I hogged the table's pitcher of wine. Would have picked the mission clean if Lemuel hadn't announced the meal was over.

"Brothers in Christ, we're at the crossroads this afternoon. Some of you have elected to pass your lives with the idols of the pen, thinking you could weave immortality around yourselves with words. Brothers,

Satan is in that pen. He guides the hand that inks the page. He's in the bowels of your Olivetti, your word processor, your copying machine. The laws of physics belong to him. He's at the bookbindery, in the printing plant. He writes the blurb on your book jacket, prepares the copyright page. Satan's a novelist, and he's a greedy son of a bitch. He wants to reconstruct the world according to his own image. What does he care? It's only ink. And so he spins out lines and lines of romance. He has this craving, you understand, this need to catch the moment by the tail. He's had thousands of years to practice with.

"He's the whore that lay with a blind man, Homer, and while the blind man was asleep, Satan dipped Homer's pizzle in octopus ink and wrote about that philandering sailor, Odysseus, who took the devil's own time returning to his wife. And that, my brothers, was the beginning of this nasty business, the novel. Satan rested a few thousand years, pleased with himself and his design of words. But he's a fornicator and couldn't lie still. He thrust his hateful image into a one-armed Spanish soldier who was in and out of debtor's prison, and we have *Don Quixote* by Satan and Miguel de Cervantes. It's the tale of a hairy boy who isn't smart enough to grow old and die, like everybody else. He picks at people with a lance, lets dangerous convicts escape, and falls in love with a terrible witch. Satan has the idiot ride a horse for fifteen hundred pages. The whole world laughed.

"The whore had his masterpiece. But he could only rest for two hundred years. Satan went into a fury of novel-writing. *Oliver Twist*, *Emma*, *Moby Dick*. Stories, stories, stories, until he fell in with a fat Norman, Gustave Flaubert, and wrote *Madame Bovary*. He was sick of romance. Satan discovered form. He took a dreary woman, Emma Bovary, and cloaked her with high art. And brothers, we've been suffering ever since. Satan and a filthy little Jesuit, James Joyce, built an enormous novel on twenty-four hours in the life of a landlocked Jewish sailor. The whore went full circle, from Homer to Leopold Bloom.

"Where will that stinker go next? He's doomed to begetting masterpieces, like a whore that can never be satisfied with her lot. Satan has to keep on swelling out. And you sinners, you book writers, with your pregnancies of ink, what will you ever find in Satan? One more masterpiece? Is Cervantes happier now, floating with the dead on a barge of a million books? What price *Ulysses*? Fame, brothers? Immortality? Until the next masterpiece comes along."

Lemuel searched the tables with a frown that settled on me.

"Jerome Copernicus Charyn. There's a name to reckon with. The new immortal of Dominick Street."

Must have had too much wine and sponge cake. I blinked and Jesus climbed the wall. His nails were yellow from living so long at the mission. He had lots of wrinkles for a man of thirty-three. His beard ran wild on the ceiling.

I stood up and sent the bowls crashing off the table. "Super, it isn't fair to mock those of us who are down on our luck. If Satan was Cervantes' ghostwriter, that's good enough for me."

"Don't negotiate with the devil, brother Charyn . . . sit down."

And I sat. That was the power the Super had. Jesus slept in the walls and grew long yellow fingernails. The devil didn't have a chance on Dominick Street.

"There's vanity in the pen. I hung on every phrase of Flaubert's until I was Madame Bovery in a cold-water flat, believing the written word was everything. The wind that spilled out of my head made a stuttering song. Satan's sweetheart, looking for the single right word."

"And you, you, you," he said, glancing from table to table, so that everybody seemed included in Lemuel's eye. "Will you go with Satan, ride his carrousel of books? Beware. If you wait too long, there could be no getting off. You'll whirl into hell on a wooden horse. And what will you have accomplished, my Madame Bovarys? Futile work, futile work."

What did I care if the devil wrote *Ulysses*? The music in that novel was like my mother's milk. Something deadly and accurate, that could lull a boy to sleep.

I returned to Jane Street. Lived like a petty bandit, eating Swiss cheese at a restaurant and escaping the cashier. But I couldn't go on the road. The Superintendent had ruined my gig at the universities. I kept seeing Satan in Herman Melville's pants.

I waltzed from restaurant to restaurant for a month, with stops at the mission. Discovered the same faces everywhere. An army of mal-contents, trying to get through 1983.

The landlord broke into my apartment while I was scrounging a meal, changed the lock, and left the following note on my door:

> Dear Tenant,
>   You are now six months in arrears. I am keeping your junk on deposit until the debt is cleared. Meanwhile, please stay out of my building.

Couldn't complain. I'd never bothered with a lease. It was too much like getting married.

Let the landlord chew on all my ancient baggage. I could survive without dictionaries and first drafts. I had James Joyce in my pocket.

Lost my courage after five blocks. I was another one of those malcontents that mobbed the streets. I broke through the line at the rescue mission and pushed my way upstairs to Lemuel Rice's office.

"Super, I'll need a bed ticket tonight."

The Superintendent's frau, Georgina, was with him. They were having their afternoon snack. Georgina was a counselor at the mission. A scrappling girl, younger than Rice, she'd come out of a Bible college, and was known as Alabam.

"The dorm is booked for the night," she said. "You'll have to sleep elsewhere, little son."

The Super bit into his sandwich and looked at me with a sorrowful eye. "Let's make room for Charyn."

Wormed a bed ticket out of the lady before she had a chance to protest. "Thank you, Miz Alabam. I won't betray the Super's confidence in me, or say hello to the devil."

Alabam rose high in her chair. She was a magnificent creature. I could feel her swollen presence under the cotton she wore.

"Get out of my sight," she said.

Alabam's contempt dug at me with a terrible heat. I had spots between my eyes, a double vision. I dreamed of Alabam outside her cotton dress. Blame it on my mother's milk. If Bathsheba had let me and my dad have more of her nipple, he'd be alive and I wouldn't be searching for a bed on Dominick Street.

Went into the lounge and sat with the Super's other overnight guests. They had sunless faces, these sinners without a home. They smoked cigarettes with blue-white fingers that seemed about to break. They didn't mutter to themselves and twitch. These weren't outcasts from the nearest institution. They were forgotten men. They had a pronounced passivity, as if they'd arrived at the edge of the planet and were frightened of being shoved off. My brothers at the mission occupied as little space as they could. It was an attempt to fool themselves into believing they didn't exist.

I wasn't a yegg like that, growing invisible in a lounge that belonged to Jesus. I had a bit of sun on my face. And I could still lust after a lady. No wonder Alabam snarled upstairs in her cotton dress. She was perfectly safe with such yeggs.

It was time for the evening meal. One of the Super's little deacons distributed neckties. Georgina had started the tradition of ties. It was a carry-over from Bible college, where students couldn't taste the Lord's food without some kind of ribbon around their necks. The mission ties were ratty strings that had never been washed. I wore mine down the back of my neck. No one bothered to look.

The Superintendent sat at high table with his wife and his deacons, who were rehabilitated bums. The deacons wore dark blue, like their master and mistress. Alabam had changed into wool for our bums' supper. Tight sleeves made her handsome. Pinocchio nibbled his tie.

We had chicken Kiev.

The Super was absorbed in the dignity of high table, which meant napkin rings and dabs of French mustard for his chosen people, and the bums escaped without a sermon. But we had to stick around until the deacons finished the mustard. They brought us upstairs to the shower room. We undressed, put our shoes and valuables into locker baskets, and the deacons sent our clothes into the delousing room, a sweatbox equipped with its own heater. This room was invented by Rice. Our clothes would bake while we slept, and the deacons could return them in the morning, like leaden pies.

We showered belly to belly in stalls that could accommodate two sinners. I saw the whitest scrotums in the world. Jesus must have been showering with us, because He lent Himself to the mission in mysterious ways. The Lord was stingy and extravagant, depending on the circumstance and the design of things. We had silk pajamas, but the deacons were out of soap. Where had I seen such pajamas before? With soft pockets and a perfect sash. Did Jesus shop at Bloomingdale's? That rich material seemed ghoulish on the men. Dead white bodies wrapped in silk.

We entered the dormitory like wizards from another time who'd outlived their usefulness and their grace and had crumpled into slow clowns. The deacons didn't have a bed for me. They tied a hammock together from old towels and laundry bags and strung it into a corner. Pinocchio had his place.

It was good to sleep with other bodies around and hear that nocturnal coughing. It was a kind of camaraderie, not like being on a mattress with Lionel, who hogged the blankets and kicked out in his dreams. With Lionel you went to bed in a battlefield.

Hervey Long, senior man among the deacons, roused us with shots of water from a plant spray. We had to suffer that mist in the dark. Hervey got the sinners out of bed at a quarter to five. He was a sculptor who'd been saved, and he wanted us to consider Jesus early in the morning. We climbed into the showers again to scrub off the devil's loam, because Satan liked to visit yeggs in their sleep, according to Herve. We scratched our chins with throwaway razors that Hervey supplied. Our clothes had come up from the delousing room. My pants were stiff. The notebook in my pocket had melted rings. The buttons on my shirt were like baby teeth. My Portable James Joyce shed half its spine for Superintendent Rice.

We had our breakfast with the deacons. Alabam came downstairs to eat with us in a housedress that molded her bosoms into deep moons.

The deacons and I watched Alabam butter her toast. Hervey held his cheekbones in one hand. The yeggs blew on their farina without the slightest interest in Alabam. Desire was an exotic bird, outside their narrow country. It took all their strength to finish a meal.

I wasn't on that rodeo circuit. I intended to ride out of Dominick Street fast as I could. But not until I drank a little of Alabam.

I cooed at her from my end of the table. I sang Volga songs about boatmen dying for a woman's heat, songs my mother taught me. But Alabam was deaf. She buttered toast without a thought of Volga boatmen.

She got up, yawned into her handkerchief—Bible ladies didn't show their teeth—and walked from the commissary, while every deacon followed the weave of her underpants.

But Alabam came back to chat with one sinner. Pinocchio.

"The Super would like you to stay on," she said.

"In what capacity? I won't be a deacon, Miz Alabam."

"That's all right. We'll make you our writer in residence."

Had visions of floating into her housedress and hugging Alabam in some dark corner. It wasn't to cuckold Rice. I was fond of the Super, but I had to feel Alabam before I died.

I felt hot mission air and the hump of my hammock. I felt my own hard nuts. The closest I got to Alabam was the far side of her desk. I was her secretary. I took notes while she counseled the men. She was softer and funnier with those sinners than you'd expect from a mission wife. She was compassionate under her voluptuous carriage. If she fancied a sinner, she'd bring him a shirt and a hat. And she awarded bed tickets with complete abandon. She was the patron saint of forgotten men.

I clutched her fingers across the desk one afternoon and told her, "I'm beginning to admire you. I mean, you care about the men. It's more than mission work. You're the good fairy, Miz Alabam."

She let her fingers lie like sleeping squirrels in my fist, but she wasn't a woman who took to compliments. "Fiddle your fairy," she said. "It's my obligation, little son. I'm the Super's lady."

And then she asked me could she have her fingers back, and I said no, because I was like a Volga boatman, hungry for the contact of a woman's skin.

"My husband's behind the wall," she said, pointing to the Super's quarters with her free hand.

"That's no bother, Miz Alabam."

"I could knock you all to pieces if I felt the urge. Now will you give a lady back her hand?"

"Not until you call me Copernicus Charyn."

"Copernicus, Copernicus."

I opened my fist for Alabam.

Could have had a bed in the dormitory, but I preferred my lumpy hammock. It suited a boy searching for an address. Pissed twenty years away as a novelist. But I was coming out of the closet. The little son would find a better toy than books.

I decided to give myself a confirmation party at the mission. It was about time I launched myself into manhood. Pinocchio had never been bar mitzvahed. It was one of the irregularities in the house of Copernicus Charyn. My father had died long before I was thirteen, and I had no one to lead me to prayers. Bathsheba was too involved with her baby brother. She mocked the notion of bar mitzvahs. "It's for sissies," she said.

But I'd seen the scrapbook of Lionel's bar mitzvah. Bathsheba had rented an entire hall. I was two years old on that occasion. It was before my mother wrestled with Percival Newgarden, and I couldn't remember much. But scrapbooks don't lie. The confirmation cake was an enormous charlotte russe with fifteen tiers.

I waved the scrapbook at my mother and pointed to the charlotte russe. "How come it was so important for Lionel to have a bar mitzvah?"

Bathsheba wiped her eyes with a sleeve. It was her favorite trick, blubbering onto her clothes. "You're so unkind. Using a family album as evidence. I wish your father were alive. He'd take the strap to you."

But I had a lawyer's clarity at thirteen. "Bruno wouldn't have bothered with a strap. He left us, Bathsheba. Alive or dead, he belongs to the furrier's widow on Crotona Park East."

It was Bathsheba who took my father's old strap (he'd escaped to Crotona Park without his wardrobe), and worked the buckle into my neck. "Ingrate, your uncle keeps us alive. And what do you know? We were starving on the Lower East Side. Lionel picked rags when he was six and seven. He never had more than ten days of school."

The buckle was eating my neck, but I wouldn't give in. "Then how did Lionel get to be such a good reader?"

"I taught him," she said.

"And did God teach you, mother dear?"

"No. I taught myself."

The buckle went deeper.

Uncle saved my life. He'd come upstairs from one of his shylocking expeditions. He wore purple pants, called whales in the Bronx, because they flared out below the crotch, like a leviathan's body.

He seized the buckle out of my mother's hand. "Bathsheba, can't I leave the two of you together?"

Uncle leaked mercurochrome onto my neck and tried to defuse the war between me and my mother. "I'll be lonely without the kid. I can never go to sleep until he starts to snore."

"Look at Romey," my mother said. "He begrudges his uncle's bar mitzvah. Lionel, tell him what we ate when you were three."

"Cardboard and glue."

"Stolen glue," Bathsheba said. "We lived behind a staircase for a month. That's how poor we were."

The lawyer with the ravaged neck began to interrogate his mother. "Couldn't you get a job, Bathsheba?"

"What job? Where? It was the middle of the Great Depression."

I shut the scrapbook and abandoned the dream of my own enormous charlotte russe. Bathsheba must have felt the bar mitzvah bile go out of me. She took a sudden interest in my neck. "Romey, forgive your mother. I'm sorry I was so mean. We'll bar mitzvah you on your next birthday. You'll appreciate it better."

My fourteenth, fifteenth, sixteenth birthdays passed without notice. But why couldn't I have my bar mitzvah now?

Went to the Super. Told him how I'd missed my manhood. Lem wanted to help, but he was leery of bar mitzvahs. "What will it take?"

"A bottle of wine, a rabbi, and some charlotte russes."

"We're a rescue mission. Can't we skip the rabbi and confirm you on our own?"

"Not a chance," I said. "Super, we were pagans in the Bronx. My father was a junkman. Hebrew never entered the house. I'll need a rabbi to give me Torah lessons."

The Super recommended a Christian rabbi who had his own tabernacle, Jews for Jesus. I wanted an old-fashioned rabbi who could pull me out of that rotten swamp, forty-five years of being a child.

Alabam wouldn't hear of it. There would be no mission bar mitzvahs while she was mistress of Dominick Street. She derided Lemuel and me. "Should we prepare skullcaps for our trustees and all the brothers in Christ? Husband, we'll be out of business in a week."

I withdrew to the dorm, dismantled my hammock, and started to pack. Then I remembered that I had no belongings other than James Joyce and the pants I was in. It was either the mission or the street. I put the hammock together again.

Had to face my enemy, Miz Alabam. I did my secretary work, but I wouldn't clutch her hand. It was no concern of mine that she was the good fairy. Let her go and lie down with yeggs.

Soon as I turned from Alabam, she produced a couple of sparks. She stopped wearing underpants during interviews. Alabama was her own contour map. Could have picked out every bump and crease under her counseling clothes. Once, after an afternoon of yeggs, she told me, "Take off your shirt, Copernicus Charyn. I'd like to see your chest."

"It's nothing special, Miz Alabam . . . except for the birthmark I have, a nipple under my heart."

It was the sign of our house. Uncle also had that third nipple. Did it come from our Tatar cousins, a thousand years ago in the Mongolian steppe? How did Lionel, Bathsheba, Bruno, and I get those Mongol cheeks and dark, dark eyes? We had nothing to do with shtetls. Bath-sheba never lit candles on Friday night. Bruno's only shul was the junkyard. We were big city people, out of the Christian part of Odessa. Both my great-grandfathers were olive merchants. Their father's fathers must have traveled up across the Black Sea from Sevastopol, where the Tatars ruled. There was a conversion somewhere along the line, from the enlightened class of Tatar traders to the backward, stubborn laws of the Jews. Judaism never stuck to the Copernicus Charyns. I have my Tatar nipple.

Alabama climbed onto the desk, crawled over to me, unbuttoned my shirt, and fondled all three nipples. She sucked on the upper ones, and I began to feel like a mamma goat. I grunted out my pleasure. The nipples were erect.

I lifted Alabama's skirt around her hips, saw the tiny blue mission veins on her legs, and started to play with her.

"Not on the desk," she said, her eyes like Volga water, with deep brown spots. "Lem will hear us."

I trusted myself to Alabam. I was a Tatar's boy. I didn't need bar mitzvahs. She led me to the delousing room, which was deserted in the afternoon. Alabam fiddled with the heater, brought the temperature down to a hundred degrees, and undressed the two of us. She was worthy of a Tatar's wife. Her shoulders had a strong, delicious sweep. Her bosoms were two complicated worlds of flesh, with a beautiful dark grave between them, where a man could sink his head and die for half an hour. Her mound was blonder than the rest of Alabam.

The floor was too hot to serve as our cradle. We had to hug and kiss in a standing position. We didn't fumble, or damage each other with our knees. Me and Alabam made a perfect fit. She was the wall that held Pinocchio tight.

I could dream inside Alabam, feel that Charyn sadness go out of my body. Didn't need to lose myself in novel writing. I could taste galaxies with my eyes cloaked in Alabam's chest. I wasn't a goddamn alien, whirling around in a scummy ball that disconnected me from everything. I was the fist inside a flower that never ceased to open. I was Jesus. I was Jerome.

I was a selfish, stinking yegg who took his satisfaction and didn't stop

to think of Alabam. Oh, I could give her pleasure, all right. I had a
Tatar's brutal finesse. But I wasn't into galaxies when we put on our
clothes. We'd obeyed the laws of friction, coupled and come apart. She
was the Super's lady and I was the boy without a bar mitzvah.

One afternoon, while I was in the hothouse with Alabam, I felt a
bitter wind blowing on my back. The wind got worse. Alabam and I
began to broil in our own sweat.

"Somebody switched on the music," she said. "We're getting de-
loused."

I went to the judas hole in the door, slid the panel, and peeked at
that other planet outside the room. Hervey Long was at the controls,
feeding hot air through the ducts over our heads. Herve had the whole
mission as his audience, deacons and yeggs. And the Super.

Tried to put on my clothes.

The touch of material burned my skin. I was trapped in my naked-
ness.

"Alabam, will our eyes melt first?"

"Don't be foolish. The door is open."

I didn't believe her. The Super wouldn't have staged this affair with
an open door.

Alabam walked out of the room. I followed behind her, looking at
the two marvelous dents in her lower back. Men were sloppy bears with
shoulders that didn't match. God must have made us with one purpose,
so we'd pull His wagons until we dropped. But He gave women delicate
pots of flesh that were useless for wagon-pulling.

I held my scrotum, thinking that's where the Super's men would
attack. But I wasn't trifled with. Deacons and yeggs didn't lay their
scummy paws on me. I was the mission's forgotten man.

The Super took Alabam in his arms and rocked her sweetly in front of his men. I was moved by his gentleness.

Shuffled to the dorm in my bare feet and climbed into the hammock, waiting for Herve to expel me from Jesus' house. Herve wouldn't come. I had the dorm to myself. Felt a chill and put on the mission's silk pajamas, tying a great bow with the sash. Jesus was up around the wall with his yellow nails. The Lord had tears in His eyes. He was crying for a yob like me, a sinner under the delusion that telling stories was the same as being alive.

Had a revelation while Jesus hugged the wall. I know now where I'd seen those mission pajamas before. On my uncle Lionel. They were the spoils of a company he'd acquired, a pajama outlet. Lionel was as ruthless as the Viet Cong. He'd gut a company's merchandise, absorb every pajama top, and declare bankruptcy.

I spoke to the ceiling. "Lord, are You in cahoots with my uncle? Because if You are, I'd like to hear about it."

I fell asleep with a turmoil in my head. The hammock started moving. I was some tired boat getting shoved out to sea. I turned shrewd on that swaying hammock. The shover was Copernicus. Uncle had come to give me a ride. He undid the old laundry bags that held my hammock in one piece and I fell to the floor in a bundle of shrouds.

"Lionel, did the devil bring you here to comfort me?"

"Not exactly. The Super had me on the phone."

"Then Dominick Street is one of your toys, and Lemuel is on the board of Copernicus Industries."

"Ridiculous," the uncle said, picking me up out of laundry bags and beach towels and dressing me over my pajamas in charity clothes from the Super's closets. Uncle understood Pinocchio's needs. He'd rescued my Portable James Joyce from the delousing room. But I was wise to him.

"You can't trick an old roommate, Lionel. My pj's come from your barrels. I shouldn't have been so dumb about the chicken Kiev. All the Super's specials are out of Bathsheba's recipe books."

"It's no secret. Mamma helps the mission in her spare time."

"Lionel, there's no listing under help in your little black book. What's Dominick Street doing for you?"

"The Super lends me his deacons now and then."

"Is Herve your medicine man? Does he rail at Jesus over high interest rates?"

"You're in some time warp, kid. I win when the rates are high or low. The deacons take care of my bills."

"Fine," I told the uncle. "Put me on their collection route. I can go into the scrap heap and lie with my father, around old rags."

"Not a chance. You're coming with me."

Did I forget to tell you that Lionel, near to sixty, is a handsome son of a bitch? He never grew much after he stopped living in the hull. That's what happens to former submarines. One shoulder is slightly bent. But it adds to his charm. He's a black-eyed, slouching Paul Newman with a hint of Delmore Schwartz.

"Uncle, I'm staying here."

"The Super doesn't want you, kid. He'd have smacked your brains if you weren't Bathsheba's. He's fond of her. You get through this world on your mother's good graces. You count on that."

"Lionel, I'm not going back to the baby carriage."

"Schmucko, you never left."

"I'll sell toothbrushes on the street. I don't care."

"You'd still be working for me. Street peddlers get their merchandise from my trucks."

"I'll run to another mission."

"They're all on Copernicus' tit."

"Well, I'm not drinking that sour milk."

"You don't have to. You'll live with us and make sure Edgar learns to read."

"Marie-Pierre's been influencing you, Lionel. I didn't get out of teaching high school to wander around in a jungle of children's words."

"Romey, you shouldn't have abandoned Bronx Science. We were proud of you. I'd tell everybody, my nephew fucked the civil service. He has a lifetime job, teaching the smartest kids that ever lived. Now that was something useful."

"Yeah," I said, "busting my hump on thousands of compositions."

"You should have told mamma and me. We'd have given you a scholarship, let you take off a year. But you chucked it in, gave up the old security blanket, dental insurance and everything, to do your stinking books. Is that fair? You could have carried mamma and me under your health plan."

"Uncle, with all your millions you mourn the loss of my health plan?"

"It's the principle of the thing," Lionel said. "Never pay for what you can get for free."

Couldn't argue with uncle's philosophy. We went down from the dorm, the stairs thick with deacons who saluted uncle and grimaced at me. The Super was guarding the front desk. He got up to shake Copernicus' hand. They discussed the weather, hard times in the country of missions below Fourteenth Street, allotments of sponge cake and chicken Kiev, the best tailors for mending silk, and I understood where Jesus got the power to run Dominick Street. From Lionel and Bathsheba.

Apologized to Lem, told him how Satan had led me into the delousing room, and that I was awful sorry for the harm I'd done to his marriage, but the Super shook me off and wouldn't allow me to mention Alabam. I was just another yegg to him.

Lionel nudged me out of the mission. I swore to whatever bloody Jesus controlled the earth that I'd make my mark. I wouldn't die unnoticed. Forty-five? I had years to kill.

Lionel shoved me into the Checker cab he hired around the clock. That was the bit of extravagance I admired most about my uncle. He scorned traditional limousines with their bullet chassis. He'd fallen in love with the Checker during his days and nights on Charlotte Street when he'd whore and gamble and ride a cab around the corner to Boston Road. He demanded comfort on that ride, the interminable rear cushion of a Checker cab. Lionel understood quality, and he didn't grow out of this need. A Checker was the continuation of Charlotte Street.

"Romey, I want my son to read," Lionel spoke from the cushions, not as my enemy uncle who monopolized Bathsheba and crowded me off a bed, but as a papa with a problem child. He had a mouse in the webbing under his eye. The mouse traveled up and down his cheek.

Wanted to assure the uncle. "Didn't I take on the worst readers at Bronx Science?"

"Yeah," he said, "the worst in a school of geniuses. Edgar can't recognize his name in print."

"He'll recognize, Lionel. I promise you."

And we both sat back in the cushions that rocked with the traffic like an enormous baby carriage.

FOUR

SINISTER PEOPLE

I had the maids' wing, a tiny reservoir of rooms in the lower extremities of the tower. Two tubs to bathe in, but no closets or bookshelves. Now I understood what oldtime business magnates on Washington Square must have thought of their maids who weren't allowed books to fire their hearts, or closets for frilly underpants. But they could wash as often as they desired, in different tubs, and store their maids' shirts under the bed. That was capitalism below Fourteenth Street, circa 1922.

The maids were gone from the maids' wing, and it was given to the family tutor. I adapted to the premises, used that second tub as a library. Put my Portable James Joyce under the soap dish, and I could go about the business of educating Bathsheba's nephew.

The boy had other tutors, reading wizards with a million techniques to cure Edgar's wordblindness. They had vocabulary builders, breathing exercises, records to inspire him into "the wonderland of reading and writing," notebooks with lightly ruled lines for boys with "anarchy in their fists," crayons that wouldn't bleed on a page, and a lexicon to describe their pupil's condition.

He suffered from dyslexia serioso, an acute disturbance of his ability to read. He was also dyslalic, confused in his powers of speech. He could talk in perfect paragraphs, and then his sentences would begin to unravel and he'd plunge into nonsense syllables and obscene nursery rhymes. His writing, the wizards said, was "an altogether different horse." Here Edgar had no lucid beginnings. His lettering was utterly malformed. Hunchbacked on the page, the wizards called it. His language grew in crooked spirals that dropped off the line. *For all practical purposes his penmanship doesn't exist.*

Like other dyslexics, he was "sinistrally inclined." Couldn't the wizards say that Edgar wrote with his left hand? They had a prejudice against lefties. *Sinistrality is the most common trait among imbeciles.* You mothers, what about me? Should I have hid my left hand? Edgar and I were "sinisters" to them. Edgar was their "sinister child."

The wizards had prepared a salad bar of Edgar's disorders. They talked about his strephosymbolia, the way he would add or drop a letter here and there and twist words around, so that bird became dribb, poor was roope, Bathsheba was Abeshtab. *It's best to read our little sinister with a mirror in your pocket.*

He had a fondness for neographisms, strange, incomprehensible words and texts, brought on by his disease.

> Llomo nimaz Abeshtab
> Bumbly memah amam em mo
> Dada doodoo bulow

They encouraged "little sinister" by making lists of notable dyslexics: Hans Christian Andersen, Winston Churchill, Thomas Alva Edison, Guy de Maupassant, Albert Einstein, Napoleon Bonaparte, George Patton, Marcel Proust, Woodrow Wilson, Ludwig van Beethoven, Nelson Rockefeller, Voltaire.

It seemed cruel to burden Edgar with such lists. Why should my nephew have to stand in the same room with Voltaire?

He had to copy the texts of stupid children's books. No wonder Edgar couldn't make it. I couldn't have copied *Dolores and the Magic Elephant*. It was full of bourgeois notions about saving your pennies, keeping your mouth clean, and marrying the right elephant.

I'd watch his body hook itself into the chair while he was into *Elephant*. His pupils roamed the page. He started eating his mouth.

I fired the wizards.

Lionel screamed at me. "You were supposed to work with his tutors, bring them along . . . Romey, he'll die if he can't read."

"Who says?"

"He wants to go to Bronx Science."

Little sinister nodded his head.

"You've been laying a number on him, Lionel. It isn't fair. My father was a junkman, remember? He survived without words."

"Bullshit. He had Spinoza under his rags."

"What did Spinoza ever do for him?"

"It got him Bathsheba, you idiot. You wouldn't have been born without Bruno's philosophy books."

"Forgive me, uncle, but he should have married another woman."

Lionel began to drive spit with his mouth, as if he were reading *Dolores and the Magic Elephant*. He must have been sorry now that I'd escaped the delousing room with all my skin.

"Don't speak like that in front of Edgar. Bruno was crazy about Bathsheba."

"But that didn't keep him alive."

Uncle leapt on me. Climbed my shoes and took me by the throat. "My sister never killed your stinking dad."

Thank God for Edgar, who clung to Lionel's arm and broke the force of his attack.

Shouldn't have provoked the uncle. With all his wrecking companies, his pickle factories, the pajama outlets he chewed to pieces, his child, and his tall, beautiful French-Canadian wife, he was Bathsheba's boy, and I was some changeling out of the dark.

"Romey," he said, "swear to me you won't run away."

"Run away when I have work to do?"

I had the boy collect James Joyce from my other tub, and I set him to copying *Portrait of the Artist.*

He didn't pull himself into the chair and nibble at his mouth. His lettering was erratic, but he scribbled with a smile:

Once p^{on} t^{i}m an a ver d$_{oo}$ g t^{im} it woss ther woss a w$_{oom}$o^{w} com don the road a$_{n}$ tis w$_{oom}$o^{w} tha^{t} woss don the roadd mete a nice ens lit boy nem Abe^{sht}a$_{b}$.

I admired the bumps and hills of Edgar's James Joyce. He was the artist of the family, not his cousin Jerome. Was it the voice of Abeshtab in my head that told me not to tamper with his lettering, to leave him as he was? But he couldn't have gotten into Bronx Science with woo-mow and doog tim.

So I unwound little sinister's text, stood the letters in their proper place, cleaned off the bloody scales like a fisherman's wife operating on a flounder. It was an act of carnage, intruding upon Edgar's designs. But whatever I did was in the name of normalcy and Bronx Science.

Couldn't devote all my energy to Edgar. The kid wouldn't have lasted. I had this terrible hunger to swallow what was around me, enter the cracks in a wall, like a maddened hedgehog canoeing in and out of surfaces while he smells the terrain.

My mother nursed her blue hair in a suite on the tower's second floor. She took in boarders from time to time, men of fifty and sixty years (Bathsheba was seventy-two), failed plumbers, stevedores with a smashed shoulder, pensioned cops. She'd buy them polo shirts and slacks from Italy, then discard them in their pastel colors. My mother couldn't stay with such men. They were disappointments to Bathsheba.

She never found another husky philosopher like my dad. Her boyfriends couldn't recite Descartes. She didn't understand a word of Descartes, but she loved the sound of my father warbling notions about negative roots.

I'd drink a martini with her in the middle of the day, after steering Edgar through Ulysses in Nighttown or bits and pieces of Molly Bloom. Caught her between boyfriends this past Monday, when she didn't have to sulk and feel guilty about the plumber she was banning from the tower.

Her eyes fluttered into the ceiling after the fifth martini. She had Gershwin in her record hop, and she danced around the room with some invisible bear.

"You Jesuit," she said behind the bear's shoulder. "How come you never married?"

"I was about to marry Marie-Pierre when Lionel stole her."

"Bite your tongue," she said, trotting to Gershwin in her silk pajamas. "Romey, you were her teacher. It's forbidden to touch a student in your class. She was a high school girl, for Christ's sake."

"It didn't stop uncle from proposing to her."

"That's different. Lionel wasn't her teacher."

"Mamma, you ought to run up to Harvard and offer seminars in symbolic logic, because there isn't a man alive who can reason with you and win."

She gave up her dancing for a minute to look at me and probe the stem of her martini glass. My mother had lovely hips under her pajamas. The plumbers couldn't have been unhappy with her while they lasted.

"Go on, make fun of me because my father died and I couldn't continue my education. I had Lionel on my hands. I could have lived on strawberries, but he was a growing boy . . . I love you, Romey, but this is from the horse's mouth. Marie-Pierre wouldn't have married you even if Lionel hadn't come along."

"He didn't come along, mother, that's the point. He thrust himself into my situation with Marie-Pierre. Don't you remember? I brought her home to dinner, and uncle wouldn't take his eyes off her."

"It's not so simple," Bathsheba said. "There was electricity at the dinner table, coming from both parties . . . Lionel and Marie-Pierre. Can't you admit that you're not her type? Marie-Pierre enjoys strong men, tycoons like her father."

"Her father was a drunken Canuck who sold shoelaces in central Texas."

"And you were a high school teacher who lived at home."

"Bathsheba, your loving brother also lived at home."

"Look how you distort things. Lionel could have had the Ritz in Monte Carlo or Madrid. He was devoted to me. He wouldn't forget how I'd slaved for him. Your father deserted us. I did without a man . . . and you, you were in love with that other Jesuit."

"What Jesuit?"

"James Joyce. He's your husband and your wife. You don't need another person."

She licked inside the glass like a young American bride. "I'm sorry . . . I shouldn't have said that about you and James Joyce. But you didn't marry and Lionel did."

She twirled in pajama silk, her back to me. It was hopeless. I was her son in the baby carriage.

Bathsheba whispered to herself. She had the ankles of a girl. She wouldn't paint her toenails like some feeble witch who had to attract men.

I'd never please her. My father was the enemy she happened to love. Lionel was the one she could adore without the complication of marriage. If I'd won the Pulitzer, she'd have said it was a trick of fate. I was a phantom outside the baby carriage.

Bathsheba smiled. She was more than a Bronx-Odessa beauty. She had wonderful teasing eyes that warmed up the witch in her.

Should have been Bruny the rag. Then I'd trot with my mother, drink martinis on her chin, and go off to the rag farm.

"You look like your father," she said, wobbling on her feet to martini music. "You have his curly hair."

"Bruno's hair was straight."

Her eyes went the color of octopus ink.

"I slept with your father, I listened to his heart at night. Wouldn't I know if his hair was curly or straight?"

"All right," I said. "Bruno was a curly Tarzan."

"You have to spoil it, don't you? So damn superior. Just because you had a teaching license. Well, there's more to the world than Bronx Science."

Might have argued with her over that, but she fell out of Gershwin and dropped to the floor. She'd end the afternoon in a martini stupor. My mother was her own *Rhapsody in Blue*. Put a blanket around her, so she wouldn't catch her death on the rug.

Like some large miracle it was, watching your mother breathe in and out. I was the fruit of Bathsheba's loins. She couldn't deny me while she slept on the rug. She didn't have Lionel to blabber about. It was as plain as Descartes. *My mother breathes, ergo I exist.*

There was a flaw in that little maxim, a wrinkle, but I can't figure where. I bent to kiss Bathsheba. She opened her eyes, hugged me, and for a moment I thought she was unclear about me again, that I was a lost plumber coming back into her life, but she mumbled *Romey, Romey* in her sleep.

A chill in Edgar today. His lettering was violent. His text spilled off the page and he withdrew into his old habit of imaginary words.

Mooda amam boobill

I didn't need a mirror to interpret that. His mamma was coming home. Marie-Pierre had gone to Paris. Seems she was always in transit, traveling for the old corporation. It had something to do with hats or shoes. My auntie Pierre was on the Paris–New York circuit, with special loops that took her to Dallas, Rome, and Montreal.

Edgar got rid of James Joyce when "amam" was in town. He clung to her culottes, as if he could make Paris disappear with his own two arms. She was his prisoner until Lionel chased him to bed.

"He can't go on treating you like a super diaper, Marie-Pierre. The boy's nine years old."

She wouldn't answer Lionel. She sat in her culottes, her legs like long gracious pins, her hair wound inside a scarf, so that you had nothing to look at but the bones of her face, and I wondered, would she have come to this, a tall lady in million-dollar pants, if I hadn't brought her home to my mother's cooking and Lionel's grubby eyes? Auntie Pierre couldn't have worn turban scarves on a high school teacher's salary.

Uncle welcomed her with a bottle of wine from Rothschild's own cellar. Auntie put her nose to the bottle. Uncle and I were Tatars. We had to depend on auntie to find the right bouquet. We only bottled vinegar in the Bronx. I could declare the value of a pickle, come to terms with the bouquet of a charlotte russe, but that's about it.

The wine was only a teaser. Lionel had booked a table at La Tulipe. I borrowed one of his suits, because I didn't have restaurant clothes. Marie-Pierre changed from culottes to harem pants. It was seven blocks to La Tulipe, but uncle insisted on his Checker cab.

Auntie rode in the middle. I drank up her perfume and got dizzy in the restaurant. She jabbered in French to the table captain, uncle and I like her little sons lost in the English language. I saw auntie's flesh under the harem pants.

She introduced us to the captain as "mes cocottes."

She ordered our food, talked wine with the sommelier, brought the sous-chef out of the kitchen to argue a point on the menu, and we sat like yobs with napkins in our laps and stuffed our faces. That was our reward for thirty years of kasha. Bathsheba hadn't prepared us for cold potato soup and rabbit in a coffin of lettuce. She wouldn't come with us to La Tulipe. Bathsheba wasn't the type to have a meal accomplished without her. She scorned vichyssoise from her tower rooms. But I know my mother. She'd have gone to Mongolia for a new recipe. It wasn't the lack of French that intimidated her. It was auntie Pierre. Mama couldn't control that tall bitch.

Bathsheba didn't dare come between Lionel and his wife. She could never be sure of Lionel in matters of Marie. Uncle loved that bitch to distraction. His eyes didn't stray from her at La Tulipe. He wouldn't eat papillote de red snapper without Marie-Pierre.

Then why was he always sending her to Paris? There's the rub. Uncle had his own wife play Ulysses. Marie was the wanderer in our family. Uncle brooded over Edgar's wordblindness while he bought and sold another company and took Marie to La Tulipe or Chanterelle during her stopovers between flights. Bathsheba could afford not to bark. She only had to contend with Marie-Pierre six or seven days a month. She was Lionel's chatelaine more days than Marie.

The tarte au chocolat at La Tulipe was baked "on command," and auntie Pierre was invited into the kitchen to help the sous-chef. I shoveled paper and fish into my mouth. "Uncle, couldn't we keep auntie Pierre with us another week? It's for Edgar's sake. He might gallop into reading if his mamma is around."

Lionel ripped the paper kite around his red snapper with a fingernail. He was concentrating hard, and I thought he hadn't heard me. He could ruin a kite the way he ruined Percival Newgarden's lower shelves, forty-one years ago. My uncle was like a surgeon with that fingernail, the surgeon of a wrecking crew.

"Marie has business abroad," the uncle said, after cutting under the heart of that kite. He wasn't interested in red snapper. He had auntie order papillote so he could wound the paper dressing. "Romey, we can't have her running around New York with no occupation. She'd get tired of us. Marie's my right arm in Paris, London, Rome."

"What exactly does she do?"

Lionel shoved the papillote to the side of his plate. "Your aunt has her own line of rainwear. And she buys for me when she gets the chance."

I'd seen those children's galoshes with the label *Marie-Pierre*, but that was only a small pinch of Copernicus. Lionel was indulging his wife, giving her a tiny star in his Milky Way.

"Romey, your aunt's a goddamn storm over Europe. We wouldn't be eating at La Tulipe without her."

It was my turn to scratch the kite with a fingernail. Uncle didn't have to lie. I wouldn't have reported him to Internal Revenue. He could plunder with or without my blessing. And it wasn't my affair if Marie was the baroness of children's galoshes.

Auntie wheeled a chocolate tart out of the kitchen. The tart was on fire. I watched the chocolate burn with a vapor of delicious green smoke.

After the smoke went off she cut into the tart with a silver trowel. The tart had white chocolate tiles. It made you want to die, because nothing on this earth could have tasted better than a soft white tile.

"My two darlings," she said, getting up to hug Lionel and me. Our faces were busy with chocolate, and then the uncle started up. "How shall we spend the next twenty years? Marie, will you marry this kid after I'm dead? He can't forgive his uncle. He still thinks I horned in on his property."

"Shut up and eat your cake."

"He's all daggers, look at him."

"Shut up," auntie said.

But he was right, of course. I'd have carved his Adam's apple with the silver trowel . . . probably not. Tatars are terribly thick when it comes to family blood. But that didn't make me stop loving the bitch. It was curious, because I wasn't eager to steal into her harem pants. I wanted to trace the curve of her neck, feel the little hairs at the top of her spine.

I swallowed bits of rubble off the edge of the tart.

Auntie didn't have the black eyes of Copernicus. Auntie's were aquamarine. And those pale underwater eyes went from uncle's face to mine. Didn't have a clue what auntie was thinking.

"Mes cocottes," she said. "Darling boys."

We ate slower with auntie purring like that. She rescued a bit of tart for Edgar before uncle and I finished the bloody thing.

Not even the richest chocolate from La Tulipe could satisfy the boy. He mourned his mother after she left and wouldn't go back to Joyce. He idled with his pen in hand, refusing to letter or to read. He began to draw a nose in his composition book. The nose resisted margins and lines. It crept between pages like a rubber beanstalk, a caterpillar with ears, a submarine with several mouths.

"Edgar, is that a portrait of your family as a nose?"

I'd slighted the boy. He wouldn't have turned his mother into a nose. He was much too melancholy.

"It's Pinocchio when he lies. His nose goes crazy and swallows up ears and mouths and other noses."

This was Bruno's nephew, all right. He'd inherited the junkman's feel for logic. Pinocchio's nose made him miss his mother less. He'd copy nothing, he said, but the story of Pinocchio as told by me. I collected my wits. I had to find a Pinocchio who was a little like him, so he could grow with the story, and I couldn't neglect history and geography, horses, kidneys, and hearts. Pinocchio would have to be a complete lesson in the manners and mores of the world. I dedicated my story to Bitter Morris, who was faithful to Madam Andrusov unto death. He was the man of Charlotte Street, with his trust in simple fascism and laissez faire.

To honor Morris, I installed Pinocchio in the slightly antiquated time of Mussolini. I had an inkling Edgar would enjoy the blood, thunder, and castor oil of Mussolini's Blackshirts.

He watched me scribble and scratch out.

"What's the problem, uncle Romey?"

Flaubert had a special table, a special pen, a special writing gown. He'd work on a paragraph for a week and recast it again. He'd brook no interference from milkmaids at his door. He grew fat in his gown, only pausing to help his young friend, Guy de Maupassant, who was like a nephew to him, a nephew touched with dyslexia. He taught Guy to sharpen pencils and erase words that fell outside the music of a text. Language is a cracked kettle, he said, on which we teach bears to sing. But it's the only kettle we have.

Well, I had my little Guy de Maupassant, but I didn't have a writing gown. The boy couldn't understand the terrors of starting a story. And then I took a plunge and swam along, inside the text. It's Montegrumo, a small Tuscan village in the foothills of Siena. And . . .

CHAPTER 1
How Pinocchio, Born in a Bread Basket,
Discovers Giacomo Joyce and Learns to
be a Creative Writer

He was born with his eyes open, alert to everything, and with a vocabulary of a hundred words. He understood walls and shoes and brown bread, but he didn't know the word for wood. Pinocchio assumed he was a boy like other boys. He arrived one morning in Geppetto's panetteria, jumping out of a bread basket in his bare feet. "Daddy," he shouted, "I'm here."

The old baker, whose scalp was bone white from half a century of flour dust, was startled to hear a voice call him daddy in all that white dust. He'd never married. Geppetto was a socialist. His theories forbid him to take a wife. Women were sisters to him, and comrades, under socialist law. He wouldn't enslave sister comrades with a wedding band. Had the Blackshirts come to mock him by saying daddy in the dust?

And then he saw the wooden boy. The baker trembled. He couldn't recall a chapter in Bakunin or Proudhon on the subject of wooden boys.

"Who are you?"

"Pinocchio, your son."

Geppetto began to wonder if old sins were being shoveled on his head. In spite of his theories on the comradeliness of women, he visited Brunhilde, the village prostitute, twice a month, when he had his usual attack of vigor. But Brunhilde couldn't have given birth to a wooden boy behind his back.

"Who sent you here?"

"No one, babbo."

Confound it all, he liked having a son, even with such questionable roots.

But the village got wind of Pinocchio, and people weren't enchanted with the idea of magical boys in Montegrumo. They thought Pinocchio was another socialist trick. Geppetto had been a troublemaker before Mussolini's march on Rome. The local militia would feed him castor oil and a tub of coffee at the Casa del Fascio to quiet his socialist mouth. The baker erupted every five years, and the Blackshirts had to repeat the castor oil.

Now the Montegrumesi searched for castor oil again. Pinocchio was a devil boy, concocted in Geppetto's oven, by some socialist formula.

The baker swore to the fascisti that he found the boy in the panetteria and decided to raise him as his own child.

"Mongrel," the fascisti said, "do you have a permit to raise a child?"

The baker kissed their boots, mumbling prayers to Gesù, Giuseppe, Maria.

The fascisti laughed. "The bastard's gone religious." But they allowed the baker to keep his devil boy.

Geppetto brushed his knees soon as the Blackshirts were gone and set about to educate his son. Pinocchio had never gone to school. The boy didn't even have a past. His memory began in the panetteria.

Geppetto took out the socialist books he hid in the false bottom of his flour barrel, and he read with Pinocchio, but the boy dropped off in the middle of Proudhon. And Geppetto despaired.

Pinocchio was determined to become a socialist like his dad. "I swear on the holy fingers of little Jesus that I'll learn. Babbo, I will."

"Wooden head," Geppetto muttered. "We're socialists. We don't believe in God."

And Pinocchio pulled books out of the village library to show his babbo what a wooden boy could learn by himself. He didn't pay attention to titles. He seized the tallest books, imagining he could get the most out of them.

He raced from book to book. Paragraphs couldn't hold in his wooden head. His mind would spill back the words on a page. He opened the last book and read with a grinding fury, determined to stick with the paragraph, hell or holy water.

> Once upon a time there was a cauliflower coming down the road, and this cauliflower was named cavaliere Marco Polo . . .

Pinocchio had stumbled upon the first delight in his existence as a wooden boy. He glanced back at the title page. *Piccolino* by Giacomo Joyce. It was almost as if Giacomo Joyce had invented a history for Pinocchio. The hero of Giacomo's book was a boy with bad eyes who suffers neglect at a boarding school on the outskirts of Florence. Priests and nuns step on Giacomo's eyeglasses. Other boarders hurl him in the mud. His parents don't send for him at Christmas and Easter.

Piccolino could just as well have been born in a bread basket, the son of a socialist baker. But he becomes a terrible prig, harping on Dante Alighieri and people called the Ghibellines and the Guelphs. Piccolino declares that all of life is a struggle between Guelph and Ghibelline, the forces of clarity and the forces of mud. Pinocchio cries when Piccolino goes off to China on the last page, to "overthrow Ghibellines everywhere and find the fearsome beauty of the Guelph."

That was Pinocchio's mission. Fight the fascist Ghibellines and bring a touch of Guelph to Montegrumo. He prepared a speech in the plangent rhythms of Giacomo Joyce, a speech he meant to deliver at the Casa del Fascio. He climbed the steps of the Casa in the bowtie his babbo had given him and curtsied to the Blackshirts, who were preparing to slaughter a baby pig and roast him in their fire.

The piglet squealed and ran between their legs. Its frantic noises, like a cauliflower learning to breathe, reminded Pinocchio of Piccolino, and he resolved to save the pig.

"Signori," he shouted, "once upon a time and a dreary time it was there lived a pig, and that pig was more than property. He had a heart that was no less human than your own. Put down your knives, you Montegrumesi, and treat your brother the pig with respect."

The Blackshirts abandoned the idea of their supper to fall on Pinocchio with the desire to whittle down his private parts. Then they wouldn't have a wooden boy to lecture them on the virtues of a pig they intended to eat.

They cut the pants off Pinocchio, pulled down his drawers, and discovered the boy had no genitals, not even the slightest bump. "Guido, did he lend his dick to the king?" They marveled at Pinocchio and then lost their interest. He was something to be shunned, like a city woman who shaved her legs.

They seized pig and boy and flung them out of the Casa del Fascio. They'd rather starve on macaroni and cheese than traffic with Pinocchio's kind. Pigs with human hearts were impossible to chew.

Flaubert cleaned his pen, while little Maupassant copied the first chapter. His eyes were rooted to the pages I'd done. Maupassant was perfectly calm. He didn't dream of his mamma, Marie-Pierre. He copied, scratching his letters into a straight line. The humps were gone. He could have been a scribe in B. Dalton's window.

Edgar learned the sentences by heart. He'd fallen in love with the Guelphs and the Ghibellines, and he'd run after his mamma's maid, Harriet, the moment she arrived from New Jersey, and scream in her ear, "Are you Gib or Gelf?"

Whatever she answered, Edgar would take the opposite side. He was Guelph to Ghibelline, Ghibelline to Guelph. Harriet didn't blame him. "Monsieur Jérôme," she said, "you will ruin the boy with such histoires."

Harriet was a Canuck out of central Jersey who had obscure family ties to Marie-Pierre. She'd vanish into uncle's rooms for hours at a time. I didn't question uncle's seignorial rights. It was his privilege, I suppose, to enjoy the maid when auntie Pierre was on a different continent. She could scold me about the bad effects of Pinocchio, but I never saw her dust the lamps or clean a dish. She had her own maid's closet, filled with hand-me-downs from Marie. I snooped in the closet. Auntie's name was sewn into all the collars.

I wondered if some of Lionel's privileges trickled down to Marie. Did she have a wind-up butler waiting in her closet? A servant she could undress? It was no good contemplating her marriage to uncle. I'd think of how it could have been if auntie had stayed with me. I wouldn't have left Bronx Science. Need an income to maintain a wife. Can't have red snapper at La Tulipe on a writer's salary. I'd have married her on the afternoon of her high school graduation. We'd have honeymooned in Montreal, so Marie-Pierre could practice her French on the yobs of that old city. Patient husband, I would have devoted a week to parting her thighs. We'd have had pralines on top of Mount Royal and gone into the old quarter for bouillabaisse, or whatever the Canucks like to eat. I'd have given up James Joyce and papa Flaubert for the love of Marie. Moby Dick could swim into whale's heaven without this Ahab. I'd be an immortal at Bronx Science: Jerome Copernicus Charyn, who explained the madness of his century to leagues of young scientists . . .

"Brunhilde."

Little Maupassant had come into my bed. The copy artist was eager for chapter two. "I want the bad lady."

"Don't you dictate to me. I'm the storyteller. I decide where a chapter has to go."

"Brunhilde, Brunhilde. I want the bad lady."

Edgar carried me out of my sleep. He fixed breakfast for the old man, since Harriet was on other business. I took my coffee dark at the beginning of a chapter to jolt me into the text.

CHAPTER 2
How Brunhilde Meets Pinocchio
and Instructs Him in the Art
of the Nose

It was a fact of village life that Brunhilde was the last to learn of Pinocchio. She trafficked with the entire male population over eleven, but since boys started being fascists at five and six, and men of eighty swore that Montegrumo didn't begin until Mussolini, even her greatest admirers had no confidence in a whore who smelled of socialism. Why else would she sleep with the baker and river rats wandering in from nowhere? The rats couldn't have come to Brunhilde by boat. Montegrumo was riverless, and these were pirate scum.

The fascisti entered Brunhilde without bothering to take down their pants. They used her as a snarling iron on which they could strike their passion for a few moments and then go home to their mothers, sisters, and wives. It was a way of thinning their blood and getting out of the hot Siena sun. They couldn't fish in Montegrumo. Brunhilde was their only sport. They had their Casa del Fascio and an undernourished whore. They never drank coffee with Brunhilde. They pulled up their pants, paid her, and said goodbye.

Such was Brunhilde's isolation, her distance from the daily weave of Montegrumo, that months went by without her being conscious of Pinocchio. One afternoon, while the baker was in her lap, marking Brunhilde with his flour dust, she happened to look out the window and notice a boy in a soft three-cornered hat sitting on the wall outside her hut at "land's end," a hummock that served as Montegrumo's borderline. The Blackshirts had put her where she couldn't incriminate them, poison their wives, or corrupt young girls into following her trade.

That boy on the wall disturbed Brunhilde. He seemed to exist in his soft hat without any particular need. He didn't have the least fear in his eyes, or the worry lines that went with being a boy. Brunhilde said nothing until the old baker had spent himself.

"Who's the piccolino on my wall?"

"Pinocchio."

"That's a fancy name for an apprentice."

"He's my son," the old man said.

Brunhilde clapped her knees and started to laugh. But she stopped soon as she saw that Geppetto wasn't smiling.

"Babbo, do you have another sweetheart that you're hiding from Brunhilde?"

She could talk this way to the old man, tease him, because they were the pariahs of Montegrumo.

"I have no other sweetheart," he assured her.

"Did a fairy visit your bed and leave you the boy?"

"Not a fairy," the baker said.

"Then a fishwife."

"We have no fishwives in Montegrumo. He was born in a bread basket."

Brunhilde made the sign of the cross on her bare chest. "An immacolato, a holy boy."

The old barber gritted his teeth in disappointment and scratched his white scalp. "A socialist, and you cross yourself? Jesus is the first thing that enters your head . . . he isn't an immacolato. He's a wooden boy."

It's true, Geppetto had converted her to socialism during his visits to her hut, since he was the only man in Montegrumo who ever talked to her. But Brunhilde had no doubt that wonders did exist, even in a socialist universe. She ran out to meet the boy in her oldest, roughest housedress.

Brunhilde waved hello.

He didn't leave the wall.

She parted her housedress, but he wouldn't take advantage of his position on the wall to peek down Brunhilde.

She'd been right about him. He had no worry lines . . . but he didn't have glass eyes to go with the wood. They were irregular and wet inside their painted sockets. The left eye was a little darker than the right. His teeth were wooden teeth. His mouth was uniformly red. His jaw could have been ripped from a geometry book. But whoever manufactured Pinocchio had put much more trouble into the eyes.

Brunhilde trembled below the wooden boy.

"Please come down."

Pinocchio stared into Brunhilde's window without a word.

"Answer the lady, wooden head," Geppetto shouted from the window. "Brunhilde, it's my fault. I trained him to speak only with his babbo . . . Pinocchio, do what the lady says."

Pinocchio removed his hat, climbed down from the wall, and shook Brunhilde's hand. She was astonished by the feel of Pinocchio, whose hand had all the bumps and abrasions of human skin. She wondered who his manufacturer could be. Brunhilde wouldn't insult Geppetto, but she understood in an instant that Pinocchio's creator wasn't a socialist. The socialists were too involved with politics to concentrate on the texture of a wooden boy's skin. Brunhilde was dying to hear him speak. She buttoned her housedress so as not to excite the boy. Pinocchio hadn't developed an attitude about Brunhilde's chest. He assumed that women were like his babbo, but with longer hair.

"Pinocchio, are you enjoying school?"

"Babbo is my school, signorina Brunhilde."

Brunhilde shivered at the sound of his voice, trying not to show the palpitations under her housedress. Pinocchio was slightly nasal, like the rivermen who would visit her from time to time, coming off their barges for an afternoon with Brunhilde, and then trekking thirty miles to that mad river, the Tiber, which changed channels every five years, sat in its own sluggish waters, or moved at will.

"Geppetto," she called to the window, hiding her agitation with a fist over her heart. "Why haven't you registered Pinocchio at school?"

"And have him taught by fascists? *Mussolini says ten minus five is fifty-three. Mussolini says the Italians are brave, the French are overcooked, and the English are a race of boiled beef* . . . my son attends school at the Piazza Proudhon."

"Pardon me, Geppetto, but have the mapmakers been to Montegrumo again? I don't remember a Piazza Proudhon."

"It's the back room of my bakery," the old man said.

"But he'll have such a narrow opinion of the world if you feed him nothing but socialist talk. School him with me . . . once or twice a week."

"Good idea," the old man said from the window. "Pinocchio, will you behave with your schoolmistress?"

"Yes, babbo."

"Will you keep out of her hair if she has sudden callers and retires to her curtain for ten minutes?"

"Yes, babbo. I will."

"And if she contradicts anything I've taught you, will you promise to let your babbo answer what she says?"

"I promise."

"Then I'll leave you here with the signorina."

Pinocchio didn't seem to object. He rose up on his heels to kiss his babbo goodbye, and then he followed Brunhilde into her shack.

Her heart thumped as if she had a squirrel inside, mean and big, that gnawed at her, so she couldn't swallow air. She tottered around the hut, worrying that if she fainted, she might fall on the boy and crush all reason out of his head. She offered him a piece of mozzarella dipped in oil. Pinocchio ate the cheese.

She drank a glass of lemon water.

She fanned herself with a broom.

She didn't bother teaching Pinocchio about doilies and pins, combs and nailbrushes, all the mysteries of a woman. She threw off her housedress.

He never looked between her legs.

"More mozzarella, please."

She fed the boy, hoping his appetite would waken him. And then she succumbed to a short, wild swoon. Brunhilde felt ashamed of her body. She wasn't pretty enough for Pinocchio. That's why he preferred mozzarella cheese. She had no meat on her arms. Her legs were bowed from lying under fascisti. Her eyebrows weren't properly plucked. Like two timberlines that met above her nose. She had bruises on her thighs where those big fascist horses sat on her.

"Signorina, why are you crying?"

"Because I undress for you, and you stand in your clothes."

"But that's nothing, signorina." And he relieved himself of shirt, pants, socks, etc., as if he were preparing for bed.

Brunhilde recovered from her swoon in time to study Pinocchio. She wasn't amazed by the genitals he didn't have. Genitals were the hardest things to mimic. She realized that his creator wouldn't bring him to the village without a piccolo. She simply had to find it.

The boy was superbly formed. He had strange little buds for nipples. Another bud curled into itself at the point of his navel. His right toes paired marvelously with the left. Needing no veins in his neck to carry blood, he had an unblemished sweep from his gorge to the bells of his shoulder blades. His buttocks, when Pinocchio turned for Brunhilde to see, were pears in the act of ripening. Pinocchio had the sweetest symmetry, with little dents in place of kneecaps and holes with ripples around them to mark his ears.

Brunhilde surrendered to old Christian habits, begging the Infant Jesus to point where the piccolo was. Then her eyes fell on Pinocchio's nose, and she thanked the Infant for leading her out of her ignorance. It wasn't the peculiar length of Pinocchio's schnozzle that convinced her. She'd seen other long noses on boys and men. But this was a serious schnozzle, with a delicate tip that curved into the sky.

Brunhilde walked around him, while the boy stuffed himself with mozzarella. "Pinocchio, the air is so dry, I have an itch. Be a good boy and scratch me . . . with your schnozzle."

"Of course, signorina. Where does it itch?"

And with a tender struggle, she guided Pinocchio from her ribs to her waist to the fluting of her groin. She swooned again as the nose pulsed inside her and grew. She cursed that devil of a manufacturer who lured Pinocchio to her wall, and then she thought the better of it and decided not to curse. The boy plunged in and out, his hands braced on the rotting floor. Brunhilde's legs went higher and higher as she sat around his nose like a toy and bit her knuckles to hold down her screams.

Brunhilde began to die of Pinocchio.

She was used to men at intervals of five or ten minutes. Pinocchio plunged without a stop, since wooden boys weren't susceptible to orgasms. If she hadn't squeezed her bosoms to remind her where she was, Brunhilde might have gone out of this world with Pinocchio's deepest plunge. Finally she pressed a finger on his head.

"Gesù Cristo, your teacher has to rest."

The boy pulled his nose away, and Brunhilde shuddered like a crazy serpent, deprived of Pinocchio.

"Are you in pain, signorina? Should I tickle you again?"

"No," she said, hugging her kneecaps to force the serpent out. Her body was quieter now. She was able to stand up and help her student into his clothes.

"Pinocchio, will you tell your babbo how I educated you? He'll think I took up too much of your time with unimportant matters."

"But signorina," Pinocchio said. "Tickling is important."

"Your babbo wouldn't understand. Trust me, Pinocchio. We'll tell him after you finish the course . . . can you come tomorrow?"

"Why not?"

Pinocchio shook his teacher's hand, put on his soft hat, and trotted out of the hut, climbing onto the wall that led like a series of broken circles into the heart of Montegrumo.

Brunhilde stood at the window and followed the line his hat made. She grew remorseful without Pinocchio. She'd sinned against the Holy Ghost, cohabiting with a wooden boy in the most unnatural of ways.

She searched for wrinkles in her mirror, convinced she'd aged a lot after Pinocchio's nose. But the fascisti had scraped the silver bark off her mirror, and Brunhilde appeared like a pregnant spider in a darkening web. She began to cry. Socialism couldn't save her. The most she could expect was a union card, and the unions hadn't come to Montegrumo.

She left the hut, ignoring the fact that she was still undressed. How could Brunhilde have been aware of her missing clothes? All sensation had gone out of her skin. She marched along the wall with a floating step. She didn't have a destination. She took the bends in the wall and landed on Via Copernico, the village's main street. Women and children weren't abroad at this hour. The Blackshirts whisked her off Copernico and dragged her to the Casa del Fascio, where they threw water in her face, slapped her prettily, and demanded what she was doing in their village.

"My village too," said the whore of Montegrumo.

Achille, the fascist mayor, felt her hot skin and was merciful.

"Signorina, what could you be looking for in this part of town?"

"The Blood of Jesus."

The Blackshirts had a terrible fit, rubbing their bellies and stamping their feet.

"Silenzio," said Achille. He stood erect on the polished floor and drew his image out of the wax. That was his glory as mayor of Montegrumo. Achille could write his impression on the floor with the boltlike design of his body. He asked Brunhilde why she'd come without her clothes.

Brunhilde looked at herself in the wax. "Cavaliere, I'm a whore. What good am I to you in clothes?"

Achille smiled at the sense she made.

"But we didn't summon you."

"Cavaliere, I summoned myself."

"That's impossible," Achille said. "You can't summon. You're a whore. We pay you."

"Cavaliere, I've come for free."

And she overwhelmed the Blackshirts with fierce wiggling of her hips. These men were too aroused to murder Brunhilde. They undressed in

the corner, folding the red, white, and green garters of Mussolini into
their shoes, the way the cavalieri had done since they were children.
They didn't fall on top of Brunhilde. The cavalieri allowed Achille to
go first. He lay with her on a blanket in the middle of their meeting
room, Brunhilde rocking under him like a deranged boat.

The cavalieri took their turns clapping themselves to Brunhilde.
"Achille, she's deep today, the skinny cow."

"A little too deep," Achille said, watching her writhe.

None of them listened when she called *Pinocchio*.

Six more lay with Brunhilde.

Her body turned quiet. Achille had to shove at the candidate who was
on top of her.

"What's the matter, chief?"

"Get off," Achille muttered. "She's dead."

They got into their garters, and then they took her pulse, covered her
with a blanket, carried her out to their motorcar, and delivered Brunhilde home to her hut.

FIVE

LES FRÈRES

L UCKY for Edgar that he had Pinocchio to entertain him, because Marie-Pierre forgot to come home that month. The boy copied and chewed on his tongue over Brunhilde's death. I didn't have endless resources. Couldn't go on weaving chapters like a bloody spider until his mamma decided to come back.

Little sinister looked at me with a clever fix in his eye.

"Brunhilde's ghost," he said.

"That's impossible."

He flapped his arms and drove himself around my bed like a sturdy engine.

"Brunhilde's ghost."

I ran from the child in order not to think about that third chapter. But Lionel trapped me in the sunroom on the second floor of his estate.

"I need you, Romey."

He was handsome in a gray velvet jacket and tan slacks: Paul Newman as a dark-eyed loanshark and eater of small companies. He handed me a blue airline ticket on the Concorde. The sun king was sending me to Paris.

"Lionel, can't you rescue Marie-Pierre on your own?"

"Stop flattering yourself. You're not going as my ambassador to Marie. It's business. You'll deliver a package to someone at Charles de Gaulle."

"Grand," I said. "A messenger boy flying Concorde."

"You're missing the point . . . I need someone with an educated look."

"Lionel, please don't start that shit about Bronx Science. I'll take the Concorde."

Been dying to go to Paris, but I couldn't get off my ass. It seemed overwhelming to get on a plane, land in the country of Voltaire and Guy de Maupassant, eat croissants instead of charlotte russes . . . might have gone if I'd married Marie.

"Uncle, how can I pack for the trip? I left Dominick Street in a hurry, without my underwear."

"Go into my closet and take what you want," Lionel said.

His closet was almost as big as the maids' wing. Lionel didn't have sixty sports coats in the Bronx. He lived in one leather jacket, with whole populations inside his little black book. Uncle was his own Sears, Roebuck catalogue. People would buy an icebox from him and have their names entered in his book. Uncle charged you pennies a month, but it was impossible to get yourself erased. It was like having your name in Deuteronomy or the Book of Kings. You and your heirs would owe him seventy-five cents a month until my Tatar uncle died.

He'd still be in his leather jacket without Marie. Auntie lured him from charlottkas to the land of papillote. His new sensibility is like a hump on his back. Lionel can't go home to kasha. He'll have to sleepwalk in La Tulipe the rest of his life.

But I wasn't a prisoner to auntie's style. I chose the softest shirts, scarves from Damascus, linen trousers from Milan, a belt that had been cured on two continents. My trenchcoat was a Swedish beauty with trunklike pockets and storm flaps that could have substituted for a sleep-in tent.

I had to memorize instructions while Harriet the maid packed for me. It was the only time I'd ever seen her do work in the house. She had a lovely strain in her calves as she bent to fold my linen trousers.

Couldn't devote myself to Harriet's calves. I was uncle's courier. We drove to JFK in the Checker cab, uncle quizzing me along the route.

"Yes," I said, "a tall man, Alain San Angelo, with a Corsican moustache."

Lionel shook his head. "There's no such thing as a Corsican moustache."

"Okay, this Corsican with a moustache will be waiting outside customs with a chauffeur and a cardboard sign. Can't I give him the briefcase and kiss San Angelo goodbye?"

The briefcase I had to deliver was a big cloth envelope that could have come from Woolworth's. I didn't ask uncle what was inside.

"Don't talk politics with Alain. He's a Bonapartist. Thinks France won't find herself until she has an emperor king. But Alain won't bite. He's our friend."

"Our Corsican friend with a moustache."

Lionel hugged me outside Air France.

I shot upstairs to the Concorde lounge and was given a shoehorn in the sleek humpbacked shape of the Concorde jet.

I understood more about aerodynamics and Icarus' wax wings as I watched the Concorde fueling from the window of the lounge. It was a tiny birdlike plane with a needle at the end of its nose. Icarus' needle. That boy had to soar over his father, fly into the sun.

I sat cradled in an empty row, with blankets, slippers, champagne. There was a mirror built into the front of the seat that could make your head large and small, and for a minute I thought I'd gone through the Looking Glass with Alice, into a supersonic zone, where time was liquid and you could drink it out of your hand, invite dead fathers on board. And then I hid the mirror behind its leather ears. Icarus got a sunburn and fell into the sea. I inherited his wax wings. I was breaking the sound barrier into my own past. The Concorde was only a sleeker baby carriage.

Got through customs without having to open Lionel's briefcase for some bloody wog behind a glass wall. I was the Bronx pilgrim, Icarus reborn, with wax under his arms, the residue of old wings. But where was the Corsican moustache? Other pilgrims walked around me. Children wheeled their own prams at Charles de Gaulle. Men and women would loiter behind a column and thrust cardboard lozenges at the nearest pilgrim. I read each lozenge like a hungry man, prepared to chew cardboard from a fist, but none of the lozenges was related to Alain San Angelo.

Icarus had fallen into his own dry sea. From where I stood, close to customs, I couldn't find an exit out of Charles de Gaulle. It cooked my blood, being Lionel's soldier, with a cloth envelope, fat as a pillow, crowding my heart. I had a suspicion this airport was the only Europe I'd ever meet.

With one eye still on America, I saw the twin of my Swedish coat lumber in my direction. The twin was chewing gum. He had a pimple in the cleft under his Corsican moustache. He'd come without chauffeur and cardboard sign. I couldn't feel Corsica in his handshake. San Angelo had a Bronx-Manhattan-Hoboken grip.

I was a little off. He'd spent five years in a Rhode Island correction facility. Alain San Angelo was a Corsican who'd never been to Corsica. He was the cousin of a cousin to a powerful Corsican family, also San Angelo. He had this habit of landing in jail. San Angelo was the little saint of some prison called la Santé. A yegg is what he was, a small-time hood who wandered in and out of penal colonies all over the map. That's how San Angelo did his traveling. From pigeoncoop to pigeoncoop.

La Santé was his pigeoncoop in Paris. San Angelo's sense of the streets came from a red prison wall. He'd gone from children's homes to bishops' schools to shelters to hobo camps to the can. He was jumpy away from institutions, nervous, morose.

I didn't know all this when we met at the airport. San Angelo delivered his biography in the car. We drove out of Charles de Gaulle in a souped-up Dodge, a gift from my uncle Copernicus. He paid no attention to the cloth pillowcase I was holding for Lionel. He wouldn't conduct business. He talked jails, jails, jails.

San Angelo was thirty-nine, and he'd been inside the monkeyhouse thirty-one of those years. His education had come from priests and older prisoners.

We were on a highway called the Periphérique, and though San Angelo swore this was Paris, I couldn't see much. I looked for the Eiffel

Tower. All I found was the bumpy shoulder of a highway on top of the streets.

We got off the Periphérique, and I sat at the window like a dumb-struck child. I didn't get my Eiffel Tower, but I had buildings with uninterrupted balconies, barrels of them, that followed the line of an avenue and curled around corners like an amazing ribbon, or some wire snake. Entire cities seemed to break out of every street corner, where buildings would narrow and almost come to a point. You could catch bursting fields of stone on both sides of that point, with chimney pots and porches, castles and hotels, swelling from the corner.

And with this swelling went the names of the streets, like heroes in a stone book: rue George-Sand, avenue Mozart, boulevard Marat.

San Angelo reserved a room for me at his hotel, le Wigwam, on the rue Pascal. He must have had the monkeyhouse in mind, because my room was like a prison closet, with a bed, a bureau, and a foot of air between them.

We dawdled in the neighborhood. I didn't have to ask San Angelo why he chose a hotel on the rue Pascal. Le grand hotel Wigwam was three blocks from la Santé. The monkey had to live near the monkey-house. La Santé was his college, his church, his shrine. It was a steep red wall to me, a house for yeggs that covered the four crooked corners of a Parisian city block.

The trees around the prison had red leaves that beckoned San Angelo. The son of a bitch wanted to climb over the wall, into la Santé. I had to hold him by his pants.

"Alain, why are you so ready to leave me for la Santé?"

"It's nothing. I wouldn't have climbed to the top. I was showing off."

"To whom? I'm a button on Kafka's underpants."

I jumped down from the wall. Both of us had red hands. We must have sensed our own marginal grip on this planet. Alain was at the edge of history, hanging on to the tail of a clan that wouldn't have him, and I was a forty-five-year-old ex–high school teacher on a slow barge between Lionel and Bathsheba.

Alain sought prisons, I dove into books. It was easy for Lionel to announce himself as a millionaire. He had Bathsheba. Alain and I had to surface without my mother's milk.

He took the cloth pillowcase and me to his distant cousin, Raffe San

Angelo, who was called "Monsieur le prince." Raffe did his business in a tabac near the parc Montsouris. It wasn't so easy to tell that Raffe was Monsieur le prince, because he posed as the tobacconist. He had the same money vest as my father, and Raffe kept digging into the pouches to provide change for his customers. It was twenty minutes before Monsieur le prince could sit down with us.

Raffe shook my hand, but he was more interested in the cloth pillowcase. He took it behind his cigarette counter, sold stamps to a spinster lady, and then returned the pillow to us. It was a touch thinner now. Monsieur le prince had switched pillowcases.

He had uncle's Tatar hair, but he was browner than Copernicus. He looked at you with the confidence of a man who had his place on the planet. He was Monsieur le prince.

We took our bastard pillowcase out to the car. "Alain, I don't like that guy switching envelopes on us."

"Stupid, it was a trade."

"A Corsican trade . . . that's some Monsieur. He has to sell tobacco and stamps."

"A tabac is the best cover in the world. Raffe doesn't go to warehouses and secret rooms. He works right off the street, so the cops can see his business. Paris is a Corsican town. Half his cousins are in City Hall. The other half launders his money. They're doctors and lawyers and tobacconists."

"What about you?"

"Monsieur doesn't count me as his cousin. When I land hard, it's la Santé. I prefer it like that."

"Maybe he thinks you're a little strange for living in America."

"Wrong. Monsieur doesn't think about me."

We parked across the Seine on the boulevard de Sébastopol. I expected to meet Russians over there. The Russians I saw carried baguettes. San Angelo pushed me onto a street that could have been an outdoor modeling school; the models stood in raincoats with nothing underneath. One of them whispered to me as she displayed her wares.

"Faire un pipe," she said.

"Alain, what's that?"

"She's a pipeuse . . . her job is to play with your pipe. But I wouldn't negotiate with a pipeuse on the rue St. Denis. She belongs to the pieds noirs."

"Pieds noirs?" I muttered, with my last look at the pipeuse.

"The black foots. Nigger Jews from North Africa. The worst trash. I piss on the pieds noirs whenever I visit la Santé. It's become an Arab beauty parlor."

"But what's it got to do with the pipeuse?"

"She'll lure you into a hotel, start her gobbling act with your pants around your ankles, and the pieds noirs will come . . . they'll steal your wallet and cut off your pipe for good luck."

"Hombre, let's get out of here."

We landed on the rue Sainte Foy. It was San Angelo's block. The models of Sainte Foy rubbed up against him. They touched me on my linen trousers. I wanted to hire them all, but San Angelo led me up the stairs of an ancient hotel. The son of a bitch had scared me with his song of the pieds noirs. I began to see black foots everywhere, little heartless men hunkering in the stairwell. But they didn't hop out at us. They lived in the meat of a wall.

We arrived at San Angelo's favorite bordel. Two rooms in a rotted house. The local pipeuse jumped on San Angelo's lap. She was Blondine, a girl with golden down on her thighs. She had a raincoat like the other models, and nothing I did or said could induce her to take it off.

San Angelo left me with Blondine and shopped for his own pipeuse. I heard him scrambling on an upper floor. Blondine had an unmarked oval face. She could have walked out of an earlier century. She didn't grind her hips or croon filthy songs. She was a good-natured girl who happened to play with pipes. There were no beds that I could see in this bordel. Blondine rolled my trousers down, unbuttoned my boxer shorts, got onto her knees, and cradled her head in my thighs. I lifted the skirts of her raincoat, looked at that wonderful bow her back made, the dimple where her buttocks began. I could hear a pulse beat in her head while she was my pipeuse. Blondine had an elf's mouth. She held you with magic dust. It was as if my pipe had fallen into an endless universe and swam in that dust.

San Angelo returned soon as the pompier was over. He wouldn't let me pay the pipeuse.

"Can't I leave her something . . . a few hundred francs?"

"Romey, it's on the house."

"Whose house?"

San Angelo twitched his eyes at me. "She's with the corporation."

I groaned. "Copernicus is multinational now."

"What do you expect? A corporation has to grow."

"Lionel's a slave trader. Alain, how old is that girl?"

"How can you ever tell with a pipeuse? She could be thirty-five."

"Or twelve."

I warbled to San Angelo on the stairs. "Alain, I'd like to bring her to America as an au pair girl."

"She'd starve. She's the best pipeuse in Paris."

I'd misjudged San Angelo. He might have been an outlander with Monsieur le prince, but he was inside uncle's economics. A soldier and a pimp.

Still, I could see how important it was to have your own pipeuse. Blondine was better than a nerve tonic. Could have slept like a baby, but Alain refused to drive us home. The soldier had his errands. We went down Sébastopol to the place du Châtelet. The city was wrapped in blue light, as if we were moving in and out of soft wool at one in the morning.

Barges rode on the river's boiling black juice. The Seine was like a stinking little canal between us and the huge stone huts on the Ile de la Cité. We passed another island, with chimneys that stood like a chorus of penguins out on the roofs. I'd swear those penguins never broke wind. Only perfect creatures could have lived among all that sanctity of stone.

We got to the boulevard Diderot, parked, and walked into the African quarter behind the gare de Lyon. It's lucky Alain and I were like Bedouins with our dark eyes, because there wasn't a white face on the rue de Chalon. We marched between old and dirty walls. Alain took me into alleys that weren't wide enough for the two of us. We entered houses where blacks slept in the halls. Alain didn't say pardon me. He climbed over bodies, knocked on doors. Blacks in Hawaiian shirts came out to greet him. They talked French with a music that was much finer than my Corsican friend's. America must have corrupted Alain.

He opened the cloth pillowcase for the blacks, like a bride's treasure bag, and they stuffed wads of money into its neck. I'd peek around the treasure bag during this transaction. I saw nothing but faces. I'd swear fifty men slept behind each door. The rue de Chalon was a giant boardinghouse where every black inherited enough room to lay his head.

These men were *clandestins* from the Ivory Coast. They worked as dishwashers and tubmen in cellar laundries. My uncle paid their passage, found them lodgings in the "Côte d'Ivoire" behind the railroad station, supplied them with prostitutes, rice, and beans.

I wondered where they were situated in uncle's little black book and under what heading? *Slave trade, Côte d'Ivoire, Paris.* He collected his fees from the black gangsters in Hawaiian shirts who watched over these *clandestins.* His bagman was Alain, and his protection was Monsieur le prince. Monsieur stroked the Palais de Justice and the police.

"Alain," I said on the stairs, "was it cabbage I brought from the States in that bloody pillow, cabbage for Monsieur to stuff the mouths at City Hall?"

"Not exactly. Lionel and Monsieur like to play the currency markets."

"And what's inside the pillow we got back from Monsieur? Trinkets to quiet witch doctors on the rue de Chalon?"

"Stolen airline tickets," San Angelo said. "How do you think you traveled Concorde?"

"My God," I said. "Lionel does own the world."

"With a little help from Monsieur."

I was a slave trader too, stuck in Lionel's machine. A yegg with a pillowcase.

But we didn't get to keep it. A boy crept out from behind a garbage barrel at the bottom of the stairs and whisked the pillow away. I started to run after him, but San Angelo clutched my Swedish coat.

"You could die running on the rue de Chalon. Rest awhile. I know where the pillow went."

"To the pieds noirs?"

The son of a bitch hugged me in the middle of that African colony. "You're getting to be a soldier," he said.

"But couldn't that boy have been an ordinary beggar thief?"

"He's with les Frères, a gang of miserable North African brothers. The pieds noirs have a hundred little gangs, but only les frères Montesquieu would take property from Raffe San Angelo."

"How many brothers are there?"

"Two. Philippe and Antoine. The cops think there's nine brothers. And les Frères like to prolong that myth. It's healthier for them."

We had some ham and cheese on the boulevard and drove to the north of Paris, into the Goutte d'Or, a nation of Arab bars, couscous joints, peddlers wandering in the street with bags of merchandise. I smelled the air of the Goutte d'Or. It was home country, the casbah. Charlotte Street had moved to Paris.

We went into a giant cafeteria, Des Poissonniers, on the boulevard de la Chapelle. Where were the nigger Jews Alain had talked about? I didn't see a skullcap or a prayer shawl in the restaurant. The black foots didn't rush out at us from behind the huge counter at Des Poissonniers. Arab men sat alone at the tables drinking beer. Alain ordered pommes frites without signaling to any of the waiters. The frites arrived. That's how things were accomplished in the Goutte. Des Poissonniers was a swamp with a hard floor. You could sink if you weren't careful, or lose your french fries.

We stole salt and pepper from a table and had our frites. And then we searched for the brothers Montesquieu. They sat near the window, without a retinue. Philippe and Antoine were identical twins. There wasn't a freckle or a frown that the other brother didn't have. Black foots with blue eyes. They were the blondest niggers I'd ever seen.

Antoine aped his brother's expression, but he was a frozen wall. His blue eyes were off in some eternity of the injured. He'd recast what his brother said, but he wouldn't start a conversation.

Philippe chatted in English for my sake.

"Cunt," Alain said, "you took from me."

"It was my way of saying hello . . ."

"Philippe, I don't need introductions from you."

"That was for Jérôme," Philippe said.

"Jérôme," Antoine said with his blue eyes. "We did it for Jérôme."

"What the hell is he to you?" Alain asked.

Philippe answered for his brother. "We had to welcome the nephew of Lionel Copernic."

"It's like the secret service," Alain said. "Les Frères know our business before we do. Philippe, give us the package you stole."

"You'll have to ask my brother."

"Stop joking. Antoine's been in too many wars. He doesn't move without you."

"Ask him."

The Corsican smiled. "Le paquet, cher ami."

Philippe barked at Alain. "Say it in English. He'll understand you better. He doesn't remember that Corsicans can speak French."

"And I forgot that the pieds noirs are comedians . . . Antoine, do us all a favor and give me the packet, please."

Antoine reached under the table and fished out the pillowcase with his blue eyes. "Pour toi," he said.

"Would you like to count your goods, Corsican?"

"I trust you," Alain said, turning from the brothers Montesquieu.

"Wait. We haven't talked with Jérôme."

"I'll lend him to you next year . . . put a move on it, little Romey."

I couldn't help liking les Frères. I stood out on the boulevard de la Chapelle and watched the brothers in the window. All that blondness was amazing to a Tatar like myself.

"Did Antoine lose his mind in Algeria?" I asked San Angelo.

"Don't get taken in by the baby blue eyes. He's cleverer than you think."

"But where did it happen?"

"It happened in Corse."

"What were the pieds noirs doing in Corsica?"

"That's where they went from Algiers. The black foots became gentlemen farmers . . . they built private roads in the maquis, made villages, moved in other pieds noirs, until the Corsicans threw them out."

"And now they're on the boulevard de la Chapelle."

"Forget about black foots. Little Romey, look at the sights."

He pointed to a young street performer near Des Poissonniers who was spitting fire from his mouth. The man went up and down the boulevard with a torch in his hand, a blue and yellow whirlwind coming out of his face.

"Is that another black foot?"

"He's a fire eater. Worse than the pieds noirs. Fire eater is as low as you can get."

"But is he an Arab from the Goutte d'Or?"

"No, it's a kid from la Santé, or a student out on his ass. When you can't find a job you become a fire eater. It's like being with the dead."

The fire eater had little scars on his lips. He'd hold the torch close to his head and suck fire at it.

I took ten francs out of my pocket, but San Angelo made me put the money back. "It's unlucky to tip a fire eater. It connects you to him and his rotten mouth."

"Alain, that's an old wives' tale."

"Not in Paris. Fire from his mouth can break your back."

We left the fire eater and rode out of the Goutte d'Or.

The pillow for uncle sat on my bureau at the Wigwam hotel. Had my ticket to America. Could have gone Concorde, but I stayed in my room and dreamt of Philippe and Antoine. I had blond eyes in my sleep and that single face of the brothers Montesquieu. Les Frères were eating fire. I didn't worry. An old high school teacher could handle the confusion of dreams.

I got on the Métro to Stalingrad. That was my stop for les Frères. The names on the Métro lines were like medallions to different countries, battlefields, and treasure grounds. Italie. Austerlitz. Babylone. Pyramides. Stalingrad. You could travel the bloody world in the Paris Métro and never have to venture above ground.

No fire eaters on the boulevard de la Chapelle. The casbah was asleep. Goutte d'Or. Drop of Gold. Drop of Gold. Goutte d'Or.

I had my recompense in the window of Des Poissonniers. Only one of les Frères was in his seat. He had that frozen look of Antoine, an empty blue sea in his eyes. But Antoine wasn't alone. There was a woman at the window. My lovely aunt. Marie-Pierre. I squatted low to make sure I hadn't ridden into the Goutte on the tails of a dream.

It was auntie. Auntie in her culottes. And it wasn't like neighbors having tea in the same Arab restaurant. Her hand was on top of Antoine's. She laughed. The black foot's eyes cleared. The blue sea went away. I'd been mistaken. This was Philippe.

Stalingrad could go to the devil. Marie-Pierre never looked that way at Lionel and me. Auntie was in love with the blond black foot.

Was I supposed to defend the family honor and duel with Philippe? I didn't go inside Des Poissonniers. I sneaked back into the subway and got the hell out of Paris.

SIX

BRUNHILDE'S GHOST

EDGAR was all over me. "Romey, Romey, did you write about Brunhilde's ghost?"

"I was on a business trip. I didn't have time for Pinocchio."

He took on that look of Antoine Montesquieu. Frozen in the face.

"I'll be Brunhilde's ghost. Give me a chance to recuperate."

He ran between my legs, got out his copying book, and I was rid of Antoine.

"Where's your dad?"

Edgar didn't know.

I rocked on my bed, hoping to catch some musical fish by the tail and ride her into the next chapter. But my mind wasn't on Pinocchio. It was on auntie and the Goutte d'Or. And I had to begin the chapter with Corsica and culottes on my back.

CHAPTER 3
How Pinocchio, an Orphan Now, Meets
His Fairy Godmother on the Road and
Mends His Rotten Ways

It's 1937, and Mussolini is bullying the Albanians and the Greeks. The Duce dreams of a new Roman Empire that will allow Italy to walk straight to Egypt. He beats up twenty socialists in Ravenna with his fists. He boasts of a "concentration colony" he intends to build in Jubaland for royalists, niggers, and Jews. "Whoso is against the Party is against me, and will get his neck broken."

But there is a wooden boy in Montegrumo that il Duce doesn't know about. The local Party boss, Achille, has tried to keep Pinocchio a secret from the outside world. The boy doesn't appear on the village registers. He's not part of Mussolini's census. The Montegrumesi don't want attention drawn to themselves. All of Italy will invade their village and worship in front of a wooden boy that talks. Better to hush up the little bastard, confine him to the borders of the village. Blackshirts and carabinieri pasture him like a dumb cow and watch that Pinocchio doesn't stray.

And so he was the prisoner of Montegrumo, without a playmate. He had nothing but his babbo. After Brunhilde died, there wasn't a soul to initiate him into the mysteries of his nose. The boy started to go downhill in his three-cornered hat. He drank tubs of coffee, he stopped searching for library books, he smoked cigarettes until his mouth turned black.

His babbo mourned Pinocchio. The boy was a lazy rascal who wouldn't even tend his father's ovens. The loaves burn while Pinocchio farts around in the bakery.

"Would you like another babbo?" Geppetto asks. "I can give you to the fascisti. They'll shave your skull and teach you how to salute."

"No, babbo, no, no, no," Pinocchio says, hugging his father and scattering the white dust on Geppetto's head.

The boy can't explain his listlessness. He has no interest in the matters of Montegrumo. He begins to wonder why he was ever born in a bread basket. He should have been left alone to sleep whatever sleep he was having before he woke up in the bakery with arms and legs.

But it was sinful to have such thoughts. His babbo fell asleep in the back room and forgot to wake up. The boy blamed himself. Geppetto had died of an unhinged heart, disappointed in his village, his country, and his wooden boy.

The Blackshirts arrived and buried the old baker in a disused vegetable garden where pariahs and idiots were put to rest without church rites.

Achille touched the boy's hand. "Come, you'll live with me."

Pinocchio was passive in his grief and went along with Achille. Blackshirts congratulated Achille and whispered in his ear. "Boss, it's a perfect way to watch the little bugger."

"Silenzio," Achille said. He was almost fond of that sad boy. He had five greedy daughters at home and a greedy wife. He welcomed the chance to eat macaroni with another "man" at the table.

Achille introduced Pinocchio while the macaroni cooked. "This is the orphan, Geppetto's boy. I will not tolerate sneers. He's made of wood, true, but he reasons like one of us. He will be pitied and loved in this house, capisce?"

The daughters and the wife trembled at Achille's emotion and the length of his speech. He hadn't delivered four whole sentences to them in years.

They filled the boy's plate with macaroni and tried not to stare at his woodenness. But the daughters still frightened Pinocchio. They kept stuffing pasta into their faces and burping behind their fists. This is what his babbo had warned him about. The bourgeoisie.

He escaped through the window that night, his stomach swollen with signora Achille's macaroni. He had no sense of the countryside, and he couldn't read a map. Pinocchio lumbered in one direction, sleeping in trees and stealing cabbages when he was hungry. He didn't bother to discard the dusty outer leaves. He'd dig with his nose until he arrived at the heart and then he'd swallow bits of cabbage, leaving the husk at the side of the road. Anyone clever enough might have discovered Pinocchio by these "pages" of trash. But the village of Montegrumo decided not to look for the boy.

He followed this existence for months, sleeping, eating cabbages, and walking with no purpose in mind, when a bear fell out of a tree and almost smothered Pinocchio. But it was the strangest bear, without claws and a big wet snout. The bear wore an old smock. It was Brunhilde's ghost.

"Please, please," the boy said, "don't murder me."

Brunhilde the bear climbed off Pinocchio.

"Piccolino," she said, and her voice was much thicker as a ghost. It seemed to spill up from her chest. "Will you reform and become the socialist child your babbo wanted you to be?"

"Yes," he muttered, but he didn't know how to address a ghost. "Signorina, can I call you Brunhilde?"

"If you like," the ghost said. "I'm not a signorina any more. I'm Madam Brunhilde."

The boy began to calculate in his head. "What does a socialist do, Madam Brunhilde?"

"A socialist breaks up fascist rallies and becomes Mussolini's enemy for life."

"I swear, Madam. Mussolini's enemy for life . . . but how did you come back from the dead?"

"Gesù sent me," Brunhilde said. "I'm your fairy godmother, Pinocchio. And I have the power to turn you into a live boy if you make good as a socialist."

The boy was confused. "Is Gesù a socialist?"

"No. But God hates Mussolini."

"Madam, why doesn't Gesù hit Mussolini with thunder and horse manure?"

"Pinocchio," his godmother said, "Gesù has other ways of working . . . listen now, and don't be so impertinent. That's how you'll get to be a human boy."

"Madam, should I tickle you today?"

Brunhilde socked him on his wooden head. "Are you an imbecile? You can't do such things with a fairy godmother."

Pinocchio started to blubber. It had nothing to do with the ringing in his ears from Brunhilde's fist. The boy was mortified. "Madam, I only wanted to be nice . . ."

"I forgive you, piccolino," she said. "But you must remember we're not allowed to touch like that."

And his fairy godmother vanished into the trees. Pinocchio felt cheated. Brunhilde rises from the land of dead people, tells him Gesù is a socialist, and socks him when he tries to continue the education she began in her hut.

He runs away from Brunhilde's trees and finds himself on the road to Parma . . .

He arrives at the Casa del Fascio, which is the old charterhouse. The Young Fascist League is holding a rally behind the house. Boys and girls wear black shirts and salute each other in the Roman way, with a wide sweep of the elbow. Pinocchio moves among them. He can't be from the Party. He doesn't have the emblem of a lightning bolt on his sleeve. The girls are shrewder than the boys. Perhaps they've already taken an interest in his nose. He's not a simple gangster of the socialist class. He's a wooden boy.

The girls would love to fondle him. "What's your name?"

"Pinocchio."

The boys don't care for this intruder. They snap their armbands at Pinocchio and lunge at him. But he's slippery.

He slaps boy after boy with his arms, solid as cricket bats. He's softer with the girls. He pulls out a few hairs from each girl's scalp. They run into the Casa del Fascio, crying, "A socialist!"

The fiercest Party members come bullying out with long knives and sneaky little guns. These fascisti shoot at Pinocchio. He has the gift of ducking under a bullet. They hurl their knives at him. The points break on contact with his skin. Geppetto must have dipped him in amazing shellac while Pinocchio was still in the bread basket.

A fisherman happens to see Pinocchio dodging bullets. He whispers to the fascists. They follow him home and bring out the fisherman's net. They whirl the net around Pinocchio and trap him inside.

Now that Pinocchio belongs to them, the fascisti can't decide what to do. They could torture him under the net, turn him to splinters and dust with carpenter's tools. What if the Duce hears about that slow murder under the net, and genius that he is, could have used a talking puppet for propaganda purposes? All of Parma could disappear.

The Party has the chief of police call Rome. Mussolini likes policemen. And so does his secretary, Count Jacobo. Jacobo answers the call from Parma. "Puppet?"

"Yes, excellency, a boy of wood."

"Shall I wake the Duce over your problems with a wooden boy?"

"No, excellency . . . but this Pinocchio talks. He's a socialist tool. He interfered with the Young Fascists. He knocked down the strongest boys and left two girls bald in the head."

"Where is the monster?"

"We have him, excellency. He's under our net."

The Blackshirts of Parma wait twenty, thirty hours.

An armored car with a candy-striped turret comes to their door. The Duce steps out in boots and black knickers, accompanied by Jacobo. The fascisti understand the need for an armored car. Assassins are lurking about. Hired guns from Great Britain and France.

Mussolini hops up the charterhouse stairs without extending the Roman salute. He has little use for the men of Parma. They're cuckolds and poor thinkers.

He sees the boy under the net. Pinocchio's eyes are bulging with hunger.

"What's wrong with him?"

"Duce, it's obvious," says the count. "They've been starving the brat."

Mussolini digs his knuckles into his sides. "He's no good to me dead . . ."

The fascists rush over with a salami, cucumbers, bits of cheese, and a bottle of red wine. The Duce hands these things to Pinocchio, his elbows lost in the net.

"I can't do business," he shouts. "There's too many people." He shuts the door on the fascisti and watches Pinocchio gobble his food. The salami vanishes into Pinocchio's mouth. The cucumbers are gnawed to pieces. The Duce admires the way this boy eats.

"Jacobo, you got me out of bed . . . prove to me this isn't a hoax. Any fool can varnish himself and swear he's made of wood."

The count goes up to the net. "Pinocchio, wiggle your fingers, will you?"

Mussolini hears the clack of wood.

"Cheap stuff. My gardener can do better than that . . . if he's a local boy looking for attention, I'll burn his feet. I hate Parma. What am I doing here?"

"He's wood, Duce. On my life, he's wood."

"Question him . . . see if he's a cretino."

Jacobo asks the boy if Italy has a king.

Pinocchio doesn't answer, but Mussolini begins to rant at the mention of a king. "It's not my fault if the king has to borrow a ladder to climb on his horse."

The Duce prances over to the net. "Sonny, who am I? And be quick."

"Prince Benito."

"Ah, the boy has a sense of humor. That's rare these days. Pinocchio, are you sure you're made of wood?"

"Yes, papa."

"How does a wooden boy become a socialist?" Jacobo asks. "Well, puppet, talk to your father, Mussolini. He won't hurt you."

"The man who discovered me was a socialist."

The Duce takes a small notebook out of his pocket. "What's the man's name?" he shouts into the teeth of the net.

"My babbo was a baker, Prince Benito . . . and he's dead."

"It's a treasonable act to teach socialism to a puppet . . . I'm the Duce, and what's under the ground is also mine. We'll dig him up. In Italy the dead can die again and again. What's his name?"

Pinocchio calls the Duce papa and prince to flatter him and get more grub, but he wouldn't snitch on the only father he had.

"Benito, he died when I was a baby . . . I don't remember his name."

"Quiet!" Mussolini says, thrusting out his jaw. "You were never a baby." Then he pulls on his knickers and sits down near the boy, his temper moving into a fit of despair.

"What is Mussolini? A cow? A dog? The pope eats cooked prunes, the king sits in his palace, and I'm the cow in the middle . . . Pinocchio."

His secretary tries to reassure him. "Duce, how can you compare yourself with this little freak?"

"I'm Pinocchio . . . that's why we get along . . . the two wooden boys. Jacobo, help me crawl under the net."

"And if one of the king's spies should look through the window? What will they say at the Quirinale?"

"The Duce loves his people so much, he crawls under the net with the least of them."

"No! They'll say Benito sits in the dust inside the charterhouse of Parma and ruins his parade pants."

"Quiet!"

Mussolini has gotten over his fit. He starts to slap the dust off his knickers. Jacobo lures him into politics.

"Duce, Aldo has been doing a lot of talking at the German embassy."

"Liquidate him," Mussolini says. "I can't stomach a tattletale."

"The Germans might not like it. Aldo's their pet."

"Then we'll liquidate the embassy. I don't care."

"And what should we do about the boy?"

"Which boy?" the Duce asks, wars rushing into his head with a maddening howl. He would like to dismember Turkey, claim Syria and Iraq, and march to Alexandria with his men, make the Suez an Italian boatyard.

The count says, "Pinocchio."

Mussolini has a fever in one eye. How can he build up the Italian race if that silly count goes on and on with the affairs of a wooden boy?

"Liquidate him!"

"But Duce, it was your idea to convert the puppet and bring him to Rome."

"That was yesterday's news. I'm sick of hearing him eat salami."

"Think of the thunder we can steal from Pius . . . a puppet who is more devout than all the holies . . . and an excellent little fascist. We'll show him off at parades. He'll ride a pony. Hah, he'll be taller than the king!"

"Then convert him, Jacobo, for Christ's sake."

The count spreads his knees and stoops over the wooden boy.

"Pinocchio, listen to your father . . . will you come to Rome with us and behave? You'll live at the Duce's palace. You'll have a man to undress you, a woman to wash your clothes. You won't have to share a toilet. You'll eat at the Duce's table, chat with his friends, spit on his enemies. You'll have a title, commander of the Young Fascist League. The Duce will take you to Germany with him. The Führer will be jealous. They don't have boys like you in Berlin . . . a puppet who can talk with a chief of state. Pinocchio, swear to Mussolini that you'll give up socialism."

"I swear," Pinocchio squeaks, his schnozzle swelling with such a lie. But the Duce and his secretary aren't watching Pinocchio's nose. They're thinking of the trip back to Rome, and all the booby traps that foreign agents might plant under the Duce's wheels. The count cuts the thick string that binds the net.

"Come out, my little commander."

Pinocchio leaps through the open net, knocks down Jacobo with his cricket-bat arm, and jumps out the window of the charterhouse . . .

Edgar had enough material to hold him for a week. I was the one with nothing to do. I'd returned to an empty tower. Bathsheba must have picked up with a plumber. Her door was shut to me, and Lionel wasn't around.

Then I fathomed why Bathsheba was incommunicado all of a sudden. She was ashamed of the plumber in her rooms. It was Hervey Long, the grand deacon of Dominick Street. Herve had come up from the mission to spend his days over Washington Square. Never mind that he was forty years younger than my mother. I had no right to condemn Bathsheba's lovers according to their age. But Herve was a sadistic bastard. He'd brutalized the mission yeggs. Bathsheba had found a lulu for her bed.

I caught him skulking around the premises with a bottle of Seagram's. He had to clutch the walls.

"Have a suck of whiskey, Jerome. Calm yourself. I'm gonna be your new pappy."

"That's decent of you, Herve, to tell me all about it."

"Yes sir, your mamma proposed, and she's just about the darnedest lady."

This wasn't Dominick Street, where Herve commanded an army of deacons. I hit him once behind the ear. Herve tumbled onto the floor with his bottle and had himself a whiskey sleep.

I guiled my way into Bathsheba's rooms, pretending I was her lulu. She was all tarted up for the deacon. Her eyes were painted silver to go with the blue hair. She had little orange specks in the eye shadow. Cleopatra would have felt naked in my mother's gown. You could see all her goods under the silk. She covered herself with a long sweater from her closet. That was her hello to me.

She understood the streak of violence in her only son. "What did you do with Mr. Long?"

"Not to worry, mamma. I walloped him with the soft side of my hand. He'll wake up fresh. I promise."

"Why didn't you stay in Paris, France?"

"Well, I was worried about Lionel, mamma. He's my uncle. He taught me to swim and ride a bike. I'm in his debt. And I didn't want to abandon him . . . seeing how auntie has disappeared."

"She hasn't disappeared. She's on a leave of absence. Lionel's better off. It's like a holiday for him. He isn't so moody without Marie. But I'll have you arrested if you hit my fiancé again."

"Careful, mamma. I'll summon up Bruno's ghost. He'll know what to do with Hervey Long."

"You're heartless," she whispered in her long sweater. "You wouldn't strut if Lionel were here. You're lucky he went to the Hamptons."

"Hamptons? Uncle hates sea water."

"Romey, where have you been the last ten years? Marie taught him to like the beach. They have a cottage on the water."

"That's rich. A change like that, a different style of life, and nobody gives me a clue. Don't I count for something, mamma? Shouldn't I have been consulted, or offered a share in the cottage?"

"What good would it do you? You're like your father. You can't drive a car."

"That's inconsequential. I have a license. Don't you remember? Uncle bribed the Motor Vehicle Bureau. I have a legal right to be on the road. I'd have made it to the cottage if someone had told me it exists."

"You're a devil," she said. The silver around her eyes began to smear. The orange specks swam under her Tatar cheeks. "I knew that even while I was carrying you. You clawed my insides . . . Lionel never clawed."

I looked at her. "That's the whole point, Bathsheba. Lionel wasn't in your belly. He was only under your dress in Percival Newgarden's shop. Babies like to claw in the womb. It's a fact. Prepares them for the outside. Bathsheba, couldn't you kiss me for old times' sake?"

"Which old times? We never got along."

"What about when I was in the baby carriage?"

"Do you always have to wound your mother? It was wrong what I did. Are you happy now? I shouldn't have taken you along when I went stealing in the stores."

"But I would have felt left out. It was you, me, Lionel, and the baby carriage . . . mamma, one kiss."

She pulled on her sweater and kissed my mouth. I could feel the heat of her dissolving eye shadow. My mother smelled of peach skins.

"I'll try to be nicer to your fiancé, mamma, I will."

Old Herve was gone, but I found his bottle of Seagram's. I pulled at the bottle like a bloody infant until my eyeballs hurt. Must have taken a nap because the walls got dark. Had whiskey in my brain, and I couldn't stand up. So I started to crawl.

Somebody's buttocks got in the way. Hearts and moons it was. Figured the moons belonged to Harriet the maid, because my mother's cheeks would have had a more pronounced fall by the age of seventy-two. Harriet clutched the stairs to uncle's boudoir. Lionel came out to greet her. "Darling," she said, touching his mouth. She was taller than uncle. But this was no maid. I caught her under the blue nightbulb in uncle's wall. It was Miz Alabam from the Dominick Street mission.

Blood banged like a tom-tom in my eyes. I didn't charge up to the boudoir. I waited a bit, let the door close behind uncle and Alabam, swiped a cigarette from the dining room table, as the tom-tom boomed.

I wasn't shivering. I was perfectly calm when I climbed up to uncle. He was on the bed with Alabam, eating her back in a kind of ravenous foreplay. I jumped on him. Alabam started to scream. She wiggled out from under Lionel and tried to shove me off. I slapped her forehead from my perch. Uncle made little moaning sounds.

My mother came huffing in, her face streaked with broken silver lines.

"Romey, get off."

"Not a chance," I said.

Bathsheba approached the bed, thinking to save uncle. It would have been a pretty sight, ripping Bathsheba's blue hair while I smothered Lionel.

"Bathsheba, outside with Alabam . . ."

That was Lionel bellowing under me, his chest squeezed to the summer quilt.

"He'll murder you," my mother said.

"Never mind."

The two women walked out of the boudoir.

"Shut the door," Lionel said.

"Uncle, who's the injured party?"

"You are."

I climbed down from his back.

"Lionel, Dominick Street is run from Washington Square. I didn't seduce Miz Alabam. She was following your instructions. You staged that ceremony in the delousing room. What the hell for?"

"To get you here."

"Couldn't you have asked me, uncle?"

"You'd never have come."

"You are the sun king," I said. "Every damn thing conforms to your private clock."

"Not everything," he said.

"Yes, Marie got away . . . how did that happen?"

"She fell in love with an Arab farmer."

"Philippe Montesquieu?"

"I don't remember his name."

"I do. And he doesn't farm in Paris. He sits in a cafeteria with a brother who's in shell shock from some foreign war. This Philippe is a moneylender and a pimp . . . he smuggles black men into Paris, same as you. Uncle, it's not that healthy being your courier. Suppose the customs people realized I was taking hot airline tickets out of Paris."

"You don't get frisked riding Concorde. That's the beauty of it. But I didn't send you over to mingle with Raffe."

"Then why did you send me?"

"To establish some tie with Marie."

"That's lovely news. Lionel, what went wrong with the marriage?"

He began searching for his clothes. The disorder in the boudoir was beyond his capabilities. I found a sock of his hiding in Alabam's underpants.

"We had troubles," Lionel said, wearing his one sock. "She was fond of traveling, and it was hard for me . . . I couldn't abandon your mother. You were on the lecture circuit."

"Lionel, are you saying I ruined your marriage?"

"Don't get jumpy. I encouraged Marie to go out on her own and discover new markets in Paris."

"And the market she discovered was Philippe Montesquieu . . . uncle, forgive me, but would auntie stray without a reason?"

"She had reasons."

"Was Alabam one of them?"

"Let's just say she was a side effect . . . but I'm worried about Marie. She abandons Edgar, gives up her whole line of rainwear, everything, for the Arab. That's not like Marie-Pierre. She's a cautious girl. Help me, Romey."

"Uncle, you have your own artillery in Paris."

"You're her high school teacher. She respects you . . . that's the best artillery I have."

"I won't fly on a stolen ticket. You'll pay for the Concorde out of your own pocket."

And he did. But you'll never make him suffer over money. He's the sun king, and he can scratch dollar signs until his arm turns blue.

SEVEN

MADAME COPERNIC

I was like an old sailor in the Concorde lounge. Ate a sack of peanuts, had bourbon on the rocks. But I should have sniffed disaster when they fed me chicken Kiev on board that humpbacked silver bird.

Rode on down to the rue Pascal in San Angelo's Dodge. Had my old room at the Wigwam.

"Alain, did the uncle tell you why I've come?"

"Yes, to scratch for Madame Copernic. She's trouble, little Romey. She started out as Raffe's companion and then she switched to the pieds noirs."

"She was with Monsieur le prince?"

"How do you think Lionel got to Monsieur? Madame Copernic made the connection. I was the chauffeur once upon a time for her and Monsieur. They formed this company for children's clothes. And then she flitted out."

"Alain, do you know her address in Paris?"

"Try the Goutte d'Or."

"I'd rather not surprise her at Philippe's restaurant. Isn't there another way?"

"Madame moves from hotel to hotel. Right now she's registered at the Scandinavia. But she's hardly ever there."

"Come on, let's gamble. She might be having crumpets at the Scandinavia."

San Angelo chauffeured me out of the rue Pascal, towards the Gold Coast of Paris. Up the hill to Gay Lussac, across the boul' Miche, around the bend of the Luxembourg gardens, with their cornucopia of sand paths, and into the rue de Tournon. The hotel Scandinavia had old wood in its window, like the wreckage of a Viking ship. I didn't badger the patronne about a certain Madame Copernic. I booked a room, shoving my passport at the lady behind the desk. Told her in choppy French that my luggage had gone to Morocco by mistake.

"That's a great pity," the patronne said.

Went outside with San Angelo, called the Scandinavia from the street, asked for Madame Copernic, got her room number, and then sauntered back into the hotel. Auntie was situated near the roof. We broke into her room with San Angelo's penknife, taking care not to leave bruises in the wood. We couldn't come up with signs of Madame Copernic. Oh, she had a few skirts in the closet, but that was to satisfy the maid that Copernic did exist. There were no crumpets on the night table. Not even a hairbrush.

The room had its own terrace that looked onto an old church and a field of chimney pots. We borrowed two chairs and sat on the terrace, while the church below guarded each quarter hour with a carillon that seemed to rock the Scandinavia.

We waited for Madame, the carillon eating up quarter hours until the roof tiles darkened one by one in that long summer night.

"Told you. She's having couscous with les Frères."

San Angelo closed up the room with his penknife. I sent him home to the Wigwam, and I sat two days in the Scandinavia, watching the stairs. I ate my fingers in the room, fearing I'd miss auntie if I ducked out for some chicken soup at the restaurant down the block. Had stomach cramps and church music, but no Madame Copernic or soupe saigonnaise.

Gave up my quarters at the Scandinavia and returned to the Wigwam. Would have slept like old Gulliver in Lilliput, but I had a guest. Madame. She wasn't in culottes or harem pants. Her hair was pulled strict around her head. She was no millionaire's wife in my room at the Wigwam.

"Auntie," I said. "Lionel sent me here. He's under the illusion that old high school teachers have some pull with their students. But we live on a checkerboard, and you're always three jumps ahead."

"That's because you had a late start. Boston Road retards the blood."

"Then why didn't you teach me at Bronx Science?"

"I tried," she said.

"Isn't uncle retarded too? Why'd you marry him?"

"I was sixteen, you idiot. I was kept like a prisoner in Texas. Why do you think I made my daddy give me a year in New York? . . . Lionel was my way out."

"You didn't love him?"

"Yes, I loved him. And I loved you too. But I couldn't wait around for Franz Kafka to grow up, and I didn't fancy being the wife of a schoolteacher."

"So you married Lionel, had the little boy, and then what happened?"

"Let's say Lionel isn't my type."

"Who is your type? Philippe Montesquieu?"

"Yes, Philippe . . . Antoine . . . or you."

"Auntie," I said, "am I one of les Frères?"

"You could be."

"What's wrong with Lionel?"

"He has the money touch, Midas in his hands."

"You didn't seem to mind that gift at La Tulipe. You're the one who taught him papillote. He would have been happy with kasha and charlotte russes."

"Kasha doesn't make you pure . . ."

"I know, but you shouldn't misread his millions. He's more of a Marxist than Philippe."

"Philippe isn't a Marxist," auntie said. "He peddles drugs . . . but why don't you come and meet him?"

"I'm more interested in Antoine."

"You can meet him too."

"Couldn't we meet with Antoine alone?"

"You saw him. He's frightened without Philippe."

So I went down to auntie's Citroën. She encountered Paris like a Corsican taxi driver edging in and out of traffic. I was disappointed in Madame Copernic. She didn't take me up the boulevard de Sébastopol to the Goutte d'Or. She had a different route. Over the Seine, along the northern quays to the avenue du President Wilson, and into the bois de Boulogne.

"Is Edgar somewhere in your future, auntie Pierre?"

"Yes," she said. "No . . . Lionel is a better mommy than I am. And if he breaks down, the boy can always count on Bathsheba."

She parked in the bois, and we marched into a restaurant under the trees. Son of a bitch, she'd dragged me to a wedding of black foots. Older men with walrus moustaches moved about the place, looking like Gustave Flaubert in a skullcap. Darker, woollier men without skullcaps walked up to Marie and embraced her. I peeked at the wedding invitation in Marie's hand: it was for Madame Copernic et Monsieur Copernic Charyn.

"How did the black foots know I was coming?" I said, tapping the invitation.

"Antoine invited you."

The tables in the wedding salon were marked with North African streets that conformed to the map of Algiers. We were seated at the rue Denfert-Rochereau with Algerian cousins, nephews, nieces, and the brothers Montesquieu. They seemed a bit alien in their blondness, but the entire wedding revolved around les Frères. Bride and groom stopped at the rue Denfert-Rochereau before any other street. Grandfathers paid homage to Antoine, bending around that brother's knee to whisper in his ear. Young woolly men gathered close to Philippe's chair.

We ate off china with Stars of David woven into the design. Soup, duck, asparagus, cherries in ice water, a second dish of duck, lettuce, balls of ice cream, gâteau Mazel Tov. Philippe was too busy to dance. I had to go out onto the floor with Madame Copernic. We rumbaed between the tables, around the suburbs and streets of Algiers.

My rumba was imperfect. I'd been too occupied with James Joyce to take rumba lessons in the Bronx, and I had to follow auntie's feet.

I was grateful to get back to my cherries on the rue Denfert-Rochereau. Auntie kissed les Frères on the back of the neck. They wouldn't turn towards the kiss. They acknowledged it with the bluest eyes in the bois de Boulogne. A waiter brought a silver pan with two white doves to the bride and groom. The bride freed one of the doves and held the other near her chin. This dove purred like a cat.

I grew sadder and sadder at the table. Celebrations like this reminded me of my lost bar mitzvah. I was embarrassed to intrude upon the white doves, but I wished Philippe had found a pigeon for me to neck with. I swallowed cherry pits.

The brothers must have noticed how pale I looked. Philippe put aside family matters to hold a conversation with me across the rue Denfert-Rochereau. "Jérôme," he said, pointing to that city of tables. "Forgive this extravagance. My cousins are lonely for Algiers. They remember the lemons they sucked on the sea wall, the Turkish coffee they drank on the rue Marengo. We're a rough folk, Jérôme. But my cousins have landed well. They're druggists, radio technicians, just like les goys, and still they dream of Algiers. I have different sentiments. It's Corsica I miss."

"Corsica," Antoine said. "Lake de Dianne."

"We grew vegetables in the stones. We nursed dead olive groves. I had my Turkish coffee in the maquis. My casbah was a wild nest of trees called le Billy Goat. It was so dark in there, it could absorb a summer storm."

"Chase le Billy Goat," Antoine said. "Chestnuts for my brother." His eyes went out of focus. He was in his own blue sea.

"Arrête, mon poupou." Philippe was cooing to his brother to bring him out of that frozen sea. "Jérôme, it was in le Billy Goat that we had our worst scuffles with the Bonapartistes, islanders who thought we were bringing Moses to their beloved Corse and poisoning their olive groves with our black hands and feet . . . but I was addicted to that dark nest of trees. I'm a foolish man. I kept going back to le Billy with Antoine . . ."

Marie-Pierre interrupted our conversation. She brought the brothers out to the dance floor and did the tango together with Philippe and Antoine. I was too caught up in that tango to be jealous. It was curious to me, because Antoine was the better dancer. He dipped into and away from Marie, while his brother seemed stranded in the dark of le Billy Goat. Philippe was a pegleg, like Captain Ahab. His body followed its own mechanical laws that had nothing to do with the tango.

Then I heard a loud huff, like a faulty engine, around the spot where the pigeon had flown out of the silver pan. The air thickened, and a black smoke curled above the tables. Mothers and fathers grabbed their children and ran . . . a mean little bomb had exploded under a chafing dish.

Philippe came out of the Corsican woods he was in. He jumped on top of the boulevard du Telemy and started to shout.

He told his brother and sister black foots not to worry. The bomb was a wedding gift, but he didn't say from whom.

The black foots returned to the salon and started on a salmon mousse. Then the meal stopped. All the waiters assembled in the kitchen with Philippe. I heard the crashing of pots and the sound of skin slapping skin. No one screamed during that storm in the kitchen.

The waiter who'd presented the doves to the bride and groom waltzed out by himself. One side of his face was red. He didn't gather up trays for the next course. He moved in a fever around Notre Dame d'Afrique and left the salon.

The wedding began all over again. The waiters scrambled through the streets of Algiers as if someone's blue eyes were grinding into their backs. But Philippe, who'd come out of the kitchen, didn't look at them once. It was Antoine who seemed to menace the waiters.

"Philippe," I said, "was that wedding gift from Monsieur le prince?"

"I'm on good terms with Monsieur. He helps me at City Hall, and I give him a couple of free pulls in the Goutte. The bomb was your uncle's calling card."

"That's crazy," I said. "Why would uncle interrupt the wedding like that?"

"To remind us that he isn't sleeping in America, that he's Lionel Copernic and doesn't like black foots with his wife."

I stared over a mountain of ice cream balls at Madame Copernic. She wouldn't wink yes or no. I was the lone bar mitzvah boy in a mock Algiers.

"Lionel," a voice said. I looked up. Antoine was talking to me. "Lionel's in the Goutte."

San Angelo was missing from the Wigwam when I got home. The night porter said Alain had checked out of the hotel in the company of two men. He went behind his cage and handed me a yellow scarf. It was a hundred percent silk, with black diamonds inside a yellow field. The scarf was from San Angelo.

"Did the cops run him over to la Santé?"

The porter couldn't tell me.

I knotted San Angelo's scarf, and I was like every other Frenchman who wore a silk diaper around his neck. I wore the diaper to bed.

Had a grand idea in the morning. I walked down to the parc Montsouris for a chat with Monsieur le prince. But Monsieur wasn't up at this hour. His tobacco stand was closed.

I took a stroll in the park, thinking I'd catch Monsieur if I killed a couple of hours. An old man was guarding a tent, and this old man kept signaling to me. I didn't know what the dickens he was after. I hadn't monkeyed with his tent.

Ah, he was inviting me to sneak inside. Gave a couple of pennies to the old guy and ducked into the tent. It was crowded with children. I'd stumbled onto a Punch and Judy show. But this wasn't Punch and Judy of Crotona Park. The hand puppet on the stage was a duke with a wig and a full moustache. The duke talked to the children, and the children talked back.

"Méchant," they said. "Méchant."

They knew more about evil in a puppet world than I ever would. The duke took a dive under the skirts of the stage, and a bumpkin appeared. His name was Guignol, and he was the son of a nobleman who'd lost his land and his money to the duke. The young nobleman walked in a trance, believing the duke was his friend.

The children tried to warn Guignol whenever the duke rose above the skirts of the stage with a knife. "Méchant," they cried, and the duke had to stall his plan of murdering Guignol and gathering up another noble line for himself.

That was the land of Guignol, where a bumpkin is at the mercy of children who shout an evil duke under the stage. Only the bumpkin never learns from it. He goes on and on, with the duke at his back. Mes enfants, it was the story of my life. Oh, I didn't have a duke exactly. I had a baby carriage, an uncle who lied right and left, and an aunt who'd gone over to the black foots.

Might have moved in with Guignol if Monsieur le prince hadn't tapped me on the shoulder. His vassals must have told him I'd been around. Monsieur didn't have his money vest. We got out of the park and sat on the terrace of his tabac. We talked without an interpreter, in English and French. Whenever we missed a word, we growled with our hands.

"Monsieur, was that your bomb at the wedding? Philippe Montesquieu says it was Lionel's present to the pieds noirs."

"C'est impossible," said Monsieur. Lionel couldn't plant bombs from Manhattan. The bomb would have had to come through Monsieur.

But suppose uncle had another Corsican cadre working for him?

There were no other cadres, insisted Monsieur.

"Then who planted the bomb?"

The Montesquieus themselves.

That's a bit extreme, I told Monsieur.

They were trying to woo me, he said, win me over to their side.

Monsieur told me about the Montesquieus. They were pimps in Algiers. During the war of independence, the Montesquieus jumped to Corsica. Monsieur didn't deny the brothers' conversion into farmers.

Les Frères established their crops on the rockiest land. But they hadn't forsaken whoring and drugs.

"What about le Billy Goat?"

That was their drug capital, right in the woods. Le Billy was so dense, it took years to drive them out.

And Madame Copernic?

Ah, Madame Copernic . . . Monsieur announced that it was time for lunch. We didn't rush across town to Maxim's. The tabac prepared an omelette for us in a giant pan. We had green beans and pommes frites. These weren't Arab frites. They were longer and thinner, and Monsieur scooped a dozen into his napkin and ate them out of there. We had coffee with burnt brown milk and cake maison, a large bun with bits of dried fruit in it.

Raffe seemed readier now to talk of Madame Copernic. Monsieur was in love with that tall bitch. Marie was everybody's mistress.

She stayed with Monsieur on her first trips to Paris . . . lived with him in his apartment over Montsouris. Did auntie visit Guignol? She wasn't meant for Punch and Judy. She produced a line of children's clothes with Monsieur. Hats and booties for the rain. They visited Corsica, went to Portugal and St.-Tropez. It was an ideal existence for Monsieur. He had his isolation and Madame Copernic half the month. He brought her to a meeting with les Frères, to devil Philippe and Antoine, get them to eat their hearts out over "la beauté," but the brothers didn't have to eat much heart. Madame began making trips into the Goutte d'Or. And it wasn't to sell children's hats.

Tried to console Monsieur. "She did the same to me. I brought her home to dinner, and she had a bénéfice . . . marriage with Lionel Copernic."

Monsieur enjoyed this part of the story. We were compatriots, and he didn't feel quite so alone.

I had some wine with berry juice. And then I asked him about Alain. Monsieur claimed that he would have heard from his Corsican brothers at the Palais de Justice if Alain was in la Santé. Ah, he said, who can trust that cow police? He would go directly to the source. The prison rabbi at la Santé.

Monsieur, I argued, wasn't this a Catholic country?

Catholic yes, except for la Santé.

One of his vassals drove us to the edge of the Goutte d'Or, where the rabbi lived on the rue du Faubourg Poissonnière, in back of a fur shop. I'd swear this rabbi was also a fence, but I wasn't perfect on the customs of Paris. Raffe called him mon Père, which was exactly how you'd address a priest.

Couldn't make out a word of their French. I wondered if it was the dialect of la Santé.

Raffe thanked mon Père, and we went out of the fur shop.

Alain wasn't in la Santé. The rabbi had confirmed it.

I grew bitter over mon Père. "Does he get to greet every new arrival?"

Yes.

"Couldn't someone have sneaked Alain over the wall?"

Not without the rabbi's knowledge.

I paraded on the rue Pascal in my yellow scarf, hoping pure silk might draw him home. The Corsicans had failed me. Monsieur could have talked to every prison rabbi in France. But none of them produced Alain.

I didn't chase up to the Goutte for auntie Pierre. Uncle could get himself a new ambassador to Marie. I was sick of playing Guignol in a guerrilla skirmish where friends and enemies wore the same stinking mask.

I decided to cure Edgar's wordblindness once and for all with a supreme Pinocchio . . . but I was scribbling for myself. The adventures of a wooden boy was a good tonic for my own time. I could depend on Brunhilde's ghost, who wasn't quite so ambiguous as Madame Copernic. But I had to be fair. Brunhilde's dependability might have come from her being dead.

CHAPTER 4
How Pinocchio Becomes a Socialist Spy and Worms Himself into the King's Good Graces

He was the scourge of Italy, attacking fascist houses everywhere. Ravenna one day, Rimini the next. No one could capture the wooden boy. Fascist patrols scoured the countryside. Informers posed as farm girls, but they couldn't lure his schnozzle between their legs. Village priests, told of his godless ways, searched for Pinocchio. Even the blackbirds knew of him. They would divebomb from telephone poles in an attempt to disembowel Pinocchio and pick out his eyes.

He eluded the birds, but those divebombings had begun to take their toll. He had no blood to squander, no arteries to break, but the birds had so marked his face with their beaks, he looked like a strolling smallpox epidemic. In spite of his afflictions, he'd cover the holes in his face with a hand, in order not to frighten little girls, and make a shambles of the next Casa del Fascio down the road.

Mussolini sent his secret service into the countryside. The Duce didn't want Britain and France to make capital of Pinocchio and declare that a puppet could start his own civil war. The secret service arrested socialist sympathizers and fed castor oil to anyone—mayors, shop girls, priests—who had a kind word to say about this disgusting boy who threatened the Duce's Roman Empire with internal strife.

Pinocchio trashed about with his pitted face, moving over Italy in a mad circle. He still couldn't read a map, and road signs meant nothing to a boy without religion or a historical past. He was ignorant of icons and churches and ruins along the road. But so much mischief to Mussolini's people had exhausted the boy. His legs began to creak. The pits in his face turned dark from all that weather beating on the wood. The boy had a slight limp.

He'd returned to his native Tuscany without even knowing it. He couldn't tell one alfalfa field from another. His babbo had never discussed nature with him. How could a wooden boy respond to a red Tuscan sky? A priest stopped him on the road and introduced himself as don Amedeo.

"Are you hungry, my son?"

The boy nodded his head. He knew enough to say "padre" to don

Amedeo. The priest had a long hat, and his skirts went below his ankles. A few buttons were missing from his cassock, and the boy could see that don Amedeo was naked underneath. Pinocchio assumed this was ordinary for a priest.

Don Amedeo led him to a hut, and it was only after Pinocchio found the hut's own wall that he recognized the landscape. He was in Montegrumo, and this was Brunhilde's house, but he couldn't recollect if don Amedeo had been the village priest.

The padre gave him bread and hot wine, and he grew feverish from the wine. He dropped to the floor. The pits in his face were on fire. The last thing he could remember was don Amedeo getting undressed . . .

He blinked his eyes and roused himself. The boy had an unholy headache. His hands and feet were lashed with piano wire, and he was surrounded by pirates. They had daggers in their pants and cuts in their faces.

Don Amedeo stood naked with his pirate friends. He had scars like river runs up and down his body. He picked his teeth with a dagger.

"Pinocchio, don't be afraid. I'm not a priest."

"Who are you, sir?"

"Dante Romano."

"Cavaliere," Pinocchio said, trying to be respectful to a naked man. But Dante Romano slapped Pinocchio's brains with the pommel of his dagger.

"Don't call me cavaliere. I'm a socialist."

"But we're friends," Pinocchio said, feeling his brains with a finger. "I'm a socialist too."

"We're secret socialists," Dante said. "Clandestinos. We don't make spectacles of ourselves."

"But sir, my fairy godmother told me to fight Mussolini."

"Who's your godmother?"

"Brunhilde."

Dante Romano was a socialist bargeman, like his brothers. He'd lain with Brunhilde a hundred times before that skinny woman landed in hell. This boy was a little saint, having visions of a whore who worked herself to death.

"Forget your godmother. From now on you work for me."

"But I promised Brunhilde . . ."

"Are you a socialist or not?"

"Yes, a socialist, sir."

"And a clandestino, like us. Open warfare is childish. Mussolini has the tanks. It's the age of the Apache."

"Sir," the boy said. "I don't know military science. What's an Apache?"

"Someone who leaps out of the rocks. The Apache hits and runs."

Pinocchio wiggled the piano wire on his feet. "That's what I've been doing."

"You have to hit and run the clandestino way."

"How?" Pinocchio asked, his face still burning from the drugged wine Dante Romano had fed him.

"You'll infiltrate the Savoyards, throw yourself at the mercy of the king. That will put you near enough to strangle Mussolini."

"Suppose the king doesn't want me?"

"Are we fools? The king has to like you. He's just your size."

Pinocchio, who'd never had an adolescence or a childhood, was five feet tall. And it was hard for him to consider that the king of Italy and Jubaland was his own negligible height. The clandestinos mocked the king, called him a terrible miser. "Vittorio Emanuele has holes in his pants. He eats cabbage for breakfast, dinner, and lunch."

"So do I," Pinocchio said, beginning to like this king.

"You're an outlaw," Dante reminded him. "You don't have twenty throne rooms and three hundred servants."

"But I'd eat cabbage anyway, sir."

"It shows how backward you are," Dante said, and he started to educate Pinocchio without untying his hands and feet. A wooden boy was dense enough to run away. The clandestinos were taking no chances with him.

"Listen, dunderhead. Your king, Vittorio, the Little Sword, emperor of Addis Ababa, prince of Jerusalem, maharaja of Tobruk, is the one who let Mussolini march on Rome. The Little Sword could have destroyed the Duce with a swipe of his pen. But he did nothing. Mussolini rocked his cradle into Rome, tore out the old calendars, and gave us Year One of the fascist regime. His angel sits near the throne. Vittorio's mamma, Queen Margherite, fell in love with the Duce's black battle pants. La

Mamma is the king of Italy, and Little Sword is her slave. Italy's constitution is whatever La Mamma says. She's feuding with her daughter-in-
law, Princess Josie. Josie hates the fascists and pities the king. We're
sending you to Josie. Her lady-in-waiting, donna Elvira, belongs to us.
She'll sneak you into the Quirinale, present you to Josie, and from Josie
you'll get to the king."

Pinocchio couldn't keep up with the clatter of names. La Mamma.
Little Sword. The princess of this and that. He knew less about the royal
family than he did of birds and alfalfa fields.

"Sir," he said, "I'll beat up Mussolini, but I won't lie to the Little
Sword."

The clandestinos rushed at him with their daggers. They meant to
carve up the wooden boy, but Dante Romano discouraged them.

"Pinocchio," he said, "if Little Sword is a fascist, doesn't he deserve
whatever Mussolini gets?"

"He's still the king . . ."

"Are you a socialist or a Savoyard? We don't recognize kings."

Pinocchio stared at his teacher. "In that case, the Little Sword will
have to go."

He couldn't tell this to Dante, but he approved the idea of kings.
Palaces appealed to his imagination. He wouldn't have wanted to live
in a country without a king. The one fact he knew about the French
is that they'd cut off their king at the neck and made him a mutilato.
No good would ever come from that . . .

Had to end off my scratching in the middle of the story. A queen
was in my room. Madame Copernic. She'd come up behind me while
I was changing pencils. She wasn't dressed for the casbah. She had a
velvet cape and gown.

"Another wedding, auntie?"

"No. You'll take me dancing tonight."

Couldn't walk out in my undershirt. Balzac had to get dressed.
Madame Copernic kissed me clumsily on the stairs. I held her to the
wall, could feel her heart pump under the velvet sack. My hands were
all over auntie Pierre. She didn't resist. Auntie smiled in the dark of
le Wigwam.

"If you're going to rape me," she said, "tell me in advance. I don't want to spoil my gown."

Walked her down to her Citroën.

"Had a nice lunch with Raffe San Angelo. He remembers you."

"Don't be stupid," auntie said. "I was his mistress . . . get into the car." We drove up the boulevard St. Marcel, crossed the river at the pont d'Austerlitz.

"Romey, you're a shit."

"And what if I am? I don't change partners every other season."

She stopped the car at the end of the bridge and started slapping me while traffic brooded behind us.

"You sanctimonious little man. If you got any holier, you'd give birth to Jesus. What did Raffe tell you at your lunch?"

Horns blasted at us like an orchestra of goats, but auntie wouldn't listen.

"Monsieur said he introduced you to the Montesquieus, and then lost you in the Goutte d'Or."

"That's a lovely word, *introduce*. He wanted me to go down for Philippe."

Auntie took us over the bridge and up the boulevard de la Bastille.

"Weren't you living with Monsieur?"

"I was . . . under Lionel's orders."

I banged on the dash like a gigantic baby. "Let me out of this car."

"We're going dancing," she said.

"Madame Copernic, I don't believe a word of it . . . you were Lionel's apparatchik? He sent you here to spy for him and pick up new customers under the pillows?"

"That's about it, with one or two complications . . . it turns your uncle on when I'm with other men. Lionel likes to hear me confess. I had to map my times with Raffe for him. Then he'd growl and love me into the floor . . . but I got sick of that circus."

"So you fled to the Goutte. And les Frères haven't asked you to perform any tricks. They've freed you from Lionel and Monsieur . . . auntie, where do I fit?"

"You're my oldest friend."

"Friend?" I said. "What if I steal you from Philippe?"

"He'd kiss you on the forehead."

"And cut my throat."

"Maybe not . . . that would depend on Antoine."

"Auntie, I'd rather dance than talk . . ."

She parked on the rue de Lappe. A narrow street it was, with lots of bars and bums in the alleys. I stuck close to Madame on the rue de Lappe. You could get pulled into an alley on this street and land in Saigon. There was one consolation. I'd fill myself with soupe saigonnaise.

Auntie shoved me into a dance hall. Ah, I'd gone through the Looking Glass again. Time snaked backwards on the rue de Lappe. This dance hall, le Chicago, was full of thugs that could have walked out of a wax museum. Their coats were a bit too long. Their trousers were held up by the fattest suspenders I'd ever seen. These burly men had the tiniest feet, but there was nothing quaint about them. Their women had the white cheeks of a cadaver. The cadavers danced. They pumped out their legs to greet the men of le Chicago.

The bouncer wore a sweater in July. He patroled the bar, keeping stragglers away from the dance floor. No one contradicted him. He took pity on me for auntie's sake. Everybody knew her at le Chicago.

Bonsoir, Madame Copernic.

Couldn't understand all that friendliness at first. Le Chicago didn't have the aura of black foot country. Did les Frères peddle drugs in the toilet?

"Auntie," I said, "was it Philippe or Antoine who escorted you here?"

"Idiot, I came with Alain San Angelo . . . some of the time."

Madame had an endless reservoir of dancing partners. I waltzed with her on the rue de Lappe. I didn't care if tango music spilled out of the shelf in the far wall of le Chicago, where a band in striped trousers held sway. I waltzed. The thugs thought crazy people had come to visit them. But if I had to play Alice at le Chicago, I'd do whatever I liked. Once you're on the other side of the Looking Glass, you can dance to your heart's desire.

Auntie threw off her cape, and we waltzed around the tango artists. The bouncer didn't interfere. The band in the shelf could have been on Neptune. Le Chicago was our waltzing parlor.

Accompanied her to that hotel on the rue de Tournon. The door was barred, and the concierge stared through the window before she would let us in. Auntie led me up the stairs by the yellow scarf at my throat. I wasn't some donkey she'd dragged home. I had my pride. I didn't want to be on Madame Copernic's seduced and abandoned list. She'd lost her key. I jiggled the lock open with my nail clippers.

Auntie pulled the velvet sack over her head. The moon jumped over the terrace to bathe Madame on the bed. Her bosoms were swollen in that light. She was like a delicate child with breasts she couldn't carry.

I shivered back eleven years to Bronx Science and that morning auntie had first invaded my class. A woman child in a school of genius boys and girls. She didn't have their ferocious intellect, but none of them would ever ripen the way auntie did.

I was dizzy from her in the moon.

Got out of my shirt and pants and approached her in my underwear, with the scarf still trapped on my throat. Her hands moved along my body, and my skin turned blue at her touch. She was the perfect courtesan, my Marie Antoinette. But I couldn't figure who had instructed her to romance with me. My throat boiled under the camouflage of yellow silk. I was auntie's fool, because I couldn't leave off the notion of what might have been . . . if she'd stayed with the high school teacher. A bambino of our own. Girl or boy, I would have loved that child to destruction . . .

The dead whore, Brunhilde, had come out of Pinocchio's story to whisper in my ear. *Have her, Romey. Have her now.*

Listened to my fairy godmother.

I lay down with my aunt on the bed, in the moon's own sucking light . . .

Had dreams in auntie's hotel. Philippe and Antoine shuffled past the bed. They sat out on the terrace, had themselves a moon bath, smoked with their feet on the terrace grille. They got up, went over to auntie, and kissed her. They were inches from my skull. *She's sleeping,* they said. Couldn't the brothers tell that my eyes were open? They were indifferent to Jérôme. They stood near the bureau, Philippe and Antoine, and vanished from the room.

Funny, but I couldn't remember falling out of my dream. I got up in that crazy moonlight and looked at auntie. I dressed without disturbing her. Wrapped the scarf around my neck like a flying ace. All that was missing was a snug aviator's cap, and I could have been Icarus, sailing out of the hotel. I searched behind the bureau and discovered a trick door. My dreams were shrewder than I. They'd stumbled upon the Montesquieus' secret lair. Had to get down on my haunches to enter the little room behind the door. It was equipped with mattress, chair, and three steps in the wall that took you up into the ceiling. I climbed the three steps, pushed another door, and I was out on the roof. I waltzed between the chimneys, with the moon on my back. Went down the hatch of the neighboring roof, pressed a buzzer in the wall, and landed on the rue de Tournon.

EIGHT

MYTHO-
PSYCHOSIS

HAD to find San Angelo. The hell with prison rabbis. I wasn't dumb to detective work. In the old days, when the muse of Moby Dick was upon me, and I was still teaching at Bronx Science, burdened with *A Tale of Two Cities* and *The Mill on the Floss,* I'd written a crime novel, *Blue Eyes over Miami,* about an orphan detective who relies on stool pigeons to do his dirty work. Well, I'd get me a stool pigeon, discover a source to San Angelo.

Sailed out into the rue Pascal with my yellow diaper. After three hours of groping up and down half-remembered hills, with market-places and butcher shops that advertised horsemeat in their windows, I reached the Seine. Saw the bums sequestered in the riverwalk under the bridges and quays. Clochards, they were. The bums of literature. We'd all read about them in Dostoyevsky, Dumas, and Proust . . . even Henry James had devoted a third of a paragraph in *The Princess Casamassima* to the clochards of Paris. An educated lot, anarchists and socialists, bachelors of art, brokers who'd given up the stock exchange, minters who'd disappeared from the Hôtel de la Monnaie, winners of the Prix Goncourt who'd run out of books to write, Bonapartists fed up with the decline of France, master sergeants from old, forgotten penal colonies . . . men with a past much more particular than mine.

I was drawn to these clochards, not out of sentimental longing, a need to slum. I wished I'd been a master sergeant in some old colony. Then I could have had a trade to fall back on, specific, reliable, like soldiering in French Guiana.

But the clochards under this bridge were curious. They couldn't have been master sergeants. There was nothing ancient about them. They were bums of the modern style. Half my age, with overcoats in July that must have served as blanket, tent, and chiffonier. They had no bottles of wine that I could discover. They smoked cigarettes with the confidence of bankers. They bundled up their overcoats to keep July away from their necks.

I crossed over the bridge, having to fight back this pull to join the clochards. Give it up, give it up, I heard a voice that wasn't Brunhilde's. It was more powerful than fairy godmothers. It was my own skull, the whalish noise beneath the hull of bone in my head.

I had to go on. Across some royal garden, up the rue St. Denis, into the land of pipeuses, women with merchandise under their coats. They couldn't waylay me.

Reached the rue Sainte Foy and searched for San Angelo's whore. Old Blondine. I found the building where Blondine was. Listened to noises behind her door. Opened it a trifle and peeked in. A man stood in the center of the room, with his underpants like a skirt around his knees, and he was swaying to a woman's head squirreled in his groin. He saw me and gave an obscene hiss. The woman's scalp rose out of his groin like a periscope with ears. It was Blondie, all right.

I scattered into the street. Had coffee, beer, a cupcake that could have been a charlotte russe, but the cupcake wasn't sweet enough, and it didn't have spongy flesh.

Blondie came down the stairs carrying a shopper's knitted sack. She walked that sack into an Arab grocery and left with grapefruits and a longish bread.

I kept following Blondine. The pipeuse didn't go into any alley. She arrived at that Russian district, Sébastopol, marched along the boulevard, and fell in with a crowd of people. I pinched my way into the crowd. Blondine was cutting grapefruits and pulling on the nose of the bread. A man was with her, his mouth dug into a grapefruit half. What was this public eating about? Then a face turtled from behind the fruit, and I understood Blondine's shopping list. The man was a fire eater trying to wet his burnt lips and catch a bit of food between acts. I didn't horn in while Blondie was around. I let her go in peace with her knitted sack and then I approached the fire eater.

"Bonjour, Alain."

The Corsican's yellow eyes had nothing to do with fire eating.

"Get out of Paris, you dumb prick."

"San Angelo, you should be kinder to your hotel mate."

"Pumpkinhead," he muttered. "That wasn't my hotel. I live with Blondine."

"Then why'd you bring me to her if she's your petite amie?"

"I felt sorry for you . . ."

"What about the yellow scarf?" I said, pointing to my throat.

"That's something to decorate your coffin . . . little Romey, you're being set up."

"Set up by whom? My uncle?"

"Your uncle, your aunt, Monsieur, and me. But I got out . . . I'm not acting in Lionel's life show any more."

"So you decided to eat a little fire . . ."

"I'd rather eat fire than be your angel of death. I don't give a fuck about you. You're a pumpkin who fell out of the Concorde. But I have my Corsican pride. I don't take pumpkins around and throw them to the dead."

The crowd abandoned a fire eater who preferred grapefruits to his torch.

"We're Tatars, for Christ's sake. Lionel and me . . . slept in the same bed thirty-five years."

"Dummy, he brought you here to die . . . and you talk of beds. He blames you for what's happened to Madame."

The fire eater was hallucinating on his feet.

"Alain, it's Lionel who took her away from me."

"So what? He says Madame is still in love with you. You stuffed her with notions about art, and Madame is living them out."

"With Philippe Montesquieu?"

"It doesn't matter. Get out of Paris."

"If I'm marked," I said, "Lionel can finish the job in New York."

The fire eater smashed a grapefruit with his mouth.

"He can't hurt you in New York. Your mamma's around."

So that woman with the blue hair was my savior in the end.

San Angelo picked up his torch and I walked on down from Sébastopol.

Wasn't going to be the puppet in some miserable playhouse, with Corsicans and black foots, uncles and aunts banding together to sock Guignol. I decided to face auntie Pierre.

Taxied up to the Goutte d'Or and got out across from Des Poissonniers. But auntie wasn't inside the window with les Frères. The cafeteria had its usual crowd of bachelors. Where the hell were the Arab women in this quarter? The Goutte was a city of men. And uncle's economics depended on that. He looked for casbahs everywhere. He fattened the pages of his little black book with the homeless of Manhattan and Paris nord. He could starve around people who stayed put. Uncle needed a clientele that shifted from continent to continent. He'd have brought Calcutta to Central Park if he could. And I wondered how he was related to the Montesquieus. Was auntie the bridge between Lionel and the black foots? Because I had this suspicion that uncle was stinking up the Goutte d'Or.

And while my mind was on uncle, the brothers appeared in the window of Des Poissonniers. Without auntie. I'd grown used to les Frères, and I could tell the twins apart by that oceanic blue in Antoine's eyes. One brother retreating into himself, the other a potentate in an

Arab restaurant. I stood on the boulevard de la Chapelle, waiting for auntie to join those two faces in the window. Was auntie shopping at the flea market? Let her shop. I drank Turkish coffee on the boulevard, like a lad out of Algiers. I had a hard-boiled egg. I had a Tunisian salad of raisins in a red juice. I had bread shaped like a fielder's mitt that I imagined had come from Cairo. You could fill up the mitt with red salad juice and feel you were eating God's own blood.

I had more and more of those sandwich mitts. I'd devour Jesus, waiting for Madame Copernic. But something arrived before auntie did.

The window shattered in front of les Frères. It was as if time had slowed for the brothers, and they were stuck in some Technicolor hit. The bursting glass mushroomed into a magic show. The fragments resembled a big rising hat. And then the design fell away. A black smoke pushed out the broken window like waves of octopus ink. I rushed into that smoke, plunged through the window frame. My feet kept dragging glass. One of the brothers lay on the floor in bitten clothes. It was Philippe. Little blue mouths welled from his shirt and pants, as if he had a hundred pockets, a long, long waiter's vest of blood. The bomb must have exploded near his feet. Antoine stood over him, rocking his head. His shirt hadn't been touched. He wasn't soiled with bomb flack or debris. He was talking to his brother, muttering in a dialect I couldn't understand. Was it the language of Corsican Algiers? The private correspondence of brother to brother. A song of wounds. Because Antoine was crying now. But his brother didn't sing back. Any fool could tell that Philippe was dead.

I grabbed Antoine, retrieved him from the window. "It's dangerous," I shouted.

Walked out of the Goutte d'Or with Antoine. Took a chance and delivered him to that secret closet in auntie's hotel. We crossed the roofs together, over the rue Tournon. Antoine held my hand most of the way. I sat him down in the closet.

"Was it the Corsicans?" I asked.

"Corsica," he said, his lips moving with the slightest tremble.

"Was it Monsieur?"

"Monsieur," he said.

"My uncle Lionel?"

His lips forgot to move.

"We'll stay until Marie comes."

"Who's Marie?"

"My aunt," I said. "Madame Copernic."

"Madame Copernic."

We could have been inside some deep well, where words jumped from the water like a bat's wings.

"Are you hungry, Antoine? Would you like some grub?"

He nodded at me with his blue eyes. I went up into the roofs again, down to a café near the Luxembourg gardens, and smuggled sandwiches around the chimney pots. But Antoine wasn't in the little room. I looked for blood on the mattress and the walls.

No marks and no Antoine.

Guignol couldn't pay his hotel bill.

I was stuck in my little hotel on the rue Pascal, where I had to keep pissing in the sink. The only person who smiled at me was the Arab grocer who sold me grapefruit juice at two dollars a bottle; Guignol had to sip from this bottle as if it were a kind of golden milk, and now the grapefruit juice was all gone.

I drifted up above the Seine and stopped at a teahouse around the corner from the avenue Pierre de Serbie. Could have been in Singapore. I didn't recognize the streets near that avenue of the Serbian king. My shirt and shoes had gone shabby, but I did have my yellow scarf. I sat with that yellow diaper, drinking lemon tea, wondering how many other tea salons I could visit before the coins in my pocket disappeared. There was something peculiar about this salon. It was inhabited by other men who wore yellow scarfs. Their shoes were pointier than Guignol's, and their jackets were made of velvet, but they seemed stranded like imperfect dolls.

The dolls began to shiver and shake. A woman entered the salon, wearing a piece of fur around her neck. It could have been the tail of a very large rabbit. She seemed to Guignol like a beautiful grand-mother. She looked across the salon, and Guignol wondered if she was searching for some nephew or niece. She roamed about the tables, moving from doll to doll, and then she stopped at my table and said in perfect English, "May I sit down?"

I was clever enough not to refuse this grandmother.

"You're new," she said. "I've never seen you before."

Guignol shook his head, without committing himself.

"Are you an actor?"

"No, Madame."

"Then what do you do when you're not sitting here?"

"I speculate."

"Ah, a stockbroker," she said, beginning to smile. "Do you fly over from Wall Street every afternoon to have your tea?"

Told her yes, and her tea arrived. It came with an assortment of cakes, and she invited Guignol to sample them. Tried not to show my hunger to the lady. Had six or seven, making sure not to put crumbs on my yellow scarf.

"You're a pretty man," she said. "My little stockbroker."

She paid for her tea and mine, and then she led Guignol by the elbow out of the salon. The men at the other tables glared at me, and then their eyes sank into their skulls.

The beautiful grandmother had a car waiting for her near the salon; Guignol stepped into the car with her, and it was like sitting on some glorious couch, the habitat of a queen. The grandmother never intro-duced herself, but she did clasp Guignol's hand. And they drove about in that manner, Guignol and the beautiful grandmother in a very small embrace.

It was the loveliest ride in Guignol's life. Houses looped over my head like chateaus on some street corner.

The beautiful grandmother asked me where I lived. I was ashamed to mention my rotten hotel on the rue Pascal. "Goutte," I said. "I live in the Goutte d'Or."

"With the Arab population?"

"Yes, the Arabs buy stocks and bonds from me."

"You're a wonder," she said.

She ran her hand along my scarf. "Marvelous material." Her fingers were like sweet stones on my chest. She dropped a packet of money into my shirt; the packet was held together by a pin.

"Can I see you again?" Guignol asked, not knowing how to deal with this grandmother.

"That depends on the time and place you have your tea."

Guignol shoved across Paris in his yellow scarf. I didn't dare count my money in the street. But I pulled out the pin once I was inside my hotel and counted ten five-hundred franc notes with a picture of Molière holding the side of his face. The beautiful grandmother without a name had given me ten Molières.

I bought bottle after bottle of grapefruit juice.

Had a difficult time remembering the boulevard where I'd found the grandmother; it was as if the city of Pierre de Serbie had crept into its own spider web. And then I stumbled across the tea salon. The same doll men sat with their own yellow scarves. But they weren't so passive, seeing Guignol a second time. They hissed at me in French.

"You whore, you're shitting up this place with your dirt. Find your own traffic station."

Had nine Molières in my pocket. Didn't have to answer to doll men. But the waiter wouldn't serve me tea. I sat while the other men drank from their teapots.

Different grandmothers entered the salon, but none of them would negotiate with Guignol. I didn't mind. I was waiting for my grandmother. Had to spend three afternoons at the salon. Finally, on my fourth afternoon without a teapot, she entered the place. Guignol waved to her as discreetly as he could. She was wearing a red cape. She looked at Guignol a moment, but she had nothing for him. She could have been any grandmother, coming out of a forest of red capes.

After that I walked around in a slow fever; it was as if this whore of a city held on to me with crazy threads. I was Gulliver in a yellow scarf, trapped on an island of stone streets, where other Gullivers would barely nod to me. I had only my Arab grocer and my fortune of grapefruit juice.

Guignol discovered the grandmother without a name on the rue Bonaparte.

"Couldn't you have said hello?" I shouted. "It wasn't my fault that they wouldn't give me a teapot."

But this grandmother must have forgotten her English. She refused to understand. Guignol followed her towards the river. She didn't have her red cape. She carried a shopping bag.

I touched her shoulder. "Listen to me."

The grandmother shrieked. Men began to fall upon Guignol, Gullivers with red faces and blue shirts; they pulled the yellow napkin off my neck. I screamed and kicked; they were still pulling at me when I closed my eyes, settling into some magnificent sleep of Serbian kings . . .

I expected to come out of that sleep in la Santé, with the prison rabbi at my heels, asking why a Jewish Tatar from the Bronx had to molest grandmothers on the rue Bonaparte. I figured on a convict's rough clothes, with the famous skullcap of la Santé, a thinker's hat that Pascal wore three hundred years ago. Because where else could your philosophers thrive in the last part of this century if not in jail? The next James Joyce will write his *Ulysses* in la Santé, with a skullcap on his head. Wasn't Cervantes a convict? And Dostoyevsky? Didn't Jane Austen, that very tough girl, spend a fortnight in the calaboose at Mansfield Park? Maupassant died in an asylum, trying to write a novel with his own excrement. It might have been his masterpiece. And what writer is so magnificent that a year in jail couldn't improve his style? I wish the calaboose on Henry James, Flaubert, and Marcel Proust. I felt around my ears and was disappointed. I didn't have the skullcap of la Santé on my head.

Woke up in an unfamiliar room. It wasn't a rathole at the Palais de Justice. There was a park outside my window. I was with Monsieur le prince.

Monsieur was brewing tea. Something about his apartment seemed to injure my bones. The Corsican chief had two small rooms overlooking Montsouris. Monsieur kept his palace in a shoebox with a window on the park.

He explained his apartment while we fed on our tea. His father had lived in these rooms, and his father's father. They'd all been tobacconists. Raffe San Angelo had grown up with three brothers in his bed. The brothers were lawyers in Marseilles. Raffe, the oldest son, had remained a tobacconist. I didn't have to wonder about la Santé. I never had the chance to be arrested. The cops must have given me to Monsieur. I was the nigger of Raffe's court, a worm who inhabited the end lines. I belonged in a shoebox with Monsieur.

I patted my pockets to see if I'd invented all that business about Molières. I was swollen with money. I asked Raffe about the bombing in Des Poissonniers.

He didn't curtsy away from me. The bomb was his, he said. A waiter had planted it, and not as a scare machine. It was meant for Philippe. The brothers had become too ambitious with auntie around. They'd begun to move closer and closer to the shoebox. They would have kidnapped the parc Montsouris if they could. The Montesquieus were trying to shove Monsieur out of Paris. So he quieted Philippe with a bomb, but he had no reason to hurt Antoine. A sick blue-eyed boy couldn't resurrect les Frères.

I asked him if he'd heard from uncle.

"Monsieur, did Lionel mention me?"

Yes, uncle wanted to know why I hadn't written my mother.

That was Lionel, all right, harping on Bathsheba.

I did write, I lied. But the mail is slow in coming.

Monsieur understood. He hugged me, swore that my enemies were his enemies, and I went downstairs, crossed the park, and hiked up to le Wigwam.

Something was wrong with this rotten currency. You had to bring all your bank notes to market for a peach. Only aristocrats could afford brown country bread. The rest of us ate croissants and little asparagus pies. The first pie made you hungrier for the next. I was always eating in Paris.

That's how my troubles began, finishing off an asparagus pie, licking my fingers, getting at the crumbs in my teeth. I began to drift towards Pinocchio. I wasn't writing, mind you. Just drifting. I could feel myself in Rome. Palm trees. Brown walls. Rome had the dry sweet taste of Africa. I was in the king's old palace, the Quirinale. I could hear the shout of wooden legs, touch my long nose. I didn't like it at all.

"Brunhilde," I muttered, "don't confuse me with that woodenhead. I like to play Guignol part of the time, but this is Paris, not the Quirinale."

Brunhilde wouldn't come out from where she was hiding to comfort me. I sniffed the dampness of the Quirinale all afternoon. I was in some crazy time pull. Stepped in and out of Mussolini's Rome. Walked on gray carpets. The queen mother was my enemy. I don't know why. I had ants in my head. I couldn't keep to one location. In Rome, under the flags of the king's chamber, I worried about Antoine. Would he survive without his brother? I dreamwalked through the Quirinale, without giving the king's salute. I was dressed in royal blue. Mussolini was screaming for my head. But he couldn't lift me out of the Quirinale. The king had taken pity on Pinocchio. He'd presented me with the Blue Garter, the highest order of his House, to hold me alive. I was now cousin to his majesty, Vittorio Emanuele. Woe to the man or woman who lay a finger on my head. It meant the firing squad. But immortality didn't interest me. I couldn't help Antoine if I was stuck in Rome. The palace was in a fury over the Hitler-Mussolini pact. The king's mother, blue-eyed Margherite, hurrahed. La Mamma saw Hitler as the Duce's apprentice. Her own ladies-in-waiting understood that Benito was an infant in the German war machine. But La Mamma looked to Berlin.

If I closed my eyes and stamped on the king's rug, I could will my way back to Paris and 1983. Then I'd miss that stinking palace, miss the king.

Time had dropped me in a cradle that swung here and there. I was warped. It never would have happened if I'd been bar mitzvahed like everybody else. One of these years I'll climb out of Bathsheba's baby carriage. I was determined to cure myself of Pinocchio. I loved the imperial city of Rome, although I was confined to the Quirinale like a bloody yardbird, because I was only safe on the king's grounds. But I couldn't exist in two faculties. It was fatiguing.

I marched up the Mouffetard, Hemingway's favorite route in Paris, and over to the Seine. I don't know why I should have been thinking of Papa Hemingway. I was searching for some books, you see, a primer in one of the open-air shops along the quays, a text that could ride me out of my dilemma, and then I started worrying about old Jake Barnes and his Lady Brett. They're in a cab, if I remember right, going down the Mouffetard to the place de la Contrescarpe, where the Corsicans hold sway in little bars and pancake houses. They kiss, and Lady Brett says, "Please don't do that." Because she's in love with Jake, and Jake has a war wound. He can't make love in the usual way. And what I always wondered is why Lady Brett didn't have a bit more imagination. Couldn't she have steered Jake down between her legs with his nose?

Went from stall to stall, rejecting Heidegger, Sartre, and Herman Wouk. I shunned Colette, because I might have gotten into her story, and then where would I be? I found the perfect book at the fifth stall. *The ABC's of Sigmund Freud.*

Buzzed through Freud's *ABC's*, looking for the term that would save me from having to exist as two people. All the stuff about id and alter ego didn't apply to Pinocchio Jérôme. And then I lit upon a definition that told my story.

Mythopsychosis, the terrifying need to mythologize one's existence at the expense of all other things. The sufferer of mythopsychosis seeks narratives everywhere, inside and outside of himself. He cannot take a move and not narratize it. This is a common affliction among writers. Tolstoy has sworn that in the middle of writing *Anna Karenina* he was unable to divorce himself from Anna's ideas and Anna's dreams. At her death in the book he fell into a horrible depression, from which he did not recover for half a year. He believed himself to have leapt under the train with Anna, and neither his servants nor his wife could convince him that he was still on his estate at Yasnaya Polyana. "I am that wretched woman," he told his wife. "Goodbye."

Tolstoy is not a singular case. The modern French author, Marcel Proust, mythologized his existence to such a degree that he literally drowned in his own narrative. He is one of the most severe examples of m. ever recorded. Proust could not escape from his characters. He could not leave them alone. From a ten-page story about dunking a madelaine, we have three million words. We'd have had another three million if his text hadn't murdered him.

Proust's syndrome is not as uncommon as we might think. Dickens suffered from an equivalent disease. He saw himself as hangman and bodysnatcher in his own texts. Dostoyevsky couldn't disassociate himself from his tribe of Karamazovs. Emily Brontë would have nightmares in which Heathcliff played a prominent role. These nightmares persisted until she died. Guy de Maupassant was so haunted by his stories, he had to be institutionalized. He did not have congenital syphilis, as some doctors would like us to believe. He was plagued by mythopsychosis.

The list of sufferers is without end. Marie Henri Beyle (Stendhal), George Eliot, Virginia Woolf. There is even a severer form of the disease, mytholepsy, in which the sufferer cannot escape from his own dream. He falls into the text, lives there, and dies, much like Marcel Proust. Medical science has not yet discovered a cure for mytholepsy. Once the disease begins, the single remedy is his or her own death. For mythopsychosis we have a little more hope. The sufferer can decide never to narratize again. He takes himself out of the text. This requires a long process of denarratization.

Freud was practicing foreplay in his *ABC's*. How was I supposed to denarratize my life? I'd been scribbling Pinocchio without putting down a word. How do you keep a story from jumping in your head? I told myself, I'm not Pinocchio, I'm not Pinocchio, I'm not Pinocchio.

I was instantly in the Quirinale. Court people marveled at me. The wooden boy who'd defied Mussolini. Now that I wore the Blue Garter, they had to call me Sir Pinocchio. But they snickered and called me Schnozzle behind my back. Schnozzle and cavaliere Long Nose. The Quirinale was a nest of warring factions. First there was the king's men, the Savoyards. They were loyal only to Vittorio Emanuele. They wouldn't side with his mother or his daughter-in-law, Crown Princess Josie. The Savoyards couldn't stomach the notion of Italy without a king. But they were outnumbered. There were a dozen other factions, factions of every stripe. La Mamma had her own party. Half the palace was sworn to her. La Mamma's people had no particular ideals. They were whatever La Mamma was. Devoted to the force of her personality, they would have been socialists or communists, depending on the weather in La Mamma's rooms. This year (1939) they were for Hitler and Mussolini. Stalin was the filthiest word they could pronounce. Pinocchio was next on their list. La Mamma hated the wooden boy with absolute passion. She seemed to intuit that he was a spy for the socialists. But she couldn't convince her son to throw the boy into Mussolini's arms.

"Mamma, the piccolino stays. I have given my word. He is a knight of the Blue Garter, one of us."

"Blue Garter," Queen Margherite smirked. "He is no more a knight than the stockings I wear for my varicose veins. He's quite ordinary."

"But it's a miracle, Mamma. A wooden boy blessed with a mind. I cannot abandon him."

"Then you will go to the devil with Pinocchio. He is a socialist, and I have proof. Vittorio, listen to me."

But the king settled onto the throne that was much too big for his size and clapped his hands over his ears. La Mamma had to leave the throne room.

England and France also had their clique in the Quirinale. Hitler kept a spy or two. The Vatican could count on twenty souls spread through the palace. The followers of Leon Trotsky, known as the Red Medallion party, worked out of the king's toilets. They were the most efficient intriguers in the Quirinale. The Red Medallions poisoned the zuppa inglese of the queen mother's men, built little fires in the stairwells, and worked as much havoc as they could into the design of palace living. The carabinieri tried to weed them out, one by one. But no matter how many Red Medallions were arrested, it still wasn't smart to eat zuppa inglese at the Quirinale.

And then there were the secret socialists. The head of the clandestinos was donna Elvira of Princess Josie's entourage. It was she who smuggled Pinocchio into the Quirinale and dropped him onto the king's bed. If Little Sword had not been enchanted with Pinocchio, Elvira and the puppet boy would have both ended up in the dungeon, smashed to pieces by the king's men. Donna Elvira had freckles and auburn hair. She was a foot taller than Pinocchio, and she'd shove him across the Quirinale.

"Ingrate, why do you wear the king's shirt?"

"I'm a knight of the Blue Garter," Pinocchio answered. "I have to wear blue."

"I'll garter your head," she told him and shoved Pinocchio some more.

It was her mistress, Princess Josie, who protected the boy from donna Elvira's wrath. "Will you stop plaguing Pinocchio?" And Elvira backed away from the boy.

Josie belonged to no faction, but she might have been called a blue democrat. She worshipped democracies and kings and believed in justice for the lower orders of women and men. I was troubled by Josie, even though I was her cousin and a knight. She had a husband, the crown prince, away in Abyssinia, and I didn't know how to react. Should I bring up the tickling business Brunhilde had taught me? I had to rely on my nose for play.

I boshed every servant girl who would have me. I sawed with my nose, thrusting deeper and deeper, driving the girls unconscious as often as not. That's how I got my reputation at the Quirinale. *Sir Pinocchio never stops.* But it was hard on me. I grew sad thinking I'd never get to orgasm as a wooden boy.

I graduated from servant girls to the nobler classes. I had mistresses of the cupboard in the king's private chapel, coupling with them inside the curtains of the confession box. I slept with ladies-in-waiting behind the king's throne. I had this ungodly appetite to thrust with my nose.

Once, around midnight, in the midst of sawing with a particular lady, I could feel a body attending me behind my shoulder. I drew my nose out and looked over my collarbone. The king was staring down at me. He was in the royal pajamas, blue on blue. The lady lurched in the dark, looking for her clothes with her bum in the air. The shape of her aroused my nose. She scuffled in the corners and begged the king's pardon. His majesty dismissed her without the least sign of anger in his face. Then he summoned me to his throne.

I went up to Little Sword with my shirt unbuttoned. Would I get the firing squad? I was ashamed of myself, trolloping in the throne room.

"Pinocchio, how many other women have you had behind my chair?"

"Sire, there were too many to count."

Vittorio Emanuele banged on the armrest of his throne. "Approximate, you churl. But give me a figure."

"Upwards of thirty-five, your majesty. That's my guess."

"Then you've rutted with every other woman in this damnable house."

"Twice that number, your majesty. I had another thirty-five in your chapel."

"You're a disgusting boy. And to think I knighted you, trusted you with the Blue Garter."

He sat high on his throne, and his feet were hardly near the floor.

"Should I return the Garter, sire?"

"No. Once presented, it cannot be taken back. Would you have all my knights go around saying that Vittorio is an Indian giver? The Garter would be a silly paradox. But you are unworthy of wearing it, Sir Pinocchio."

"Then I'll disappear into the street."

"And have the Duce butcher you? What kind of protector would I be? I'll never give you up, no matter how many women you whore with. But we shall not hold you as near to our heart as we did yesterday and the day before. You have disappointed me, sir."

It was the king's great generosity, his openness to a common boy, that got me to cry. Could have watered the royal gardens with the crying I did.

"End that blubbering, you hear?"

Wiped my eyes with a sleeve of the knight's coat I'd gotten from the king. We smoked American cigarettes that his majesty was able to smuggle out of the Vatican grocery store at a fabulous price. The king was a pennypincher. He went around picking up nails in the royal garage, lest his old battered Fiat suffer a flat tire. But I didn't hold this against him. It was shrewd to be thrifty at the onset of a world war.

"Sir Pinocchio, my mother tells me that you have been planted here by the clandestinos. Do you mean us harm?"

"No, sire. I wear the Blue Garter. It's the Duce I hate."

"But the Duce governs under my command. Interfere with him, and we have anarchy . . . Pinocchio, I shall never talk to you again after this night. As you are my cousin, I will nod to you. But if you engage me in a conversation, I will be obliged to screw off your head."

The king climbed down from his throne. "One last thing. Did you ever have congress with my daughter-in-law?"

I looked at Little Sword.

"Idiot," he said. "Were you inside Josie's pants?"

"No, sire. God forbid."

I couldn't tell if he was pleased or not. I tried to test him on that subject. He held out the royal fist. He had a doll's hand, smooth and veinless at the knuckle joints. "Sir, there's silence between us."

And he walked out of the throne room in his pajamas.

It got lonely in the House of Savoy. Never to address the king. Not the idlest word. *Majesty, how are you today?* We'd pass each other in the hall with a formality that seemed so unnatural. Worse than strangeness it was. He nodded. I nodded. That was it. I wanted to leap into the stairwell and destroy myself, I had such loathing for whoever it was that lived in Pinocchio's pants. I tried to eat the Blue Garter in my despair, but it wouldn't stay down. I'd chew and cough it up.

Women touched me in the royal corridors. Didn't have the slightest urge to saw at them with my nose.

Bumped into a lady in the dark.

"Go on," I growled. "The mating season is over, my dear."

The lady leaned into the light. It was the crown princess, Josie herself.

"Sorry, your highness," I said under my teeth. "I mistook you for a kitchen wench."

She was a princess, and she didn't bitch at me. She entered into a dialogue with the knight of the Blue Garter.

"And where were you going with the wench, Lord Pinocchio?"

"To the garden, highness. For a midnight stroll."

"Do you often stroll at this hour, my lord?"

"As often as I can. It's hard to be a knight without an occupation."

"But we can't have knights laboring with their hands. It would throw the world upside down."

I climbed up on my toes to get nearer the princess. "I beg to contradict." I was a bold son of a bitch. "How would it hurt to have a knighted garage mechanic? Might as well make the plumber a lord. He rules over us. We'd be up the creek without a working toilet."

The princess took my arm. "Will you stroll with me?"

I got the hiccoughs with Josie's first touch. It made me nervous, having my arm a prisoner to hers, strolling with the king's daughter-in-law.

"Where did you learn to reason like that, my lord?"

"My babbo was a philosopher."

How could I tell her that I'd studied Descartes at the public library in the Bronx? She'd have yelled for the bailiff, and they'd have put me in the asylum for knights.

"Well, thank your babbo for me. You are a formidable arguer, Sir Pinocchio."

"My babbo's dead."

I wasn't thinking of Geppetto. It was the junkman who was on my mind. I longed for a ride on Bruno's chariot.

"I'm so sorry, my lord."

She bent to kiss me on the forehead. It was a consolation kiss, out of charity. But her lips burnt a snake into my head. I went weak from Josie's toilet water. My schnozzle grew an inch.

"Pinocchio," she said, and the princess touched my nose.

Ah, it was the same mad whirl to be in love as a novelist, knight, or high school teacher. I sneezed. I had a pain in my chest. Don't think lightly of me, I wanted to shout. I'm the author of *Blue Eyes over*

Miami. But I'd have frightened her with my tale of two presences. So I stuck to Josie's time. I played Pinocchio.

She was fondling my nose. She held it like a tube in her hand. Colors shot from my eyes. I saw green. I saw orange. I saw black. A hulking thing organized itself within the black and cohered to it. That thing was a padre with a pointed hat. Don Amedeo, the false priest.

Josie removed her fingers from my nose. She didn't jerk her fist away. She had all the breeding of that royal house she'd married into. She didn't apologize to don Amedeo, who bunched up his skirts as if he were about to dance.

"Your highness, may I borrow the boy?"

"Of course," she said. She excused herself and went inside the palace. The false priest removed his hat, and now he was Dante Romano, the clandestinos' commander in chief. Dante slapped me up and down the garden with his hat.

"I didn't bring you here to play nose with a princess and cop a hundred girls. Are you a satyr or a socialist?"

"Both," I muttered. I stopped pirouetting to his slaps. He'd stroked the Tatar in me. I belted him with a wooden wrist. He toppled with a look of wonder and sat in the garden on his ass.

"Hit a priest?" he said.

"You're a stinking socialist. There's a price on your head. Don't start getting holy with me."

The clandestino returned to his feet. "I've killed men for less than what you did."

"Silenzio. I'm a knight. You'd better kneel and call me Sir Pinocchio."

Dante began to guffaw but he didn't have time to finish. Donna Elvira came out of the bushes in a great bursting run. She fell on me with monstrous fists.

Dante rubbed his nose. "Elvira, what the hell is the matter with him?"

"Comrade, he's in love."

"With the princess?"

"No. With himself. Sir Pinocchio is God's gift to the female population of the Quirinale. He's lain with everybody there is."

"Should we douse him in cold water?"

"That won't be necessary," Elvira said. "I'll put his mind on politics . . . imbecile, the princess is on Mussolini's death list."

"I don't believe you. He wouldn't hurt royal blood. The Duce can only govern with the king's consent."

"Mussolini means to change all that. He's moving closer to brother Adolf. We'll have the Reich in Rome, you'll see. The Duce will quarantine Jews and aristocrats. Josie is a perfect target. He doesn't care for princesses with a democratic bent."

"Shouldn't we warn the king?"

"King, king," Elvira said. "He'll never come out of his mother's skirts, and Margherite would love to tango with Herr Hitler at the Quirinale . . . we'll get small satisfaction from this king."

"What can we do?"

"Strangle Mussolini. We need a lovely boy who can get inside that circle of police without suspicion . . . a cousin of his, a former socialist, like Mussolini himself, who's risen out of the slime and adores the fascist state."

"But milady, I don't want to leave the Quirinale. I like it here."

"You'll leave," she said. "Tomorrow morning. You'll have your breakfast and walk down the hill to the Palazzo Venezia."

I shivered that night. It wasn't dread of Mussolini and his Blackshirts. It was separation blues. No matter that the king cut me dead. I still had a nodding relationship with him. Or that the other factions were jealous of my knighthood, that La Mamma left thumbtacks on my chair, that the Red Medallions liked to set my feet on fire, that the English-French alliance caricatured my pockmarked face on the privy walls, that the Stalinist in the kitchen put coffined mice in my pudding. It was my home, better or worse.

Had my final bath in the Quirinale. I wore a knight's shirt. Took my breakfast alone. One soft-boiled egg. I didn't want to natter with the kitchen maids. I'd never come up the hill again to the Quirinale. That much was clear to me.

But I left them all my pocket money and departed from the Quirinale, taking the knight's entrance.

I stood outside on the piazza, sunning myself, looking down at the roofs from the king's stone wall, sniffing the air as a knight of the Blue Garter was wont to do.

A band of Blackshirts spotted me.

"It's the outlaw," they said. "Pinocchio."

They nudged each other and skipped along the Via del Quirinale, overjoyed with their catch of the day.

"Pinocchio the socialist you're under arrest."

Didn't argue.

"Take me to my cousin," I said.

Had to shout through their braying laughter. "My cousin, Benito Mussolini, prince of the Adriatic and protector of Rome."

"He's a great one for titles," the Blackshirts said. "Hey Big Nose, Benito doesn't have a puppet in his family."

I pointed to the Garter a knight such as myself was required to wear below the left knee. But these Blackshirts were ignorant men. They pushed me down the hill.

I was dungeoned under the Palazzo Venezia. My Blackshirt jailors brought their kin to peek at me. I had a chickencoop all to myself.

They tortured me from time to time, dug pins under my wooden fingernails. I howled to make them happy.

"Puppet, where's your leader, Dante Romano?"

They dropped me in barrels of pissy water. I pretended I was swimming to Beirut.

I requested books from my jailors. They laughed through the chicken wire and told me to read my own slop bucket. I wasn't impoverished by them. I rewrote *Anna Karenina* in my head. I cheated on Tolstoy, took out all the chapters on farming and nature, and moved the entire book to St. Petersburg. Anna didn't mess around with a stinking soldier named Vronsky. She fell in love with a novelist, some Dostoyevsky of the minor leagues, a magician who writes for *Odessa* magazine, a hack who's paid by the word, a misfit whom Anna has to support together with the novelist's mother and sister-in-law.

I was on my thirteenth chapter when the jailors summoned me. Lost in that funhouse I was making of *Anna Karenina*, I forgot about the Blackshirts. Their serenade fell on chicken wire. They turned violent when I wouldn't answer their calls. They destroyed the chickencoop, standing on the roof until it collapsed, and then they dug me out of the wire.

I had new ruts in my face from their little trick. They mocked my knighthood, bowing to the Garter below my knee, and kicked me up the stairs. A pretty flight it was, over the dungeon level. Mussolini was no piker. I'd bet my Garter he didn't save pennies and pick up loose nails, like the king.

Footmen led me to Mussolini's door. His secretary, Count Jacobo, ruled the palazzo from a little waiting room. He had an entire bank of buttons on his desk. The buttons glowed. He would press on one and get immediate satisfaction from the soldiers, maids, and undersecretaries who were on button call. But it wasn't the same Jacobo who stepped from a candy-striped truck outside the charterhouse of Parma. He was gloomier in Rome, trapped between filing cabinets and photographs of his chief: Mussolini with a lion cub at the zoo; swimming in the Adriatic; going down a coal mine in a bell-shaped hat; riding his Arab horse, Fru-Fru; picking wheat in a sunbonnet with an army of peasants; in an airman's cap, at the controls of his private plane. It was the portrait of a leader who'd willed himself through the world. Nothing could resist his force or deny itself to him. The wheat grew in Mussolini's shadow. Lions were always cubs around him. Arab horses tamed themselves for the Duce. The Adriatic swelled in and out to his crawling in the water. Tanks and planes lived by Mussolini's touch. The photographs didn't advertise him as a god. He was ridiculous in a miner's hat much too big for his head. The sunbonnet he wore in the wheat field made him look like a girl. But it only added to his *tono fascista*. Half clown, half ape, he was a man like other men. Mussolini.

"Well," Jacobo said. "You've improved your station, my little commander. Vittorio's pet."

"The king doesn't talk to me."

"Because you've outgrown him. Should I kiss your kneecap, Sir Pinocchio?"

He forgot his glowing panel of buttons to look at me.

"You have changed," he said. "Pinocchio, what's happened to you?"

"It's the Roman air, Count Jacobo. Puppets mature faster outside Tuscany."

"I'd say it's the debauchery of being a knight . . . straighten your shoulders, puppet. The Duce is expecting you."

I sailed into Mussolini's office with my shoulders high. It was called the Sala del Mappamondo because it had a signature of the universe on the wall from Ptolemy's time. The universe was a collection of planets, shaped like shrunken heads. Mappamondo was the biggest, emptiest room I'd ever seen. It had two pieces of furniture: Mussolini's desk and chair, situated by the far wall, so that you had to cross a battlefield of carpets to get to him. The desk was as barren as the room. It didn't carry a single envelope or a paper clip. All you had to look at was Mussolini's eyes. They shone at you from the corner with such concentrated appeal, you couldn't stare into them very long. I'd forgotten that the prince of the Adriatic had black eyes like Copernicus.

He wouldn't play the clown in Mappamondo.

"I should hang you."

That's how he greeted a puppet. Not one thought of hello.

"Duce, I beg to contradict. You can't hang a cousin."

"How are we cousins?"

"From the king's side," I said, lifting my left knee to display the Garter.

He didn't frown or pull his eyes away.

"Cousin, then."

That's all he said. I had to continue the conversation.

"Prince Benito . . ."

I shivered in my royal pants. It was a memory I had. My first trip to the RKO. Early 1945. It was the newsreel that launched me into films, the bloody newsreel. Mussolini hanging upside down with his mistress. Her blouse was open and her skirt was shredded like some jungle lady. I couldn't hate that dead man, with his face jumping out at you like a halloween lantern, his coat riding down from his head, the middle of him nothing but an undershirt, black in front, his feet lashed to a lamppost, the ankles so thin, I confused them with those of his mistress. The crowds on the screen smiled under Mussolini's head, and the whole movie theatre pissed with laughter. *The most hated man in Italy,* the newsreel said. There was nothing to piss at. Bare ankles. Blood. Benito upside down could have been anybody's dad.

"Dada," I said out loud.

He studied me with his black eyes. "Do they teach you baby talk in the king's building?"

"No, Benito. I was thinking about my daddy, that's all."

"Are you going to start with that thumbtack? The wooden boy and his babbo. You're a knight . . . you don't need a father."

Ah, I couldn't help seeing him upside down, with his girly ankles.

"You're ours, little knight. My men captured you on the king's hill."

"I beg to contradict . . . your men didn't capture me. I was coming down the hill to consult with you."

"A likely story."

"But you couldn't have touched me in the Quirinale. Why should I have gone for a stroll on a public street?"

"Because you're a nincompoop and a socialist knight, and you think a Blue Garter is the key to Rome. I could have reached into the Quirinale and had you strangled in bed, but what would my enemies say? Benito Mussolini makes war on a puppet . . . why did you come down the hill?"

"I'm sick of socialism. The clandestinos can rot in hell. They envy my Garter. I can't be bothered with all the hurly-burly of socialist talk."

His black eyes took me in, swallowed whatever there was of me. Mussolini was suspicious. "You weren't this eloquent the last time we met. Who's been sticking honey in your mouth?"

"I've been around the nobility, Ben."

"Benito," he said.

"Forgive me, cousin Benito."

"What do you want?"

"To serve my prince."

"Suppose I said that the best way to serve me was to lose an arm and a leg."

"Then I'd give up those limbs to the state." And I started banging at myself.

The Duce wasn't satisfied. "Stop that noise! A clever bastard is what you are. A piece of wood that can argue like a Jesuit. But I'll make use of you, cousin. You can stay here until further notice. I'll give you a room on the top floor. But if you betray me, I'll whittle you into ten Pinocchios and feed the ten of you to the alligators in the Tiber."

Jacobo appeared at the door. I hadn't heard the Duce summon him. Were there secret wires behind Mussolini's desk?

"Jacobo," the Duce shouted. "We'll take the boy, give him the yellow room."

"Is that wise, Duce?"

"What is wrong with the yellow room?"

Jacobo got behind Mussolini and whispered in his ear.

The Duce wouldn't whisper back. "How can he hurt us? He won't live to be Claretta's tattletale. Jacobo, give him the yellow room."

The count led me by the arm.

We climbed the Duce's pretty stairs and stopped at a tiny elevator behind a niche in the middle of the flight. Our chests rubbed in the little elevator car that rode above the landing.

We left the car from a niche on a higher floor. This part of the palazzo had no staircase. We crossed a narrow corridor and Jacobo found the yellow room for me. The lighting in the yellow room was perfect. It had dormer windows that faced a pink sky. The furniture wasn't yellow. Every piece was white. It was the sky that tinted the walls and gave the lowboys a yellowish look.

It was peaceful up near the roof. I had a campanile out my window, and behind that an enormous soccer field filled with ruins.

I heard singing, a lullaby about an infant stranded in the woods. That voice hadn't traveled up from the ruins. The lullaby had come from behind the wall. Didn't have to reason hard. Mistress. Mussolini had stuck me upstairs with Clara. No wonder Jacobo balked about the yellow room. I was sentenced to live in Mussolini's love nest.

I was dusty, and I needed a bath. I found a tub in the hall, but this tub had a passenger, Claretta the concubine.

"Pardon me." Turned my eyes from Claretta and tried to close the door.

"Wait a minute."

I hung there, my nose twitching from the memory of water lapping her cleavage.

"Come in," she said.

I stared at wallpaper.

The mistress commanded me to look at her.

"If you're going to be my valet, we can't have secrets."

"Signorina, I'm not your valet. I'm Sir Pinocchio."

"The bad boy? The socialist?" But she didn't cover her body and order me out of the room.

"I've left the socialist party. The Duce has put me up on this floor."

"Then you can be my valet until Ben finds me one."

"A knight of the Blue Garter can't go around dressing women. What will the other Garters think?"

She stood up in the tub, bubbles splashing around her, her bosoms close to my head, her pubic hair like a salty diamond coming out of the sea. I dressed her, mates, wrapped her in bath towels that were thick and blue as a windstorm, and I had this disgusting desire for Mussolini's mistress, wrapping her with my hands, feeling her shoulders and the flesh of her behind under the towels, my nose beating a hard red color and curving out like an elephant's prong. But Clara was kind enough to ignore the difference in my nose.

I followed her into her room like a hungry bat. She got into pajamas while I caught slices of her flesh and tried to cope with a schnozzle that lived by its own rules. Her lounging pajamas had a mink collar and crepe that flared around her ankles and wrists like a jungle flower. You couldn't forget the print of her body under the soft material. I stumbled across her room with the thickest face in Italian history.

"Sir Pinocchio, aren't you feeling well?"

"Fine, fine. I'm allergic to bubbles."

"Then I'll have to change my bath oil, carino."

And she pulled me onto her bed. I sat in a valley of velvet, since her bedclothes were like a fort with wiggly turrets and fur giraffes that came in a freakish size.

"Pinocchio," she said, slapping me as if I was a girlfriend on a regular visit. "My Ben is always busy . . . I had to pick a man who runs the Mediterranean Sea. I worship him, Pinocchio, but I'm bored living in a castle closet . . . be a good boy and tell me a story."

I couldn't give her *Blue Eyes over Miami*. She wouldn't have understood the detective milieu. So I made up my own *Arabian Nights*: I offered her a picture of Charlotte Street and a boy born in a baby carriage.

"Carino, where did you learn of this place called the Bronx?"

"Shouldn't ask a storyteller where his stories come from."

She scratched under her breasts with a motion that was lovely to me. "But why not?"

"It's like asking a woman why she's beautiful . . . you would be in some pain to answer me that."

"If I'm beautiful it's because I love Ben and it shows in my face."

"There's more than one face under your pajamas," I muttered, and then I continued with the story of Copernicus Charyn and his convict mother. She stopped me in the middle.

"Is this a Jewish boy? Then I mustn't tell Ben. He wants to show Herr Hitler that we're as pure as the Reich, but his secretary is a Jew, and Ben can't get along without Jacobo."

"The boy in my story is a Tatar Jew, and Tatar Jews are a civilization unto themselves."

Now she could lean back in her pajamas, because she wouldn't have to lie about the story to her Ben. I kissed her warm face. She hurled me into the pillows like one of her toy giraffes.

I was Clara Petacci's girlfriend and sometimes I was her valet. I'd swear a silky potion came off her pajamas and out from her skin. What was a monster nose compared to the deliciousness of Clara herself?

She cried about the other mistresses Mussolini had. "They're sluts," she said. "Movie stars and hairdressers. He wrestles with them half an hour and shoves them away."

"You know these women?"

"Of course. I have my spies. I pay them to follow Ben . . . Pinocchio, do you think he's tired of me? His palace bitch. Would he enjoy me if I moved into a bordel? But then I'd only be another one of his half-hour girls."

I kissed the back of her neck. It was like trying to influence a battleship.

She scribbled a note to the Duce and elected me to deliver it. I stood on that tiny elevator and skimmed through her lines.

> My beloved Ben,
> Why are you so far away when we are only a floor apart?
> I am like a marble tigress, awaiting your touch . . .

Folded the letter back into its perfumed slip. I wasn't a vampire, feeding off Claretta, sinking into the teeth of her love.

Down in the Sala del Mappamondo, Mussolini's usher announced me with two bangs of his long wooden pole on the carpet runner.

"Sir Pinocchio."

The Duce was having a glass of milk. He didn't look much like the tumbler of women. His face was squeezed tight. His eyes didn't have their usual dark hint.

"Benito," I shouted across the battlefield of carpets in Mappamondo. "I have a letter from your miss-stress."

I was Claretta's girlfriend and I didn't have to play polite with Mussolini. He drank his milk.

I'd heard about the great man's ulcers, that he couldn't bear solid food. He had three bowls of minestrone for breakfast and three bowls for lunch. The rest of the day was devoted to milk.

I trodded into carpet depths. The scale of Mappamondo couldn't frighten me. It was natural that a dictator would adore a big room. He'd developed his ulcers on account of Matteotti, the socialist chief his goons had kidnapped and murdered after the march on Rome. The Duce couldn't rid himself of Matteotti's ghost. He'd been appeasing the ghost for fifteen years with glasses of milk. The Savoyards believed Mussolini had ordered Matteotti's death. But the king himself held that Mussolini was innocent. The brutal temperature of the Blackshirts had destroyed Matteotti, said Vittorio Emanuele.

Little Sword was a dreamer on that subject, or else a very practical king who didn't want to topple his own first minister. The Blackshirts couldn't have fantasized Matteotti's death all on their own. Something had to have come from their leader. A word? A gesture? A bitter smile? *My brothers, wouldn't Rome be better off without this Matteotti?* And Matteotti was beaten to death.

I placed the letter near his glass of milk. He sipped once. The letter sat.

"Duce, would you like to read in private?"

He had a problem with his lips. They moved without much matter going on.

"Benito, can't you speak?"

He stood up, his face like some pale rider without a horse. He began to gallop behind his desk. I couldn't determine the impulse that was driving him. Matteotti's ghost? The moocow in the milk? He seized himself, seemed to grapple with his waist. I understood. He was trying to undress, but his fingers couldn't negotiate the buttons under his neck.

"Here," I told him. "Let me help you."

But he went on galloping without me. He gripped the back of his chair, and I wondered if he'd ride it to Cairo or Suez. He was always talking of Egypt. But then his fingers unloosed themselves and he grabbed at nothing. Mussolini fell. He lay writhing on the carpets, his girly legs knocking once or twice.

I stood over him. "Mussolini, I'm going for a doctor."

A word bit from his mouth. "Stay."

"But you're sick . . ."

He stopped writhing. I saw the Blue Garter he was wearing in a niche of his trousers. He'd recovered the power of speech. His lips moved with the old familiar rhythms.

"Puppet, your place is with me."

"What about Jacobo? Shouldn't I alert him? He'll find you an ambulance."

"It's nothing," Mussolini said. "A gastric attack . . . I have powerful juices. Pinocchio, hug me."

I didn't understand. "What, my prince?"

"Hug me. I have to keep warm."

So I got down on my knees, took Mussolini's head in my lap, and cradled him like that.

"Pinocchio, what would you like from your Duce?"

"An occupation," I said. "I can't go lounging all the time in a knight's coat. It's indecent."

"What if I made you commander of the Figli della Lupa?"

"But they're children. Six-year-olds."

"Six to eight," Mussolini said. "I'm going to start drafting all able bodies soon as they're six. The She-wolf mothered all of us. And my Sons of the She-wolf will return that debt to mother Rome."

There's an occupation for a knight. Sir Pinocchio, keeper of little boys. No matter where I leapt and whose wooden body I was in, I couldn't get away from children.

The gastritis was gone. Mussolini resented being cradled now. He rose up from my lap, pushed the milk aside, and toyed with the letter I'd delivered.

"Puppet, do we have anything more to discuss?"

"No, Prince Benito."

"Then why are you standing in my light?"

That's how he dismissed his puppet men, making us feel guilty for being there. I shoved off on the carpets, took the long trip to the door, and was foolish enough to turn my head around. He'd put on his spectacles to read Claretta. Like any prince, he didn't want me to see him in eyeglasses.

"Shut the door."

We camped in that soccer field of ruins half a mile away from the palazzo, practicing military tricks in a stone junkyard, the remains of Imperial Rome. The paths we walked on had once been Caesar's streets. Ancient Rome felt like a tiny village, hardly as big as Monte-grumo. Caesar took the world from this choppy ground, landed in Egypt, fell in love with Cleopatra, and was stabbed to death on the senate floor. Didn't he suffer from mythopsychosis, thinking Rome was the city of his dreams? Perhaps the Rome in his head was profounder than her streets. And why shouldn't the Duce have his Second Roman Empire? He could swallow the Mediterranean in a bottle of milk.

I had the Sons of the She-wolf. We bivouacked with bows and arrows. We weren't so cockeyed in our choice of weapons. Forget 1939. My She-wolves will have to fight the Russians, the British, or the Red Chinese in a world without oil or metal alloys in 2005.

We shot our bows and arrows, aiming at broken columns, broken sheds, the little tails of Caesar. We wore black neckerchiefs with the fascist skull and crossbones. Each of us had replicas of Mussolini's own dark fez.

A priest came onto the soccer field in his pointy hat and interrupted our maneuvers. "Scusa," he said. The children deferred to his hat, but I wasn't in the mood to reckon with Dante Romano, the secret social-ist. I ordered the children to grease their bows and sharpen the heads of their arrows, and I stood with Dante behind a stone shed.

He pummeled me with his fists the moment we were out of sight. Not to worry. A mouth like mine can't bleed, but it was the principle of the thing, getting hit by a fraudulent priest. I gave him such a wallop, the whites of his eyes sank from his head, leaving him with spooky holes until his eyes reappeared.

"Stronzo," he said.

That's the filthiest thing you can say to another man. Stronzo is a turd. I walloped him once more.

"Take it easy," he said, covering his mouth with a handkerchief. He pointed to a bunch of clandestinos hiding in the ruins.

"They're waiting to pounce, Sir Pinocchio. You had a job to do. But you've decided to sleep on us. Instead of strangling Benito, you vaca-tion in his palace."

"I'm not afraid of your stinking men. I have bows and arrows on my side."

Dante forgot the handkerchief and laughed into his sleeve. "And what will your little conquerers do, Pinocchio? We wear stilettos, like the fascisti."

I didn't argue with the priest. I summoned my She-wolves with a whooping call. Told them to let their arrows loose on the clandestinos.

"Figli," I said, "these are not our friends. Show them what we can accomplish in the name of Mussolini."

The children rocked with their bows high in the air. The arrows flew. It was like a raining of pregnant lines. The arrows arced with a lovely spin and then snipered down. The clandestinos got out from under that rain.

"You're disgusting," the priest said. "Teaching infants to aim like that. What are you?"

"A fascist . . . for now."

And Dante Romano left the soccer field in his skirts and pointy hat.

Marching towards Mussolini's piazza, after one such target practice in the ruins, I noticed people ignoring us. It was a Roman holiday. All work had stopped for the prince, who was giving a speech this afternoon from his balcony window.

Blackshirts bumped around us on the way to a choice spot under the balcony, where the prince could make his colossal shouts immediately over their heads. But they had to joust with a hundred thousand other souls. The Piazza Venezia was packed from wall to wall. Romans hugged the nearest prop—a lamppost or a statue leg. Cars and bikes had to find shelter beyond the square. Romans crowded into whatever niche was available to them. A particular kind of current moved among that crowd, a rhythmic snaking of heads.

I held to the edges of that snake dance, with the She-wolves behind me. Romans grimaced at us as they pushed along the current. "Ecco —Pinocchio!"

I had nothing to tell them. Hands gripped at my shirt cuffs, tried to force me into the dance. I punched at faces over the hands, because I knew that once I was in their rhythm, I'd never leave it.

The dancing stopped. Heads stood still. The prince had appeared on his balcony. A hundred thousand souls chanted at him, "Duce, Duce, Duce." He raised his arms and we shut up. The marble railing was low, and you had the impression that Mussolini was about to fall. It was this vertigo that kept us in a fever. We couldn't be sure when the prince would land in our lap.

He started to prowl on that little balcony, his hips beating against the balcony walls, and we feared for his life. That's how a Duce delivered his speech. He'd won us before a word was said.

"Blackshirts of the revolution, hear me."

He'd given up the prowl to thrust his jaw over the balcony.

"Mussolini says there are no disloyal Italians, not one. We have only bandits and socialists, and these are not Italians. They are dwarfs in the service of England and France and the United States. We will not abide these dwarfs. We will show them the kindness of an auto-da-fé. I mean to lend their hands, their heads, their feet to the torch."

Hid myself under my clothes, trying not to accent the puppet side of my nature.

"And what about the sister states that uphold the dwarfs, furnish them with bread, guns, and lies? The democratic sisters."

He stuck his fingers in the air, using them to count the sisters. "France," he said. "Blackshirts, this is not the France of Napoleon Bonaparte, a glorious tribe. Napoleon would weep in his grave over the French nation, ruined by alcohol, syphilis, and Marcel Proust. The future belongs to people who drink water, my friends. Leave wine to the dwarfs and syphilitics who cannot spend a morning without a page of Proust."

He prowled again and peered at us with his black eyes.

The piazza screamed, "Evviva Mussolini! Abbasso Proust!"

"England," he said, holding up a second finger. "Her admirals are swollen geese. They cannot exist without five meals a day. England suffers from a displaced uterus. Water and blood drip between her legs."

"Water and blood," we chanted. "Water and blood."

He wiggled a third finger.

"America," he said. "The rich sister, with a king in a wheelchair, Franklin Delano Roosevelt. There have been bald kings, fat kings, handsome and even stupid kings, but never kings who had to be supported by other men every time they went to the bathroom. And this is democracy's sweetheart. What should we do when I capture him? We'll make him our pet. He'll feed us ice cream from his chair and tell us stories about the Wild West."

"Wild West, Wild West."

"We'll give him a holster to play with, dress him in cowboy pants, Franklin the ice cream vendor. His America cannot hurt us. Only God can bend the fascist will. Certainly not the ice cream man."

Mussolini put away his counting fingers.

"The cripple has been spreading rumors that we've jumped too close to Germany, that we are Hitler's little lion he can hold in his pocket and smother at will."

The prince leaned his elbows on the stone rail, like a babbo to his children.

"Blackshirts, do we look like little lions?"

"No," we said. "No, no, no, no, no, no."

"If any man among you believes the ice cream vendor's lies and thinks of us as Hitler's circus, I beg him to find one swastika in the Adriatic, one swastika in Rome, and I will present that man with a million lire. Friendship is not slavery. We have formed a pact to preserve ourselves from democracy's big stink. The Führer has no use for little lions."

"Evviva il Führer!"

I was Cassandra now, that Trojan witch, with a big accounting book of Mussolini's future in my head. All the debacles of the Italian navy. His ventures into Greece. The routing of his Africa corps. The soldiers he would send to Stalingrad with cardboard shoes.

Digging his knuckles into the sides of his Saharan shirt, he listed the might of his empire on land, sea, and in the air. "The English announce that Italy has no aircraft carriers, as if that were a revelation of our weakness. I say to you that Italy herself is a huge aircraft carrier, and we have no need of conventional carriers."

The Romans hurrahed Italy the aircraft carrier. I shoved the She-wolves further behind me.

The magician on the balcony seemed about to produce cannons and tanks from under his fez. He was willing to take on the universe with that aircraft carrier of his. He spoke of six hundred dive bombers housed in Sicily, secret guns he had in Turin that could catapult a thousand men to Cairo. Egypt was always on his mind.

"We will not be ruled by a collection of old vegetables. No one dare bully us."

He turned around on that narrow ledge and walked through his window. Rome was bereft without him.

"Duce, Duce, Duce, Duce."

The prince returned to the balcony, ranting at us as if he'd never been away.

"Romans, erase the word impossible from your vocabulary. We do not encourage farces, big lemonades. We dream with our legs on the ground, and then we crack the dream and take whatever is inside with our claws."

He turned around again, departed from us, and we had to recall the son of a bitch.

"Duce, Duce, Duce, Duce."

It was a monotonous, maddening song, but it got him to the window. He'd have scorned the nation, neglected us, if he couldn't have his curtain calls. He began to reverse himself, beggar his own opinions, by his ninth trip to the balcony. He praised Roosevelt, called him the grand old patrician, and grew tighter and tighter about brother Adolf.

"The Italians are a race apart. Give the German his butter and his beer and he will not fight. But we were born with daggers in our mouths."

Mussolini whipped us in five directions. We'd have declared war on everybody. My She-wolves held their fezes like the Duce, low on the head, with room for their eyebrows and a patch of skin.

I was exhausted after his twentieth call to the balcony. I gave up the count. He was buying and selling countries with each new visit.

"Duce, Duce, Duce, Duce."

A priest rocked in front of me a little, on my left. He was with a woman. Dante Romano and Brunhilde's ghost. The ghost had put on some weight. I told the She-wolves not to move from their edge of the piazza, and then I jumped out at Dante and the ghost.

"Mamma, why have you forgotten me?"

Dante curled his teeth.

Romans advised me to shut my mouth. They were screaming at the balcony window. Mussolini strutted out. I touched Brunhilde's hair. She had a thick white powder on her face. The powder wouldn't rumple even when she smiled.

"I'm still a socialist." It was only half a lie. I'd have dropped Benito in a minute, but not my girlfriend Clara.

"Copernicus Charyn," she said, "you're in the wrong place."

"I'm Pinocchio."

I could feel my nose condense. I had a sudden arthritis in the elbow. I turned to look at my She-wolves. It was a stinking mistake. I should have concentrated on that balcony. The Duce might have held me in Rome.

Nothing melted. Nothing gave. I was out in the street, on the rue Pascal. The old whore had hustled me to Paris.

NINE

COPERNICUS

I had withdrawal pains. This return to flesh. I was cold, unspeakably cold, in my room at le Wigwam. How many months had I lost, living in Pinocchio's body? I'd swear it was September outside, but my bones said February. I took a piss. It was no comfort to make yellow water in a sink. Pinocchio never had to pee. All his wastes were absorbed in wood.

Tested my pockets. No one had robbed me while I was shoving between Paris and Rome. I had lots of money in my pants, Molières that could keep a guy in grapefruit juice.

Put on three sweaters and walked down to Montsouris. Other men strolled in sleeveless shirts, but I shivered, mates. It was the climate under my skin.

Montsouris was where I'd met Guignol, but I hadn't come to commune with puppet shows. I wanted to continue my conversation with Monsieur le prince. He was lying in his bed in the tiny apartment that overlooked Montsouris. His throat was cut, but you could hardly tell. His hands were folded in his lap, like a man expecting neighbors. He had a pale string of blood under his ears that could have been a bracelet to beautify his neck. Somebody had washed him, I promise you, prepared him for his wake.

Had this funny notion that the gutting of Monsieur was staged for my benefit. I was part of somebody's orchestra, and I couldn't say whose.

A tickle in my ear told me not to go back to my hotel. I'd have prayed to Pinocchio's godmother, but Brunhilde was no longer on my side. I went to join the clochards under the nearest bridge. The bums took a vote. I was too ordinary to them, ordinary and unbroken. They decided not to have me until they discovered my pack of Molières.

They weren't the clochards of Dostoyevsky and Proust. They were stinking capitalists. Money got me into their club. We had snails at Aux Deux Magots, buttered radishes in the street. We danced with young widows under la Coupole, wearing neckties the manager gave us. We attended lectures on Lewis Carroll at the British Cultural Foundation. The clochards knew every word of Alice. And when my Molières gave out, the bastards dropped me. I was nothing to them. They'd slum with rich Americans, but these clochards had a strict sense of brotherhood. No American could ever creep into their circle.

They kicked me far from their quay. I was beginning to distrust la vie parisienne. Good old Mussolini was right about the French. A nation wrecked by alcohol, syphilis, Proust . . . and idiotic fraternal orders. Even the bums had their own union.

Couldn't go near the quays. All the different fraternities seemed to recognize me. The bums of Paris had selected me out. I wasn't an absolute donkey. I'd hidden one Molière in my sleeve. I sat in teahouses. I still had my yellow scarf, but I didn't bother looking for that beautiful grandmother who'd befriended me with Molières and then wouldn't acknowledge me at all.

But I was cursed. Having a bit of fruitcake near the window, and a woman knocks on the glass. A few months of wood hadn't dulled me. It was the grandmother without a name. How did I know? I remembered her red cape. Paid the bill and ran out after grandmère. I'd lost my familiarity with human feet. I was nimble as a puppet, but I couldn't make purchase with these damn American shoes. I slid along the road.

Grandmère kindly stopped for me. But when I got close, she'd break away with a terrific striding under that red cloth.

She led me to the river. Tried to warn her that I wasn't welcome there. But I couldn't reach grandmère with my signaling. I waved and waved and she went under the bridge.

Should have known it was an Italian trick. The cape fell from her shoulders, and I had Brunhilde in my midst. She wore that terrible white powder . . .

"What do you mean," I said, "sneaking around like that, playing the beautiful grandmother, giving me Molières when they weren't yours to give? You come marching out of Pinocchio, betray me the first chance you get, and all you are is a pimple in my imagination."

"You're the pimple. Who do you think boils the stories in your head? Brunhilde."

"So you tickled me into inventing you. Is that your stinking tale?"

"Idiot," she said, looking deprived without her cape. "I existed long before you were in your mother's womb."

"Did you also invent my father? Were you in business with the ragman? Did you pretend to be the furrier's widow from Crotona Park and sleep with my poor dad, confuse him so that he never returned to my mother? No wonder Bruny kept away. He bought himself a witch."

She socked me on the cheek. They must have outfitted her badly in heaven and hell. Brunhilde had marshmallow hands. Her socking was the closest thing to a kiss. I had the mind to throttle her, make that witch ride me back to Rome. I missed my yellow room.

I danced with Brunhilde, forced her into my embrace, and did the foxtrot two feet from the Seine. The old whore was soft under her clothes. She started to whimper.

"Any other theories, Brunhilde, about who's the boss of our frigate? You're the queen of invention, dearie, the stoker girl, and you live in my hold. When you're rotten, I whip your ass."

Tried to eat her marshmallow skin, but she wasn't so mushy up around her neck. She had the usual bark of a woman.

She danced me into the clochards, who had wet newspapers rolled into billy clubs bound with wire and the straw of a broom. You wouldn't think newspaper could hurt so much. They whacked my shoulders and my neck while Brunhilde clutched me in her spider's dance. The constant sound of wet paper was like the cannon booms that Benito had dreamed about. He'd sent his war to France with a socialist witch.

And I discovered the sights of Paris. I'd close my eyes to the whacking and see the Eiffel Tower. The tower struts were high. There was a field in front of it. Blood whipped from my nose. It felt like the end of the story. Children, I had nowhere to go.

A man rushed up to the clochards. I saw him out of the one eye that was still half open. He waded through the bums, received their hits of wet paper, and slammed their foreheads until they fell away. That was some punch my savior had. The punch of Charlotte Street.

"Romey," he said, "did I send you to Paris to run with sewer rats?"

Copernicus had come for me.

Woke in the Concorde, a stewardess babying me with napkins and water. I wasn't allowed to drink champagne. Had bandages up and down my body. I was wearing one of uncle's pinstripe suits with trousers that held its line of stripes from crotch to ankle without a fault.

Uncle had herring with his champagne. I was always stronger coming out of a fog. That staged death of Monsieur le prince reminded me of forty years ago and the first two deaths I'd ever seen. Madam Andrusov and Bitter Morris. They'd died with the same look of tranquility.

I interrupted the track of Lionel's herring. "Who killed Monsieur?"

"Hey, you're recuperating."

"Who killed Monsieur?"

"Those nigger Jews."

"But Philippe is dead, and Antoine is too crazy to fight."

"Then they must have brought a new brother up from the minors. Because the niggers got to Raffe. I arranged the funeral."

"Didn't he have a family to bury him? . . . what about Alain?"

"That jailbird?" Lionel said, gobbling champagne with the churning of his mouth. "Alain doesn't know to bury."

"I thought he works for you."

"Strictly part time. And he's jumped. Alain's a missing person right now."

"No he's not. He eats fire on the boulevard de la Chapelle. Alain told me something. He said I wasn't meant to survive Paris."

"Do you believe everything a jailbird tells you?"

"That depends. Alain is persuasive with fire in his mouth. He feels you were trying to punish me."

"Punish you? For being Henry James? Schmuck, who taught you the alphabet? Who read you *Bambi* in bed?"

"But you think I prepared Marie for the pieds noirs with my lectures at Bronx Science."

"You did. You ruined her fucking mind. You taught fifteen-year-olds Marxist shit."

"Lionel, you were a Marxist last year."

"I can afford to be a Marxist. I have twenty million dollars. You gave my wife the Kafka complex. Marie wouldn't have fallen for that scumbag in the Arab quarter without you."

"So you figured it was time I took a rest. And Alain wouldn't have any part of it."

"Romey, if I wanted you, I wouldn't go to Alain. I have better resources. Didn't I save you from the sewer rats?"

Took a sip of uncle's champagne and went back to sleep.

Bathsheba stood at her door with a tower of blue hair. "Who crippled my baby?" she asked.

I could smell martinis on her breath.

"Romey, they wrapped you in bandages like King Tut."

"It's nothing. A misunderstanding with some grandmother."

"Grandmothers? You're growing up."

Damn it all, I didn't have a present for Bathsheba. Could have saved her a fascist stick, some toiletries out of Claretta's medicine chest, but how did I know I'd be wrenched from Italy?

I was careful with Bathsheba. I had a tick in my nose that registered death masks. Andrusov. Bitter Morris. Monsieur. I smelled a pattern in the forty years between Andrusov and Raffe San Angelo. So I started to dig. I was a crafty son of a bitch. I let mamma feed me turkey sandwiches. I had a pint of mustard. Cucumbers and dill. I licked my fingers and counted her martinis. Six.

"Where's Hervey Long?"

Bathsheba stared at me as if I were the dumbest man in America.

"Hervey," I said. "That Bible salesman from the Dominick Street mission."

"I know who Hervey is. He's been gone at least a month."

"Sacked him for another suitor?"

Mamma rose up high on her heels. But she couldn't tolerate the altitude near her son's head. Her left heel caved in, and I had to carry her across living rooms to her settee.

"Didn't have time for Herve. Someone has to look out for Lionel. He's a man without a wife."

I understood the lay of the tower. Bathsheba had turned herself into Marie-Pierre. I don't mean incest. Lionel and my mother kissing under the stairs. But she must have gone with him to La Tulipe and tolerated Miz Alabam in his bed. Did they attack the other side of the menu without Marie? Salmon mousse instead of papillote?

I mixed her a small barrel of martinis, sinking olives into her glass. It was wicked to ply Bathsheba like that. But I had to get that tick out of my nose.

"Mamma, do you remember Belinda Hogg, the secondhand girl from Texas?"

Bathsheba pretended to be involved with her olive pit. She didn't enjoy my waltzes into the past. They reminded her of Bruno and the baby carriage.

"Belinda Hogg," I said again. "She lived in the casbah with Madam Andrusov."

"Romey, there was no secondhand girl from Texas. You made her up."

"Mamma, I wasn't writing novels at seven."

"You made her up."

"But I followed her to the casbah. That's how I met Andrusov."

"You met Andrusov through your mother."

Impossible. Bathsheba had stopped going to Charlotte Street when my dad made her give up the baby carriage. That was years before Belinda Hogg.

"The baby carriage," I muttered. "Mamma, those times you went to Charlotte Street with the baby carriage, did you visit Andrusov's nicknack shop?"

"Yes. She handled the stolen goods."

Andrusov was my mother's fence!

"She gave you lollipops," Bathsheba said.

"How did I get to meet her again?"

"Lionel took you to Charlotte Street. He worked for Andrusov behind your father's back."

"Uncle never played with the secondhand girls and boys . . . mamma, did Andrusov have a pet octopus, Tatiana, that the pickle merchants killed?"

"Romey, I couldn't say."

"But mamma, you can't invent an octopus out of nothing. Tati had to exist."

My mother shook the martini barrel; that blue tower shivered on her head.

"After Andrusov died, you came home with the story of Belinda and the octopus. I didn't see any harm in it. I used this Tatiana to help you read."

"What about Edgar? Why haven't you been reading with him? You could have given him Tati too."

"Edgar can get along without his aunt Bathsheba. He's cured."

"Cured? He couldn't spell his name before I went to Paris."

"It's Pinocchio," Bathsheba said. "Pinocchio cured him. He'll be going to the Dalton School this winter."

"But when did he start to read?"

"About a month ago."

"Just like that? He picks up a book, the signals bump in perfect order, and dyslexia hides in the closet. I don't believe in that kind of business."

"See for yourself."

Ah, my mother had used the martini barrel to pull me from Tati and Belinda. I'd swear on my life that Andrusov had an octopus in a pickle barrel, made black with Tatiana's ink.

Kissed Bathsheba and went down to Edgar's room. Gesù, Giuseppe, Maria. He was sitting in front of a word processor, punching out his autobiography on the screen.

I'm Edgar Copernicus.
Manhattan is my terrestrial home.
I live on mother earth, a moving ball.
I believe other creatures are signaling us,
And we are much too deaf to hear.
One day

The little cursor on the screen that drove him to spell had stopped after "day." He must have noticed my shadow in the backfield of the screen.

"Don't let me inhibit you," I said.

He wasn't so happy as a word magician. His lunge into spelling had given him dark pouches under his eyes. He looked behind my back for Marie.

"Didn't my mother come home with you?"

"I was in Italy most of the time. I hardly saw Marie."

"Lionel said you were bringing her."

"Then your dad told you a lie."

The cursor bled white on the screen: that blinking god of words was waiting for Edgar.

"Aren't you glad to see me?" I had to ask.

"Not without my mother. You were supposed to bring her."

"Grateful little bugger, aren't you? Didn't I write Pinocchio to help you out of your blindness on the page? Look at you. You're a bloody genius."

"It had nothing to do with Pinocchio. I woke up one morning and I knew how to spell."

"That's called osmosis, Edgar. Your mind absorbed my text."

"I know all about osmosis . . . why didn't you send me chapters through the mail?"

"I told you. I was in Italy. I had things to do."

Marie came home to Washington Square with a companion from the Goutte d'Or. Antoine Montesquieu. It wasn't Antoine's presence in the tower that troubled me. Why couldn't auntie bring a guest? It was the sock in his blue eyes. Antoine had Philippe's elegant power. I'd misread the vocabulary of les Frères. Antoine was the important brother.

Uncle welcomed him into the fold. The four of us had dinner at La Tulipe. Mamma stayed home. Headache, she said. She'd rest with a magazine and rinse her blue hair.

I watched uncle for signs of unrest. The bastard was enjoying himself. He attacked the papillote, didn't leave a morsel of red snapper.

Antoine came without his speech affliction. He had no brother to parrot at La Tulipe. He argued sweetly with Lionel about currency markets. Did the Montesquieus have their own bank behind the counter at Des Poissonniers? Antoine must have lived on a gravy of gold.

Uncle turned impetuous, reaching out to muss my hair. "This kid couldn't tell a dollar from a graveyard. Gives up a lifetime job at Bronx Science to put ink on his nails."

"Molières," I muttered.

Lionel made a cuckoo sign and returned to his ravaged kite of fish.

I had an anger in me that could have swallowed a restaurant, but I didn't touch the green beans on my plate.

Uncle went off with Antoine on a trip to the toilet.

Saved my bile for auntie Pierre. "It's marvelous how Antoine has recovered from his sickness."

"He was never sick," auntie said. "He had to confuse people, make them think only one of the brothers was dangerous."

"I get the picture. Philippe was the duck in the window."

Auntie broke a carrot stick.

"Did you want Antoine to advertise himself? He was surrounded by enemies."

"The Corsican brothers, I suppose. But Raffe San Angelo still died without a friend. Auntie, who cut his throat? Lionel says it was the black foots. That means Antoine."

"Antoine couldn't walk the streets. It was difficult enough smuggling him out of Paris. Don't add murder to the list."

"But if Monsieur was dead, why should Antoine have to leave Paris?"

"Poupou," she said, "Monsieur wasn't the problem. It was jealousy among the pieds noirs."

"The black foots were fighting themselves?"

"Yes. Monsieur was killed because he was Antoine's ally."

I leaned across the table. "Tell me," I said, clutching her hands, "if Antoine and Philippe had the same blue eyes and brilliant complexion, how come you loved one and not the other?"

"I loved them both."

I begged the blue fairy not to blow on my head that night. The whore of Montegrumo could pull a web around you that was impossible to penetrate. It wasn't any old wrapping, like her red cape. It was the knotted silk of your past, a silk that bound you the more you tried to uncover it. But I had to get under the silk.

I started with the outer web, thinking I'd tickle that pinup queen of mythopsychosis. You can't tickle a witch. Her silk held like the toughest hymen.

"Belinda Hogg," I said, because one or two words, spoken correctly, might create a tear in the silk. Belinda Hogg. Belinda. I could feel a disturbance in that hymen the whore had wrapped around my head. I must have broken through. Belinda, Belinda, Belinda, but I couldn't find my uncle in Andrusov's storefront church. Only secondhand girls and boys.

I was in memory's armpit, stranded in silky hair.

I pulled on my nose and found Lionel, but he wasn't skulking in the casbah. He was in our old flat on Boston Road. I could lend you a diagram of every room. I could recite how each wall smelled, with chicken Kiev in the woodwork the closer you got to my mother's kitchen. Uncle wouldn't depart from Boston Road, even after the firebugs arrived on our roof. The building had emptied around us. The landlord begged uncle to move. His name was Ivanhoe Bonaventura, and his begging had something to do with the insurance he could collect if the building was unoccupied. Our family, the Copernicus Charyns, was spoiling his plan. He offered uncle a thousand dollars to vacate.

"Ivanhoe, fuck yourself."

The landlord tripled his offer.

"Not three thousand, not ten thousand, Ivanhoe."

"Tell me why? It's not even a nigger neighborhood. Lionel, you're the last human beings on the block. You have to go a mile for a lousy piece of cake."

"I'll go the mile," Lionel said. "This is the home my sister made for me. I grew up here. I copped my first titty in the hall."

"Be reasonable. There are imbeciles on the roof. They play with matches a lot. You get my point? Your sister could wake up one morning with her pajamas on fire."

Lionel threw the landlord down a flight of steps. Ivanhoe gripped the walls with his fingernails and managed to recover himself. Blood seemed to drip from the nails.

"Lionel, I have a big family. They'll learn how you mutilated me. They'll never control the firebugs. These rooms will be a coffin for you, your sister, and the brilliant one from Bronx Science."

My uncle chased Ivanhoe into the street. The landlord shook his fists from the mounds of rubble at the corner.

"You can scratch your own obituary in that little black book of yours, Copernicus. Put it in for tonight."

Uncle had his own enforcers. But he wouldn't summon them to babysit on the roof. Copernicus was the single knight of Crotona Park. My gallant uncle would never bring hired help near his door. He tried to hand me a baseball bat. I wasn't that eager to fight with Ivanhoe. The firebugs could have our building. The Bronx was a burnt-out case.

"You can garnish my salary, Lionel. Let's move."

"Not for that shit and his insurance policy."

"But he'll win in the end, with or without his firebugs."

"He won't win tonight . . . Romey, take the bat."

He had that mad Tatar gaze. He could have been canoeing on the Black Sea. He'd have beaten my brains and then gone up to the roof. I took the bat and we went to meet the firebugs.

We had to wait. They weren't hairy children, refugees from some delinquents' camp paid to menace us with their fire. They were grown men with barrels of kerosene. Lionel didn't attack until they crossed onto our roof. Say I'm heartless, but I thought Willie Mays, my uncle beats on firebugs with Willie's swing. I didn't have to rush the bastards. I protected Lionel's rear. He socked them towards the hole between the roofs. Three of the firebugs got away. The fourth dropped into the hole, still clutching his head.

I heard him bump against the walls and then hit the ground with the lush noise of a tank. I couldn't conceive that a body would have such a thick fall. I wanted to run to Cairo out of excitement and shame. We'd killed a man, socked him over a roof. The side of my face pulsed like an owl, but Lionel could have been buying vegetables, or picking weeds from the garden he didn't have.

I slept beside Copernicus on our bed, with that silly pulse in my face.

A police captain visited us in the morning. I smelled Attica and Sing Sing, maximum security and all that. The captain had Bathsheba's tea and a baked Alaska. He asked us if we'd heard an uncommon noise the night before.

"There was a lad playing on the roofs with a kerosene can. He slipped, the poor devil, and broke his ass."

"We were asleep, Captain John."

"Right," the captain said. "You have to retire early around here. Nothing walks on Boston Road past noon. But Lionel, do us a favor. Listen to Ivanhoe. It's a savage street you're on."

Uncle ignored the captain. "Had a bird on my window yesterday. It's like the country . . . see you, John."

The captain applauded my mother's baked Alaska and pulled on his tunic as a goodbye.

"You shouldn't have been rude to him," my mother said.

"And he shouldn't side with the landlords."

Bathsheba wagged her head. "Karl Marx."

Ivanhoe razed the buildings on both sides of us. We were the only piece of real estate standing on the block. It was like coming home to a castle. Rats played in the rubble by the front door. Captain John sent lackeys with shotguns to blow them onto the next block. Lionel's Checker cab carted Bathsheba's groceries. A castle, I'm telling you. A country estate.

And then I brought Marie-Pierre home to dinner. Uncle's complexion changed. He didn't want his future wife to live around the corpses of other buildings. He moved his country estate to Washington Square. Ivanhoe didn't profit from it. Lionel wouldn't confuse love and economics. He hired a deputy to squat in the apartment until the landlord came up with eleven thousand dollars.

I'd ruptured the silk that had to do with Lionel as a grand seignior, but no matter how hard I begged Brunhilde, I couldn't seize his image in Andrusov's shop. I fell asleep with my head inside the hymen Brunhilde had prepared for me.

I woke with a shouting in my ear that made me think I was in the Quirinale, listening to La Mamma badger her son the king. But it was only Harriet the maid. She'd found Bathsheba lying in bed with her martini barrel and a tray of club sandwiches. My mother had choked to death on martinis and turkey meat. She must have been upset by the return of Marie. I should have forced her to go with us to La Tulipe, convinced her that she was chatelaine, with or without Marie.

I was the evil son who couldn't cry for the swollen blue face on the coverlet. I'd changed mommies. Brunhilde was my mother now. That blue face was like an old furloughed aunt. But Lionel wept and wept for his sister. Antoine tried to console him. He gathered my uncle in his arms and rocked him with a force that resisted the violent pulling of uncle's body.

Put out my hand, but I was afraid to touch Lionel, as if I'd killed Bathsheba in some perverse, magical way. Auntie stood with Edgar. He was crying. He swooned my mother's name.

"Bathsheeeeeba."

All I could concentrate on was the swelling of Harriet's calves.

My uncle couldn't end his grieving. Miz Alabam came up from the rescue mission to take his mind off Bathsheba, but Lionel sent her away. He paddled around in silk pajamas that had begun to stink. It was as if the clothes he wore when his sister was alive couldn't be tampered with or washed. He made no entries in his little black book.

Antoine watched after Lionel's receipts. He sat in the main parlor and met with those who'd come to see Copernicus. Soon he had his own black book, with the crisscrossings of uncle's accounts. Lionel had built his empire promoting other men. He juggled a thousand businesses, and Antoine had to relocate inventories that were lost in uncle's hieroglyphics. It was a wonder we didn't grow poor.

Uncle slashed his throat. He might have been shaving in the middle of a dream and suffered the wicked, accidental pull of his razor. He wouldn't go to the hospital in an ambulance. I put a sweater over his pajamas and rode with him in the Checker cab.

Lionel was delirious. Nothing could console him. Not his millions, not Marie. He hardly said a word to Edgar in the hospital. He'd fall asleep while Antoine recited the finances of his pickle factories. He only allowed himself to cry in front of me.

I'd sit and hold his hand in a hospital room that was a ward with one bed. Bankers and deputy commissioners rang him up. He wouldn't answer their calls. I'd wipe his eyes with a great big hospital napkin. He'd blubber for an hour and turn lucid again.

"Alain wasn't wrong, you schmuck. I planned a stiff vacation for you in Paris."

"A hole in Montparnasse?"

"Not that stiff. I told you. You're like a kid brother. French justice suits my style. No bail. We were preparing a nice morals rap for you. Molesting an old lady . . ."

Son of a bitch, was Brunhilde in on the deal?

". . . you could sit five, ten years in that old red prison until you come to trial."

"Like a lettre de cachet," I said.

Lionel understood my French. "Exactly."

I was still clutching his hand. "Uncle, all that for the sake of jealousy? Marie would have gone to the Montesquieus without my ravings on Kafka and Joyce."

"No. She was your child. You created her at Bronx Science."

"But the girl I created married you."

"She was listening to Kafka and Joyce," my uncle announced with his neck in bandages.

"And what did Kafka say?"

"That Marie should marry the old entrepreneur and find adventure outside the marriage."

"But why should I have to sit in la Santé? She didn't have her adventures with me."

"A high school teacher with haunted eyes? She's not that sick. But you were the monkey that gnawed at her."

"I never encouraged her to go to Paris, uncle. You did."

"She'd have gone without my encouragement. You witched her head."

I swear on Brunhilde's ancient tits that auntie would have left Lionel without Kafka, Joyce, or the Bronx High School of Science. I wanted to punch his ears back. Tatar Jews are a paranoid race. And there's little to remedy that.

"What saved me from la Santé? Alain's running off?"

"Never. He's a meaningless kid. It was Raffe San Angelo. He didn't love the idea of an American writer camping out in his territories. The French are scared of scribblers, didn't you know? He thought you'd do a manifesto and smuggle it to a magazine. I told him we'd take care of all the smugglers, but he wouldn't listen. Raffe liked you."

"It's a disease, liking me. And Raffe died for it."

"That's a different story," uncle said. He took my hand and put it to his eyes. "I was a moron in pursuit of money. I pulled nickels from every pocket . . . the wild boy of Boston Road. Until I met Marie. I groomed myself to keep her. I learned Lords and Taylors. But it was never enough. She had the dream of Paris. Maybe that happens when you're a little Quebec girl living in Texas, with wheat and cow sheds. So I bent to her dream. I built connections around her. I won't lie. I made dollars helping Marie. I'm a trader. I can't stop."

"Why didn't you go with her to Paris?"

"Charlotte Street and Paris don't mix."

"They mixed for the Montesquieus. Antoine kept his Charlotte Street in the Arab quarter."

"But he's the golden boy. Antoine has the European touch."

"He's no more golden than you are, but you gave up."

Uncle pulled my hand from his eyes. "He's the golden boy, I said . . ."

"Uncle, I'll go back to Bronx Science and manufacture another beauty, but stop grieving. Mothers and sisters have to disappear."

"Not my sister. You wouldn't know. You arrived late . . . we sifted through the garbage together. What did I need my millions when I had Bathsheba? She could have married and gone to Portugal or Cleveland without me. Your mamma had plenty of beaus."

"And she picked the ragman, that philosopher with the handtruck."

"Don't say bad about your father," Lionel warned me from his hospital bed.

"Of course not. We're one big family playing ring-around-a-rosy on the rubble of Boston Road."

"It could have been worse. You had *Bambi* and bottles of milk."

A nurse arrived with a peach in yellow water. Lionel begged me to go down and bring him papillote.

"La Tulipe doesn't have take-out service, Lionel. It's haute cuisine."

"Wanna bet?"

He dialed La Tulipe and charmed some superchef, my uncle who'd slipped on his razor. And I had to fetch him his meal, sneaking in the papillote under my sweatshirt, because the hospital wouldn't tolerate another caterer on its premises.

The papillote couldn't soothe him. Uncle started to cry.

"Romey, I'm scared without Bathsheba."

"Scared? Deputy mayors call you on the phone. You turn La Tulipe into the corner deli."

"That's the song money sings. I'm scared without Bathsheba."

He wasn't Benito whooping up a crowd from his balcony window. He was my uncle in bed. I told him we'd resettle after he got well, go to some neutral spot where he wouldn't be reminded of Bathsheba.

"I am well. I nicked my throat, that's all. And there is no neutral spot. Can you come tomorrow with a candle? They don't let us read late at night."

He'll burn the hospital down, I thought. He's had too intense an affair with firebugs. I brought the candle, but uncle wasn't in his bed. He'd started to climb out the window an hour earlier. Three black nurses had to pull him from the wall. He was under sedation upstairs in a holding pen. I got to uncle through an iron gate. It was the psychiatric wing.

"Did my aunt Marie sign him in here?"

The nurses said no. Uncle had committed himself.

"From the top of the window? Did you give him a pencil while he was hanging overboard?"

I was cruel to those black nurses. They'd kept my uncle alive. An intern showed me the paper he'd signed. *Copernicus needs a rest.*

He was taken out of the holding pen and put in a room with wire windows. He could look at the Chrysler Building from a world of hexagons. He'd clutch me in that wire room and scream that I was his only kinsman.

"You have a son and a wife."

"Traitors," he said, biting his mouth. "Black foots."

"They are not. Marie's a Canuck. And Edgar's a Tatar, like you."

"Black foots."

Lionel was king of his wire room, and what could I tell the king? His empire flourished without him. Antoine gave me documents for uncle to sign. His signature had authority, even from the madhouse. But that signature was beginning to change. It curled larger and larger on the page, the more uncle drew into himself.

I brought him seven pairs of silk pajamas, but he wouldn't get out of the ones he was in. The nurses and I had to tear them from his back.

"Romey, live with me here."

"They wouldn't allow it."

"I'll make a telephone call," he said, but he didn't have a phone in his wire room, or he'd have gotten the governors of the hospital to agree to let me in. Lionel sniffed the air, and I think I understood. It was only nature. My mother's smell must have comforted him. Is that why he was so reluctant to leave Boston Road? Because he was frightened that it would take a couple of years before Bathsheba could penetrate the walls of another apartment?

"You smell like Bathsheba," he said, falling asleep on my shoulder.

Uncle suffered a heart attack while he was in bed. Nurses sucked his mouth and sat on his chest, but Lionel had already gone to Bathsheba.

He could have made billions in the madhouse, but his empire crumbled the moment people knew he was dead. Customers preyed on Antoine with promissory notes. He was deluged with a constant traffic of paper. We shuffled through the tower for cash and uncovered half a million dollars in the baseboard on the bottom floor. The half million went.

Auntie rummaged through all her closets. She wasn't searching for money. She was deciding what to wear.

Auntie said our blood would get spilled if we stayed in Manhattan.

"Where you going?"

"Does it matter? Honduras. Antibes."

"You could lose your head in Honduras."

"Look around you. There's plenty of banditos on Washington Square . . . Romey, come with us."

"And be Edgar's nanny in Antibes? Someone has to finish uncle's accounts."

She pulled her face out of the closets. It was angry, beautiful, and red.

"You're like a stranded child . . . you don't know the first thing about money. Lionel's been floating you since you were five. You'll be dead in a month."

"I didn't die in Paris, I won't die here."

"Oh lucky man," she said. "You should have died in Paris."

"What did my dying have to do with you?"

She dug her face back into a closet. ". . . hopeless goose."

I walked into the clothes with her and dragged her out. "Who's a hopeless goose? Auntie, you were with the Montesquieus. You'd lost touch with Lionel. He sent me to make contact with you."

"We were always partners, idiot, no matter where I went. I'm the one that hated you."

"Hate me?" I said, with auntie's skirts and blouses hanging over my ears. "Hate me, why?"

"Because I saw very fast that I'd get crushed being around you. You couldn't even write a book that would sell."

"*Blue Eyes over Miami?*"

"Who remembers? Why didn't you court me after I got married?"

"Court my own aunt?"

"Lionel wouldn't have noticed."

She stroked me under the left eye. ". . . the doomed little boy with the exquisite cheeks. You'll never age. You're the Tatar prince."

"You should have married me."

"Yes, I'd become a clerk at Bendel's and you'd lecture at Bronx

Science. What a sweet little life. And where do you think I'd have spent my lunch hours? In bed with every buyer that came into the store. I'd have found my way to Paris."

Couldn't help it. I started to cry. "I might have had a success. We could have lived at the Plaza-Athénée."

"Poupou," she said. "I never wanted the Plaza Athénée. I wanted the lecturer to take his words into the street . . ."

"Well, if you hate me so much why don't you kill me now?"

"What for? Lionel isn't here to see it."

The Tatar prince had the tower all to himself . . . and Harriet the maid. Didn't know what to do with Harriet. Could I order her to undress? Harriet took it for granted that I'd inherited her. She undressed the two of us. Harriet had the tiniest navel I'd ever seen. Like the head of a thumbtack. I licked it for an hour, and her belly began to open. She was quebecoise, and you had to move slow with her.

I didn't get the chance to ride on her French-Canadian calves. Two men squatted behind me and put a gun to Harriet's head. How'd they get in? I swear I'd bolted the front door.

Funny what happens once you've been a knight. Couldn't even shiver for these guys. "Don't hurt her," I said. "She's only the maid."

I didn't want Harriet killed. They could have been pickle men out of my past, the Jennings Street mob, come to murder Andrusov . . . or me.

They weren't pickle men. They were shills without their kerosene cans, the same uglies from our roof on Boston Road. That landlord, Ivanhoe Bonaventura, peeked around their shoulders. "I have a lien on you, kid. Your uncle owes me eleven big ones. I'm not hungry. I won't ask for interest. I want what I paid to buy your uncle out of Boston Road."

I sat with my ass on the pillow. "I'll never negotiate. Not with a gun on Harriet. Let her go, Bonaventura."

The uglies hardly menaced her. They were too involved with Harriet's tits. Ivanhoe agreed to let Harriet get dressed. She wasn't in much of a hurry to escape these firebugs. Harriet preened for Ivanhoe, stood around with that naked fork between her legs.

She wasn't whoring. Harriet winked at me. She had all the desperate courage of a quebecoise. She was trying to draw the uglies' attention, so I could run away.

"Harriet," I told her. "Go on. Get out of here."

She stepped into her clothes and kissed me with her tongue deep in my face.

"Hey skirt," Ivanhoe said. "Push off."

I followed the progress of her calves from door to door. No one did a thing until Harriet was gone. Then the uglies pounced on me.

I mocked Bonaventura in some quiet corner of my heart. I wasn't crazy. I was convinced Harriet would return with the cops. The firebugs punched and kicked, and Harriet didn't come. I remembered the children of Montsouris during the puppet show, trying to warn Guignol. *Méchant, méchant.* I was caught in the same wicked world.

"Bonaventura, I'm out of bread."

"That's a pity, sweetheart." The landlord stooped over me. "Then we'll sell your lungs and your liver to the first junkman I find in the street . . . but your uncle was a bit of a miser. There has to be money around."

"We pulled every dollar out of the walls," I told him.

"Maybe you didn't pull enough."

And his uglies proceeded to tear and scrape with the chisel knives they kept in their coat pockets. They deposited scars in my mother's wallpaper. These rippings in the wall reminded me of Matisse.

The firebugs arrived in Edgar's room.

"Ivanhoe, stop this dumb joke. Uncle's fortune slipped away. So shove your matches between my toes and I'll kiss you goodbye."

"What's that?"

"A word machine. It processes language."

"Show me."

"Ivanhoe, it's not my machine."

Edgar wasn't a dope. He'd taken his memory discs to Antibes.

"Show me, I said."

I poked into Edgar's storage box. He was a kind little bastard. He'd left one disc for his teacher. I blew the dust off and shoved it into the console. Nothing happened.

Bonaventura began to pull on my neck.

"Are you making fun of me?"

I managed to light the screen. But I couldn't understand its simplest circuits. The mother kept asking me for a menu.

I tapped the keyboard by mistake. I must have found the right menu, because that mother broke into song.

> Once upon a time
>> Twice
>> Three times and four
>> There lived a high school teacher
>> And this high school teacher that was named Jerome thought he could teach children how to read. He was arrogant and in love with the love of words. He valued words over people and every other thing. Words were his children, and they kept him a child. He sobbed about his absent bar mitzvah, but the truth of it is that he wasn't ready to have one . . .

Mamma must have given my secrets away before she choked in bed. She'd conspired with Edgar to write that song.

The landlord shouted, "I've had enough." But I wanted to hug that menu on the screen. I had facts to learn. How deep had Edgar carved into the high school teacher?

The firebugs threw the console off its table in their avarice to wreck things. They'd stumbled upon a treasure trove. The back of the console fell away. The machine had hundred-dollar bills attached to its spine. The firebugs laughed at Lionel's banking system. Ivanhoe assembled the bills by himself.

"You're still on the short side of my eleven thousand. But I'll forgive you, seeing how Lionel is dead."

He pulled the memory disc from the broken console.

"Ivanhoe, what's on that disc is a family matter."

"I am your family. Sweetheart, you belong to the Bonaventuras."

He signaled to his firebugs and left me alone in that wreckage. I was Robinson Crusoe on a wallpaper island. I was Sinbad the sailor. Pinocchio without a crew.

Could have tunneled in. Ivanhoe didn't come back to seek more treasure. But I had an itch for human company. Went down to Dominick Street. Superintendent Rice didn't have any psalms in his window. The window looked eaten alive. Rice's mission had fallen on hard times without Copernicus' money. There wasn't a single sinner inside. Lemuel Rice sat in the commissary with his deacon, Hervey Long, and Miz Alabam.

Lemuel invited me to sup with him. I shared a spoon with Miz Alabam.

"Sorry about Lionel and your mamma," she said. I felt the progress of her ankle under the table.

"We're moving out," the Super said. "Going to Texas."

"How come?"

"Texas is kind to mission people," Hervey said. He pressed my hand. "Your mamma was the decentest woman."

They treated me to a bed for their last night in Manhattan. Miz Alabam lent me a blanket and I took it up to the old dorm. It felt odd to lie down in a room of empty mattresses. But I didn't have a troubled sleep. I imagined sinners on those mattresses, sinners like myself.

TEN

IN THE LION'S MOUTH

T HE noise of a baby crying woke me during the night. Couldn't recollect how a baby had sneaked into the dorm. I searched under all the mattresses. Was it a changeling left by some evil fairy . . . a deformed child crying for the fairy's blue milk?

"Hush now. I'll be your dad in the morning. I'll scream for Brunhilde. She'll fairy you . . . let you suck her own blue tit."

I kept peeking under mattresses. Looked and looked until I realized the baby was me.

What the hell did I have to cry about?

I wasn't deformed. I had fingers and toes. I groped around the dorm, listening to myself sob. Noticed a body on a mattress. The body had blue hair.

Brunhilde wore a fuzzy graduation gown.

"Madam, are you coming from the Lord's prom?"

"Don't irk me," Brunhilde said. "You're not my only godson."

"Who else is in your stable? García Marquez?"

"None of your business."

"Brunhilde, I want my other family. Benito, Clara, and the king."

"That's over with. I can't whirl you into the same slot."

"Are you running a supermarket?" I asked the witch. "I need Pinocchio's skin."

"Impossible," she said. "I can let you be Napoleon Bonaparte for a couple of weeks."

"Pinocchio."

"Not a chance."

"Brunhilde, do you shiver people in and out of skins? Am I stuck in a gigantic pinball game between fairy godmothers?"

"What would you know?" she muttered to me out of that gauzy costume.

"Are you going to give me some extraterrestrial crap? E.T., E.T."

"Not at all. The universe is dead. There isn't the slightest vegetable on Mars. No carrots anywhere. It's earth swimming inside a bottle without a beginning or an end. And you play with sonic cups, big fat ears listening to the music of dead things."

"I'm not a scientist," I said. "I have no interest in sonic cups."

"Keep still. There is music all around you, a music you can't pick up. You have the awareness of a dwarf, my darling. You live in the interstices, in the dullest, emptiest space."

"Hold your horses," I said, having a sudden revelation on the properties of a witch. "You're the one who taught Edgar how to read."

"I did. I won't deny it. He was dependent on you, and I wanted him out of the way."

"And my mother? You strangled her in bed?"

"She did that on her own. I'm not an orchestra leader. I only have one Jerome."

"Tell me about the interstices," I said.

"There isn't that much to tell. The molecules of a particular moment never disappear. They push into different holes, holes that are too fine for you to see."

"So Sophocles is around the corner, and the Battle of Waterloo is

on the next block. Not a moment of history is ever lost . . . it's recorded
in your precious molecules, locked in."

"Yes. All I do is ionize them, shove the molecules into place."

"What do you ionize them with, a magic wand?"

"No. My blue hair."

Should have figured that Brunhilde would carry lightning rods in her
scalp. "And if I asked you, you could bring me back to the moment
my father and mother first met."

"Of course."

"You are a witch," I told her. "I want Pinocchio."

That old whore gave me the smile of a graduation queen. "You can
have him, but on one condition."

"Go on," I said. "I'll bargain with you. I come from a family of
traders."

"The condition is that you kill Jerome."

"Easy," I said. "Give me a necktie and I'll hang him from some
simple hook."

The witch refused. "Not that easy . . . once you're Pinocchio, you
can never get back to Copernicus Charyn."

Tried to shake her hand and call it a deal. I was prepared to sail out
from Copernicus bay. What did I have in forty-six years? The corpse
of a stinking book? Bruno dead. Lionel dead. Bathsheba dead. The
witch wouldn't shake on it.

"Is it clear? No trips to your mother's grave. No lusting after your
widowed aunt. No conferences with Edgar. No charlotte russes. It's all
Mussolini."

Wanted to ask Brunhilde if I could say goodbye to Miz Alabam, but
my mouth hardened and my tongue couldn't catch the words. I felt a
strange sundering in my groin. I wasn't stupid. I was Pinocchio again,
and I'd lost all the traffic between my legs.

Somebody had painted the street lamps blue, and Rome was like a
giant blackout shelter . . . or an alchemist's shop, because the lamps
hurled you into a terrible fog.

"What year is this?" I said. It was an innocent question. I couldn't
get my bearings in this blue-black city, thick as Tatiana's ink.

There was a boy at my shoulder with a silver skull on his fez. I remembered him. He was one of my own, a Son of the She-wolf who'd grown tall. He didn't have a bow and arrow on this trip. He carried a bludgeon and a dagger.

"What year is this?"

"Colonnello," the boy said, giving the fascist salute. "It's Anno 20."

The boy was feeding me the Duce's calendar. We were in the twentieth year of Mussolini's reign. But I wasn't going to count on my fingers back to Mussolini's first months in office.

"Give me the old calendar," I said.

The boy seemed perplexed. "Colonnello, it's 1943."

That made sense. This child had sprung up in four years. I blamed Brunhilde. The witch wouldn't allow me a continuous line. I had to jump from Mussolini's blusterings on his balcony to the bleakest part of the war.

"What's your name?" I snarled at the boy.

"Colonnello, why do you joke?"

"Your name, I said, or I'll have you shot."

"Sottotenente Piero Volpe, your second in command."

Why the hell were we trotting into the fog?

Other boys trotted behind us in the murderous uniform of Piero Volpe. Black boots, black pants, black coat, with a bit of silver on their heads. The colonnello examined himself. He had the same black sleeves. I was holding a bludgeon, like them, a leather pipe.

"Piero Volpe, who are we?"

The boy didn't hesitate. He was getting used to his mad colonel. That was the delight of fascism. Complete respect.

"We're the Giovani Brigade."

Ah, an Italian Youth Corps. I'd graduated from the She-wolves to my own brigade.

"And why are we running so fast?"

"Colonnello, we're collecting leaflets that the miserable English have dropped from their planes."

"Propaganda," I said, sounding alert.

"That swine, Churchill, is asking our people to surrender. Ecco!"

And my junior lieutenant showed me a sample of Churchill's bloody prose. Piero was correct. Churchill was a swine. He singled out the

Duce and a certain leader of the Giovani Brigade, who was pretending to be "a marionette out of literature" in order to fool the Italian people. "This Pinocchio is a charlatan and a war criminal. Italians, I promise you that Pinocchio has regular hands and feet."

I ripped the leaflet and tossed the remains at one of the blue lamps. "Who am I, Piero?"

"The Ducellino," my tenente piped. "Cavaliere Pinocchio, knight of the Blue Garter and cousin to the king."

"Touch me, tenente. Tell me what you feel."

The lieutenant groped under my cuffs.

"I feel a very remarkable wood."

And we hurled our way into the fog with all my titles intact and my wooden skin established once and for all.

I wasn't blind to the extravagances of the Giovani Brigade. We were a children's police, unwavering in our love of the Duce. We handed madonna lilies to mothers who'd lost their sons in Mussolini's war. We intimidated bachelors who had no sons to give. We attacked men and women who wouldn't wear a fascist badge in the street. That's what I picked up in my first half hour with the Brigade. We were the guardians of fascism, yes, but mostly we drifted through the fog.

The witch must have assumed I'd fall, give my human character away, and have the Giovanis bludgeon me to pieces, so cavaliere Pinocchio could retire into a wilderness of print, the safe and familiar hero of a children's classic, the walking, talking puppet who saves his babbo from the stomach of a whale, and is turned into a real boy by the blue fairy as his reward. The smug little bastard beats his chest and declares at the end of the book: "How stinky it was to be a puppet! And how glad I am to be a good little boy."

My whale would have been Moby Dick; I'd leave Moby lurking

under the Tiber, like a British submarine. And Pinocchio wouldn't get out of my whale so quick. He'd suffer with his babbo. He'd have a hundred years of Moby Dick. His nose would shrink from starvation, and his babbo would die in the whale. He wouldn't end my book with platitudes. He'd say: "How miserable it is to be a wooden boy married to Moby Dick."

But I wasn't a children's writer under the blue lamps of Rome. I was a cavaliere in a stinking war, having to learn the business of Pinocchio.

Couldn't do a complete about face. I had to let these fighting children beat up a few fat yobs.

We passed under a stone arch, into an alleyway that brought us to a fontana of old Triton surrounded by a snake. Triton struggled, but he couldn't win. Near him were angels and nymphs. Water shot from a goose's head. A pair of demented giants labored above the goose, but I wasn't so sure what that labor was about. Behind them were horses peeing white foam.

Blackshirts stood beneath the horses with pails and were selling water to old men. It seemed like a gross injustice to make old men pay for public water.

"Sottotenente," I said, "commandeer the pails. I'll teach those fatheads to take advantage of the weak."

Piero did what he was told. The fascisti complained, and my children smacked their heads. The old men were too timid to seek water by themselves and I had to fill their pails.

"Grazie," they said.

The fallen Blackshirts muttered to me from the ground. "Ecco—Sinbado!"

"Who's Sinbado?" I asked.

"You are, colonnello," my tenente said. "Your friends have christened you that. It pleases them to think that you have come from the sea. It's a sign of great respect. You are the fierce man of the sea."

"Sinbado," the Blackshirts screamed, and my children bludgeoned them some more.

"They'll learn," I said. "The old are still safe in Italy . . . Piero, how come Blackshirts steal water from a fountain?"

"Because half the city is dry, colonnello. The Blackshirts have a license to sell water."

"Who gave them such a license?"

"Mussolini. The old men are water boys. They buy from Mussolini and sell water to housewives. It's a common practice."

Had to wiggle out of my ignorance of Roman ways. "The Duce's been misled. Fountain water should be free."

"That's what the socialists say, colonnello, when you can find a socialist."

"The socialists are using our propaganda against us. Fountain water is for free."

And my children kept commandeering water pails. We had sixty of them by the time we reached the Tiber. I watched the seaweed drift under the general gloom of blackout lights. There were small grass islands in the Tiber. The islands moved.

Men worked near the mossy Tiber wall. They picked at the moss with their fingers; imbecile work. It was wet here. Moss was native to this wall. Blackshirts stood around them to keep them at the moss. The moss gatherers had yellow dunce caps.

"Are they convicts?" I asked Piero Volpe.

"No. Jews."

"And Benito has sent them to beautify the Tiber, I suppose. Tenente, will you free them from this imbecility?"

Piero chased the Blackshirts from the Tiber wall. The Jews didn't seem content. They would have pounced on Sir Pinocchio if it had not been for the presence of my children. These weren't Tatar Jews. They had pale gray skin and could have come out of some medieval Roman closet.

"Why do they frown at me?" I whispered to Piero. "Tell them to take off those ridiculous hats."

"Sir, you're the one who ordered every Jew to wear a yellow cap outside the ghetto."

That puppet had educated himself in the four years I'd been absent from his body. Pinocchio was an anti-Semite. He'd given up his babbo's socialism and gone to school with Mussolini. He stank like the dead fish under the Tiber wall. But I was stuck with the little bastard, and I couldn't trample on all his policies with Piero.

"The yellow caps," I said. "Aren't these Jews on the ghetto side of the Tiber?"

"Yes, colonnello."

"Then that settles it. They needn't wear yellow caps."

And we marched away from the Jews.

"Tenente, what will happen to the moss gatherers? Will they reach their ghetto alive?"

"I think so, sir. But other fascisti will knock their heads in if they don't have an organized escort of Blackshirts."

"Are you saying that the Blackshirts at the wall were protecting the Jews?"

"Precisely . . . and obligating them to work for the state."

Damn me and Crotona Park. I was out of step with the modern world. Jews should gather moss. That was reality near the Tiber.

I followed the children to our home base, a converted pensione on the Via Bocca di Leone. What a metaphorist my Pinocchio was. He established residence on the Street of the Lion's Mouth.

Five past midnight, according to the pensione clock. The children existed without sleep. A group of them held daggers near the front door.

"Ragazzi, are the clandestinos that close?"

"Not the secret socialists," my elite guard sneered. "The Italian SS."

I milked Piero on the stairs, cleverly as I could. The Italian SS were our biggest rivals. They were older children in German uniforms. But they hadn't come up through the ranks. Not one of them was a She-wolf. They were graduates of the Minorenni Corrigendo, Rome's reform school. Their headquarters on Via Principe Amedeo was known as Villa Triste. It was a torture palace. The Italian SS was fond of pulling antifascisti off the street and grooming them at the Villa Triste. Everybody was an antifascist to the SS. Communists, socialists, Savoyards, and Jews, and the chief of the Giovani Brigade. They reviled me in the language of their borrowed uniforms. *Der Pinocchio ist ein Schwein* (Pinocchio stinks).

They hated us because we stole their secrets. Had to learn from Piero that I ran a school for spies at Via Bocca di Leone. We tapped every phone on Prince Amedeo Street. We'd infiltrated their dirty ranks with younger boys who posed as delinquents. We had their coded messages and their torture lists.

I searched the current list and discovered Dante Romano on it. The Italian SS had that false priest.

"Ragazzi," I said. "We're going on a trip."

I didn't have to tickle up the brigade. My children were ready for a march on the Villa Triste. We took to the alleys, loping behind the Quirinale. Up and down the king's hill and across to Prince Amedeo Street. The boys of the Italian SS stood in front of their pensione, teasing the neighborhood with their long whips. It was two in the morning, and no one fell into the path of their whips. They ought to have been more alert.

They couldn't recover from our blitz. We drove them into the pensione, disarmed two floors of SS, and took over the Villa Triste. The SS had a jail near the attic, and we ripped the jail apart. I found Dante Romano. The SS had stuck his toes into the hopper of a mimeograph machine.

I locked the stinking yobs into the attic and then I gave Dante back his toes. It was an evil sight. The toes were twisted, and they'd turned black in the machine. He gripped the collar of my uniform and demanded an American cigarette.

"Dante, what do I know about cigarettes?"

My children scratched their noses. Ah, Piero had neglected to inform his colonel that we were black marketeers. He removed a carton of Chesterfields from his military bag and cracked through the cardboard with a dagger. I emptied the carton into Dante's pockets.

The children rolled their eyes. Who cares if I was giving a fortune away? I hardly smoked.

Dante's fingers twitched, and I had to light his Chesterfield. He was wearing old trousers and an undershirt. I whispered to the Giovanis, and they returned with an SS uniform for Dante Romano.

He was greedy with the cigarettes, biting into the stubs. Had a whore of a time getting Dante into a pair of boots. He didn't show the slightest gratitude to the Giovani Brigade. "Stronzo," he muttered.

The Giovanis would have plunged their daggers into his throat but I signaled to them. Dante stood up. He had to clutch the walls. "Stronzo," he said from the stairwell.

The children barked at him. "Stronzo yourself."

I loitered until Dante completed his lame walk out the Villa Triste and then I tore into the fog with my band of boys.

Had a cot upstairs in my office and I stayed there the rest of the night, too timid to show up at Mussolini's palace. I suffered from dyslexia in Rome. It was hard to find a puppet's vocabulary. Had to learn who Pinocchio was before I could encounter Mussolini, Clara, and the king.

Slept like a baby in my cot.

Woke and went around the corner to a caffè on the Via Condotti. The caffè had green curtains in the window. You could stand at the coffee bar or sit at a marble table in a labyrinth of rooms. Rome was out of coffee and this caffè lived on the black market like every other establishment. It bartered, bribed, and let Pinocchio drown his nose in caffelatte.

An old man began to bother me from the next table. He had coffee in his beard and a cape around his shoulders. He wore eyeglasses with one black lens. He slurped his caffelatte and wouldn't stop winking at me.

"Sinbado!"

"It's Colonel Pinocchio to you. Drink your coffee and shut your face. I'll teach you not to pester a military man."

The old boy sobbed into his cup. I'd have torn out his head, but it was too early in the morning.

I summoned my waiter. "Who is this guy?"

"The scribbler, Giacomo Joyce."

Pinocchio had turned me into a fascist pig, because I screamed the waiter out, out to the window and I damned the whole caffè. "Why didn't you tell me?"

"Excellency, the scribbler is one of your friends."

"That makes no difference. I'm groggy in the morning, you dope."

And I went up to the old man. "Maestro, please forgive me. I was distracted."

Giacomo Joyce rubbed his black lens. "Sinbado, sometimes you're so cruel."

I was dying to tell him I was a scribbler caught in Pinocchio's body.

"Maestro, it's brutal running a brigade. We hit the SS last night."

"What were you doing on Prince Amedeo Street?"

"Jesus, they had Dante Romano, and I let him go."

The master grew agitated over his coffee cup. "You let Dante go? He's a murderer, a pawn of the capitalists, criminally insane."

Had to lie to get his liver down. "It's nothing, maestro. We have him under surveillance. He's in our goldfish bowl."

The master grabbed his beard. "Sinbado, you love to torture me, throw me into a panic, keep me in suspense. What about the Jews?"

"The Jews? They have their yellow hats."

I couldn't find a way to please this old man. He was boiling under his cape. His one black lens could have been the bitter eye of God. "Don't speak of yellow hats. How many agents do you have in the ghetto?"

Giacomo was beginning to make me nervous. I wanted to talk shop, get involved with his early oeuvre, and he was treating me like an ordinary runner of spies. What better homage could I pay than recite to him the glorious opening of *Piccolino* that had killed the nineteenth century and broke into the twentieth like the strongest caffelatte in the world, invented modern literature in one dark sip, shaped a puppet's prose style in the village of Montegrumo. *Once upon a time there was a cauliflower coming down the road, and this cauliflower was named Marco Polo . . .*"

"Stop it," he said. "Don't mock me, Sinbado. We mustn't forget the Jews. They're a miserable folk, doomed to wander everywhere. But they control the senate in the United States. Roosevelt is in their power. That paralitico is married to a Jewess. Eleanora, the ugly one. She's his commander in chief. They'll drop parachutists into the ghetto, and the parachutists will tunnel under Rome. Sinbado, we'll have the enemy under our feet. That's why they must be met with agents of our own. We'll deal donna Eleanora a mortal blow."

"But maestro, will you ever write again?"

"I am writing . . . for Mussolini."

He got up from the table. "It's time for my broadcast," he announced, holding the cape to his neck.

My master had become a puppet for Radio Roma. The author of *Piccolino* was the Duce's toy. I paid for his caffelatte. I wiped the dark milk from my nose. I'd lost the urge for Italian coffee. Asked the waiter for English Breakfast tea. He laughed at my joke, then he stopped laughing.

It took half an hour to comb the black market for British tea. He served it in a silver pot.

Pissed tea out of my ears until a visitor arrived. Questore Manganello, Rome's chief of police. Figured he was a waiter from another part of town, but then he introduced himself. He didn't question my involvement with British tea. The Questore had a cup. He was embarrassed about something.

"Cavaliere, I must have a consistent policy, or we cannot have a police. You introduced the yellow hat, but this morning, when my men tried to enforce the rule, the Giovanis chased them across the Tiber into Trastevere. They put the yellow hats on my men, arguing that all Romans must wear the yellow hat on your advice. If it is a trick to confuse the Anglo-Americans, shouldn't I know?"

"Questore, give my condolences to your men. The Giovanis went too far in their zeal. I have outlawed the yellow hat."

The Questore touched my hand. "Cavaliere, I always thought the yellow hat was medieval . . . what about the Jews that are hiding in the old people's home? Should we flush them out?"

"Not for the moment," I said.

"Cavaliere, I have permission to disobey the other laws?"

"As much as you like."

"I can close the Jewish section of Regina Coeli?"

Romans loved to play on words. Queen of Heaven is what they called their yellow jail on the Tiber. It was quite a hotel.

Couldn't go overboard with the Questore. He might have snitched to some other arm of the police.

"Close it as judiciously as you can."

"And Count Jacobo, what shall we do with him?"

I must have jailed Benito's secretary along with a hundred other "political" Jews. Pinocchio had a bigger appetite than Moby Dick. He swallowed wherever he went.

"You will bring Jacobo to Bocca di Leone."

"Cavaliere, I'll need your signature for that."

I scribbled *Pinocchio* on a blank piece of paper, and the Questore shut it inside his briefcase. Children, such was the power of my fist!

"I have your word, cavaliere, that you won't reverse yourself the minute I'm out the door?"

"More than my word," I told him. He seemed perplexed. I had to stroke the chief of police.

"Questore, let there be an end to all yellow hats."

He thanked me for the cup of British tay and he strode out of the labyrinth, looking like a waiter again.

Heard Giacomo's voice rise over the table tops. The caffè had switched on Radio Roma. I'd abused the maestro. His words, over the air, had the same plangent tones of *Piccolino*. He'd become a lunatic with literary style.

He began his speech with the legend of Pinocchio!

Once there lived . . .
   "A king!" my little readers will say in an instant.
   "No, ragazzi, you're wrong."

And now the master pushed out of Pinocchio and into fascism.

Once there lived a fountain pen in the gutters of Rome, an educated fountain pen. It had earned its doctorate at the University of Bologna. It would talk to gente in the street. And what an aria it had. "Romans, come pick me up. I'm a magic pen. I can keep you company while you write. I'll whistle you a song."

The best class of people knew not to believe a fountain pen. They left it in the street to try its song on the gullible of Rome. It was a seductive pen. It nearly charmed a dozen children on its first appearance. But the children held back. Their Duce had told them not to talk to strange objects in the street.

It's the misfortune of our empire that one child was gullible enough. His name? Burattino. He lived in the slums of Trastevere with a churlish father and a mother about whom it's better to be silent. He didn't have the simplest toy at home. Burattino had to suck his thumb for pleasure. The fountain pen talked, and it's no surprise that it made a big impression. Burattino wasn't a total fool. He circled the fountain pen and talked back to it.

"Como sta, signor scribacchino?"

"Molto bene."

"Why do I have the good luck to meet a talking pen?"

"Because I favor boys from bad neighborhoods."

"Will I catch a disease if I take you home?"

"What disease could you catch from a scribble pen? I'll help you with your homework. I'll iron your shirts. I can see that your mamma doesn't take good care of you."

It was talk of his mother that ruined Burattino. He went down on his knees to pick up the pen and it exploded in his face.

Burattino died.

He hadn't listened to his Duce. The chief warned of little talking bombs that the Anglo-Americans were dropping over our empire. But since his home was sad, Burattino didn't have the sense to walk away.

I searched this blasted coffeehouse I was in to see what effect the maestro's broadcast was having. The waiters stood with handkerchiefs in their eyes. None of them had the slightest thought of delivering caffelatte to the tables. Customers could have gone to hell and these camerieri wouldn't have cared. "Burattino," they blubbered, as if they'd stumbled upon the story of their lives.

Got up from the table, shoved around the camerieri and out to the curtained window of the caffè, because if I listened to the end of

Giacomo's speech, I'd have given up all allegiance to the democracies and my king. I'd have forsworn Cervantes, Flaubert, and Proust, and followed Giacomo Joyce inside fascismo's bitter root. I'd have loved it in there. Seamstresses would have worked night and day sewing yellow caps for every cockroach that lived outside the fascist party. I'd design a special cap for the king and crown princess . . .

There were radios out on the balconies, and Giacomo sang from the street.

Clapped my fingers over my ears and headed for Bocca di Leone.

Questore Manganello was as chivalrous as any knight in the new Italian empire. He smuggled Jacobo from Queen of Heaven jail. The count was in a convict's shirt. He had stubble on his cheeks. Mussolini's war had made him a pinched little man. He'd lost his last connection with the Italian race: the reliability of a prison number. Once the Questore had snatched him, Jacobo ceased to exist. He belonged to the *sepolti vivi,* invisible people who were buried alive in Rome. If the *sepolti vivi* ever surfaced again, they were liquidated in a quiet way.

"So," the count said, "you're the master I've inherited, Sir Pinocchio . . . first you poison the Duce against me, sign me into that temple of Jews at Regina Coeli, and then you have the police kidnap me and conduct me to your headquarters. If this is a plot against the Duce, I won't stand for it. I'm a fascist, Pinocchio. I always was."

"Burattino," I said to that crumbling man. "You're a Jew."

"Yes," he said. "I might have had a Jewish aunt hundreds and hundreds of years ago, but we were counts before the Medici arrived in Florence. We have palaces and roads named after us. Cousins of mine sat with the popes in the sixteenth century and kept them in office with our family treasure."

"And I'm a cousin to the king," I said. "But we're invisible men, you and I."

"Don't you dare put me in the same sentence with yourself. My family helped finance the crusades, and you don't even have a father you can speak of."

It's lucky for Jacobo I didn't have human blood to boil in me. I felt sorry for the son of a bitch.

"My babbo was a socialist baker."

"Puppet, I recruited you. You were born in a bread basket. It just happened to be a socialist neighborhood."

"I could kill you for that. There was only one socialist neighborhood in Montegrumo. My babbo's store . . . should have left you in Regina Coeli."

"Then take me back," the count said. "I prefer the Jews to Pinocchio."

"It's too late. The Questore would get into trouble. And they don't allow returnables at Regina Coeli. The fascisti would beat you to death."

"Then how shall we live, Sir Pinocchio?"

"We'll share this room."

"What will the ragazzi say?"

"I'll tell them you're my manservant."

"I'd rather be dead. I'm a count."

"A count who was a convict."

"Thanks to you."

"Silenzio!" I screamed into the count's face. "I'm the boss at Bocca di Leone. Jacobo, you don't have to clean up after me. Manservant is just a title to satisfy the boys. Write your memoirs. You'll have a long time sitting in this room."

But suppose the Italian SS returned our compliment and raided Bocca di Leone while I was sipping black-market tea on the Via Condotti? They wouldn't bother to torture Jacobo or use him to turn Mussolini against me. Sir Pinocchio was a bit too secure in this regime. They'd have dragged him off to an alley on the Via dei Portoghese and shot him in the ear with a snubnosed German gun that would crackle between the walls like an ordinary firecracker. How come the Via dei

Portoghese? Because it sounded a little Jewish and it was far enough from their headquarters on Prince Amedeo Street.

I had the Giovanis build a fake wall in my room at the pensione to house Jacobo whenever I was in the street. But the count chose this walled-in existence to my company. He stayed in his secret closet most of the time, coming out only to exercise his legs. He'd circumnavigate my office without uttering a word. I had to draw him into conversations.

"Jacob, shall I get you some books? . . . Cervantes?"

"I know him by heart."

"Flaubert?"

"Polished and beautiful, but a little too dry."

Ah, the crusader count was also a literary critic.

"Dostoyevsky?" I said.

"Too much fainting."

"Tolstoy?"

"I don't care for adultery in the upper circles."

"Giacomo Joyce?"

"I can live without cauliflowers coming down the road."

"Then what do you like?"

"*Anno 85.*"

Anno 85 was Mussolini's ten-volume comment on the twenty-first century. It came to three million words, and it took a hundred ghostwriters to prepare the text. *Anno 85* was translated into sixty languages. It flopped everywhere, except in Rome. In Rome it became an instant classic.

Mussolini and his ghostwriters didn't rant in *Anno 85.* They simply put you to sleep. It was one long ducian dream, with Rome as the capital of the world and Italy a giant cradle in the Mediterranean Sea. Germany was our own blond stepchild. The rest of Europe contained distant cousins whose single reality was their contact with Rome. Great Britain was a series of islands sinking out of sight. The Soviets were learning Italian in order to survive. The United States had succumbed to revolutions by Negroes and Jews. All of South America was adopting ducismo. Australia had wanted to rebel; Rome returned it to the aborigines.

Anno 85.

That's what the count picked to read over Cervantes and Flaubert. I had all ten volumes delivered to his closet and then I closed that trick wall. God forgive us, Jacobo never seemed to tire of Mussolini's book.

Thinking of him behind the wall, squirreling into *Anno 85,* drove me out of my office. I wandered in the Borghese Gardens. I didn't have to worry about curfews and identity cards. I was Pinocchio. The fascist police slapped out their arms in salute. You didn't find a soul other than policemen after six . . . except for the beggars who came here to starve. I'd bring chestnuts and paper cones of dried fruit from our private stores on Bocca di Leone to feed the beggars. But soon the beggars became ambitious. They tried to rob Pinocchio. Their daggers began to notch my skin.

"Sinbado, fork over your money belt."

"Professori," I said. "I'm a colonel. I only carry enough cash for caffelatte."

"Then we'll take your uniform."

I wouldn't undress.

Their daggers hacked a little deeper.

Policemen arrived. There were so many competing departments, I couldn't tell what secret branch they belonged to. They were kind enough to knock the beggars down and gather them up for Regina Coeli.

"No," I said. "It was nothing. A puppet show."

Their superior officer bowed to me. "Bene. But the scratches on your arm weren't given to you by Pulcinella."

I didn't admire his tone. Then I understood why such men had found it convenient to rescue Pinocchio from the rabble. They were spying on me. It was the Duce's dreaded undercover police, the OVRA, Organizzazione di Vigilanza e Repressione dell' Antifascismo. They reported on everything from bombs in public buildings to graffiti on the Tiber wall. They posed as cab drivers, gravediggers, and simple policemen. OVRA was much more efficient and murderous than the Italian SS.

"Colonnello, be so kind as to come with us."

They'd already shuffled the bums to another section of the park.

"And if I refuse?" I said.

"It would cause us great embarrassment."

"I'm not coming with you," I said. "Go on, saw my wrists. But what will the people think if Pinocchio is a mutilato?"

"Cavaliere, you forget that we're in the middle of the war. You would be one mutilato among many . . . you're our brother and we will not harm you. But we'll lay gelatina in the sewers under Bocca di Leone, and we will blow your Jewish count up into the air to meet his ancestors."

They knew about Jacobo. Was the Questore one of them?

"Professori," I said. "I'm coming with you."

It was in the car, going down the hill with the OVRA, that I decided to murder Mussolini. They hadn't brutalized me. They sang from *The Barber of Seville*. The Organizzazione di Vigilanza was filled with opera buffs. I was short on opera, having been a gluttonous savage about books in my years as Copernicus Charyn. And I couldn't hold on to the singing of such hoodlums. They had no sense of shame in front of an amateur like me. *The Barber of Seville* grew into *The Marriage of Figaro*. The hoodlums were ordering their own opera straight out of the oven, like a pizza pie.

They stopped singing and talked of Verdi and Rossini, as if Herman Melville were sitting in the car. For an hour the Duce's secret agents struggled with themselves to comprehend the silence Rossini fell into during the middle of his career. They posed one theory after the other as we missed the Palazzo Venezia, crossing and recrossing the Tiber in a mad, aimless drive under the blackout lamps. They talked of Rossini settling in France. Money troubles. The French impresarios were notorious pennypinchers. *Aldo, he was composer to the king.* Now they searched like agents among the fish bones of Rossini's life. Ah, he shouldn't have gone to Paris. His first wife should have been fatter. No, thinner, they said . . .

"He was like Melville," I told them. "Melville after *Moby Dick*."

"Hey, you with the big nose, shut up . . . Aldo, imagine him. He compares an American scribbler to Rossini."

The yobs turned on me, slapped my forehead with the thick of their hands. They weren't out to hurt Pinocchio, but to humble him. "Burattino, opera is everything. Not the costumes and the orchestra. Not the little dancing interludes that the French admire. It's the human voice . . . the audience is never lonely. And you babble about words on a page. Can a page do this?"

Mussolini's whores improvised the saddest, sweetest aria in the Italian empire. They took on the voices of beggars, clowns, courtesans, kings, and grocers' wives. They were Verdi, Rossini, and Shakespeare's brother. The hoodlums were right. What was a whale in a long book to such an aria? But that's not why I wanted to murder Mussolini.

It's what I saw in the middle of that opera lesson, as we drifted through Rome. Old men with nothing to eat sucking lead off a lamppost. Delirious women licking the clay from a wall. Rome hadn't succumbed to simple starvation. People were mad with hunger. Those who didn't have candlesticks to sell on the black market for a lump of cheese, began to devour metal, clay, and stone. They were getting whatever nutrition they could in Mussolini's town.

I wasn't escorted to Mappamondo. The boss was too busy to see Sir Pinocchio. He still had pieces of the war to lose. His African colonies were gone. He had to give up the idea of a Roman Egypt. The great aircraft carrier, Italy, had developed sores and holes.

I was deposited in the elevator car that traveled up around the attic. My old yellow room was much as I'd remembered it. White furniture close to the sky. There wasn't any sun at midnight to tinker with the walls. The yellow room was octopus blue in the blackout.

"Sinbado!"

My nose bloomed into a frigging tree. It couldn't mistake Clara's throaty syllables. She had a wonderful hoarseness that made no attempt to conceal the luxury of her chest.

I carried my face into Claretta's room. She was naked on her bed, with her bum in the air. She didn't have a thought about my feelings. I was her girlfriend, Pinocchio, and she could display her buttocks in my presence, behind the blackout curtains.

"Sinbado," she said without looking up. "Why have you abandoned me?"

On that bed, with all the flutings of her body, she was like a blondish whale resting out of the water. I was dizzy with the urge to bite her bum, which lay in perfect order.

"Clara, don't be selfish. I've been out with the ragazzi, defending Rome."

"You're not my Pinocchio any more. My Pinocchio would come to me every night after his raids. I can't survive without your tickles."

What habits had Sinbado picked up all on his own?

"Darling, tickle me!"

I didn't undress.

Before I murdered the Duce, I'd cuckold him.

Her bum wiggled out from the bed.

I'd enter madame in the crusader position, with my nose slipping under her legs. But when that schnozzle of mine got near her button, the lady screamed.

"Dio!"

She swung around to sock Pinocchio between the eyes. "Is that what they taught you in the street?"

"Scusi!" I said.

The beautiful lady began to blubber.

"Clara, I slipped. My nose fell in by mistake."

"A nose doesn't fall," she said. "You have to push with it."

How had she discovered the dynamics of Pinocchio's nose? But I had to plead bloody ignorance.

"I'm a puppet, and my nose can fall."

"Don't play on your wood," she said. "Gesù delivered you to us like a human boy." She wiped her eyes and offered up her bum again. "Tickle me!"

So I rubbed my nose along the heel of her spine and onto the shelf of her buttocks. Her neck rose with delight. Her fingers clutched the summer quilt. Shiver marks appeared on her back like the ribs of a whale. Then she dropped down, exhausted and happy, and hugged me to her chest.

"I'm not a bloody eunuch. I have the desires of a man."

"Shut up," she said in her throaty whisper. "You've seen me without my clothes all these years, and now you pretend to suffer, Sir Pinocchio. What an ungrateful beast you are!"

How did Pinocchio manage? Did he wash his nose in ice? No wonder he invented yellow hats.

"Where's the licorice you promised me? There's nothing to eat."

Did the mistress of the attic have a depraved appetite like the old women in the street? She didn't have to feed on clay. Her butler arrived with a boiled potato and a marzipan bread.

I took the butler aside. "Professore, couldn't you come up with something better as a snack?"

"How?" His eyes were on Claretta. She wouldn't dress for her own butler. "Things disappear from the cupboard the minute they're locked inside."

"But this is Mussolini's house."

The butler laughed with his eyes still on Clara. "Cavaliere, Mussolini is dead."

I struck him on the mouth. "I'll give you to Prince Amedeo Street. They'll know what to do with you at the SS."

His mouth hurt, but he hadn't stopped laughing. He took all of Clara in with his stinking eyes.

The butler excused himself.

Clara dug around for silverware. She found two forks and a knotted napkin on one of the cantons in her quilt. She hacked the potato in half but the marzipan wouldn't yield to the prongs of her fork. I cursed the fascisti who ruled an empire but couldn't negotiate on the black market.

The telephone rang.

Clara hugged herself, thinking she might be summoned to her Ben.

But the call was for Pinocchio. Some undersecretary said the Duce was prepared to see me now.

"Is he sick?" Clara asked, suddenly shutting herself into a housecoat, as if the first mention of Mussolini demanded that his mistress be dressed.

"No, no, Claretta. He's occupied . . . with maps, I think."

She hadn't gained much ground with Benito since the beginning of the war. She was at the mercy of his telephone in her upstairs room. That's why she had me tickle her bum. So she could forget that love had made a marionetta of her life.

Went down to the Duce. He had three secretaries and eight guards outside Mappamondo. The guards were his Musketeers, dressed in black. They carried their submachine guns the Italian way, tied to their wrists. They were devoted to Mussolini. Half the Musketeers were blond. The Duce mistrusted dark-skinned people. He would have preferred albinos around him.

I entered Mappamondo and shut the door behind me.

Benito wasn't behind his desk. He was in the corner with his Stradivarius. This was how the Duce planned his battlefronts. He hacked on an orange violin.

I crossed the room to Mussolini. The genius hadn't shaved. He had a field of stubble sitting on the violin. The shifting of his head wasn't about battlefields. He was avoiding the war with his Stradivarius.

He finished his tune and sat the violin on a little shelf in the molding. But he wouldn't come out of his corner. His eyelids were pale. He had a pulsing in his leg.

"I saw Matteotti last night."

Now he was meeting with socialists his men had killed.

He left his corner to clutch at me.

"Not Matteotti. Matteotti's ghost."

"What did the ghost say?"

"That I should end this war and go back to farming."

"But you were never a farmer."

"Idiot," he said. "Matteotti came in a dream. I'd like to listen to the ghost but I can't. We have to go on fighting. If the Anglo-Americans win, they'll exhibit me in the Madison Square Garden."

Benito smiled. "Don't think you'll get on with the Americans. They'll put you in the cage with uncle Ben . . . the wooden boy of Italy and the old dictator. Remember. You're my Ducellino."

How can you murder a man who's willing to share his old age with you?

"It won't be so bad. Babbo, you have fans in America. Millions will come to see us."

"But in a cage, Pinocchio." He knocked his girly hands together. Then he marched to his desk. Matteotti's ghost seemed to have gone out of his head. The Duce turned to business, but the business was unclear. Fascism had lost the old familiar tone that wouldn't have allowed a surplus pin on Mussolini's desk. It was littered with papers, bundles of wheat from some forgotten farmer's drive, fascist party badges, volumes of *Anno 85*, sprinkled with the pulpy hearts of half a dozen chestnuts.

"Start arresting bachelors," he said. "Those who cannot provide Italy with sons will have to sit in jail or go to the front lines."

"That's impossible. I don't have enough boys to interview every bachelor in Rome."

"Liar! You protect the bachelors because you are a bachelor yourself."

"Shall I marry?" I said, clutching the groin I didn't have. "With what?"

"Save your sad history. You wouldn't have given us a son even if you had the right equipment between your legs."

A shrewd son of a bitch that Benito was. He understood my problems. I wasn't in Pinocchio's skin by some random act of God. I'd picked the little bugger. You can't create sons and daughters with Pinocchio's nose.

"Will you arrest the bachelors?"

"I will not."

"Good," he muttered. "We'll prepare a kitchenette for you at Regina Coeli."

"It's a stinking yellow box. I'll jump through the windows."

"That's a treasonable act in Rome."

He summoned his Musketeers. The eight of them surrounded me

like a clock in leather boots. These birds were in the habit of arresting people out of uncle Ben's office.

"Liquidate him!"

They could have chipped me into a wooden soup. The blondest bird spoke for the rest.

"Uncle, he's the Ducellino."

"Not any more," Mussolini had to shout. "He's a bachelor who talks treason."

"But you'll miss him when he's gone."

"I'll take my chances. He doesn't show the slightest bit of gratitude to his leader. He was nothing but an unemployed knight when I found him. I gave Pinocchio a career."

"Wonderful," I muttered. "The weaver of yellow hats."

Duce wouldn't listen. He turned his back on Pinocchio. He had an audience of eight private guards and he could be charitable to a puppet he'd thrown onto the civil service list. I was a fascist colonel. No more than that.

"He's comical," Duce said to his Musketeers. "A burattino with the Blue Garter. What other nation in the world ever adopted a wooden boy? Hitler has midgets in his salt mines, and we have Sir Pinocchio."

"Sì," the Musketeers said.

"He exists in my shadow, the Ducellino. I don't have to take him seriously. He's my jester, a common buffoon."

"Uncle, it's better this way."

The Musketeers marched out, and Benito was gloomy away from them. He searched for a report on his desk. All of Rome was under the eye of Duce's vigilanza police. But it took him most of the day to digest the simplest acts of disobedience: he kept a trace on old men drawing genitals outside a public toilet, but he couldn't have told you where the navy was.

"Pinocchio, you will reinstitute the yellow hat."

"Babbo, what for? The Jews are starving like everybody else."

"Quiet! No one starves in Rome."

"Babbo . . ."

"I insist. There's plenty of food. I keep calendars of every warehouse. People are hoarding. That's the picture."

"Your calendars tell lies."

Uncle Ben reached out to strike me with the reports on his desk. I
yawned once. I could have waited until his shoulder dropped off. But
I cuffed him on the ear. The Duce couldn't believe it. He made to
touch his ear, to sweeten the hurt with a finger, but a Duce had to show
that he wasn't subject to human pain. Duce, Duce, Duce. I cuffed him
again.

"Brutus," he said. "Brutus is a wooden boy."

I cuffed the other ear.

"It's treason," he said. "Striking my person is punishable by death
. . . go away, Pinocchio. You've made me cross."

He was in a state of fever. That's how it is with dictators. They never
prepare themselves to take a slap. And once you cross that threshold
of insolence with them, you can go up the old ladder to murder itself.

"Stronzo, I've been in the street. Old women are sucking clay, and
you have inventories that can't even come up with an egg. Rome
governs around you. You sit in Mappamondo with your charts, sentenc-
ing people to death, and your echo never arrives to the end of this room.
Your ministers feed you what you want to hear, and they run to the
black market for food."

"Dummy," he said, "I've outlawed the black market."

"The black market is every man and woman with a turnip to sell.
It starts in your kitchen and circles Rome."

"Then I will resign from being an Italian. Italians are no good. I gave
them a revolution, and they cry for pasta and soup. It will take centuries
for them to grow up."

"Babbo, it takes a century for any man to grow up."

His ears were red from the hiding I gave him, but he hardly noticed.
One pull on his earlobe and the dictator moved on to other things. "I
don't have a century. I have days. I'm not so complete a fool. Whenever I sign a book, I write *the late Benito Mussolini* . . . I'm playing
dead for the Anglo-Americans, so they won't bomb Rome."

He took a towel from inside a drawer and twisted it onto his head
to mock Vittorio Emanuele. "Look what baggage we have. Italy makes
a revolution and holds on to her king. Mussolini has two masters
. . . Vittorio and the pope."

"Babbo," I said, "all of us are under Pius' gown."

"Speak plainly."

"Churchill doesn't want to lose the Catholic vote. That's why he hasn't sent his parachuters down on our heads. They could spill into the Vatican and frighten the Sacred College. Babbo, we'd be dead without Pius."

"That's what a puppet thinks."

Mussolini dug his fists into his sides in that dictator's gesture he'd used on his balcony to harangue the city of Rome. Now I understood his secret agents and their *Barber of Seville*. Italy wasn't an aircraft carrier, it was an opera house. And the Duce was its own falling star. He survived by gestures. He delivered his arias in a black uniform; under that uniform were more Mussolinian gestures that flew at you until you reached a hollow bone with yellow fuzz. That was the pith of Mussolini. A bone for toothless dogs to suck on. And what was I? Another toothless dog, wearing wooden furniture.

"You should study more, piccolino. Pius means nothing to the British. Churchill is afraid of me."

"How's that?"

He swayed with the towel twisted on his head.

"Because he knows that the Italians will rant and scream at my death and refuse to recover from the war."

The witch of Montegrumo, Brunhilde herself, stung my left ear with the image of Mussolini hanging upside down in Milan. That's the mourning he would get. Women squatting to pee on him and his mistress.

"Babbo, let's go and hide."

He plucked at his crown. "A Duce has nowhere to hide."

The old dictator was right. The people would love him while they swam in caffelatte. But even in Italy the opera has to end.

"Babbo, kiss me."

"What for?"

"In case we ever have to rush our goodbyes."

"I've wronged you," Mussolini said. "You're a kindhearted boy."

It was a wet kiss. Mussolini's mouth was moist as a witch.

Couldn't have murdered him. He was the only babbo I had left.

ELEVEN

MAMMA MADRIGALE

I tumbled into Pinocchio. It was easy. I learned most of the puppet's tricks. He was a scoundrel, far as I could tell. He'd succumbed to fascism. He dipped into the black market to finance his operation on Bocca di Leone. The government had run out of hard cash. It was Pinocchio who paid for the silver emblem on the Giovanis' hats. He had his own terror shop in the basement until I took over his skin.

I blunted Pinocchio's designs as much as I could. Started a little network to smuggle Jews into Switzerland. Told the ragazzi this was part of the war, exchanging Italian prisoners for Jews. But I had to sweat blood on the black market to come up with the silver to bribe border guards. Money flowed like castor oil. And here I was, a puppet that never had to move his bowels.

Pinocchio was a stinking mystery. I couldn't crawl deep enough inside him to come upon the interiors of his life. I discovered women, of course. Fascist contessas and chambermaids. I schnozzled them, but I wouldn't call it love.

I was lonely, mates. All this pretense eats at you. Figured if I tried hard enough, I would seize who Pinocchio was, catch him on the move, get at the contours. Love, guts, and all that. But I never broke through the fog. Pinocchio's or mine. Then I wondered if Pinocchio had an interior life. He was blank as a bread basket . . .

I'd give him a soul to dream about. Pulled a rabbi from the ghetto, got him alone in my office, and ordered him to bar mitzvah me. I frightened the man. He assumed it was another form of ridicule, like the yellow hat. I offered him whatever silver I had around.

"Colonnello, are you a Jew?"

"Yes," I told him. "A secret Jew."

"How secret? Are you conversant with Torah?"

"That's not a problem. I don't expect to be bar mitzvahed on the spot."

I asked him for Torah lessons. The rabbi refused. He could teach me Torah, yes, but as "a senseless decoration." A puppet wasn't Jewish in God's eyes. I was a golem, a twisted thing, brought to life by other men.

"Rabbino, I was born in a bread basket."

"Perhaps, but you're still a mutilation and not complete."

Could have found another rabbi who wasn't so punctilious. But I didn't want a bargain bar mitzvah. The law was the law.

I returned the rabbi to his ghetto seat.

Off to the Quirinale I went. I had business in the king's house. Not with the king. He'd promised never to speak with Pinocchio again. I wouldn't forget a slap like that. It was Princess Josie I was after. I announced myself to her lady-in-waiting, donna Elvira, that socialist with the freckled face who'd bullied me four years ago.

"You're hateful," she said. "You come here flaunting your fascist uniform. The princess will never see you."

"Milady, I have the absolute right to seek an audience with her by the Blue Garter I wear. Josie is my cousin."

The crown princess wasn't so happy to learn of Pinocchio's desire to see her. Josie was dressing for dinner, and the audience would have to be brief. The Anglo-Americans must have forced an early dinner on the palace. It was an hour after lunch. I was ushered up to Josie like a stinking rat. No one wanted a fascist colonel around in July, 1943. Sir Winston might come to one of the king's early dinners by parachute next month.

The princess received me in her anteroom. She'd gone a little gray in four years. A touch of the old beauty was gone. I remembered to curse myself. The whole world aged around a puppet.

Josie didn't have much kindness for the silver skull on my fez. She asked me if I wanted something to drink.

"I am thirsty, your highness. Thank you. I'll have a cup of English tea," I said, removing a tin of Earl Grey from my pocket. "Compliments of Bocca di Leone. We're tea drinkers, your highness."

"Why do you come to us now, Sir Pinocchio, and impose your cousinage on me? The king isn't fond of you. You must know that."

"I have a piece of business to discuss."

"What kind of business could I possibly have with a fascist policeman?"

If I'd gone down on my knees and appealed to Josie, said I was a human like her, with ideals and everything, imprisoned in Pinocchio's suit, she wouldn't have believed a word. It's the baser instincts that connect. You can always win with the right piece of business.

I scratched along the pike of my nose. "Well, your highness, I'm in the smugglers' union at the moment. The ragazzi and I have developed our own underground railway."

"Whom have you been smuggling?"

"Rich fascists with an urge to disappear."

"And you think we have some at the Quirinale?"

"No, no," I said. "It's just that you're in contact with the battling priests."

"What battling priests?"

"The ones who help to hide British airmen and antifascist Jews. The pope can't shut his eyes on them for too long. Rome's becoming a German town. Pius has to keep in the middle, or he'll lose his operation to the Luftwaffe and some British air wing up from Sicily."

"You are a disgusting boy," she said.

"No doubt, but the point is, your highness, I can take a little pressure off the battling priests."

"And what's your price?"

"Well, since the Brits and the Yanks are coming, I was hoping you might adopt a few of my boys, take them into the Quirinale as vassals or cooks."

"What a lovely way to penetrate a palace."

"Not at all. We're finished. The Americans will hang my ragazzi as war criminals, and half of them are under thirteen."

"And what will the Americans do to you, Sir Pinocchio?"

"I'll manage," I said. "It'll be hide and seek."

The maid appeared with our tea. The king's cups and saucers had five gold stars. Could have cashed them in on the black market, but I wouldn't swipe teacups behind the princess' back.

"I'll adopt your children, but I don't trust you at all."

"Your highness, it's satisfaction guaranteed. Bring us an airman, and you can hold me hostage until he's out of the country."

"And what does the Provolone have to say about this?"

She meant Benito, the Big Cheese.

"Duce doesn't have to know."

"Finish your tea," she said.

I returned the cup to its saucer. I wouldn't smack my lips near a crown princess. I'd humbled her, and she could hardly feel it. That's what you call finesse. It's practiced on Bocca di Leone and Boston Road.

I stood on the king's gray carpets and whistled what I remembered from *The Barber of Seville.* A door opened downstairs. Through the door was another door, and in that door was the king, grooming himself in front of a mirror. He had his ceremonial sword attached to him. The sword had been cut down to fit the dimensions of his body. That's why Vittorio was the Little Sword.

He went on grooming himself. Then he looked out the first and second door.

Vittorio had to have seen me. But he groomed his moustache as if I was his bloody kitchen maid, some creature that existed outside the courtesy of kings. Didn't thrust my kinship at him. Didn't salute his moustache.

I walked out of the Quirinale and went back to *The Barber of Seville*.

Couldn't convince my own filthy boys to take on a situation at the palace. "Ragazzi, you'll be Sinbado's ears to the king."

The boys refused. They didn't want to become Sinbado's ears.

"Stupids, the inglesi are coming. You'll be safe in the Quirinale. The inglesi won't harm the king."

"Colonnello, we'll beg the Madonna to start a miracle and have the inglesi lose their way to Rome."

"We can't beg the Madonna."

"Why not?" the boldest of them asked, my subaltern, Piero Volpe. "Because soldiers never beg."

"But we're not exactly soldiers. We're the fascist youth patrol, free Italian boys. We can beg and pray with impunity."

Should have sacked him. That little son of a bitch will grow up to be a lawyer.

"Colonnello, we'll go to the Quirinale if you go too."

"Good thinking, Piero. And what will the inglesi do after they discover my nose? It's a giveaway. I can't go to the Quirinale with you."

"Then we'll stay here and piss on the inglesi from our front wall."

"The Giovani Brigade isn't a latrine. You'll go, or I'll pitch you into the gutters."

"We'd still be your ragazzi," said Piero Volpe.

They were whorish boys, ungrateful to their Ducellino. I could have demoted Volpe, made him into a corporal. But he'd have gathered sympathy around him, and I'd be the stinking old man of the brigade. So I had to drop the idea of a residency for them in the Quirinale.

Needed a bit of vacation from these boys. I went to the black market. Oh, it wasn't a steady place, a seat somewhere, like the stock exchange. It could be around the corner, under a bridge, or in St. Peter's itself. My black market was wherever Mamma Madrigale happened to be. She was the widow of some forgotten private who fell in Greece. Madrigale was the name she used with us. The Gestapo or our own SS could have delivered her to Queen of Heaven. Mamma Madrigale was an outrageous profiteer. She was also a Jewess. She insisted on wearing a yellow hat. The Gestapo would have destroyed anyone who touched the Jewess. They wanted the figs and oranges that were impossible to get without Madrigale. She had chestnut candies and strawberry tarts that her own bakers prepared. She had peaches and nectarines. She had the hearts and livers of fattened calves that Churchill would have dreamt about. She had kidney pie, and she wore a yellow hat.

Her marketplace this morning was a gelateria at the end of Bocca di Leone. I only had to cross the street to find Mamma Madrigale. The gelateria was out of ice cream. Twice a month Mamma put it back into business, servicing it with tubs of gelati and a small barrel of whipped cream that went into the mouths of the Gestapo and the Italian SS. But she hadn't come with her tubs today. She sat in the deserted gelateria. The Jewess troubled me. I'd get near her and think of Charlotte Street. She smelled of soap and sardines, like Andrusov, the pirate lady. She had Andrusov's thick shoulders and rutted face.

Mamma was my fix. She supplied me with charlotte russes.

"Do you have to embarrass me?" I said. "With that yellow hat."

"It's your invention, Pinocchio, your device."

"But the Questore must have told you. It's been canceled."

"Not for me," Mamma said. "The hat is convenient."

I drummed my wooden arms on the table top. "What's convenient about a dunce cap?"

"Clients can spot me from far away. I'm the last one in Rome with such a cap."

"Mamma, you have a wide appeal. You don't need inducements like that."

"How would you know?"

Ah, she was hinting at the anti-Semite in me.

"Haven't I reformed?" I asked that powerful lady.

"Yes, because you can't exist without a charlotte russe. The tedesci gave you that habit. You picked it up in Berlin."

"Berlin's not my city. I discovered charlotte russes in the Bronx."

She laughed in the deepest portion of her throat. "How would a burattino travel to America? Not even your master has been there."

"I dreamt of it."

"Did you also dream of what the Gestapo will do with Rome after your master falls down?"

"Mamma, the inglesi aren't that close. They'll sit awhile in Sicily with their American cousins."

"Dream some more, Pinocchio. Mussolini won't last out the month."

Did Madrigale have Brunhilde on her side? Were they witches together?

"Sinbado, is there anything you'd like to say?"

"Mamma, you've been slow in sending me up cigarettes. I can't bargain with the shopkeepers if I've got nothing to bargain with."

Ah, she was a witch, because Madrigale spat in my bloody stinking face. Me without a handkerchief in my pocket.

What had I ever done to Mamma? Could have arrested the witch, chained her to a wall in the Lion's Mouth, but then you couldn't have found a fig in Rome. The fascisti would come to shoot my windows out. We'd have had a lovely civil war.

Out in the street with spittle on my face. It clings to wood. Heard the old familiar whistling of the air-raid sirens. Three harsh whoops in a row. Metal she-wolves screaming in your ear. Women and children around me ran towards the bomb shelter underneath the fascist ministry on the Via del Babuino, Street of the Baboon. Couldn't find any men. You had a delicious manhood in the Second Roman Empire. You labored for the Reich in Bavaria like a bloody wog, or took your chances in Mussolini's army with cardboard shoes and cannons that had to be mounted on garbage trucks, or you sat out the war in somebody's closet.

The gelateria closed around Mamma Madrigale. The padrona had gone to Baboon Street. Mamma held to her table while the sirens barked. I heard a thud like some pimple falling in the sky. The thud turned into a cough. It could have been a giant with bronchitis a hundred miles from here. The giant developed a louder cough. The sky smudged a bit. The smudges went away. And we had the bluest sky in Italy, Roman blue, with a nibble of green to acknowledge the piss of the Tiber and the brown walls. Points of silver appeared in that blue field like a bloody miracle; the silver melted into gold soon as it caught in the sun, and then the gold hardened into silver points again. Silver to gold, gold to silver, like an alchemist gone amok.

It was the inglesi and their American cousins. They'd come to bomb Rome. But I couldn't tell where by the pull of the smoke. The smoke didn't have any tails. The sky was still blue as Jesus. I ran home to the brigade. The ragazzi were watching from the windows, binoculars in their fists. We went down to the radio room. My operators picked up whatever signals they could from the war office. The radio boys at the war office must have been out to lunch. Their transmitters were only a hill away, but it was like looking for Alaska. We had to get our signals from the krauts. The biggest antenna in Rome was on top of the German embassy near the Porta Maggiore. The Germans had their own little park at the Villa Wolkonsky, an independent state as removed from us as the Vatican was. The Germans enjoyed their sovereignty inside the villa. Their Sacred College was a bunch of admirals who'd given up the Atlantic for a political life. They were a company of blue-eyed fish away from the water. We'd catch them riding incognito on the tram, the only men in Italy with perfect creases in their trousers. But their antenna didn't lie.

Die Brüder, as Villa Wolkonsky called the Anglo-Americans, were bombing the freightyards of San Lorenzo. Die Brüder had five hundred boats in the air. Villa Wolkonsky expected die Brüder to say hello and bomb its little park. The admirals wondered over their frigging radio if they should climb onto the roof and drink champagne to die Brüder. Ah, these were sailors with style. But they didn't have much respect for us. They'd sing on the radio how the Führer was a lunatic to give Mussolini a piggyback ride right through the war.

They knew our agents and theirs were listening to them. They mocked the Duce, his policemen, and der Pinocchio. A nation of Pinocchios, they said. But how could I have admonished them? They recited Goethe over the radio, Thomas Mann, and Moby Dick. The admirals played radio chess with their counterparts in Florence. Ishmael was their code name for an unprotected king. Ahab was a queen that departed recklessly from its lines. They called a pair of cooperating bishops die Brüder. Mussolini was a pawn that was doubled-in. Der Pinocchio was a knight that fell asleep at the edge of the board. There's your game of chess at the Villa Wolkonsky.

Couldn't dawdle, mates. Had to rush out to San Lorenzo. We didn't keep a car in the Lion's Mouth, because none of us, man or boy, could drive. And we didn't trust a chauffeur from the outside. Somebody would have beaten our chauffeur into spying on us.

The alleys were the only accomplice we had. We could trust the dirty stinking vicoli of Rome, where the sun hadn't crept in a thousand years. We turned them into riverboats, paddling with arms and legs. The humpbacked avenues were islands we had to cross. We avoided Quirinale mountain and got to the freightyards from Prince Amedeo Street. The Italian SS hadn't come to the party. They were in the basement, hugging their heads.

Die Brüder would come and go in thick formations. It wasn't a random silver pin in the sky. It was thirty pins flashing down on us. Their engines would grind, and we could spot their noses. The bombs came whistling like the curl of an elbow. Idiot that I was, I thought of the admirals' trousers. Because the bombs arrived in the same perfect crease.

They chewed up the yards and the small streets around them. Matériel broke into the sky. A freight car landed on a roof, and then the roof disappeared. Bits of track formed crazy letters in the sky. It was like a new Jerusalem with its own picture language. A spaghetti factory crumpled close to our feet, burnt flour spitting a golden red from the windows. We stood near a fence outside the yards. The fence fell. We wouldn't budge for die Brüder and their bombs. Dust socked at our eyes. The bombs whistled down. None of us was hurt.

We began to hear screaming in the rubble. We moved onto the mounds where the screaming came from. We'd find a hand and pull.

A body would emerge in blood. We whimpered, but we didn't abandon people. We wrapped them in our shirts and carried them down the rubble hills. Soon there wasn't a shirt left. We had to give up our undershirts. What the hell? It's no thrill being half naked in a fire storm.

We clopped on the rubble in the dark boots of the fascist elite. Never even noticed that die Brüder were gone.

Soldiers didn't arrive to dig for bodies. A few old women climbed on the hills, screaming for husbands, daughters, sons. We helped them search, but we couldn't come up with the right body. It was always someone else's husband, daughter, son.

A black limousine rode into the rubble, flying a yellow-and-white flag. I knew the duchy this flag had come out of. My children didn't have to stare into the car.

"Ecco—il papa!"

They covered their nipples with their hands, thinking it rude to be undressed around that black Mercedes. Two priests let a man with a long nose out of the car. I'd swear it was another Pinocchio, with gold-rimmed glasses. It was only Pius.

His Holiness blessed the children for their labor in the ruins, and he didn't bother about their lack of shirts. He walked in the rubble, tears under the gold rims. The two priests distributed money and little bags of food. Pius went from mound to mound and absolved those who lay dying, his white cassock spotted with blood.

I liked that other Pinocchio, mates, even if he was il papa, whom my babbo had warned me about and told me to disregard. Pius wasn't a stinking yob who sat in St. Peter's. He was the first soldier to reach San Lorenzo after the all-clear.

Felt like a bloody criminal in his presence, a drifter posing as a wooden boy. I marched the Giovanis to a different hill of ruins. We gathered in the dead and shoveled for the living with our hands. A second Mercedes paused at the bottom of our hill. Its bumpers wore the five gold stars of Savoy. I climbed down to greet Vittorio, even if he wouldn't talk to me.

A window opened and the king shouted, "Get in."

There must have been an edict for bombings, whereby Vittorio could break his silence and talk to a cousin in times of crisis.

I entered the Mercedes. Vittorio sat with Princess Josie in a green uniform, as marshal of the empire.

"Pinocchio, do you parade like this for the inglesi? Where's your shirt, boy?"

I liked him better during the silent years.

"We had no bandages, sire. I had to lend my shirt to a wounded man."

He gave me his tunic to wear with ribbons and medals that made me emperor of Ethiopia, king of Sardinia, king of Cyprus, and prince of Jerusalem. But I wasn't the king of Cyprus very long.

Vittorio had to reclaim the tunic once we got out of the car, since his shirt was ordinary and didn't have the markings of the realm. His bodyguard distributed lire, like the two priests, but he didn't have Pius' success.

Old women pitched the lire back at the king and cursed us all. They must have confused Pinocchio with the king's aides. And they didn't spare the princess. "Putana, go to the palace and paint your nails."

Vittorio's bodyguard picked up the lire and we got into the car, the women cackling behind us.

"Look at Little Sword!"

"What can I do?" the king muttered from his window.

"You bastard, end the war."

They wouldn't allow the barest notice of his station. He wasn't their majesty or king. He was as common as the rubble of San Lorenzo.

"But this is Mussolini's war."

"And who is Mussolini? Your servant."

Now they called him majesty. They curtsied to the limousine and strode off to the next mountain.

Vittorio squeezed himself into the corner. Josie held his hand. His kingship had been questioned, and Vittorio didn't know what to do. He'd come to assist the people of San Lorenzo, and they'd ordered him home.

"Sire, suffering has turned them crazy."

"Not so crazy," Vittorio said.

He wasn't a bad king. But he'd fallen under the sway of Mussolini and the dazzle of empire, and he couldn't free himself. He would have loved to fish somewhere at the side of the war and console himself with his coin collection. The Duce had made it impossible. Uncle Ben brought the inglesi down on our heads.

I was about to quit the limousine when I discovered the princess looking at my chest. Was I a curiosity to her highness? I knew the goods I had. Nipples softer than any man's, with a burr on the wood that could have been chest hairs. But then the princess' eyes went off Pinocchio, and I shoved out from that ship and returned to the rubble.

I couldn't find the brigade. One mound was like the next, and the Giovanis might have been on a whole other planet of ruins. People walked around me cloaked in plaster dust. They weren't too friendly at the sight of my nose.

"Hey," I said. "Help me dig out the bodies trapped in the dust."

"And who put them there? Benito and his puppet."

These dust people began to push and shove. Pinocchio hadn't lost his cricket-bat arms. I walloped the dust people, but they picked up burning cinders and threw them at my head. The cinders caught. My ears were on fire. The dust people grabbed my legs and tossed me over the ruins.

"Ecco—Churchillo!"

The wind spread the fire like maddened snakes. My ears belched a green smoke. I dashed about, clutching my head where the fire hadn't bit.

I screamed at the burning wood.

The dust people laughed. It took their minds off their own misery to have Pulcinella with green ears. I wandered from hill to hill. Gesù, Giuseppe, Maria. I was searching for Pius. Pius would have gotten the dust people to slap the fire out of my head. But the smoke curled around me and I couldn't see Pius.

All I could remember was Mamma Madrigale's spit. Was it spit to put out the fire? She must have had a reason to spit at me. How could I have disappointed Mamma Madrigale? It had to be more than the black market. I'd swear the answer was locked into Charlotte Street.

In my agony I saw a charlottka. Old firehead was dreaming. The dust people threw more cinders. I begged them to stop. I was growing clever with all my new fire hair. These weren't dust people. They were underground men, the sepolti vivi of San Lorenzo. Die Brüder had bombed them out of their secret closets, and they blamed Pinocchio. I was the Ducellino in their eyes.

I ran and ran, but I couldn't get outside the green smoke. The pits in my face where the blackbirds had wounded me years ago began to burst from the heat. Sparks landed on my nose. The liquid in my eyes had begun to evaporate. Pinocchio was near to blind. Why the hell were my last stinking images about Copernicus? Me and Lionel in the baby carriage.

"Colonnello."

Ah, I must have crossed another mountain and met with my boys. They took off their trousers and used them as brooms, beating me around the ears. They hugged me with their bodies to kill the fire. They turned their spittle into a kind of salve. They carried me out of San Lorenzo.

TWELVE

OUR LADY OF MONTEGRUMO

THE ragazzi fed me bouillon cubes purchased on the black market. I lay upstairs in a room full of ointments. I could see out to the balconies across Bocca di Leone. I had sun and soup.

It was a short vacation. The ragazzi appeared without a bouillon cube. "Finito," they said. Piero was crying.

"Volpe, what's wrong?"

"The king arrested Mussolini."

"It's nothing. We'll go with the Italian SS and fetch the Big Bastard."

"Colonnello, there is no more Italian SS."

"Then we'll call in the Blackshirts."

"The Blackshirts disappeared an hour after Mussolini. Their uniforms are floating in the Tiber."

"And Duce's Musketeers?"

"We checked on the radio. We're the last fascisti in Rome."

"One brigade?" I said.

251

"Yes. Everybody is practicing to be an Englishman."

"The Germans too?"

"No, colonnello. Not the Germans. But we have to be quick."

"Why? I'm not afraid of the inglesi."

"I wasn't thinking of the inglesi," Piero said. "It's the converts I'm afraid of. The ones who are preparing for the English. They will kill you in your bed."

"Who told you?"

"Our radios aren't asleep. We've been getting signals from the Villa Wolkonsky. The admirals warned us this afternoon."

"Why should they care? The admirals aren't fond of der Pinocchio. I'm a fool to them."

Piero had to explain the basics of war to me. "Colonnello, they're still on our side. They've offered us asylum in their villa. But it's not safe for you. The inglesi consider you a criminal. And some of our countrymen will collect the reward. We'll have to smuggle you out of Rome."

The little bastards pulled me out of the pillows. I didn't have a chance to exit from Bocca di Leone in my black uniform. They dressed me in rough farmer's clothes. I'd become the victim of my own smuggler's route. We had an idiot farmer and his horse bus at our disposal. This farmer, Tullio, wasn't clever enough to inform against the Giovanis. We paid him a pittance to smuggle out a handful of Jews and deliver contraband to our door from Mamma Madrigale's supply depots.

I asked the ragazzi where I was going.

"Colonnello, we found a fascist to take you in. The mayor of Montegrumo."

Ah, they were exiling Pinocchio to his home town. But I didn't intend to live with fascist Achille and his five battling daughters.

"Piero, please, send me somewhere else."

"There is nowhere else. Only the mayor of Montegrumo."

"Will he adopt the entire brigade?"

"We're not going with you," Piero said. "We're going south to look for Mussolini. We think the inglesi have him, and we intend to recapture the old man."

I shouted in my farmer's suit. "I'll die before I let you fight the inglesi. You're children, you hear? Children."

Volpe's mouth twisted with contempt. "Colonnello, it's obscene for you to treat us like that. We're Mussolini's brigade."

How could I argue? These children were blonder and braver than Pinocchio. Saluted them, touched Volpe's shoulder. "Addio," I said.

"Addio, commendatore."

They went up and hugged me beyond the obligation of their rank. They were the best stinking boys in town. I got into the horse bus, under a blanket. It was good timing. As the cart squealed out of Bocca di Leone, a herd of republicans arrived at the Lion's Mouth to arrest Sir Pinocchio.

"Abbasso Sinbado!" they shouted into the windows. "Evviva Matteotti! Evviva il papa! Evviva il re!"

Little Sword had become a hero again. That was politics. Our fortunes went up and down like a frigging commodity on the open market. If I lived long enough, I might be emperor of London, Rome, or Addis Ababa. My calendar was a bit off. I must have come out into the street during carnevale. Romans danced in their pajamas. There was more kissing than I'd ever seen in Mussolini's empire. Grandfathers were knocking fascist emblems off the walls. Children dragged a stone head of Mussolini in the gutters. Our cart had to wait for the head to cross Bocca di Leone.

Tullio, the idiot farmer, sat sniffling up in his seat. He wasn't a fascist or a republican. He was a farmer with respect for a man's stone image.

"Cavaliere," he called into the blanket. "They shouldn't handle the Duce like that."

"But it's children playing in the gutter, children hauling stone."

"I agree, but a man's face is holy."

And the farmer turned back to his horse.

The Giovanis must have instructed him well. He dropped me off at Brunhilde's old hut. We'd passed a German armored column on the road to Montegrumo. The inglesi couldn't have come this far north, not even with their parachutes. I'd shared a dozen portions of bread and cheese with Tullio on this trip. The farmer liked to eat in silence. It wasn't fair to call him an idiot. He was someone who paid strict attention to his horse.

I tried to feed him another hundred lire. The farmer said no. He could accept nothing beyond the price he'd contracted for him and his horse. I got down from the cart while Tullio went off on another mission.

He clucked at his horse.

I wouldn't waltz into that hut at the end of town. It had the stink of witches. I'd find a better place of exile. I followed the witches' wall into the Via Copernico. Women stood outside their doors and made the sign of Jesus over me. Bambini kissed my farmer's sleeve. I was Montegrumo's holy boy.

I stopped at the Casa del Fascio. Its bronze lictors had been ripped from the wall. It was now republican headquarters, with the five gold stars of Vittorio Emanuele. There wasn't a black shirt or silver skull in the rotten place. The fascisti were decked in midnight blue, Vittorio's favorite color. They were snide about the farmer's suit until they discovered my nose. Never saw so much hand-kissing in my life.

Achille spoke for the yobs. "It's an honor, commendatore. I insist. You're the hero of Montegrumo, the most famous citizen we've ever had."

"Achille, I'm a wooden boy. Remember, you wanted to adopt me after my babbo died and I ran away."

"But not every wooden boy that runs away lives to become the Ducellino."

"And what's a Ducellino in today's market? Dust. Achille, there's a price on my head. Churchill would love to parade me in Piccadilly."

"We know that, excellency. That's why we have to take precautions. The Germans aren't so fond of you either. Their generals say you corrupted the Duce, but we don't believe that. You're the great Sinbado. You turned Italy's children into fighters. After the Duce, you're our noblest son."

Noblest son? I was a shill from Charlotte Street.

"Achille, should we fight the inglesi together and show Churchill what he can do with Piccadilly?"

A gloom settled on Achille's republican face. "Pinocchio, we're trying to steer between the Germans and the inglesi."

"Sir Pinocchio," I said.

The mayor bowed. "Yes. Sir Pinocchio. You're a knight. But unfortunately, fascist knights are out of style . . . almost a nuisance. We'll have to hide you."

"Hide a nose, Achille? Are you a magician?"

"No, but we could upholster you with rouge and wigs . . . for the inglesi. Perhaps a carpenter could help."

I grabbed him by the collar. "I'm not fresh out of the basket. My nose has developed the properties of skin."

It grew tense between us. I'd have strangled him before any carpenter could have whittled me down.

The Montegrumesi clamored near the window. "The Madonna," they yelled. "Achille, the Madonna is outside."

Achille moved over to the window and went pale. "The Madonna."

"Lunatics," I muttered. "You all belong in a republican asylum. The Madonna wouldn't come to Montegrumo. She has better things to do."

I hopped across the room and flexed my body out the door. Brunhilde stood naked in the street. She wasn't grinding her hips. Nothing provocative. She stood. Just as I started to ponder her visitation, Brunhilde disappeared. That's the problem with witches. They're bloody unpredictable.

"A miracolo," Achille said, wiping his face with an immense handkerchief. "The Madonna is punishing us for our sins. That old whore was a holy person . . . Our Lady of Montegrumo."

"You're only the mayor," I said. "You can't declare a miracle. You have to petition the Holy Office. And what would Pius think about a town that whores a woman into her grave?"

Achille was firm in spite of his fears about the Holy Office. He was ready to take on Pius and Pinocchio. "It's clearly a miracle. The Madonna is among us now . . . commendatore, where are you going?"

"To meet with your Madonna."

"I forbid it," Achille said. "You're a renegade. You cannot walk in the street."

I left the republicans and took the trail back to the witch's hut. The little house was dusty. It hadn't been in service since Brunhilde's day.

My godmother the witch was inside. She must have stolen mozzarella from the town. I never realized that witches had to eat.

I looked between her legs. She had a silky, symmetrical mound for a witch. And her thighs weren't very wrinkled. She'd prospered as a ghost.

"Madam, why did you come here?"

"I have to have some fun. Why shouldn't those fascisti sweat a little? This was my town. I might have been happy as your school-teacher."

"You were never my teacher. You tutored me once, explained the engineering of a nose."

"Pinocchio," she said, "dear Pinocchio, tickle me."

"Stop it. You're my godmother. I'm in enough trouble as it is."

"Tickle me."

"I will not."

But my schnozzle betrayed me. That little mother grew and grew. Wish I had a carpenter, some Giuseppe to plane me into oblivion.

I tickled the witch.

Can't help it. I'd developed a solid technique in my time as Pinocchio. I could enter her standing, sitting, or lying on my face. I picked Brunhilde up into the air, rested her thighs on my shoulders, held her by the buttocks, and schnozzled the witch while I carried her across the hut in my own variation on the fireman's grip. She sighed for twenty minutes. And then she was gone. Out the roof, like a bloody dervish. The idiot boy was holding buttocks and thighs that weren't there. It was phantom copulation. Brunhilde had put me on her angry list. She was taking vengeance on the whole town and Sinbad, the landlocked sailor.

But I wasn't going to surrender to a witch.

I inherited her cottage. I slept. The wounds in my face healed. War widows arrived with rations. I drank their soup. God forgive me, they were young and pretty girls. Widows at nineteen and twenty. We took our pleasure in that dusty place. Afterwards, the widows swept up with a broom.

Wouldn't have minded being a renegade for the rest of my life.

The Germans moved into town. They occupied the one caffè, shut republican headquarters, and broke into houses, bathing in washtubs and begging the pardon of widows, grandmothers, and wives. They bullied, but they didn't steal. They paid for whatever produce they took with blue bank notes printed in Vienna. These bank notes were worthless to the Montegrumesi, who accepted them because they weren't at liberty to call the Germans thieves.

The soldiers whistled in the streets at night. They sat on Brunhilde's wall. They peeked into the hut and smiled at der Pinocchio.

I was the puppet of a government that fell. Their commanding officer invited me to a tea party in an alfalfa field. He spoke of the British as der Tommy. And he had no doubt that der Tommy would win the war.

"You should practice your English," he said in an Italian that was no less fluid than mine.

"I'm a criminal to them, Herr General."

"It makes no difference. They're a clubby sort. If you speak their language, they'll warm to you."

The general's aide was drunk on alfalfa and tea. He said the Germans ought to sell me to the British. The general banished him to the next alfalfa field and protected me from der Tommy. It was like having my own Musketeers. I could go unmolested through town, drink with Germans at the caffè.

When individual inglesi dropped from the sky in their silver chutes, the Germans would pick them out of the fields like blackberries. I had nothing to fear from der Tommy, long as the general was around.

Die Brüder would strafe the village from time to time, attacking chimneys, gunning donkey carts and German tanks. Children would sing songs, begging the inglesi to bomb and gun down the road from Montegrumo.

It was almost a sleepy war . . . until the goumiers. These were French colonial troops, Berber irregulars who maintained their own wild packs. They were mountain fighters, scorning tanks and armored cars. The goums came on donkeys or by foot. They wore striped gowns, with pigtails under their helmets. The goums prayed to la Allah and cut your throat. They believed that every woman was their wife. It was in their province to claim grandmothers and young girls.

The village was deathly afraid of them. No one ventured out to pick blackberries. The Germans began to hold their picnics and tea parties in the village square. I was told to move from my hut.

"Find a more central location, Herr Pinocchio."

But I wouldn't relocate for warriors in pigtails. I'd match wits and weapons with the goums. My body was a wooden shield.

I'd become a pariah with my decision to remain in the hut. Young widows wouldn't visit. No one brought me soup. I clutched at berries near the wall. I made my own leafy soups. I had dialogues with the dead in my life, Lionel, Bathsheba, Bruno, and that Corsican, Monsieur le prince. I was as rational with the dead as I was with the living. Would have addressed the goums in the same crisp tones. But the goums didn't come.

I asked Copernicus to clean up the mystery of octopuses and second-hand girls. "Lionel, was there a Tatiana and a Belinda Hogg? I couldn't have manufactured Tati's black ink and Belinda's Texas drawl. I'm a storyteller, yes, but my brain isn't the Nile. It's a stinking box with bloody wires."

Uncle had nothing to tell.

I walked to Florence inside the hut. The Florence I saw didn't have mountains and Jewish streets. There's not a frigging city the mind can't conceive.

I lived on blackberries.

It snowed once.

I lost my faith in the goums.

And then those mothers arrived at my door. They had lighter skin than I'd imagined. Their pigtails were gone. The goums carried Italian knives.

"Entrez, mes amis. Pinocchio à votre service. J'adore les goumiers."

They looked at me as if I were some camel driver. These goums couldn't unravel my kindergarten French.

"Colonnello, are you sick?"

It was Volpe and the Giovani Brigade in ragged clothes, without a single marking on their sleeves. They could have been deserters or common bandits.

We had uncooked macaroni on the floor of the hut.

"Why has the village abandoned you, sir?"

"Everybody's afraid of the goums."

"We didn't see one goum on the road."

"They're mountain fighters. They attack from the hills. But they send their harems along the road. They capture women, the goums. Once you're kidnapped, that's it."

"Is she from the harem?" they asked, hurling a creature with pigtails into the hut. "We found her begging in the fields."

"That's a goum," I said.

They hadn't bothered to notice that their harem lady had a beard. They poked under the Berber's gown, touched him like a gang of surgeons. "A man," they concluded. "But colonnello, where's his harem?"

"He must have gotten lost," I said.

His eyes were milky. We fed him whatever noodles we had. He ate them Berber fashion, sucking on the noodles as if they were bones with meat. He was a hairy little bugger, and I couldn't tease much information out of him. I addressed the goum in English, French, Italian, and German. "Bist du ein goumier?"

This goum had no identity tags. His only rank was his pigtails. He was just another stinking refugee.

"Should we lend him to our German brothers? They'll tickle his feet. That could be a goum trick, holding his eyeballs up in his skull."

"Where's your compassion? He's been dropped by his own outfit. He's a Berber with nothing to eat."

"Suppose his harem is in the woods."

"Piero," I said, "sometimes I can't tell if you're a lawyer or a priest . . . let the Berber go."

They spun him out the door, pulled on his pigtails, and shoved him over the wall.

"Ragazzi, now will you tell me why you're in Montegrumo?"

They frowned. I could have been a goum in their eyes.

"Commendatore, we've come to rescue you."

"But I have the Germans for company."

"The Germans are not our own people," Volpe said.

"I don't understand. Didn't you go south to look for Mussolini?"

"We did. But Mussolini is up north, near Lake Como."

"You mean the Big Cheese is back in business?"

"You could say that, colonnello. He's mostly free."

"Mostly free," I muttered. "Will you tell me what's going on?"

"He's starting a new republic under German supervision."

"Then why didn't the Germans here say something?"

"It's still a secret. Hitler sent his gliders into the mountains to rescue him from the king's men."

"And now he's a prisoner with his own republic?"

"Yes," Piero said. "A prisoner with his own republic."

THIRTEEN

SALÒ

HE was cavaliere Benito Mussolini, president for life of the Repubblica di Salò. He reigned in Lombardy, where the goums and the Anglo-Americans hadn't arrived. He was half a step from Switzerland, but the Duce couldn't leap. He had German guards in his house. The guards fixed his bicycle, brought his mistress up from Rome, but they would have shot his head off if he'd tried to run away. He danced a German polka. He signed decrees. He couldn't get beyond the toilet without his German guards.

They were there to protect him from the communist and socialist rabble. It's true, mates. He would have been murdered in a week if the tedeschi hadn't upholstered his little republic with their bodies and their armored cars. They weren't evil boys. They acted as barbers and shaved his skull. They sat in on his telephone conversations. They chauffeured his mistress around. The Germans were bored with Mussolini. They wanted to meet with die Brüder in an open field and finish the war.

But they were locked out of the struggle. They had to guard uncle Ben.

He was sequestered in the village of Gargnano without his government. Mussolini lived on a lake. His ministers were in Salò, a town he never visited. He sulked from room to room with his Germans behind him. "Sinbado, I consider myself a man three-quarters dead."

"Duce," I whispered. "We could revive you."

"No one can revive me," he shouted. The Germans went on muttering to themselves. It didn't matter what Benito said. He could have planned a world revolution. They'd stopped listening to him or der Pinocchio and his gang of boys. The Giovanis were nothing but a nuisance, mouths to feed, children to entertain a Duce.

I whispered a little louder. The Germans laughed at the sight of two puppets walking in a big dollhouse by a lake that was the Repubblica di Salò.

"We'll go to Val Tellina with the ragazzi. We'll make our stand."

Val Tellina was the Italian canton that uncle Ben would dream about when he stopped behaving like a ghost. At Val Tellina he would be rid of the Germans and fascisti who'd thrown their uniforms in the Tiber. He'd fend off the Anglo-Americans and make a new flag with enough lions, lemurs, and skulls within its borders to populate a country.

"Val Tellina," Mussolini said, as if he'd never heard about his canton. He had milk stains on his collar. His boots were muddy from having gone nowhere but around the lake. His undershirt had started to shove out of his uniform. He'd forgotten to wear a shirt. He stood still in one of his living rooms and sneezed.

I scolded him. "Duce, you should wear a decent shirt. You could get a chill."

He rubbed at himself. His black eyes seemed to bolt from his skin. He pulled the collar up around his neck. He was the dictator again. "In such a moment of history, a Duce doesn't catch a chill."

"Val Tellina," I told him.

"That's a mythical country."

His shrewdness had come home to the dollhouse.

"Duce, Salò is worse than a myth . . . it's a stinking German fantasy."

"Never mind. I'm the prince. I have things to do, Pinocchio. I have to end the civil war. Italians are destroying each other over me . . . I'll surrender to the socialists."

"Your cousins will never permit you to surrender. They'd look too much like invaders without you. The Germans need a Duce at Salò."

Benito clutched his undershirt. "Foolish boy, I could discharge the Germans from Italy with a stroke of my pen. They have no sovereignty here. But listen to your uncle. It's better to be on the side of Berlin."

He lapsed into that brooding world of Salò, shuffled with his German escorts. He had a screaming in his ears that shut out every other music.

I went to his mistress in a cottage down the road.

Clara had unpacked all her lounging pajamas. She could have run to Switzerland. But she'd arrived with black and red pajamas to please the president of Salò.

She wasn't the old Claretta who lived according to Mussolini's whims. She understood which country had rented her the cottage.

"Sinbado, will the tedesci strangle him in his sleep?"

I felt like a witch. Could have told her that she'd die with her Ben, but I didn't. What if I kidnapped Claretta and forced her into Switzerland? She'd have scratched my eyes out and come back to Salò.

I wasn't allowed to bathe her or tickle her back. The somberness of Salò must have eaten into Clara. She wouldn't walk naked in a German cottage.

I assured her as much as I could without dancing into lies.

"Clara, the tedesci won't harm Ben."

We played backgammon in this country by the lake. You could hardly hear a cannon pop. The goums were far away. No enemies drifted into our camp. Die Brüder never bothered to strafe Mussolini. We didn't even have a parachute scare. It was indecent how both sides excluded us from the war. We could have frigged ourselves and the world wouldn't have noticed.

I left Clara to her pajamas and consoled myself with the ragazzi, who had their own living room in the Duce's dollhouse. They were restless without a war. They sat near the mantelpiece with their shortwave radio, trying to gather in news from Rome.

"Are you picking up the Villa Wolkonsky? Let's hear what the admirals have to say."

The boys came out of their stupor to pity me. "Commendatore, the admirals were arrested months ago. They're in Queen of Heaven."

"Hitler put his own admirals in jail? Why?"

"They wouldn't round up the Jews."

Ah, I couldn't blame it all on drowsiness. Hitler had reached beyond the Villa Wolkonsky to shut the ghetto. "Where are the Jews?"

"In a colony outside Trieste. A special work farm."

I picked that moment to remember the Jewish count behind my wall at Bocca di Leone. "Whatever happened to Jacobo?"

"He's at the Jewish farm."

"Then we don't have a choice. We're marching on Trieste."

Had no trouble sneaking away from the house. The Germans yawned at us. Mussolini was their measure. We could come or go, and chew on dried apples from Mussolini's larder.

Got halfway round the little lake when an armored car shoved us off the road. Mussolini jumped out of the car in battledress. His boots had been shined. He had silver skulls on his collar, and he wore a regulation shirt.

He stepped in front of my boys and told them I was a whore.

"Stronzo, are you on a picnic? Why did you steal apples from me?"

"Duce, we're going to Trieste."

"It's lovely how you inform me of this and that. What's in Trieste?"

"Count Jacobo. And the Jewish colony." I could have said concentration camp. But I'd only have confused the boys.

"You're disturbing state business," the Duce said. "Jacobo is where he belongs."

"Good. Then I'm going to Trieste."

He bruised his girly hand slapping Pinocchio.

"My brave tactician, how will you get there?"

"On foot. I have maps. An idiot can find Trieste."

Uncle Ben parroted me. "An idiot. Only an idiot. Do you have military papers? There's thirteen war zones from Gargnano to Trieste. Pirates occupy six of them and we have seven."

"Pirates?" the ragazzi asked, interested all of a sudden.

"The socialist front and every other brigand. They've been waylaying people on the roads, demanding tribute. They're crawling with inglesi. Fortune hunters. They've turned my revolution into profit. Pinocchio, they'll sell your ears to any interested party."

Had to remind the Duce that my ears were wood. This time he slapped me with his gloves. "Wooden ears won't stop the pirates. They'll chisel into your head."

"I'll take my chances."

"Will you take your chances with the boys? They'll steal the whole troupe. There's a market for ragazzi in America. Warriors like that will become servants to rich old men."

Couldn't escape my past. It saddened me to think of the ragazzi going to Scarsdale. "Brutale," I said.

The Duce bargained with his brother puppet. "You want Jacobo, you'll get Jacobo."

He pulled a field telephone out of the armored car and spoke to the dollhouse. "Herr Corporal, be so kind as to ring up the concentration colony at San Sabba. Tell the commandant that I would like him to locate my former secretary, Count Jacobo, who is his guest. He is to prepare the count for shipment to Gargnano. I will send him the proper papers this afternoon. Evviva Hitler! Evviva Salò!"

The count rode out of Trieste in the sidecar of a German motorcycle. He wore the green uniform of Salò. Mussolini had made him a private. That's how you graduate from a concentration colony. He looked bizarre in military clothes, like a butler who'd lost his station. He wouldn't kiss the Duce or any of my boys. He suffered our presence and remained aloof. The count always ate alone. He prepared the Duce's social calendar, but he never offered advice. He didn't exist outside his obligations to the republic. He was a shadow in a soldier's uniform.

I cornered the shadow a few nights after he arrived. The shadow was reading Dante and Proust.

"Jacobo, you needn't live with us. I can arrange a ride to Switzerland."

He put down Dante and Proust to stare at me. "I wouldn't dream of running."

"Believe me, Jacobo. The Germans aren't interested in us."

"I'm comfortable here, Pinocchio. I have my books. And I'm a servant of Salò."

"What are you talking about? You won't get your sergeant's stripes working for Mussolini. Go to Switzerland, man."

"I have nothing to do with the Swiss. I'm a Roman count."

"Forget Rome. Rome's a province of Bavaria right now."

"Then I'll stay here."

The shadow returned to his books, read and whimpered to himself. It was odd crying for a shadow. The sounds could have been issued from a child of six.

"Jacobo, I'm sorry about the colony you were in. I might have saved you earlier but I had a bit of amnesia. We all get the sleeping sickness in Salò."

He wouldn't give up that terrible whimper, soft as a little girl.

"Did you lose some people at the colony?"

"We didn't lose people. We played shuffleboard . . . I'm crying over you."

"What for? You have nothing to cry about. Wooden boys don't depreciate. They hold their value in hard times."

"You're the worst rascal in Italy. You belong to no one. A monster without a family."

"Maybe so, but what can I do that will keep you from crying?"

"Come out of the wood and show me the moorings of a human face."

"I have pockmarks. Isn't that enough?"

"Pinocchio, it's not a matter of cosmetics. There's nothing, nothing in your eyes."

"Gesù, I'm a puppet. I was made without the right fluid."

"It's not the fault of your carpentry. You've grown evil as a puppet. Your eyes swim in an empty sink. Damn you, Italy is swollen with wooden boys, boys begging for the chance to turn human. You've gone the opposite way. Someone or something is possessing you."

Copernicus Charyn. But hadn't I gentled Pinocchio, bumped him off fascism a little? I couldn't help it if I'd become a golem on the way from flesh to wood.

"Count Jacobo, should I run to a priest and make him smoke the devils out of my bark?"

"I'll smoke your devils. You can do without a priest."

"Will you stop crying then?"

He whimpered, "I will."

The count laid his hands on my shoulders and administered a squeeze. I felt his fingers go under the wood, as if he carried an electrical current in his skin. Ah, the count must have picked up sorcery at San Sabba. He was something of a witch. Because I started to cry with the touch of him. It was a curious thing. He was making me mourn myself. I'd always been a stinking puppet. Pinocchio or Copernicus Charyn. I was a bloody outcast who hoarded whatever he had, the burattino that wrote *Blue Eyes over Miami*.

"Jacobo, that's enough."

He dabbed my eyes with a military handkerchief. Must have developed a couple of tear ducts, because the handkerchief went away wet.

"I think I'll go to my room . . . thank you, sir."

I left the shadow where he was, crossed Mussolini's living rooms, and lay down in my own bunker; we all had bombproof boxes to sleep in. It was 1944, the year I'd rediscovered Charlotte Street through Belinda Hogg . . . until my mother told me there was no Belinda. Even with tear ducts I couldn't puzzle it out. But if that shadow count had become the conscience of Pinocchio, I might get lucky and push a little closer to my past. I breathed through my nose, which is half a lie, since puppets don't have to deal with that oxygen business. But we can hold air in our noses, spooning it into a nostril with our hand.

I spooned and spooned. And then I shivered. All that air was like an hallucinating drug. I smelled half-sour pickles. The Duce didn't keep pickles in his larder. An image cradled into my head. Lionel sucking on a pickle in Madam Andrusov's shop. And then I recalled how Copernicus got his start. He was financed by the pickle men of Jennings Street, Andrusov's enemies. Uncle had his own beanstalk. He climbed over the pickle men with it, became a millionaire, and bought them out of their pickle barrels. But why did they help uncle in the first place? I was Detective Pinocchio, high on the air in my nose. No wonder Andrusov and Bitter Morris had been murdered in their sleep. They'd had the comfort of knowing Lionel was in the house. Uncle was their watchdog. He borrowed ice picks from the Jennings Street mob and dispatched Morris and Andrusov while both of them lay in bed. It was the same expertise that had served him in the belly of a baby carriage. Lionel was always a submarine. He knew how to crawl without getting noticed. The wind over Charlotte Street must have been his abacus. He sniffed it and counted up his future. His future was with pickles.

There's the blow. I must have guessed the conspiracy as a kid and couldn't bear to see Lionel as the ice-pick man. So I began to weave the fabric of Belinda. That's how it seemed to Pinocchio's nose.

I wish the count hadn't laid his hands on me. I couldn't sleep. Kept thinking of the ice-pick man.

Couldn't get back into the ordinary swing of Salò. The republic ran on a clock that was no longer Pinocchio's. Yes, I could offer the republic's salute to our German conquerers. Evviva Hitler! Evviva Salò! But it was the brain marking time, spitting out its necessary slogans.

I was in the casbah, licking charlotte russes. The Giovanis had to shove me during dinner. "Colonnello, eat, eat, for Christ's sake."

"I'm already eating."

"But you haven't tried the tortellini."

"I prefer a charlotte russe."

The Duce left his end of the table to comfort me. "Piccolino, is it some woman who's poisoned your appetite? She's not worth the bother. Finish up and we'll go to the brothel together."

"Don Benito, will you take your wife?"

His black eyes lost their friendliness. Donna Rachele, the Duce's wife, was in a villa up the road. He preferred the dollhouse to the villa.

"Oh," I said, "if not donna Rachele, what about your mistress? Why can't Clara watch us at the brothel?"

Blue worms appeared on Benito's forehead. He pulled at the table-cloth and we had a feast of tortellini on the floor. "Where are my guards? We'll hang him from the roof."

Piero Volpe hopped around Mussolini's shoulder. "Forgive him, Duce. He's not in control. He often says things that don't make sense. His head was on fire in San Lorenzo. It hasn't properly healed."

"How can I calm him?"

"With a charlotte russe."

"That's impossible," I muttered. "Mamma Madrigale cornered the market. And she's probably dead."

The Duce warned me with a finger. "Shut up, you." He clutched a phone and got his radio room on the line. "Herr Corporal, put a rush on one charlotte russe . . . I don't give a damn if it comes from Geneva. I want it here within the hour."

We sat around the table like supplicants at our own Last Supper. The tortellini stayed on the floor. I tittered at don Benito.

"The charlotte russe will never come. We'll sit until Anno 85."

Mussolini drummed on the table. He scratched under a boot. A German arrived with a pastry box.

"Go on," Mussolini said. "Show the republic how to eat a charlotte russe."

I opened the flaps and peeked in as if I were looking for a holy cup. The universe had to be correct, because this charlottka had the usual cardboard battlement. Cream ran on my finger. I licked at the roof. It made no difference having a puppet's tongue. I tasted Lionel and Bathsheba. The jelly in my eyes disappeared. It was something new. I'd had fire in my ears, birds ate my cheeks, but I'd never swooned before . . .

I woke with a bandanna of towels on my brain. Wood has a damaging sweat, and the boys were keeping me dry. Didn't recognize this bunker until I realized I was in Mussolini's bed. The Big Bastard was being neighborly to his wooden boy. He had a photo of Claretta on the wall.

He brought a chair into the bunker so he could sit and read Dostoyevsky to Sir Pinocchio. He fell in love with Grushenka and ranted about the stinking way old man Karamazov was killed. Mussolini believed in a beautiful death, morte nella belleza. He wanted to die fighting the inglesi.

"Pinocchio, Churchill will never capture this old man. He would like to put a Duce in the Tower of London and hide the key. But we will go to Val Tellina and hold off his dogs another five years."

"Babbo, when should we pack?" I asked, while the towels ate up sweat.

"Soon. Soon."

But he wouldn't orchestrate a move to Val Tellina. He was trapped in that timeless webbing of his republic. I got up after a week and returned to my own bunker.

The towels did their work. I stopped smelling half-sour pickles. I had to pull back from the human chalkline. I learned to accept my puppet nature, even if it meant blank eyes.

I avoided Jacobo, and Jacobo avoided me. He had his own portions of the dollhouse to shadow in and out.

Rome had fallen to die Brüder, and refugees arrived in Salò. That radio announcer, Giacomo Joyce, was among the first refugees. He'd come with his little daughter, Bianca Joyce. She was half-blind, like her dad. Bianca wore the same frigging eyepatch. Her good eye rolled in her head. It didn't take me long to discover that the daughter was a bit unbalanced. She was frightened of candles, rain, and Englishmen. Bianca would only take food from her father's hand. The maestro was insanely devoted to her. He'd rock her to sleep in his arms, and buy candy for her from the Germans, who had their own black market in Salò. The maestro gave up the gold in his mouth to this schwarzer Markt. He sold his vest and all his ties until Mussolini heard about it. The Duce screamed at his guards, who had to return it all, including a maestro's neckties. The guards swore to the Duce that these goods had nothing but sentimental value. "Herr Mussolini, Giacomo is your greatest living artist. We wanted souvenirs."

"Souvenirs? So you went like dentists into his mouth."

He paid them a benefice for guarding him, and he cut this benefice in half. His Germans didn't complain. They upped their prices on the schwarzer Markt and had most of Giacomo Joyce by the end of the month.

The maestro would broadcast from the radio bunker. It was the old malicious song about Jews and mad-dog Englishmen. He didn't bother to preach in a narrative form. He cursed the democracies for bringing about il finimondo, the end of the civilized world. He would not live among the English, he said, or eat their barbarian food. The English would make a circus of Rome. Finimondo. He would hold his daughter's hand and hide in a cave.

We had reports of goums appearing in the neighborhood. I elected myself Bianca's bodyguard. I was fond of that little girl, and I didn't want her to become part of some harem. But the goums hadn't foraged into Salò for women. The pigtails were desperate for food.

"That means we're winning the war," Mussolini muttered.

"Benito, these are stragglers who've left their raiding party. You can't divine a war by the route of their pigtails."

"We're winning, nonetheless."

More and more refugees arrived. The guards grew restless. After they bought up everybody's gold teeth, they turned inward and wouldn't hunt for goums.

"Cavaliere, we have to leave right away. The Germans can't protect us, and we're growing short of food."

"Food?" the Duce said, twisting that word under his tongue. He had milk stains on his collar again and he'd abandoned *The Brothers Karamazov.* "I don't read, I don't think, I don't consume calories, and therefore I have no desire for food."

"But you still dream," I said. "And it takes calories to do that."

"Then I'll stop dreaming."

"Duce, we have to go now."

I shook Benito's collar. "I'm arresting you. You're unfit to govern."

"Unfit? I'll break your back. My guards will sink you into the ground with machine-gun bullets."

"Your guards trade bullets on the black market. They couldn't sink a mouse . . . Duce, remember the man that once said, *If I retreat, kill me; if I fall, avenge me; if I stand still, abandon me forever?*"

Mussolini picked at his undershirt. "That was before Salò. You have to act different in a republic."

"Your republic is a big lemonade."

The Duce slapped me and howled from the pain of knuckles on wood. He could never seem to learn who I was.

"Duce, we have to get out."

We gave the Germans Salò and bought six trucks. I couldn't understand what they intended to do with the republic. Put it on the market? They didn't seem so eager to sell. The Germans lounged in Mussolini's living rooms while we packed ourselves into the trucks. None of the refugees chose to stay. We were all fascists together. We'd make our stand against the banditi in Val Tellina.

Duce didn't take his wife. The English wouldn't harm donna Rachele. Churchill might store a dictator in the Tower of London, but not the dictator's wife.

He took Clara because he wasn't certain how the inglesi would treat

a mistress. She packed her pajamas and wouldn't consider the conse-
quences of selling Salò.

I was in the sixth truck with the Duce and his mistress, Giacomo,
Bianca, the count, and a dozen refugees. Our driver was a Dutchman
who'd fallen under the Duce's spell in 1939 and moved to Italy at the
age of fifty-seven. We called him Hals, and he was the only man
who'd ever been convinced by the rubbish of *Anno 85.* That bloated,
stinking whale of a book had changed the Dutchman's life. Hals
adored the idea of a Mussolinian universe. I pitied the bugger and
the pages he'd had to read. He was a walking bible of ducismo, and
he drove our truck.

We didn't occupy the rear of uncle Ben's little wolf pack out of
weakness. We were hoping to confuse our enemies. I'd encouraged the
Duce to become a man without a republic, and now he was vulnerable
from every side. There were a million scalphunters in Italy who would
have enjoyed seizing his head. So I forced Benito to wear a pillbox hat
and military cape of the carabinieri. He didn't want to disguise himself.
He couldn't have a beautiful death in such an outlandish uniform. But
I told him it was for the good of the caravan. While we were in transit,
we didn't exist as a state. We were invisible people until we got to Val
Tellina, and we couldn't afford to lose our uncle Ben.

He grumbled under the pillbox hat and accepted the cape.

I was another war criminal, but I couldn't become anonymous with
my nose. I sat buried in a German greatcoat, my nose pushing out at
the chest buttons until I looked like a pregnant soldier. Claretta
laughed, her face hidden in a crash helmet.

The ragazzi were in the other five trucks. They'd asked to ride with
their colonel, but I thought it prudent to segregate them from Sir
Pinocchio. I'd rather they weren't under my greatcoat if the banditi
captured us.

Bianca sang songs about the Infant Jesus. The maestro stroked her
hair. I couldn't understand why he'd delivered his genius to fascism.
Mussolini's politics had become his masterpiece. I was still in the land
of Flaubert. Art was a surgeon's knife that cut through politics. But
who knows? Push that old Norman into the future with his walrus

moustache, and he might have been the Duce's minister of Home Affairs, in charge of wiretapping. We're all bloody ice-pick men.

Jacobo did paper cutouts for the little girl. He was less of a shadow around her. Ah, I could have had my bar mitzvah on the truck. All we lacked was a fascist rabbi.

We'd entered bandit country, one of the socialist zones, but we didn't come upon their checkpoints. We climbed into the mountains, stopped and relieved ourselves behind the truck. I pissed with Mussolini.

"Duce, the German guards will catch it when Hitler finds out they bought Salò from you."

"Moron, they'll maintain the fiction that I'm in Salò."

"How will the Germans manage that?"

"With a ragazzata," he said. "A mean trick. They'll radio Berlin every night that the Duce is asleep."

Now I grasped why Giacomo Joyce picked the radio over books. Radio was the supreme fiction.

But these mountains were as porous as Salò. We drove into the bloodiest fog. Hals wore a miner's lantern clapped to his skull. Bianca was enthralled by the light. She said it was Jesus' eye. She sat down in her father's lap and prayed to the Madonna of the Mountain. "Madre di montagna, pensacu tu . . ."

All that piety under her eyepatch made us feel like wretches. We were floating towards a kingdom that was imbecilic compared to hers. We were stupid exiles on the road.

The fog had lifted, but our Dutchman began to drift behind the other trucks.

"Hals," I said, "you're losing ground."

"Will be all right, sir. We'll catch them on the downgrade."

Mussolini was paring an apple for our truck. One growl from him, and we might have caught up. But he was beyond the gradations of a mountain road.

We dragged further and further behind until the five trucks were pinpoints in some valley slope. I had a bit of Mussolini's apple, and then the bandits struck. They dropped from the trees. Some of them had pigtails. The rest could have been deserters from the Duce's African corps. They put a knife to Mussolini's neck. It was strange how such undisciplined yobs recognized him under the pillbox hat . . . until I smelled the rat.

Hals was one of them. We'd had a pirate in our lap.

The yobs plucked me out of my greatcoat and stepped on top of me. I told Bianca not to cry.

We had to abandon the truck. They marched us through a field of wild flowers. The pigtails were eying Bianca, and I warned Hals.

"You'll have a mutiny on your hands if the pigtails bother the little girl."

"Yes," he said, with a stinking smile. "Pinocchio's revolt. The pigtails are under orders. They don't attack blind girls."

"Where are we going, Hals?"

"Stuff it," he said. "Since when do we owe you an itinerary?"

"We took you in. We adopted you."

"Bully," he said. "We'll give your master the passion medal."

It was a rough mountain walk. The hills were full of hurly. The flowers clawed our feet. It was like dragging chains along.

"Why did you betray us?"

"That's darling," Hals said. "Your kind murders people, and you expect to cash in on every little loyalty that's coming to you. Sir Pinocchio, you stink."

I had no sense of geography. Was this the bloody Alps, or another mountain chain? We stopped at a bungalow colony in the hills. Hals ordered us into the head bungalow.

I kept Bianca away from the goums and cursed myself for imposing the chimera of a mountain fort on Mussolini. Val Tellina was a bubble in the mind. We should have wrapped ourselves in Salò, challenged the inglesi to work us out of that web.

Bumped into a bandit lady. It was the freckleface, donna Elvira, formerly of the Quirinale. I could sniff who her escort was without having to look up. That secret socialist, Dante Romano. Dante had a red scarf today, not a church collar.

"Buon giorno, Sir Pinocchio. Grazie for bringing your friends to us."

Ah, now the witch's veils were gone. I was the tool of time. Brunhilde's pet. The witch had used me to capture Mussolini.

Dante pulled at his scarf and pranced on his lame foot, that souvenir from Prince Amedeo Street, when the Italian SS put his toes in a mimeograph machine. Here I'd rumbled in my past, discovered the ice-pick man, when I was caught in history's underpants. Brunhilde had been coy with me. The old whore lent me Pinocchio's skin so I could become an accomplice to Mussolini's execution.

Son of a bitch.

FOURTEEN

ANNO 85

THEY fed us rotten macaroni and put us to bed. We lay in Dante's bungalow, having to share army blankets. The count was my blanketmate. A shadow gives you lots of room. The maestro slept with Bianca in the hook of his arm. Clara lay with Mussolini. It was the first time I'd seen them together at night. Until the pirates got him, the Duce would crawl into his private bunker, or return to his wife.

They held each other in that powerful sleep of lovers and children. Clara warbled to herself. Duce touched his nose.

The pirates woke us at five and immediately fell into an argument. They couldn't decide whether to ransom Giacomo Joyce to the Americans or the British.

"The inglesi are moribund," Romano said. "The Americans will pay much higher for literature."

"I disagree," Elvira said. "The English have better taste."

"We shouldn't bargain over him," said the Dutchman. "Give his head to the inglesi, and his balls to the Americans. The crows can have the rest."

I drank their bandit coffee, which tasted like the bark of a worm-infested tree.

Those pirates exercised a slavish democracy. They took a vote on Giacomo Joyce. The Dutchman changed his mind and stood with Dante. The maestro was now American merchandise. Hals pushed him, and the old master shivered, but it wasn't on account of his skin. "Cavaliere," he said to Dante Romano. "Let me take my daughter with me."

"Bianca stays here."

"What purpose will she have in pirate country?"

Dante slapped the old master. "Fascisti like to think of us as pirates. It makes them feel they've surrendered to chaos and not a genuine army. We're socialists, you fool. It's that Big Bastard who sent us underground and obliged us to become pirates."

"Still," the maestro said, "she's a one-eyed girl. What could you possibly do with her?"

"Teach her socialism," donna Elvira said. "Our future lies with Bianca's generation."

"I beg you. Let me stay with my daughter. I'll write for the clandestinos. I'll prepare a socialist novel."

"Maestro," the Duce said. "Don't degrade yourself. Romano, I offer you the kingdom of Italy if you sell my scribbler to the Americans with Bianca Joyce."

"That's not a deal you're in a position to make. You've lost your kingdom and your republic. You're as shabby as Pinocchio."

"I'll go on the radio for you, tell Italians to forget their Duce."

"They have forgotten you," donna Elvira said. "You're the most forgotten man in history."

"Signorina . . ."

"Drink your coffee and shut up."

"I can't drink coffee. I have an ulcer, signorina. I must have milk."

"Find a mountain goat and suck her tit."

They tied the maestro's hands behind his back so he would be a willing cockatoo for the Americans. Bianca mewled in the corner and rumpled her eyepatch. It was time to go to war. I made to lunge at Hals, but Elvira put a gun to the little girl's head.

"I'll blow her brains into the Matterhorn. Mind yourself, Sir Pinocchio."

They shoved Giacomo out the door, into some America over the mountains, and meditated on Mussolini. Dante wanted him killed on the spot.

"Comrades, it's best he disappears. If we present him to the British, they'll have one of their interminable trials, and it will bring sympathy to the old man. The Americans are worse. They'll coddle Mussolini."

"What about the woman?" Elvira asked.

"She's nothing to us. We'll let her go."

"You can't release his whore," the Dutchman said. "She'll write a book about him, and ducismo will start all over again."

Dante laughed. "The whore can have her book."

"And the puppet?"

They all agreed that Sir Pinocchio had to fall with Mussolini. The Dutchman told Claretta to bundle her pajamas. The Popular Army would drive her to Chiavenna, where she could whore her way to Rome.

"Hals is the whore," I said.

The freckleface glared at me. "No one asked your opinion."

"I'm not going," Clara said. "I live with Ben."

Dante shouted at her. "Can't you hear? He's about to lose his license."

Her blue eyes swerved from the pirates to Ben and me. She must have understood years ago the grave she was in.

"I'm not going to Chiavenna."

"Good," said the freckleface. "You'll suffer like his squaw." And then she remembered the shadow that had traveled with us from Salò. Elvira told the count he was free. The pirates didn't have a grudge against him.

The shadow did a funny thing. He declared himself like any bar mitzvah boy. "I live with Pinocchio. I live with Clara. I live with Ben."

They couldn't understand his litany. He was a fascist count who deserved to die.

"We don't have time to kidnap Pius," Dante said. "Mussolini, should we find you a fascist priest?"

"The girl will absolve us."

Duce knelt in front of Bianca, who tickled his neck. She was waiting for her babbo to return from the American side of the mountain.

The pirates marched us into that thick veil of wild flowers. I could have galloped into the next field. But Elvira was shrewd about Sir Pinocchio. She had her machine-pistol on top of Bianca's head. I wasn't sure how a puppet died. Did it have something to do with bread baskets?

The Dutchman volunteered to be our executioner. He stood a yard from Jacobo and ripped him under the neck. His machine-pistol barked like typewriter keys. The count took three steps in the wild flowers and dropped without clutching where the bullets went. Bianca trotted over to him in the grass. Her guardian, donna Elvira, stooped behind her, while she played with a dead man's buttons.

Now the pirates elected Mussolini. Clara jumped in his way, and she died with him as the Dutchman ate up their clothes.

Then Hals bowed to me. "Come, my little friend. We'll destroy this myth of a fascist wooden intelligence once and for all. The Americans will think that you were just another boy."

The bullets hurt. I bled whatever sap I owned. It was like having the worst bronchitis there ever was. My chest splintered out of my shirt. I had fragments in the flowers. Bits of Pinocchio arrived in the trees. I twisted twice, lost the locomotion in my legs, and crashed like a complicated log with carvings on it and sleeves.

But someone's been making a fool of us all. Because I could think and sniff and hear and see as much as I ever could. My features were frozen tight. The old voice was gone. I had a mummy's mouth, but I was the same philosopher. Bullets hadn't robbed me of Flaubert.

We were corpses in Milan.

The pirates delivered us by truck. I'd listened to their debate while we rode down from the hills. The Dutchman wasn't our driver. He sat with us in the bed of the truck. The goums were eating some Berber pie that stank from here to Berlin. They cupped the pies against their lips like an invading army. I kept hearing the smack of their teeth. But it was a disadvantage being dead. I couldn't swing around and survey the truck. The pirates had cropped me in the corner, over a flour barrel. I could see Jacobo and his torn chest. I could see Bianca and the goums. But the pirates themselves were hidden from me. I had to clutch at their words with the ears I had left.

—Comrades, we should dump this Pinocchio. If we hang him in the piazzale, we'll create a morbid puppet show.

—But if we don't exhibit him, the Milanesi will wonder if he still exists. That could be dangerous. What's the harm of ruined wood dancing from a lamppost? People can piss on him, whatever they like.

—There's something human about his proportions . . . and his wounds. People will ask why we had to machine-gun a puppet. And what shall we say? Sir Pinocchio was a desperate character?

—We'll say nothing. Citizens will see the Duce and his puppet hanging together.

Ah, they argued well. To dump or not to dump. That was the burning question. I would have flung the puppet in some ravine, if I'd been in their shoes. Because there was no mistaking the force of my construction. Even with bullet holes, I wasn't Pulcinella.

Bianca was playing with something. That's as far as my eyes could travel. It was Claretta's hair in the little girl's hand. She was nursing the dead. But I couldn't see Claretta beyond her hair. I'd have sacrificed all the lire in my pocket for the gift of turning my neck around.

I was getting angry. Bianca's skirt was up around her knees as she rummaged in the hair, and I didn't have the right vocabulary to lower that skirt. A goum abandoned his pie to meddle in Bianca's business. The bugger pulled on Clara's hair to disarm the child. He did a slow Berber dance in the truck, looking at her thighs. He was a bloody magician. He knotted Clara's hair and produced a kind of doll.

I called on the witch. Brunhilde, will you stuff time under your bloomers and throw that pigtail off the truck?

But it wasn't Brunhilde's bloomers that got touched. The pigtail was exploring Bianca's skirt. He groomed the hair doll with one hand and plumbed Bianca with the other.

We had a holy accident. The wheels must have slapped a giant stone. The truck lurched, and the barrel rocked, and I plunged into the pigtail. The commotion drew donna Elvira. She found the goum with his elbow in Bianca's skirt and she smacked him with her pistol.

"Bruto," she said. "I'll kill you if you ever go near that girl again."

Elvira picked me up and placed me on the barrel. She was much more tender with me now. It takes a corpse to invoke a little kindness.

And then we got to Milan.

The pirates lashed our feet with wire and strung us from the neck of a lamppost. Men, women, and children came to shout and piss. It was the rarest circus. Old men clutched their genitals near the Duce.

"Duce's dead, Duce's dead, Duce's dead."

The fattest women showed me their buttocks. But they hardly remembered Sir Pinocchio. I was part of the fascist entourage. Children danced over to spit. As they knocked at me, I spun around and saw Claretta's face. Her eyes were open. She could have been a woman in a long, hard dream.

"Duce's dead, Duce's dead, Duce's dead."

Rather be a fascist with crumpled knees than a member of that mob. I prayed for a miracle so I could drink their piss and blow it back at them like a bloody whale.

Lovely Brunhilde, let me hang here for a century. It takes time to absorb a landscape with all the spit. I was growing comfortable with my head near the ground. But leave it to a witch! Brunhilde whored me out of Milan.

It was like jumping around in a cradle. I'm no bloody child. I was in a silver bird, flying Concorde. The whore had sailed me back to Jerome. It felt peculiar. I don't mean the ordinary pull of human flesh, the withdrawal pains you'd suffer after leaving your wood behind. Asked the stewardess for a magazine. She brought me the *Washington Post*. I'd landed in April, 1993, a lad of fifty-five. Why should the whore worry if I lost ten years of Copernicus Charyn?

I was like an invalid, cut off from his neighbors on account of a witch.

The stewardess curtsied in the aisle. "How are you, Pinocchio?"

Passengers looked up at this Pinocchio Jerome. They had computer terminals in their laps. I wasn't dumb to 1993. Had my own terminal, sitting on my lap like an obscene toy. I didn't have to pluck at the keyboard to find myself. I must have dreamt through the life of Jerome while I was hiding in Pinocchio. I'd given up adult novels and written a children's book, *Pinocchio 1945.* I was rich, but I'd never be Moby Dick or Molly Bloom.

It hadn't been easy. I'd starved for seven years, scribbling away at a novel. And then I turned to my children's book, finished it in five weeks, and now I was on a safari to France. The entire planet wanted to interview the son of a bitch; journalists had to touch my skin, test how a wooden boy might feel, as if Pinocchio had come off the page to sit on the Concorde with a terminal in his lap.

I'd accepted an invitation from a French magazine, *The Shrunken Overcoat,* to come to Paris. The magazine's editor in chief, Solange Merci-Gâteau, promised there would be no touching. I hadn't agreed to come out of any damn nostalgia, the urge to find chateaus in the street and waltz on the rue George-Sand. I didn't want to rediscover Corsicans and pieds noirs. I preferred the clean, neutral lines of the Eiffel Tower. I was looking for a children's Paris.

Meantime I sat in the belly of a silver bird and drank champagne while the toy in my lap blipped words at me.

    MEET MERCI-GATEAU
    MEET MERCI-GATEAU
    MEET MERCI-GATEAU

I shut the mother off and finished my champagne.

Had a bit of trouble with my passport, which was under the name of Copernicus Charyn. The man in the customs booth would only recognize me as Monsieur Pinocchio, auteur. How could I enter a country as Pinocchio? I'd have to write my next book at la Santé. The man looked sadder and sadder behind his booth.

"Yes, yes, I'm the Pinocchio that you want."

Madame Merci-Gâteau was waiting on the other side of customs. She was a freckleface, like donna Elvira, my old enemy from the Quirinale. Taller than Pinocchio, she had wild red hair that aroused me in a terrible way. Tried to shake her hand.

"Where's your luggage?" she asked. But I was traveling light; I had extra underwear in my coat pocket.

I entered Solange's car, and she drove us onto a highway that could have been in the heart of New Jersey. "When do we get to Paris, Madame Gâteau?"

"Soon," she said, and I was grateful she didn't paw me, like other journalists did.

We passed enormous concrete bunkers that bit into the sky, bunkers with clouds painted on them, clouds and candy stripes. Ah, these were the suburbs of Paris. They'd become cliff dwellers in the old banlieue.

We landed on a boulevard, and Solange stopped the car. We were outside le Palais des Cocottes, a restaurant that reminded me of the Bronx Botanical Garden. It had plants and trees and a great glass wall; I could see people eating and drinking wine between tall plants. But Solange wouldn't take me into the arbor house; she pointed to a terrace at the side of le Palais des Cocottes that was slim and had no plants at all.

"Madame, can't we eat in there?" I asked, looking inside the glass wall.

"Don't be silly, Jérôme. That's for hillbillies, tourists, and clowns."

"But it's so much prettier to eat in the middle of an arbor."

"This is Paris, mon coco. Who would you like to meet?"

"The hunchback of Notre Dame," said Pinocchio Jerome, whose entire history had come out of books.

"Idiot," she said. "Just keep your mouth shut and we'll both be better off. Let me do the talking for you."

And Solange led me into that narrow zone of tables and chairs, away from the arbor that I liked. We had a table in the corner, with our own computer terminal, but Pinocchio couldn't get away from other people. They breathed and talked right near my nose.

Solange presented me with contracts to sign. Tried to scribble *Copernicus Charyn*, but she insisted on the signature of Pinocchio.

"What am I signing, tell me, please?"

"It's nothing. Some people want to use your name on a bar of soap."

Then a man with a napkin around his neck approached me and whispered, "Would you like to be kidnapped, old boy? It can be arranged. You'll never have to work another day in your life."

Before Pinocchio Jerome could answer, Solange kicked at the man and scolded him in French.

"Who is that guy?" I asked.

"Nobody," she said. "An Arab gangster."

"He doesn't look like an Arab," I said. "He isn't dark."

"What do you know from dark? He powders his face, that's all. Under his powder, he's blacker than Othello."

People kept brushing against Pinocchio. It was worse than Rome in this little casino, with everybody wanting to lay a hand on me and feel if I was human or not.

"Yes," I finally shouted. "I'd prefer to be kidnapped."

Solange told me to shut up. I had a piece of lettuce and the bill arrived on the terminal screen. Solange ignored the bill. She used the screen as a mirror for her lip ice, shoveled me out of my corner, returned me to her car, reached over, kissed me on the mouth, with her tongue slapping inside my face and her lip ice all over me, and then she pushed Pinocchio aside.

"Please," I said. "The Eiffel Tower. We don't have to climb to the top . . . just one little look."

"It's being repaired, you idiot. It's all bandaged up."

She drove me to the wild lands near the airport, and I was more downhearted than I'd ever been. It wasn't a very kind thing to be human, with a redheaded woman kissing you and chauffeuring you around, as if you were some lousy article, like a bar of soap. Wished someone would restore me to the tranquility of wood. But my fairy godmother wouldn't listen. Here I was, a fancy bar of soap with human eyes and ears, an article called Pinocchio, being returned to the USA . . .

But I disappeared from the Concorde lounge. I wasn't finished with Paris. Pinocchio Jerome hired a taxicab. "Parc Montsouris."

Had an urge to witness Guignol one last time, but the puppet tent was closed at Montsouris. Guignol must have gone out of fashion in an age of computer toys.

I strolled up to the tabac of Monsieur le prince. I hadn't come to greet the new tobacconist. Felt sorry for the dead Monsieur. He'd ruled Paris from his tiny flat until he got his throat cut in that endless war with the black foots. Monsieur le prince was like some Guignol who didn't have children in the tent to shout for him. His crime was that he loved Marie-Pierre.

Poked my head into that Corsican tabac, and I had a fright. This tobacconist was the ghost of Montsouris. He had a grizzled beard around his moustache, but I wouldn't forget a fire eater. Alain San Angelo occupied the seat of Monsieur le prince.

He called to me from his tobacco counter. "Pinocchio, you've risen in this world. Come inside."

Now I was feeling like Guignol, in need of a chorus to shout, "Méchant, méchant." But I went into the bloody tabac.

Alain wore his cousin's vest with the different money pockets. We sat in the corner and drank cognac.

"What happened to your mistress Blondine?"

"Blondine retired to Bordeaux."

"Who retired her? The church or the state?"

"I found her a little handkerchief shop."

He could have been one of Balzac's merchants, or Balzac himself, creating a handkerchief shop in Bordeaux with all the thievery of a novelist.

"Liked Blondine," I said. "She was a good accomplice for a fire eater."

"Stupid, why do you think I have a beard? My mouth is still raw from the fire."

"So you climbed into your cousin's shoes. Alain, is it a tight fit?"

"Dumbo, I could shoot your eyes out before you got to the street."

Ah, I had the son of a bitch. He wasn't Balzac. He was a yardbird looking for his fix. Bet my life as a children's novelist that he wasn't happy outside the walls of la Santé.

"Tell me, Alain, who cut Monsieur's throat?"

"I did. He was about to slip. He'd decided to protect an errand boy named Jérôme."

"You didn't cut his throat. He'd never have allowed you to get that intimate. It was either my uncle or my aunt. He'd have let Marie near enough. He was crazy about her."

Alain marched behind his shelves and returned with something that was bloody familiar. "I've been holding this for you . . . until you got famous. You left it on your last trip." Alain had my yellow scarf. "Put it on, will you? I didn't throw arsenic into the silk."

I wore the scarf with a fluff at my throat.

"Where the hell is my aunt? Are you hiding her, Alain?"

"You crazy? She's on a scholarship from the San Angelos . . . Antoine is part of the package. She's still in love with that nigger. You can look for them at le Wigwam."

"My old hotel? Couldn't you have done a little fancier than that?"

"They have the best suite," Alain said. "We own le Wigwam."

"What about a room for me?"

"Can't have Pinocchio running around the halls. You're too popular this season. You'll excite the clientele. Come back when you're obscure."

"What if this Pinocchio madness never ends?"

"Pray it does, or you'd better keep out of Paris."

I wondered which name Marie was using at le Wigwam. Copernic or Montesquieu? But then I figured that a black foot who'd gone out of business wouldn't want to advertise himself. I asked for Madame Copernic. The concierge fell all over Monsieur Pinocchio. I had to sign her little black book of illustrious guests.

Went up to discover my fate in Madame Copernic. Alain wasn't fooling. Marie-Pierre didn't have my old closet at le Wigwam. Her suite came with toilet, fridge, and color tv.

She was more beautiful in this stinking hotel than she'd ever been on Washington Square. She served me Russian tea in a metal holder. All that was lacking was a charlotte russe.

"Romey, why the hell are you crying?"

"Family," I muttered. "Can't help it." I touched my nose to the yellow scarf.

Going into wood can teach you things. It was clear to me why auntie could never have been with Jérôme. It had nothing to do with Bronx Science. Auntie might have loved a high school teacher. I was part of the sepolti vivi, those who buried themselves alive. I'd lived in the belly of the whale, a stinking mytholeptic, a golem producing golems on the page.

"Forgive me," I said. "For hurting you. I poisoned your head at Bronx Science. I told lies. Kafka was a bedbug."

"Romey, you were the best teacher a girl could have."

"But look how you ended up . . . a prisoner to the San Angelos."

"We're not prisoners," Antoine said. "The San Angelos pay us to keep the pieds noirs out of their hair."

I watched this Montesquieu. He was as fluid as an opera singer. I was jealous, because the black foot had Marie.

"Where's Edgar?" I asked. My little cousin had taken to the streets. He ran with the lulus, bad boys from the suburbs who'd descend upon Paris and return to those bunkers I'd seen in Solange's car. Their favorite targets were Arabs and older people. The lulus had a dash of politics to them. Their plunder wasn't without purpose. They were practicing war drills, preparing for the time when the Russians or Bulgarians invaded Paris.

"Does the boy ever come home?"

"When he feels like it," Antoine said.

"But couldn't you get a tutor for him?"

"Yes," auntie said. "Your answer is always some kind of school. Edgar doesn't want schooling. He wants the street."

"Ask him to visit me in America, please."

Hugged her and Antoine, and I sailed out of the hotel. Couldn't tell where my natural country was.

Walked a bit, got away from the boulevards.

Heard footsteps behind me. Figured Alain might have come up from Montsouris to climb on my tail. But it was only the blue-eyed nigger, Antoine Montesquieu. He'd followed me out of le Wigwam.

"Jérôme."

Ah, he'd gotten his old shivering voice back. Was it camouflage for the street? His eyes weren't so frigging blue. They had that deep stranded color I remembered from the Goutte. He was Philippe's brother again, a victim of the Corsican wars. And the son of a bitch had no one to soothe him. Pinocchio couldn't have played Philippe Montesquieu.

"I lied to you. We're San Angelo's bowwow, his pet dog. We bark in our rooms, and he pays the rent."

"Why can't you and auntie bark on your own?"

"Not in Paris, Jérôme. We still belong to Monsieur le prince."

"Monsieur was killed ten years ago. How can he hold you in his debt?"

"He howls at us, howls from his grave. We all murdered Monsieur. Alain, Marie, your uncle, myself."

"Then it was Copernicus who paid Alain to eat a little fire. Uncle was grooming him to become a tobacconist."

"Yes."

"And you visited Monsieur with auntie. It was perfect. Monsieur figured you were harmless without Philippe, a black foot who'd been his brother's echo. He ogled Marie and forgot about you, and you cut his throat. But what the hell did uncle have to gain?"

"He couldn't manipulate Monsieur. They'd been quarreling. Your uncle wanted to expand, Monsieur was in a contracting mood."

"So you retired him for uncle."

"Monsieur killed my brother. I had every right . . ."

"And auntie Pierre?"

"She didn't have much of a choice. Monsieur would have claimed her for himself. Didn't he put a bomb in the Goutte d'Or to get her back?"

"Yeah," I said. "Love does that to people . . . makes them into killers and gets them killed. Uncle offered her Paris and you for Monsieur's life. But he didn't live long enough to find auntie a good umbrella. Bathsheba gummed up the works. She died, and uncle's house fell apart. You should have kept away from Paris."

"How? Alain couldn't afford to have us too far from him. He threatened to kill Edgar if we didn't become his permanent guests at le Wigwam. He was being charitable. Alain could have given us a plot in Montparnasse, and there would have been no one to link him with Monsieur's death. But he made a promise to your uncle."

"So you all sit while Monsieur howls from his grave. What if the howling gets too much for him and Alain decides to murder you in spite of the promise? Or suppose his house happens to fall. You'd be at the mercy of the next tobacconist."

"Marie still wouldn't leave Paris. She's been a wanderer too long. Her home's le Wigwam."

"Then help me kidnap Edgar, for God's sake. Why should Edgar be caught in your little doom machine?"

"He'd never go with you. He has his gang."

"His gang," I said. "Antoine, should I buy a revolution? You could reorganize the Goutte, push Alain below the parc Montsouris."

"I'll stay in le Wigwam."

The black foot scampered to auntie Pierre. Ah, I'll revive the Giovanis and raid Alain's tabac. Or should I beg Brunhilde to quiet Monsieur?

I was pondering this when I discovered a gang robbing peaches and pears from an Arab grocer. Could have waltzed around these lulus. The street was wide enough. But how could I get clear of the grocer's screams? The lulus were whacking him with old, bundled-up magazines.

The grocer still had plenty of fruit. I hurled soft peaches at the bad boys. The peaches came home with an ugly plop, hitting lulus high on the shoulder. They screamed as loud as the grocer did. They must have thought some gang from a fiercer neighborhood was going to seize them by the pants.

The lulus whirled around and abandoned the grocer to knock on my skull with their magazines. Then the pounding stopped.

The lulus jabbered among themselves. Each of them was carrying a pocket book with a big nose on the cover, *Pinocchio 1945*. They surrounded me and took a deep sniff. I was another bad boy, Pinocchio Jérôme, their cousin from the Bronx. They hugged me like crazy, while I cast about for their leader. The little bitch finally surfaced. He'd been skulking behind his fascist friends. Now he stood tall as auntie Pierre, but with Lionel's mug on him, like a flag to ruin Pinocchio. He signaled to the lulus and escorted me away. We drank Schweppes at a local fascist dive.

"Come to America," I said. "You don't have to cannibalize the streets."

"Cannibalize? I'm a Parisian boy."

"But your gang lives out in the bunkers."

"They wouldn't if their papas could afford Paris."

I remembered Edgar as an infant, and here he was with whiskers on him, reasoning like a bloody adult.

"But you can't believe the Bulgarians will grab the Eiffel Tower."

"Not unless the Americans bag it first."

"What would Uncle Sam want with the Eiffel Tower?"

"Booty. Something for the treasure chest. Isn't that why *Pinocchio 1945* was so successful? The wooden boy who loves to go to war."

"Jesus," I said. "It began as a story to cure you of dyslexia."

"Uncle Romey, you published it years after I was out of your life."

"I'm not your uncle. I'm your cousin. Can't we be friends?"

"Friends with Pinocchio? Where were you all these years?"

"Absorbed in a novel," I said. "It failed. But now I'm a children's writer. I have more time."

"And what are your plans, cousin? To become a lulu like us? You're too old for that. Go to America where you belong."

"What about your future?"

"My future's here," he said, pointing to that fascist bistro, with its alley of computerized pinball games, like a road to Venus. He paid for the Schweppes, kissed me on the cheek, and caught up with his gang of lulus. And I was left with bubbles in my glass, the old fart of Paris. I meant to take off my stockings and go up to Normandy. Not in homage to Flaubert. I'd walk into the Atlantic and join a school of whales. Because Pinocchio was a sea animal, in the end.

But I didn't get to Norman country. I found a freckleface in the street.

"Solange, have you been following me?"

"Imbecile, this is my quartier. What are you doing here? I delivered you to the Concorde."

"I couldn't stay. I had urgent business in Paris."

"Come," she said, clawing my hand, and this time she delivered me to a concrete waste disposal plant. Wrong. It was a housing development on the rue Commandant Mouchotte. The caverns near the bottom were garages, not mouths where the garbage went in. Our elevator had slogans lipsticked on the wall.

Toujours les lulus, les lulus toujours!

We arrived at a concrete terrace, adorned with concrete flower pots, and strolled into a garden of metal trees, tinseling in the sun. Don't kid yourself. Metal can bloom on the vine. The trees were as alive as Pinocchio's nose.

Mounted another elevator and rode up to Solange's flat. She had six keys to open her lock, and I wondered if anarchy could ride an elevator. But I shouldn't begrudge the trip. Solange had a view of the Eiffel Tower. It looked like an enormous radio bird, ready for Anno 85. Solange hadn't lied about the bandages near the top. The Eiffel Tower had a wounded skull.

"What are you gaping at, mon coco? I have to leave for a dinner party in fifteen minutes. Undress me, you dope."

Couldn't make much sense of Gâteau's commands. Because she stripped herself like a bloody whirlwind, and did much the same to me. I was delirious about the freckles on her front and rear. We lay on a bed that occupied most of the flat. A simple black-and-white tv grew out of the blankets. The fridge was in the bed frame. She had pencils and lamps around the pillows. Solange's bed was a self-sufficient ark.

I was afraid I'd bollix things. I couldn't schnozzle her with that rude fountain pen I carried between my legs. It didn't feel right. I was cumbersome in the flesh. But Solange wasn't cross with me.

"What's bothering you, Jérôme?"

I remembered to bite her neck. Her freckles deepened. And I started to travel with the pen. It was peculiar, lying face to face, as if we were having a conversation. I tell you, orgasm is an overrated thing. My head slapped the stars for half a minute, but then the stars were gone, and you were stuck with a fountain pen that dribbled useless ink.

Solange didn't bully me about it. She kissed Pinocchio. Merci-Gâteau had the sweetest fuzz on her lip. It was like kissing a unicorn, or some other magical beast. I was beginning to enjoy the human way, mouth to mouth, lip to lip. And then Solange hopped off the bed.

"Donkey, I have to dress."

She was lovely in that map of freckles on her skin. The old pen was acting up, but Madame Gâteau wouldn't hear of it. She got into her clothes, piece by piece. Solange was in a big hurry. She ironed her skirt while she stood in it, the steam iron fitting the contours of her body like a toy train married to a hill.

"Don't bother with your pants, darling. Wait for me."

Solange was out the door, and I remained on her ark, with the Eiffel Tower in her window, trying to guess what the bandages were about. The old tower was being tarted up to introduce the twenty-first century to France. But I couldn't get into a heat over Anno 85.

I was hungry. I'd have gone into the street and scared up a croissant, but I couldn't solve the machinery of Solange's locks. The door wouldn't open from the inside. I was condemned to that concrete bunker until the freckleface returned from her party. But I willed Solange back to Commandant Mouchotte. The locks turned with all their counterweights, like a mysterious heart, and I had Madame Gâteau.

This Solange smelled different. The freckles were too perfect on her face. Pieces of geometry. The red hair burned a little too deep. It wasn't Solange at all. I had the witch of time.

I played with Brunhilde, pretended not to see beyond the freckles.

I nuzzled her the human way, valleying under her chemise. I laid Solange's steam iron on her chest and practiced ironing her skin. But the old whore wasn't susceptible to a human boy.

Gave up pretending and confronted the witch.

"Brunhilde, why'd you take me off that lamppost in Milan?"

She shrugged and pulled on the freckles until she had the bone-white color of a witch. "You should have accepted me as Solange. I'd have made you happy."

"I'm tired of tricks. What happened in Milan?"

"Nothing special. I had to get rid of Pinocchio. He wasn't meant for the history books. Philosophers will say he was an example of Italian hysteria, a fascist myth."

"But I wrote about him."

"Certainly. He's allowable in children's novels. But we can't have Pinocchio be the number-two fascist. People will get the idea that magic exists and they'll never go back to the ordinary. The planet would fall on its ass."

"One thing, Brunhilde. Why did the black-market lady, Mamma Madrigale, spit in Pinocchio's face? It's like a tick that eats at me."

"She wasn't spitting at Pinocchio, my dear. Madrigale was spitting at Jerome."

"That's preposterous. Madrigale couldn't have known about the pact I had with you."

"She didn't have to. She realized you weren't the same Pinocchio. Imbecile, you meddled in their business."

"How could I have meddled with a black marketeer?"

"That was only one of her ventures. She saved Jews on the side."

"Madrigale was with the underground?"

"She worked alone. But she did have one hook into the fascist war machine."

"The German admirals at the Villa Wolkonsky."

"No. She had an accomplice much closer to Mussolini."

"An Italian fascist. Who?"

Brunhilde looked at me with her witch's eye. "Sir Pinocchio."

Didn't feel a fist in my heart. Nothing blunt as that. But I was getting giddy. The ark seemed to lift off the ground, into a concrete paradise. Then I caught myself and forced the ark back down near Brunhilde. "Pinocchio was an anti-Semite, you lousy witch. He introduced the yellow hat."

"Poor dear Jérôme, the yellow hat was a means of placating Mussolini and also smuggling Jews. The fascists fell asleep over that yellow hat. They thought Pinocchio was tagging every Jew outside the ghetto. He gave them yellow hats so they could walk from the ghetto to the military vans Madrigale was buying with her black-market money."

"I don't believe you. He was a vicious hollow boy. I had to undo his harm, stop the Giovanis from beating up old men."

Brunhilde took me by the hand. "Come with me."

"What will you prove? You're a witch. You can decide on any scenario from the past. You have no respect."

"Come with me."

She caressed her blue hair and we drove through Solange's wall like razor blades. We were in Rome, on the Via Catalana, nicknamed Stinking Heart Street because of the old Jews that bled out their lives in its alleys. Brunhilde had put a veil over us on the Via Catalana. Jews and gentiles couldn't see the witch and her disciple. I discovered a lad with a yellow hat. It was only optional headgear in the ghetto, and the boy stood out. He wore a mask, like a medieval Jewish clown. But this was a cunning mask, a rubber mold of Pinocchio's face to frighten Jews, or so it seemed. But I wasn't fooled. What better way to be anonymous? Pinocchio disguised as Pinocchio. He was free to wander as he wished. No one would have disturbed this gruesome clown.

The clown had Pinocchio's handle on him. The fingers below his cuffs were wood. He was ticketing Jews for Madrigale's vans. He'd brush men and women on Stinking Heart Street, crumple slips of paper into their pockets, with rendezvous points written on them, points where the vans would load up with Jewish passengers.

He got rid of all his tickets and strolled out of the ghetto. Pinocchio took off his rubber mask on the far side of the Via Arenula and marched for half a block with the softest face you could imagine on wood. This wasn't the puppet that grew out of my Pinocchio book. He was a different creature. His eyes weren't short of liquid. They shone like bloody jewels against the burnished wood. Then he put on his fascist face, assumed a vicious sneer, and Romans acknowledged him.

"Ecco—Sinbado!"

And all I'd ever bothered with was that sneer. I'd lived in Pinocchio as my own loveless phantom.

"Brunhilde, let's get out of here."

"Shall I take you to Merci-Gâteau?"

"Niente," I said. "I'll try America."

FIFTEEN

GEORGE MILLS

MISSED that little bugger. Mourned Pinocchio. I dreamt of a new edition, *Pinocchio Perfect.* But how would customers respond to a bad boy who wasn't authentically bad? Ah, I kept Pinocchio to myself.

Had a new home, a penthouse over Abington Square. It was the spoils of successful authorship. I could prance around Manhattan from my terrace. I didn't preen over the long tube of Empire State. I preferred Ninth, Tenth, and Eleventh avenues, a circus of red and brown caves that seemed to have no end.

Earned a million in royalties last year. Only one other writer earned more. George Mills. But he didn't do it on children's novels. George was a serious bugger. He deals with the Literary Guild. He's the successor to Dickens, Kafka, and James Joyce. "Mills has the true arc of comedy in his writing," says the Literary Guild. "Mills has no equal in America."

I was a stinking children's artist. I couldn't compete with George Mills. All I had was *Blue Eyes over Miami*.

Got an invitation to attend a writers' conference in Austin, Texas. I would be the star children's writer. I was about to decline the invitation. Who needed seven thousand dollars? My accountant was ordering me to earn less and less, or I'd float away on income taxes. But then I looked down the list of divas who'd promised to come:

> Raphael Canker
> Marvela Ming
> Byron Paderewski
> George Mills

Wired the conference: I accept. Donate my fee to the Fresh Air Fund. Pinocchio.

The mothers who ran the conference must have misinterpreted the wire. They sent me my fee in advance, with hotel reservations and airline tickets. These arrived the old-fashioned way, in a stamped envelope, because I wouldn't keep a bloody terminal on Abington Square.

I shivered in Texas. The sky was Roman blue. Austin didn't have palm trees, or I might have wept for Pinocchio's lost home. The stars of the conference were put up at the Burlington, an old cattlemen's hotel with an ancient portico on one side and a modern glass entrance on the other. It was like having Anno 85 and early Texas on the same street.

I lived on the grubby side of the Burlington, over the shoeshine parlors, the Mexican bars and cowboy inns, the dry cleaner's that sold root beer while you waited, the finance companies and secondhand furniture shops. That was Texas from my window.

The other writers shunned me. Raphael Canker wouldn't be seen with Pinocchio. Byron Paderewski and Marvela Ming were escaping from their husbands together. They sat in the Burlington coffee shop and never even nodded when I arrived for my morning ice cream soda. And the great man, Mills, kept to his suite at the Burlington. He wouldn't answer his phone. The Guild hadn't been wrong about him. He did have a comic arc. He was Kafka in St. Louis. But I couldn't get near the son of a bitch.

Our conference was held in the senate chamber of the state capitol. I wondered where the senate was while we were gathering. The chief of the conference, Taylor Stern, assured me that the senate didn't convene more than once or twice a year. "Mr. Charyn, we're not stepping on anyone's toes. Texas is glad to have us."

Stern was a lecturer at the University of Arizona. I didn't dare ask what he was doing in Austin. He looked like some transplanted Pinocchio. We got along, but I had the bastard's end of the conference, the children's hour. Students of adult fiction wouldn't come to my lectures. I had mad-eyed men and women. They sat in the chamber, and I stuffed them with the wisdom of writing for young readers.

"Never write down, my dears. Children won't stand for it. Give them the whole blast. They'll either love you, or hate you. Dickens was a children's writer, but he never realized it. Mark Twain is mediocre in the books he triggered for grownups. *Lolita* is a children's novel. Kafka never cared about adults. Swift had a bitter root that children admire. His Gulliver belongs in Lewis Carroll. What is it that children love? Stories, mates. They expect to die with laughter or fright. That's what they desire from the page . . ."

A man blundered into the chamber in the middle of my speech. He had green suspenders under a bald head. His fly was open. A dinner napkin was attached to his waist. His skin was whiter than a witch. The yob had a cane, but wouldn't walk with it. The cane was hooked under the napkin. He wobbled to the front row and sat near the lectern. I knew him from his book jackets and the conference brochure. I'd bagged the great man, George Mills.

Once he got to his chair he unhooked the cane and sat with his chin on the handle, staring at me. I wasn't going to let him win. I had a right to exist with my Pinocchio book. Mills had written an epic about a lost Russian whaler that captures St. Louis from the American navy. It was a genius idea, and in my own bloody heart I wish I could have written *Captain Fyodor,* by George Mills.

"Mills," I said. "Mills is the quintessential children's writer." I waited for him to challenge me.

"What is *Captain Fyodor* about? Politics? No. Morals? No. It's a children's story. What's a whaler doing in the Mississippi? Mills' answer is why not? And how can one ship overcome an entire navy? Through the persistence of dreams. The author willed it so. It's the logic of a line on the page, crafted with its own authority. Children are the first to spot a fake. They'll look at you and tell you if you stink. But I'd bet my life they wouldn't speak dirty of Mills."

We had a question-and-answer period. Mills said nothing. Taylor Stern initiated a round of clapping. Mills didn't clap. The mad-eyed came up to get my autograph. I shook hands, promised to read manuscripts. The chamber emptied. Mills sat.

I was alone with him on the senate floor.

"I'm Pinocchio Charyn," I said, under the strain of his silence. There was, after all, a frigging line from Joyce to Faulkner to Mills.

"Will you have some coffee with me, George?"

His chin hadn't moved from the handle of his cane. "The trouble with you, Charyn, is that you have no guts. I liked *Blue Eyes over Miami.*"

"Then you're an audience of one. It sold six hundred copies. The book was remaindered two months after it came out. Shall I tell you what *Newsweek* said about it? Nothing. *Time* put it on its obituary list. The only real review was in the *Miami Herald.* Two hundred words about my references to Miami Beach."

"Don't give me hard-luck stories. I've had books buried worse than that. I learned how to write from *Blue Eyes over Miami.* You were my hero until you fell into Pinocchio. You went for the quick buck."

I was getting angry at the guy with the green suspenders. "Look who's talking? The sweetheart of the Literary Guild."

"The Guild has nothing to do with me. It dances with my publisher. I write the books."

"What's so bad about Pinocchio, George?"

"You copped the story, smoothed it out, peppered it with Mussolini and his mistress. I grew up on Pinocchio. I didn't want it tampered with."

"But Pinocchio is the story of my life."

"Ah," said George Mills. "Aint we all bad boys. You didn't have to steal him from us."

He got up, hooked his cane into his pants, and wobbled out of the senate. The great man had skewered me on my own stick. *Blue Eyes over Miami.*

I sat in a Mexican bar on Old Pecan Street. I wasn't an author to the yobs who drank with me. The bar was flooded with "undocumented people," aliens who'd missed out on the last census, invisible men and women clutching bottles of dark Christmas beer in February. I ate migas at the bar, eggs fried with onions, tomatoes, crumpled taco chips, and white cheese. I had it for breakfast, dinner, and lunch. I nursed my sorrow with migas and Mexican Christmas beer. George Mills. Couldn't he have let me go my way as a children's writer? George Mills.

I'd come to Texas, hadn't I? Austin wasn't the Panhandle, but I'd find Belinda Hogg, prove she did exist, and make peace with my past. There had to be a Belinda and Tati, the octopus. Boys of seven don't manufacture myths. Why wouldn't Brunhilde help me? She could have whirled me back to 1944. But I'd do without the witch. I had magic left, in my migas. I sat with all the undocumented women and men and prayed to the original Pinocchio, the Pinocchio of George Mills.

"Brother, let me be my own good fairy tonight."

I blew on the migas and muttered 1944. Nothing shook. Tables didn't shiver under me, but I was back on Charlotte Street. The first smell I caught was minestrone. Then I smelled sardines. Andrusov had

to be in the neighborhood. She'd gone to her bedroom to lie down with
Bitter Morris. The secondhand boys and girls were asleep in their little
dormitory. I peeked in. There was no Belinda. I looked around for
Tatiana's barrel. Where the hell was that lovely girl with her dark ink?
I found one stinking barrel with brine and cloves and half-sour pickles.
I dug with my hands. Tati wasn't under the pickle juice.

I sniffed another presence in Andrusov's narrow parlor. Didn't have
to turn and look. I saw him with that secret eye any child of Charlotte
Street had in the furrows at the back of his head. It was a man-boy in
a pink striped suit, with pink tie, pink shirt, pink vest, pink suede shoes,
the mark of 1944, when soldiers had to wear shit brown. Pink defied
everything.

Lionel was sucking Chesterfields. He had silver rings and a gold
tiepin. Uncle bribed me with a cigarette. I smoked like a fiend at seven.

"I'll get you pussy," he said.

"Lionel, what do I have to do?"

"Close your eyes for ten minutes."

"What will happen to Andrusov?"

Uncle slapped the cigarette from my mouth. I scrambled for it.

"Texas pussy," he said. "She'll play octopus with you."

"What's that?"

"You'll see. You'll never want to do anything again once you play
octopus."

He blew on his rings and a fat whore came out of the dark. She was
one of those women who wore bandannas on the fire escapes. She
looked enormous, wider than Andrusov.

"Sonya, entertain the kid. He's my sister's brat. Give him the octopus to play with."

Uncle went behind the big fat whore. I tried not to look at the tits
in her bandanna. I asked about the octopus. "Where is it?"

"In the barrel," she said.

"There's only pickles in there."

She told me to get undressed.

"What for?"

"To find Tatiana, stupid."

I undressed for Sonya, putting my socks into my shoes.

"You're not finished," she said. "Off with your underwear."

She wouldn't let me clap my hand to my groin. Sonya turned me upside down and dunked me into the barrel. My ears swam in the brine. My eyes burned with pickle juice. Sonya hoisted me up.

"Did you see Tati yet?"

"Noooo."

"Look a little harder."

She dunked me again, holding me by the ankles. That's how I got baptized in holy water. The pickles bumped softly against my skull. Told myself they were octopus arms.

Sonya let me up to breathe Andrusov's air.

"Tati," I said. "Tatiana. I saw the old girl."

"Don't lie," she said. "You're only trying to please me. What did she say to you from the bottom of the barrel?"

"Texas pussy."

Sonya frowned.

I was worried. The whore's eyes bulged at me, and her bandanna unloosened a bit. "What did she say?"

I took a chance with Sonya, because even at seven I could tell she was crazy.

"Texas pussy."

She didn't go and get a towel to dry me off. Sonya licked me with her tongue, drank the brine from my face. It was the nicest feeling in the world, Sonya's tongue. Then she pushed me under the bandanna, cradled me there, and I was home free, safe as a stinking little god . . . until Lionel reappeared.

His lips were gray against the pink armor of his vest. The upper lip was frozen into a curl, like a wolf. He walked with dizzy steps.

"How's my watchman?" he said to the boy inside Sonya's bandanna, riding a hull of tits.

"Uncle, what was I watching for?"

"Snoopers and brats who might have gotten up to have a pee."

"No one peed," I said. "It was quiet." I'd have said anything to stay inside the hull. But Sonya swept me out of there and ordered me into my clothes. Then she and Lionel left the parlor.

That's as deep as memory goes. Did I wake the secondhand boys and girls, tiptoe into the bedroom, and discover Morris and Andrusov lying sweetly with ice picks in their skulls? It was like old times. I was Lionel's shill, shielding him while he did the dirty. But where was Belinda Hogg?

I walked the capitol grounds. You could see that pink building through the trees, with a goddess of liberty at the top, holding the star of Texas in her hand. She had the damnedest job. This capitol never closed. It belonged to the people of Texas, and it was in service twenty-four hours a day. Pedestrians used it as a thoroughfare, foraging into the shopping district from its great hall. The governor had a mansion across the street. No one seemed to remember the governor's name. He was in and out of office every few years, and it was a public nuisance, because each time a governor got elected, it took a week to rotate the portraits of earlier governors to make room for the son of a bitch.

But the lieutenant governor didn't have his portrait on the wall. He lived in the capitol, had his own apartment on the second floor. He's the one who lent the capitol to the writers' conference. His name was Briney, and he was a distant cousin to Taylor Stern. I was beginning to understand Texas politics. Briney seemed to have only one wish. He'd been lieutenant governor fifty-six years, and he wanted Texas to become her own country before he died.

He considered himself a disciple of FDR. "I was preparing a deal with that man. If he'd lived out his fourth term and gone for a fifth, we might have gotten Texas back from him."

"Briney, you're turning Roosevelt into a man of the South."

"So he was. So he was."

His favorite writer was George Mills, and I'd go onto the grounds with Briney, discussing George. It stopped me from thinking about the boy who'd helped murder Andrusov and Bitter Morris. No wonder I'd frozen the memory of Tatiana around Andrusov's death. It was to keep me from looking at myself.

"Yes," I said, "Mills. He's done his *Moby Dick*. Now he ought to give the other guy a chance."

The old lieutenant governor gave me a hug. "Don't be irritable, Pinocchio. You and George work in different leagues."

We stumbled into a preacher burning books on the capitol lawn as a protest to the writers' conference. Briney could have had him arrested, but he tolerated this sort of thing. The preacher hardly had a following. Two men with dirty faces. Bums, I imagine, who slept inside the capitol. The preacher himself had a grubby chin.

I watched him burn Cervantes, feeding pages to the bonfire he'd built. He was quiet for a preacher. Briney dug a five-dollar bill into the preacher's pocket.

"He's a loon, but he has to eat."

That preacher seemed a touch familiar under the dirt. Had he once been a mad scrabbler in the Bronx?

Briney returned to his apartment, and I strolled further south, feeling an odd doom behind me. I was chasing my own tail. Not even migas could help. I was everybody's accomplice, the universal shill. And then I heard a funny song, like a spoon going into my ear.

> Belinda Hogg, Belinda Hogg,
> Aint she the sweetest Texas frog.

The preacher was as quiet as ever. Nothing came from his direction but the crackle of books in a bonfire.

Brunhilde must have been taking vengeance on my own poor scratching at my past. The witch was jealous of her preserves, as if she had the only copyright around.

> Belinda Hogg, Belinda Hogg
> Aint she the sweetest Texas frog.

And then I made a kind of skip and fell into that song. It was Sonya singing from the fire escape. I was sucking cigarettes with Lionel and enjoying the song.

"What does that lady do, Lionel?"

"She gives it away. Belinda Hogg."

"Uncle, can I have some Belinda?"

"Ask her, you twitch."

But I was shy about that bandanna above me, and Lionel had to ask.

"Sonya, my nephew wants to taste your frog."

"He's too young."

Lionel began to protest in his pink suit.

"Young? When he's a Tatar like me?"

"Then bring the Tatar upstairs."

"I will," Lionel said. "One day soon, when you deserve him."

And uncle drove me out from under Sonya's song. Took me fifty years to get back to Belinda, like a bloody time surgeon. Only the knife was in Brunhilde's hand. I was the witch's little commander in chief.

Began to lecture less and less. Pinocchio Freud, absorbed in the curls of his navel, a time detective. How come this Sonya had removed herself from my Charlotte Street itinerary for so long? Her bandanna was a feint, something to hurl Pinocchio off the mark.

It wasn't tits, I tell you. It was Sonya's face. She had that dark concentration of Bathsheba. Another cool witch. You couldn't win Sonya's love. She packaged herself on the fire escape, preened in her bandanna, and sang of Belinda Hogg. Me and uncle fell for the witch. We were always in love with the same fucking women. Our disease wasn't so different. We were waiting for my mother's smile. Bathsheba would hoard her smile like a miser, give it and take it back.

My father Bruno abandoned the witch, went to look for Belinda on Crotona Park East. But the furrier's widow didn't turn out to be a sweet Texas frog. Bruno died without Bathsheba.

And Lionel? He became a millionaire to avoid the bafflement of his

sister's smile. La Gioconda of the Black Sea. He married another
enigmatic lady, chased that smile. His millions brought him shit. He
should have stayed on Charlotte Street with his pink suit. Sonya could
only have hurt him a little bit. Sonya was my mother's screen.

No more Giocondas. I'd teach myself to whistle or hunt for fish.

I was standing under the cupola, on the heart of Texas, the center
stone of the state capitol, where you could see a gold star in the ceiling,
surrounded by the cupola's curving web of blue. If you hummed under
the star, you could feel an echo in your throat.

Some mad-eyed woman from the conference thought she'd earned
the privilege of trifling with me while I stood on the center stone.

"Pinocchio, why do you look at the world from its shabbier side? It's
always Mussolini and his mistress. What about Mussolini's wife? She
never appears in *Pinocchio 1945.*"

"You can't have every little character roaming around in a children's
novel," I said in my defense. "You have to select. Clara was important
to my story."

"But Mussolini spent much more time with donna Rachele. It's not
fair to seduce children's minds with the notion of an all-important
mistress."

Who was this bitch? A high school teacher from Bleeding Heart,
Texas? Couldn't get her off my back.

"Children will begin to think that wives are superfluous. They'll
never marry. Pinocchio, you're a bilious man."

And she left me alone under a blue web that was beginning to look
like a marriage canopy. But I wouldn't depart from that center stone.
The adult stars, Canker, Ming, Paderewski, and Mills passed me on the
way to their end of the conference. I could have been some undocumented man. Not even George nodded to me while he was in the

presence of those other stars. Shame on him that he had to politick with Marvela Ming and couldn't recognize me in public. Marvela did a monthly fiction roundup for *The New York Review of Books.* And old George was afraid to waltz on her bad side. She'd lacerated Pinocchio in *The New York Review,* called me "the children's drudge, that nasty champion of prepubescent erotica."

But I wouldn't play invisible for Marvela's crew.

"How are you, Marvela dear?" I shouted across the rotunda.

"He's mad," she said. "He belongs in an institution."

And she continued on with her company. I saw the lieutenant governor slip around me, under the blue web. The old fox couldn't afford to alienate Marvela. She'd have ruined the conference if she decided to run. George was the great man, but Ming was the power broker. Conferences rose and fell according to her wish. She'd crucify all of Texas in *The New York Review* if Briney displeased her.

"Pinocchio, shall I give you a key to my flat? There's secretaries floating around who are already in love with you."

"I'm leaving off the secretaries this year. I've decided to become celibate. A Bronx whore caused me grief fifty years ago, and it will take me another fifty to recover."

The fox winked. "But you can still recover on my key." Then Briney turned gracious and fingered my yellow scarf. "Don't let Mrs. Ming get you down. I'll arrest the biddy the second she starts to provoke. We'll hold her in custody until the crickets leave."

Funny he should mention crickets. We were in the middle of a cricket plague. The capitol was infested with them. You found crickets on every wall, inside and outside the building. They climbed the portraits of Texas governors. They used the corridors as their own bloody highway. But they weren't the talking kind. None of them whispered to me.

Briney went upstairs to listen to Marvela lecture on modernism in Proust, Bellow, and Mills. He'd incorporate the lecture into his plans to secede. Mills would become the spiritual father of the new Texas republic. God go with the lieutenant governor!

Had to be careful. Nearly lost my rights to the center stone. That preacher with the grubby chin set up shop beside me. He was too sharp to create a bonfire within the capitol walls. The sergeant at arms would have thrown him into the dungeon downstairs. He did all his bookburning with his mouth.

"Ladies and gentlemen, listen please. Shun that writers' conference around you. It's Satan's work. There's a desperate tunnel going from Cervantes to George Mills . . ."

Ah, I captured the preacher with the opening of his sermon song. I should have seen under the disguise of a grubby chin. He hadn't come down from the Bronx. He was Lemuel Rice, the old superintendent of the Dominick Street mission. He was still in the business of rescuing lost souls.

I interrupted his sermon, wagged at him from my center stone. "Lem," I whispered, "it's me."

He went on with the sermon.

"George Mills is the most recent costume that the devil wears . . ."

"Super," I said, "hold it for a minute. Don't you recognize a boarder from Dominick Street? Copernicus' nephew, Romey Charyn."

He finally turned to me. "Yes, you're Romey when you like. But you've picked up the devil's name, Pinocchio."

"Super, I can't help it if my book is in fashion. Readers confuse me with Pinocchio. But where's Miz Alabam and your deacon, Hervey Long?"

"Out fornicating," he said. "They got rid of my church. They've gone the way of George Mills."

"Ah, Super, what do you have against George? He's got some mysterious disease. He wobbles when he walks."

"That's Mephisto's dance. He plays the cripple, traps you into pitying him."

"George doesn't ask for pity. He's a heartless son of a bitch. He wrote *Fyodor*. That's enough."

The mention of *Fyodor* set him off. Lemuel turned away from my stone and harangued shoppers who were heading downtown to Scarbrough's department store.

"Good people, brothers and sisters in Christ, don't take another step until you listen . . ."

The shoppers didn't have time for Jesus. He could only gather in the cat's army of bums that used the statehouse as a people's park. The bums put out for Lemuel. He'd become their very own church. But the Super collected more than bums. The beetles had come to listen. They dropped from the walls to rally around Lem.

"*Captain Fyodor* is a communist tract, a godless book about a vessel that defeats the United States. It could only have been accomplished with Lenin's ghost standing behind Mills. It has the cadences of a sovietized world, the drugged language of the dead."

The bums clapped for him. "Mills is pink, Mills is pink."

Now the shoppers paused to consider Lem. He was building up a clientele. He walked around me and my stone, like a bloody tiger preparing to spring.

"Brothers and sisters, you're asking Mills and company to piss on you by letting them into your house. Do they have a permit issued from the people of Texas? They usurp your facilities, bend it to their own rotten design. And you acquiesce, you shrug your shoulders and say it's all right. All right? Do you know who is on the faculty? Mrs. Marvela Ming. And who is Ming? Doyenne of *The New York Review,* a godless newspaper, devoted to godless politics, godless authors, godless books. She comes here with Mills to plant her rubbish. She's his sister and his wife . . ."

"I'll sue the state of Texas." A shiver went from bum to bum, and a path emerged in the audience. It was Marvela Ming. She'd come down from the conference with Briney and George Mills to erase Lemuel's song. She was carrying an official state umbrella she'd borrowed from the sergeant at arms. She didn't beat Lemuel with it. She used the umbrella for emphasis.

"George, you will shut his mouth. This man is an agent of Pinocchio. We will sue Texas for all it's worth if he's not quieted and taken from the grounds."

Mills didn't move on Lemuel. The cane was in his pants. One of the green suspenders had unlooped itself. He wouldn't be shoved around by *The New York Review.*

"Marvela, it's good publicity to damn a book."

"George, you will listen to what I say, George. I will not be maligned by a clown who poses as a preacher."

"He's not a bad egg. He's floundering, Marvela, and he's hooked himself to me. I've become his personal devil."

"George . . ."

There's nothing in the history of literature that says a man or woman who's written a great book can't be a fawning fool. *Fyodor* was not George Mills. Marvela had discovered George. She could create or destroy a literary reputation. Fifty words in *The New York Review* was enough to sink the career of a serious writer. Her leverage didn't apply to children's books. I was immune to Mrs. Ming. Her attack had heightened the interest in my "criminal work."

"George . . ."

Mills became his own fiction, turned into Fyodor, the Russian captain who danced while he made war. He took Lemuel in his arms and trotted with him, the cane lolling between them like an obscene stick.

"I am going mad," Marvela said. "Where is Governor Briney?"

But the lieutenant governor had anticipated Mrs. Ming. He didn't intend to dance around *The New York Review*. He'd gone to the edge of the rotunda, outside Marvela's reach. I understood his game plan now. Briney had the bums put on badges that said SECEDE AGAIN. He was trying to brew a little storm in the statehouse. The Super was his shill. He'd brought Marvela, Mills, and me to Texas to start a second civil war.

I grabbed Mrs. Ming by the wrist of her umbrella hand. Her eyes pushed towards the capitol's webbed sky. "I won't be handled by Pinocchio."

"Marvela, it's a scam. They're trying to spear a bloodless revolution with the conference as a scapegoat."

"Don't you talk to me!"

It's then that I noticed the bluish tint of her hair under the cupola. Was Brunhilde out migrating again? I sucked with my nose and couldn't feel Brunhilde. Ming hadn't been invaded by the witch. I figured she would shove me off my stone with the point of her umbrella. But she softened to Pinocchio. Gesù, Giuseppe, Maria, Ming was almost pretty with her blue hair.

"Should we chuck the conference, Pinocchio?"

I pulled her near me for a whisper. "No. It will give Briney the excuse he needs to agitate against New York."

"Then what shall I do?"

"Take your umbrella and lead the conference upstairs."

She kissed me on the cheek, with one of her blue curls in my forehead. "Pinocchio, I've been cruel to you. You're no Dickens, but you are a funny writer . . . come upstairs with us."

"I think I'll stay in this traffic circle."

I sniffed her perfume. Could have followed her upstairs and pinched her bottom in some dark corner, but it would have been like sleeping with *The New York Review.* I'd have thought of columns on a page, bylines and everything.

I held to the stone.

Mills stopped dancing and wobbled upstairs with Marvela. Shoppers continued downtown to Scarbrough's store. The bums returned the badges to their pockets. The beetles scampered back to their walls. The epiphany the Super had expected, that moment of illumination and grace where Christ would emerge from the blue web, hadn't come. Lemuel skulked away.

Briney didn't expel me from the stone. He'd bring in new shills, finance another conference to launch the country of Texas.

"Hang on, Pinocchio," he said.

I was like the Super, looking for some epiphany to fall on my head. It's a childish wish.

Shoppers returned from Scarbrough's and left by the north wing. The conference broke up for the day. Marvela invited me for a drink in her room at the Burlington. I had to say no.

The sergeant at arms brought me a sandwich.

Signed a few autographs, long as I didn't have to leave the stone.

A darkness landed on the walls. The blue in the ceiling went a little gray. Might have slept for a minute. A voice pulled me awake, like a puppet string. I saw the wildest color red.

"What are you doing in Austin, Solange?"

"I came for the conference. You have this fantasy in America, called creative writing. I'm covering it for my magazine."

"But you'll have to wait until tomorrow."

"What do I care about tomorrow, you imbecile? Show me Texas. I want to see Santa Fe."

"Santa Fe isn't Texas. It's New Mexico."

"You're quibbling," she said. "It's all the same, my darling. Mountains and hills."

She had a bit of a point. Texas, Argentina. Plant a flag and you have a city-state. I was the tenant of some republic that included the Quirinale, the Eiffel Tower, and the goddess of liberty over our heads. And this freckleface was Gioconda with wild red hair, as bossy and unpredictable as Bathsheba had ever been.

I clutched her hand and stepped off the stone. I didn't need that umbrella of a webbed sky.

"Where are we going?"

"Santa Fe."

"But we'll miss the conference. I'll never understand creative writing."

"Trust me," I said. "I'll teach you on the road."

We took the south trail, towards the Burlington, trying not to step on crickets. Passed Scarbrough's on Congress Avenue. There was a woman on a pillow in Scarbrough's window. She had luscious blond hair. The curve of her body, down to the articulation of her pink toes, obliged me to pause and press against the glass. I forgot Santa Fe. I wanted to join blondie in the window and invite her to the conference.

Solange sensed that fierce pull I had. "Jérôme," she said, with a certain tenderness. "That's a dummy in the window."

Crossed the street with Madame Gâteau to the cattlemen's entrance of the Burlington Hotel. We wouldn't lie down on a Burlington bed. We'd make love in the deep shelf of my suitcase, like any married couple, and then we'd find our Santa Fe.

SIXTEEN

THE PEDERSEN KID

GÂTEAU was generous with her red hair. After a night at the Burlington she forgot Santa Fe and began to follow Mills and Marvela Ming. I was just another children's writer, some Pinocchio from the South Bronx steppes. Oh, she'd lie down with me, call me darling under the quilt, but it was George she had coffee with. It's a fact of the universe that frecklefaced women prefer men with masterpieces. She interviewed Mills for two days, studied his work with Ming, and didn't attend one lecture of mine. Her passion to understand *Captain Fyodor* consumed Solange. She'd scratch up the margins and come to bed with George's green suspenders in her eyes.

"Solange, shouldn't you take a rest in Santa Fe?"

"Darling, I can't. I'm in love with George."

"Then go down to his suite and declare yourself."

"I wouldn't know what to do. I don't want to kiss George . . . it would be like fondling Moses."

Had a dark ache in my loins, almost a tear under the skin, a hernia I was getting from George Mills. "What is it that you want?"

"To die in Fyodor's arms."

"But Fyodor isn't flesh. You can't crawl into George's book."

"Why not?"

She had me, of course. There'd been stranger loves than that. Dante Alighieri and a twelve-year-old girl. Proust and his married chauffeur. Why couldn't Solange disappear into a paragraph? She grew thin. I fed her migas and breakfast tacos, cursing the power that literature had on our lives. Solange was in the teeth of some enchantment, teeth I couldn't break. I took her to the Super, hoping he might work the devil out of Solange. He stared into her eyes and announced it was a hopeless case.

"Get rid of her, Pinocchio. Give her to George."

"It's Fyodor she wants."

"That's much worse. Mills is nothing. But Fyodor means that she's fornicated with the devil and can't stop."

"Super, please don't get into metaphysics. Solange hasn't strayed from my quilt."

He gave me that goddamn missionary smile. "Pinocchio's the same as Fyodor. She does sleep with the devil."

I traveled upstairs with her to Ming. The empress of modern literature crawled out from behind *The New York Review* and revealed her compassion for Solange. She hugged the freckleface.

"Marvela, couldn't we introduce her to a lesser classic . . . deflect her from George's book?"

"That wouldn't do. Only George can help her."

She summoned the great man. Mills had wearied of the conference. He was ashen behind the green suspenders, his skin like withered cakes of dust. And he was sick of *Captain Fyodor.* He wanted St. Louis, so he could lie down near the Mississippi and dream himself into another book.

"George, we cannot abandon this child."

"Sue me," he said. "I'm not responsible for Fyodor."

"George, you will do whatever is in your means to discourage her infatuation with your writing, or I shall never, never review you again."

Mills had written his classic. He wasn't afraid of Ming. But he saw that burnt-out look on Gâteau and he didn't march away from Gâteau's distress.

"Solange," he said. "Fyodor's a submarine commander, incapable of loving back. The boat's his mistress. He doesn't have time for other girls."

"Wonderful," she said. "I hate womanizers."

George unhooked the cane from his pants and beat Solange around the knuckles. "Fyodor is mine," he said. "I don't share my characters with French dames."

Solange licked her knuckles while Mills restored the cane to his pants. The freckleface started to cry. "I'm hungry," she said.

She had three helpings of migas in my room. She was tender with me under the quilt, tender and violent. She never mentioned Fyodor.

Solange's recovery was swift. She sacrificed Pinocchio and George Mills, gave herself to *The New York Review*. I couldn't prevent her from accompanying Ming to Manhattan Island.

"But darling," she said. "It's not so fatal. I'll work for Marvela and live with you."

"Solange, I'm staying here."

"Don't be silly. The conference is over. All you have in Texas are stupid beetles. I insist that you come with me."

Was it some mad wind in my ear that told me I'd meet my fate in Austin? Freckles be damned. I wouldn't go.

We smooched a long time. I'd become addicted to that Parisian witch. It was the nearest thing I'd had to marriage, outside Belinda. I didn't want to give up the freckleface.

"Couldn't you stall *The New York Review*?"

She got on the plane with Ming, and I was left with a rumpled quilt.

I took solace in the bars and bad cafés of Old Pecan Street. I drank sour mash with jailbirds and undocumented people. I rented a smaller room to preserve my capital. But it had the same bitter view of second-hand furniture stores and groceries with nothing on the shelves.

My father would have loved Texas. He could have carted his junk to the railroad tracks and made tortillas with the rags. I began to sympathize with our lieutenant governor. Texas ought to be its own city-state. Austin had that dry, burnt feel of Tuscany. It's strange how a body finds its home.

I joined the crowd of bums that occupied the capitol and used it as a recreation hall. I was part of an anonymous bundle that came under Briney's wing. The old man was our protector. We had hors d'oeuvres in the lieutenant governor's apartment. His own butler served us. The sergeant at arms treated my crowd as if we were the frigging senate.

We acquired a new member. He was from the gerontology clinic behind Pecan Street. I swear to you, he could have fallen out of *Pinocchio 1945*. He might as well have been made from wood. He suffered from a malady called progeria that mimicked the aging process. Fourteen and he looked eighty-five. He'd had a heart murmur since he was three. His arteries had begun to clog at six or seven. He was the darling of the clinic, this kid from Saskatchewan, the most pronounced living case of progeria. He'd come to die at the clinic.

His name was Pedersen, and the bums liked to call him "bird head," because he had the blue baldy head of a young bird, with a bird's thin beak. He was a kid without hair on his body. And when Pedersen took off his shirt he had two scarry spots in place of nipples. His joints were so crooked, he walked around as if he were on a saddle.

The Pedersen kid burst into tears the moment he met me. It wasn't my fault that Pinocchio had been his childhood hero.

"Pinocchio, Pinocchio."

"Lay off. That fucker is part of my past."

"Other people call you Pinocchio, and you don't seem to mind."

"But you mean it," I said, sprinting to the opposite end of the capitol, so I could avoid the Pedersen kid. It wasn't fair, running from his awkward gait. He couldn't play tag around the rotunda, like the rest of us. Pedersen sat on the stairs, the bums mocking his outsider's station. "How are you, bird head?"

He took the gibes, glad to have a respite from the worn old men at the gerontology clinic.

My mail began to arrive at the capitol, in care of the lieutenant governor's office. I'd become a child of Texas. I found myself turning from the bums to that kid. Because the Super hated Cervantes, Pedersen had no one to teach him about books. He couldn't devote his time to high school and college; children with progeria hardly ever got beyond their teens. So the kid had this terrible thirst to know.

"Who's the greatest writers?"

"Shakespeare and Mills."

"If you could have one book in the world, what would it be?"

"A good biographical dictionary."

Pedersen frowned. "But a dictionary has no style."

"Who cares? I'd have thumbnail sketches of Mozart and Dostoyevsky. That would hold me more than any fiction."

"Think a little of me," the kid said. "Why should I care when Dostoyevsky was born, if I'll never read his books?"

"Because," I said. "The weave of his life, the gambling he did, the wives he had, his quarrel with Turgenev, could be the chapters of a novel. Pedersen, I swear to God, stick with a biographical dictionary."

The kid was eager to hear the facts of my own life. I told him about the Bronx and the baby carriage and my lack of a bar mitzvah. The baby carriage didn't absorb him much; for him the Bronx was another Saskatchewan. But Pinocchio's missing bar mitzvah stuck to the Pedersen kid. It was as if he saw his own robbed childhood in that particular emblem.

One afternoon, while the others were playing catch, the kid said, "Pinocchio, come on up to the chapel."

"What the hell for? I never pray."

"The chapel," he said, with an authority I was loath to contradict. I climbed around the bums to the fourth floor. It was eleven at night, and the chapel was deserted except for a guy who could have been from our gang. He had stubble on his face, boots with broken points. But I could smell a holy man under the stubble.

"Are you a rabbi, sir?"

"Almost." He pinned a skullcap to his head. "I'm a rabbinical student from Port Arthur."

This Port Arthur man had to be my age. But who the hell was I to disparage recent conversions? A rabbinical student, then. Sixty or fifty-five.

"What's your name?"

A crease appeared in his lips. "Port Arthur," he said.

Ah, we were in the land of anonymous rabbis. Had he studied Torah in the penitentiary? Another one of Briney's shills, borrowed from some parole board. Who cared what credentials he had, long as he was licensed to perform bar mitzvahs?

"Can you give me a little Torah tonight?"

Port Arthur was indignant. "I don't know you. We haven't studied together."

I clutched him by his rabbinical collar.

"Bar mitzvah me . . . I've been waiting too long."

"But do you understand the Law?" he asked, with my fist in his throat.

"Yes, yes, I'll never covet another man's wife. I'll confess all the murders I did, I'll give up women if you like . . . please."

"The Blessed One doesn't admire idle promises. Do you understand the Law?"

I dug as far as I could into his collar.

"I swear on everything that's holy, I understand."

"Don't swear," the rabbi said. "It's the first signal of false pride. I'll bring you to bar mitzvah."

He didn't wrap any scrolls around his arm, or take out his prayer shawl. He didn't even bend in the chapel. He held his hands on my skull, turned me to the north wall, closed his eyes, and pronounced benedictions under his breath. The ceremony took five or ten minutes. That's how rabbis bloomed in Texas.

I wanted to discuss his fee.

He asked me not to interrupt the service. I trembled the moment he stopped muttering.

"Rabbi, am I bar mitzvahed?"

He looked at me as if I were a wild and ignorant man. "Of course."

"Do I get some certificate, a slip of paper to certify me?"

"Don't you dare profane what you've just gone through."

I heard titters behind the rabbi. Our bloody gang was standing at the door.

"I'll kill the man that laughs at me."

Briney waltzed into the chapel. "It's sacrilege," he said. "Talking murder after a ceremony like that. We'll get Port Arthur to cancel the whole thing."

"I'll cancel all of you," I said. "He's no rabbi. He's a shill."

"What in thunder do you mean? I scratched the state for that Hebrew man. He's legit."

Pedersen hobbled between us with his saddle walk. He had a terror in his eyes that was beyond the old governor's deceit. "Don't ruin it for yourself . . . the guv made a party for you downstairs. Pinocchio, we got delicatessen."

"I'm not going," I said. "I want a search out on this rabbi."

Briney asked the Super to declare whether the rabbi was fit.

Lem is a shill, but I trusted him on holy matters. He was too wrapped up in Jesus to lie about the authenticity of any churchman.

I didn't like the sweat near the Super's mouth.

"Will you speak up?" Briney said.

Lem turned to look at me. "Jerome, Port Arthur is in God's flock."

"But is he a rabbi?"

"A student rabbi."

"At what college?"

"County jail."

"That's good enough for me." All my comrades locked arms to celebrate Pinocchio's bar mitzvah. We traveled to Briney's apartment on the second floor. The butler served us corned beef and chicken fried steak. We drank tequila with salt on our tongues in that endless apartment the old man had. It was equipped with a servant's door, where women, single or married, could come and go without endangering the capitol's decorum.

We had a load of mammas at my bar mitzvah party, nurses, professors' wives, government stenographers that Briney had rounded up. He was the king of one-night marriages after fifty-six years in the state-house.

The rabbi picked himself a nurse. Lem discussed the meaninglessness of George Mills with a charwoman from the University of Texas, which we called the Vicarage, because its red tile roofs reminded our lieutenant governor of some lost medieval town on a hill. Briney was the vicar to that lost town. It couldn't have bought a bottle of milk without Briney's legislature. Since all professors were pink to him, he would only invite the professors' wives and certain charwomen to his affairs. This charwoman worked for the philosophy department and was an admirer of Wittgenstein and George Mills. She argued back and forth with Lem, while he slid his hand under her dress.

Her name was Alice. She argued the Super into the depths of his chair. "If language is the devil, Mr. Rice, then the devil's the saddest thing on this earth. Because no two people can ever get closer than a verb or a noun. Language is all we have."

Alice was the prettiest charwoman I'd ever seen. Her bodice was open on the chair. Her breasts moved like a sea of swollen corn, under a band of silk. The Super had plunged his elbow into the bodice. Alice looked at me.

I had worms in my legs from that creature on the chair. But I'd made a vow of chastity for my bar mitzvah, and I meant to keep it. I wasn't wood. I'd go out of my mind if I watched the Super explore her body. His fingers were like caterpillars in Alice's cloth.

I shuffled from room to room, driving tequila through the salt in my mouth. I stood near a lump of blue stone that seemed to hold up a lamp. Had too much tequila. Couldn't even tell a statuette. The stone shifted to another lamp. It was the Pedersen kid. He was all scrunched up.

"It's not polite, kid, being a wallflower at my bar mitzvah."

"It's my sickness. It's tearing at me."

"Hell, I wouldn't have had a bar mitzvah if not for you. Get on my back, kid. I'll ride you to the clinic."

"I'm happier with the guv and you."

"But they'll treat your sickness down at the clinic."

"It's not treatable, Pinocchio . . . I've never been laid. I'll die without knowing what a woman is."

"But there's women everywhere," I said, pointing to Briney's harem.

"You don't understand. I have the wrinkles, but I'm not mature between the legs."

That was the meanest trick, to give a boy heart murmurs and forget about puberty.

"I'll help you, kid."

I dragged him over to Alice. The Super had crawled under her dress. She lay over the chair with her eyes fixed on the ceiling. I whispered in her ear.

Alice shoved the Super's head out from between her ankles. She got up and went with me and the kid to the master bedroom. I wanted to stay in the hall, but Pedersen wouldn't go in without Pinocchio.

I stood in the corner while Alice undressed the kid. She was gentle with his clothing, and she didn't pretend he was Matt Dillon without an undershirt, or that she admired little hairless men more than anything in the world. She was natural with the kid.

He had little squashed testicles and a peter that was hardly there. Pedersen could have been my Italian brother, piccolino, who was born in a bread basket and had nothing downstairs. But Alice wasn't mystified, and she didn't reach for the kid's nose. She got undressed. I put a fist into my mouth. She was as beautiful as Mussolini's mistress. Alice had Claretta's blond bum.

The kid couldn't take his eyes off her, but nothing happened. His groin wouldn't burst for Alice. Reading Wittgenstein must have prepared her for the kid. She began to suck the two scars on his chest that he had for nipples. His peter grew.

I wasn't a stinking voyeur. I walked out of Briney's bedroom.

The kid wasn't the same after that. He spoke in a deeper voice. He joined our games of tag, even if his hobbling never allowed him to win. He ate tacos on the rotunda and wouldn't return to the clinic. He'd become a terrible delinquent.

"Shame," I said. "Didn't the doctors bring you from Saskatchewan? You ought to be a little loyaler to them."

"Loyal to a farm that registers how you die? I just got laid."

Pedersen shook his pants to show the heat that had developed in his groin over Alice.

"Well, why don't you live with the charwoman?"

"I might," the kid said, but I never saw him go up to the Vicarage and look for Alice. He was content to play tag with us.

"Isn't someone at the clinic responsible for you?"

"Sure," he said. "Old Belinda . . . Pinocchio, are you having a fit?"

Had tears big as marbles in my eyes, because I knew this Belinda couldn't be an accident. She was in the bloody book of my life.

"She's just a den mother," the kid said. "Belinda takes care of me and the old men."

I rushed him out of the capitol, propelling the kid by his pants.

"Lay off," he said. "What's old Belinda to you?"

"Everything."

We went on down to the clinic. It was in the heart of that scrubby district of secondhand stores. Gerontology may have been a brand-new science, but the clinic had nothing to do with Anno 85. It was a former stable that had been gussied up to give the appearance of an experimental ranch, sitting between a firehouse and a taco factory.

Old men nattered about near the firehouse in robes and blue pajamas. They stuffed taco chips into their jaws and waved to the Pedersen kid.

"Belinda is worried to death over you."

"That's not my concern. I'm no invalid. I'll hop as much as I like at the statehouse."

I shoved Pedersen into the clinic. Nurses babied him and took his pulse. "Where's old Belinda?" he growled.

"My, my, you've grown up in a week," came a voice from behind a curtain with the deep bellowing drawl of a den mother. It didn't have much of a Texas lilt. Belinda parted the curtain and shuffled out to the kid. She was a woman with a thick nose and blue marks in her legs. She couldn't have been the secondhand girl who'd passed six months on Charlotte Street.

"Belinda, Pinocchio wants to meet you."

"I'm too busy for Pinocchios," she said. "You rascal, you'll fall away and die if you don't swallow your heart pills."

"I'm cured," the kid announced.

"And so is Shakespeare and Sam Houston. But the trouble is they're dead."

"I had intercourse."

"What are you driving at?" she muttered, turning around to take me in.

"Intercourse is intercourse . . . long as it's with some woman."

"What have they been teaching you up at the statehouse? You don't have the starch in you to be with a woman. Didn't the doctors tell you? Your eggs are dry."

"It's the clinic that's dry. I had intercourse. Ask him."

"He has no business here. Who is he?"

"I told you, Belinda. That's Pinocchio."

"And I'm the Wizard of Oz. Only this is Tuesday, Pedersen. And I'm tired of you."

But she didn't have much bitterness in her eyes. You could have guessed in a minute that she was fond of the kid. Belinda bowed to me.

"Is that rascal correct?"

"Afraid so, ma'am."

"I'm not your ma'am," she said. "I'm Belinda. And why have you been introducing a child to tarts on the government hill?"

"He's not a child," I said. "He has the symptoms of an eighty-year-old."

"He's still fourteen. I can have you put away on a morals charge. But I don't believe this blather about intercourse. I've read the literature on his disease. There's not one example of consummation with a woman."

"Then the literature will have to be changed. I was there."

"Don't you listen? You've been corrupting a minor if what you say is true."

"You can't bully me, Miss Belinda. I won't deny the kid."

Belinda took a pad out of her pocket and attended to it like a police captain with a pencil stub. "What is the name you were born with?"

"Copernicus Charyn . . . of Charlotte Street."

She kept to her pad. "Where's Charlotte Street?"

"In the South Bronx. I once knew a Belinda who was brought there from Texas."

"Tarnation," she said, "do I look like a Bronx girl? Are you a private detective, snooping after people?"

"No, I grew up with Belinda. We raised secondhand girls and boys for six months."

It was lucky I didn't have wax in my ears, because Belinda muttered under her breath. I couldn't mistake the word minestrone.

"You are my Belinda," I said. "You drank Bitter Morris' soup."

She put her pad away and blew her thick nose with a hospital napkin. She told Pedersen to lose himself for a little while. "Go on," she said. "Go to a nurse and ask her for some intercourse. I have to talk with Pinocchio."

The kid looked at Belinda and me and hobbled behind the curtain.

"Romey," she said. She fell on my shoulder in the clinic's front room and we both had the longest cry. Finding her was the fruit of my bar mitzvah.

"I thought you were a detective with the clinic, poking into my past. Texas is touchy about undocumented girls."

"What happened, Belinda, when the pirates auctioned you from their truck in Crotona Park?"

"I was sold to a couple in Scarsdale that worked me to the bone. Would have died of hunger, only I escaped. I've been on the street ever since, until I got back to Texas. My last schooling was in the Bronx. Had to lie on all the applications."

"But how did Andrusov get you in the first place?"

"A goddamn uncle lent me to her. Andrusov was the nearest thing to mamma."

"She wasn't much of a mamma to those other secondhand girls. She sold them into slavery."

I must have hit a sensitive tooth, because she shoved herself from my shoulder. "I'm not to blame if Andrusov liked me more. Didn't I care for her children?"

"Belinda, I know that."

"Then why are you shoveling dirt on Andrusov?"

Ah, that old pirate of Charlotte Street had become Belinda's sacred cow.

"Andrusov gave me my first job. Don't you remember? I looked after her pet octopus."

"Course I remember. Tati. Who could forget? Tati lived at the bottom of the pickle barrel."

"But are you sure, Belinda?"

"Andrusov wouldn't have hired you to be the caretaker for a bunch of pickles."

She approached my eye with her pencil stub. "Are you calling my mamma a liar?"

"Tatiana . . . in the barrel . . . alive."

"Romey," she said. "We should have a reunion."

"With what? Those secondhand girls and boys could be in Dallas or China . . . or under the earth by now."

"Well, all you have to do is advertise. We could put out a flier asking Andrusov's children to get in touch."

"I thought you had to keep your affiliation a big secret."

"One flier wouldn't hurt."

I kissed Belinda on the forehead like an old sister and sailed out of the clinic. I'd never capture Charlotte Street no matter how many secondhand children I found. The past was like a grim feather that could tickle you in altogether opposite ways. Andrusov's barrel didn't have any bottom.

Went into a tavern on Old Pecan Street, sucked on sour mash. I danced with a lady and never looked at her face, figuring she was some gringa down on her luck. Pressed twenty dollars into her hand.

"Pinocchio," she said, "don't embarrass me. I'm not a taxi dancer."

It was the charwoman who loved Wittgenstein. She passed her lunch hours on Old Pecan Street. She'd always pick the darkest tavern.

"Sorry, Alice. I should have recognized you."

We danced in the tavern's bluish light. I groped about for the familiar design of her body. We swayed with our hands in each other's underwear. I prayed the Torah would forgive me. I'd promised the student rabbi to keep clear of lust. But I was dizzy with Alice and all her silk. Something disturbed me. Alice hadn't mentioned the Pedersen kid, not a word on his magic nipples.

That was Brunhilde in Alice's clothing. Had the urge to strangle her in the park, put an end to the whore and her monkeyings with time.

"Should have figured only a witch could solve the riddle of a boy who'd been cheated out of puberty. Brunhilde, don't you deny it. You gave Pedersen his prick. Tell me, are you the kid's godmother too?"

"Of course."

"And you settled him here in Austin so we could meet?"

"I wanted you to have a companion in your old age."

"Another Pinocchio. But that's a cruel disease you saddled him with . . . it mocks everything that's human."

"Not at all," the witch said. "Pedersen is a walking immortality ode."

"A boy starts to die the minute he's born, and you see immortality in it."

"My adorable dunce," she said. I took her hand out of my underwear. I wasn't going to pet with a witch.

"Dear Pinocchio, wash your head. Isn't he proof enough that aging can be reversed? If Pedersen has a calendar in his body that speeds him towards death, couldn't that calendar be tampered with? We could slow it down, make it go back and forth."

"Why don't you start with the kid?"

"It's much too soon. Scientists will have to grovel for a hundred years until another Mendel comes along and discovers immortality in goats and garden peas, and little aging boys. But I could adjust your calendar, if you'll promise to be my sweetheart and come away with me."

"Isis and Osiris, huh? A brother and sister team. I'll sit in some underworld while you play godmother to different Pinocchios. No thanks. I'll take my chances in Texas."

"Your hair will fall out, your teeth will rot, your scrotum will shrivel, my idiotic darling."

"I'll be a better companion to the kid."

"I'll make sure you die together."

The witch curled up into her underwear and left the tavern.

Got on a flight to Newark, hired an airport limousine, and rocketed towards Manhattan. Hurt the chauffeur's feelings when I asked him to keep off the main drag.

"We'll lose an hour, sir."

"That's fine. I'll pay you double."

For a moment, around Jersey City, we caught the Manhattan sky-line, and I shivered under my blood, because the sun on Chrysler and Empire State slanted off the roofs like a freeze of honey. Ah, I'll miss that after I'm dead.

The chauffeur delivered me to *The New York Review.* Told him to wait. I'd have another customer for him.

Shot up to the thirty-sixth floor, where Marvela Ming had her offices. The receptionist wasn't kind to Pinocchio. She must have recalled the bad notices I'd had from Ming.

"Marvela is rather busy."

"Did you tell her it's Pinocchio?"

"It wouldn't make that much difference," she said.

But I hadn't flown in from Austin to be ambushed by *The New York Review.* I waltzed behind this girl and crashed the editorial offices.

Ming stood outside her cubby with her arms crossed. "You will leave the premises, Pinocchio, or I will notify the building's police."

"I want the freckleface," I said. Merci-Gâteau had abandoned her career in Paris to write articles for Ming on Baudelaire and Noam Chomsky, Melville and Mills, semiotics and other stuff.

"Pinocchio, if you are pursuing Merci-Gâteau, please continue it outside the office."

"The only address I have for her is your bloody masthead."

"That should tell you something. She's not interested in men of rough conduct."

"Where is Solange?"

"Safe from you."

Marvela summoned her gang of copy editors and paste-up girls. They were a sneering, villainous crew. The editors lunged at me while Marvela got on the phone with the security office. Ah, I didn't have the piccolino's cricket-bat arms. But I was fierce as any gang of copy editors.

"Gâteau," I screamed in the middle of the battle, as security arrived, guards in brown uniforms. Solange crept out from under the desk in Ming's own cubby.

"I forbid you to enter into any conversation with this man," said the mistress of culture. "It is unlawful to utter a single word to him."

The guards handcuffed Pinocchio and ordered him up to their bullpen near the roof.

"Breaking and entering," they told Marvela.

"He was about to maul my employees."

"Good," said the guards, pulling on the handcuffs' little chain.

"Buddy, you'll have some song to give the magistrate."

Solange watched them lead me towards their attic. "I invited him here," she said to security. "That's my boyfriend, Pinocchio."

The guards looked to Marvela. She made the tiniest motion with her wrist, and the guards removed the cuffs.

"Child," Marvela said to Merci-Gâteau. "You have half a minute to pick between your ruffian and our review."

I pulled Solange into a cubby and slammed the door. Her freckles were blazing. She couldn't decide if I was her own D'Artagnan or her ruin.

"Jérôme," she said, "Jérôme."

"Shut up. I want you to marry me."

"That's impossible. I'm doing an article on eating, sleeping, and Derrida. But you can propose to me next month."

"Solange, you're coming with me to Texas right now."

"You are the dearest lunatic, mon coco. Why should I come with you when I'll inherit the magazine in five years? I'll be *The New York Review*."

"Because if you don't come I'll keep breaking your door until there is no *New York Review*."

"But darling, what would I ever do in Texas?"

"Live with me. We'll get married in the statehouse. We'll adopt my friend, the Pedersen kid, so he won't have to die in a stinking clinic."

We heard a voice from outside the glass closet.

"Merci-Gâteau, you've used up your time with this man."

The freckleface laughed. "Texas," she said, as if she could weigh my proposition with a Gioconda smile. "Texas, when I have *The New York Review* in the palm of my hand?"

"Yes," I said. "Texas and Pinocchio."

We heard Marvela like pebbles on the glass. "You're getting me angry, child."

Solange marched out with me. "I'm marrying Pinocchio."

"Then you'll suffer the same obscurity as he will," said Ming.

The freckleface had her own anger to declare. "I can live without Derrida."

We waltzed out to the elevator bank.

"Darling, take me home. I'll have to pack."

"No," I said. "Straight to Texas."

We hugged in the elevator, causing a commotion on our way down to the street. It was a building of editors who'd never seen such kissing in a public car.

"Coco," said Solange, with her arms around my neck. "Why do you have to be so extreme? We can make our family in Manhattan or the Bronx."

"Texas," I said.

SEVENTEEN

THE MAN WHO GREW YOUNGER

F
EBRUARY, 1994.

Married Solange.

The bums were our bridesmaids.

We began to weave a life together, Pinocchio, Solange, and the Pedersen kid. Pedersen's face turned a dark blue, as if someone had poisoned his cheeks. The clinic put him on stricter medication. His knees sank when he did his saddle walk, and he couldn't play tag or sit around in the capitol. He had to depend on Belinda, who brushed his hair when he was too drugged to climb out of bed. The kid wouldn't tolerate a bedpan, and Belinda carried him in her arms to the loo.

Solange sensed that Belinda was more than a nurse. "Jérôme, who is she?"

"My first sweetheart."

"She's thick as a bull."

"Belinda wasn't always like that."

With the kid in bed, unable to charm Solange with his one tale of intercourse, she turned to Texas politics. She stalked for Briney, became his sounding horse. She'd go around the state like a drummer girl, seeing if Dallas or Amarillo might break away from the Union. She had devotees on account of her freckles, but Dallas didn't care about an old man in the statehouse. Briney had been singing secession for sixty years.

Solange felt embarrassed about being Madame Pinocchio. She held to her maiden name. The fact is I was growing old, and I wanted a bambina to dandle on my leg, with freckles, if God could arrange it. But Solange screamed of morning sickness and the fat belly she'd have to endure. You couldn't carry a child and expect to be a journalist.

"I'll take hormones at the gerontology clinic. I'll grow tits, Solange, and nurse the child."

"And then you'll give her to Belinda, once the fascination wears off."

"I wouldn't do that."

"You will, my darling. You couldn't bear the competition with another child. You'll be living off my nipples when you're a hundred and ten."

"But it's natural," I said, "for a man to drink his wife."

We might have had a chance, but Marvela died, and Solange inherited *The New York Review* out from under her feet. Oh, she didn't dissolve the marriage. Solange would come and suckle me every month. I was grateful, even for that. You don't expect much when you've been reared as a silent runt in a baby carriage.

"Give up this existence, Jérôme. That old man will never have his empire. He'll lose the statehouse one of these days. Pedersen has Belinda. I need you in New York."

"Can't," I said. "This is home."

"Home? When you trudge between a broken hotel and a clinic for dead people."

"Don't say that. The kid's not dead."

"Darling, he opened his eyes with the curse of death upon him. He gets weaker by the hour. Soon you'll have nothing here."

"Can I have my baby if I go with you?"

"Imbecile, I slave my ass off, commission pieces, count words in a column, and you expect me to drop everything and satisfy this obsession of yours . . . Jérôme, I'll see you in a month."

But Solange canceled on Pinocchio. Woody Allen was playing Robin Hood on Broadway, and Solange had promised to interview him. Got a letter from her lawyer. Solange was interested in a quiet divorce. "Your differences are irreconcilable," the lawyer said. I agreed.

Heard rumors that Woody bought *The New York Review* as a trick to retire Solange and marry her. But they didn't marry, and Solange continued to edit and write.

She wasn't wrong about one thing. Briney did lose the statehouse. His own senate rebelled against him and scratched him off the ballot. Voters didn't object. They'd forgotten who Briney was.

I had to help him pack. The sergeant at arms gave him an hour to vacate his apartment on the second floor. The old man moved into the Burlington. But we couldn't solve the problem of where to put the bums. Briney pondered and came to me.

"There's a solution, Pinocchio. The clinic will take them, but it's a package deal."

"I'm not one of your senators, Briney. Talk straight."

"That damn clinic wants me and you."

"I won't live with yeggs."

"You can share a room with the kid. They promised."

I couldn't discern any doctor in chief. The clinic seemed to have some pendulum of its own that moved outside my understanding or influence. That Belinda had real power in the wards was as much as I could grasp.

She didn't abuse her power. She was a good mamma to all her children. I thought the kid would be happy with Pinocchio, but he growled under his blue face.

"Get out of here while you have the chance. Pinocchio, this is the place for terminals."

"Nonsense," I said. "The clinic took our gang in. Briney arranged it."

"Yeah, the guv was doing business. He gets dough for every bed he can fill up."

"Who cares? The gang is under one roof."

"Roof?" the kid said. "Can't you tell? It's a creeping mortuary . . . go back to your wife."

"She's engaged to Woody Allen."

"Who's Woody Allen?"

"Didn't you ever see *Annie Hall?*" But I'd forgotten that Pedersen was a juvenile from Saskatchewan, without a pip of hair.

"Pedersen, I won't desert my mates. That's final."

The kid turned bluer and bluer.

"It's called cyanosis," he said. "That's what happens when oxygen can't get near the skin. You go blue."

"Couldn't you exercise, kid?"

He looked at me as if I were his child.

Belinda would rock him as he shivered in bed. "Pinocchio, tell me everything you know . . . about books. I don't want to die an ignorant."

I lay across from him while the kid was in Belinda's arms and delivered Cervantes from start to finish, reinventing chapters about the old don and his nag Rosinante, his sweetheart, and his squire.

"Pinocchio," Belinda said, "please. You'll wear him out with those stories." But she wept over that don who tried to implant himself upon the world. And she wept over Cervantes' horse.

"Pinocchio," the kid said, "don't you stop."

"But it's the end of the book."

"Then start at the back and take us to the middle."

We arrived at the year 2000 with Cervantes still on his horse. There were explosions outside our window, festivities to mark one more century. We hardly heard the noise. Politicos dressed up the capitol and shot candles off that goddess of liberty on top. I went to Briney. He wasn't part of the year 2000. He sat on his bed, having a game of checkers with himself.

"Guv, the bastards in the statehouse should have invited you up the hill. You chaperoned all of them, and they never come to visit."

"Well," he said, "there's a new regime that can't afford to be sentimental about its political roots."

"But you remained a bachelor for the state. You sacrificed having children and everything."

Briney winked. "Had my bachelor apartment, didn't I? That's the breaks."

I waltzed back to the kid. "I admire that old guv. He can sit out any defeat."

Our mamma was making her rounds, and the kid grew petulant without Belinda to rock him. "Pinocchio, you ought to drop Briney from our reading list."

"What's Briney got to do with books?"

"The guv wrote a Russian novel. *Dead Souls.* He's Churchikiv."

"Chichikov," I said.

"Yeah, Churchikov. That's him. The guv collects souls for the clinic, souls in any condition, so the clinic can make up a bed list."

"Who told you that?"

"Belinda."

"Is she Chichikov's wife?"

"Near to a partner, I'd say."

I ran to Belinda while she was straightening blankets for the yeggs at the clinic. It hurt me that my old sweetheart from Charlotte Street was involved in some stinking affair. She saw that burnt look in my face, and she meddled with more and more blankets to keep her distance from me.

"Is this clinic a scam, Belinda?"

"Scam? It feeds a hundred gentlemen and studies how they're growing old."

"But the doctors must be phantoms. Are they under Briney's bed?"

"There's doctors, and don't you belittle that man. We wouldn't have a clinic without Briney."

"What does he do?"

"Helps me capture citizens from other nursing homes."

"But I don't see much of a change in your clientele."

"Well, he captures them on paper mostly . . . the guv shifts records around. He uses whatever influence he has with the county coroner. Somebody dies in an obscure situation, and we borrow them."

The kid was right. *Dead Souls.*

"Romey," she said, "we could lose our license if we can't meet our quota of beds."

I didn't have to sit on Cervantes' horse. I was adrift in somebody's fiction. Gogol or Dickens could have created the gerontology clinic.

Churchikov died in his bed. The statehouse didn't even drop its flag for him. Not one tremor from that goddess up in the roofs. Liberty girl never noticed he was gone. His gang assembled in the little chapel the clinic had. Our student rabbi recited a mass for the old man, praising his Christian soul. But I wondered about this rabbi who couldn't seem to graduate. He was another Churchikov, collecting dead souls as his congregation.

I waited for Lemuel to begin, because the Super wouldn't miss a chance to sermonize. But he didn't invoke Jesus or the devil. He muttered "Robin Hood."

"Louder," the kid said, sitting under a blanket.

"Briney was like Robin Hood. He pestered the rich, but he wouldn't take a farthing for himself."

"What's a farthing?" the kid asked.

"Money they used in Sherwood Forest," said the rabbi, who was an economist all of a sudden. How the hell did he know which coins Robin Hood's loot came in? The farthings of Sherwood Forest.

We buried the old man, but he left instructions that we not take him off the bed list. That way Belinda wouldn't have to scratch up one more soul. It was becoming a metaphysical question, the matter of where Briney was. With Robin Hood, the worms, or with us?

It was a shame he had to die, because the guv finally got his wish. Texas broke with the Union, and she didn't have to rebel. Uncle Sam went bankrupt in 2002. It wasn't on account of missions, foreign empires, or the moon. Uncle couldn't meet his social security payments or sign a check. Anno 85 had come to Uncle with a wicked slap. Texas had to bail him out. She bought her independence with a twenty billion dollar gift. And now Uncle had to write his checks without a Lone Star state.

There was dancing and singing on the cement of Old Pine Street. The firehouse next door had become a carnival. All the engines sat out front with garlanded ears and a cargo of yeggs from the clinic. But our gang had little to celebrate. Texas should have been Briney's. That was his blueprint in the street. We were all trespassing in his country.

The fools couldn't understand how much they needed Robin Hood. They fought up at the old statehouse. No one could agree on the bloody terms of a constitution. The Houston delegates walked out. Dallas camped on the lawn, while Lubbock threatened to return to the Union. It was a mad fricassee.

On the fifth night of that delegate assembly, San Antonio declared herself a separate city-state. Dallas followed San Antone, and Texas fell to the dogs. You had a republic with borders that wouldn't keep still, and seven city-states.

Austin was in a peculiar spot. She couldn't leave Texas. The country's capitol was on her lawn. She became the spiritual center of the republic, which had some of the Panhandle, most of the Pecos, and little else. But the capitol couldn't creep west of the Pecos, and with her isolation, Austin turned into a bitter island surrounded by city-states. Bitten with the urge to do something, she went on a naming binge. The capitol was rechristened Constitution Hall. Briney's Vicarage became the University of the Republic, or Lone Star U. Barrooms were renamed to fit Austin's picture of herself: Armadillo Alley, Texas Spuds and Suds, Constitution Wine and Dance. Groceries and banks had to wear a Lone Star in the window.

Since the Pecos was the one cohesive geography the republic had, it crawled into the naming ceremonies. We were now the Pecos Infirmary for the Old, the Feeble, and the Blind. Brothers, we had plenty of Feeble, but there wasn't a Blind man among us. It didn't seem to bother the doctors and bureaucrats of Lone Star U. That old Vicarage adopted us. We were deluged with ladies and gentlemen from the learned society of red roofs on the hill. They administered oaths of allegiance and a battery of tests. I'd have signed any oath to get rid of them, but I couldn't wiggle out of the tests. They put me into different cradles, and I had to live in a furnace of blue light and swallow their stinking elixirs.

They chose Belinda to announce the news. She held their print-out to her heart and said, "Pinocchio, you have the metabolism of a twelve-year-old boy."

I scratched my nose at the news, but the kid looked out from under his blanket. "Can't you hear? You're growing younger."

"The testers made a mistake."

The kid threw off his blanket, hobbled across the lane between our beds, and put a mirror to my face.

"How old are you?"

I had to think. "Sixty-six."

"Look at your neck. You don't have buzzard marks. Not a wrinkle..."

"It's my Tatar blood. Tatars age slower than other people."

"That's not retardation, it's a reversal," the kid said in the doctors' lingo he'd picked up at Pecos Infirmary. "Am I right, Miss Belinda?"

"Yes," she said, with the print-out still close to her heart. "Remarkable . . . a boy's symptoms at his age."

"I don't feel twelve," said the oldest twelve-year-old boy in the republic of Texas. It had to be the witch who was dragging me down below the bar mitzvah season. The whore mocked everything I did. But I wouldn't succumb to a witch.

"Have my mates," I whined to Belinda. "I'm not getting kicked out of the Pecos hotel."

"Who's kicking? They want you here. You and Mr. Pedersen are the prize boarders."

She took the print-out, leaving us to ponder how Texans get hurtled into time. The kid and I were at opposite ends of a looking glass that had its own cruel quotient for distorting people. We were like a comedy act, the Mutt and Jeff of this republic. But it wasn't a ripe year for comedy. All of Texas, east of the Pecos, was in a reactionary pull. The old Vicarage began to quarantine its books. They burned half their library at Lone Star U. Proctors from the Vicarage would come down into the city and demand a book check from street to street. The proctors were strict about what they would tolerate. No fiction of any kind. Nothing that couldn't conform to the codes and solemn condition of the republic.

I thought the Super would bless this burning in the street. But he was a curious son of a bitch. He didn't want to give up his books. The proctors had to confiscate his library. They didn't spare my own beaten copies of Melville, Joyce, and Mills. I hugged the Super as the proctors' whorish police tossed our books into the fire. I could feel him quicken under his pajamas. He rushed out at the police.

"I was a retailer," he said. "I never burned wholesale."

"What's he yakking about?" the young policemen asked as Lem stepped onto the fire and beat the ashes with his boots. His pajamas flamed under one shoulder, and it looked as if the Super was carrying a wing.

"Help him," I said, starting from the porch, but Belinda grabbed me by the ears and pulled me to the ground like a broken calf.

"Shush, Romey, shush now. These men are mean . . . they're like to kill you."

"But Lem?" I said.

"It's too late."

Lem danced towards a proctor with the fiery side of his pajamas and a policeman shot him in the head.

We declared war from our blankets, the kid and me. Texas would have to pay for the Super's life. We stole into the bookkeeping room and ordered a Deerslayer with a telescopic sight from the catalogues in the terminal screen. It took a month for the Deerslayer to arrive. We hid its quilting under my bed and assembled the mother while Belinda was on her rounds. We'd sit crosslegged with the instruction manual in Pedersen's lap and oil the Deerslayer, count our bullet clips, peer into the telescope.

"How are we going to shoot it?" I asked. "Do you think the rabbi was ever a soldier?"

"He soldiered in a creek," the kid said. "I'll shoot the Deerslayer."

"You can't make revolution out of an instruction book."

"Hell on you, Pinocchio. I had a high-powered rifle in Saskatchewan."

The kid suggested a shootout in the street.

"Not a chance. They'd pick us off in a minute. We'll go to the Vicarage and capture the clock tower. We can command everything east of the Pecos from up there."

The tower had been used before to hold Texas at bay. Long ago, in that prehistoric time when Texas was a state, an honor student had climbed into the shelf under the clock with a deer rifle and slapped at buildings and people for a day and a half. He destroyed two helicopters, fired on the statehouse, until an off-duty guard went out onto a window ledge a floor below the sniper and shot him to shit.

The kid and I intended to be more careful. We put together a survival kit of water and banana bread, hung a crowbar from the kid's pants, disassembled the Deerslayer, wrapped it in its original quilt, and tied it all to the kid's back. The kid sat on my shoulders, with a blanket around him, and we skulked out of the clinic.

We were two weird boys from the Pecos Infirmary on a sightseeing tour of Texas. I strode onto Congress Avenue with the kid. We looked at the dummies in Scarbrough's window, marched through the old statehouse, saluting policemen and other buggers, and went on up to the Vicarage.

No one paid much heed to some Pinocchio in blue pajamas, holding a blanketed boy. We waltzed into the tower building, a small Empire State in stone, and discovered a gang of proctors in red shoulder capes.

The kid tightened against my neck.

"Pinocchio, we'll come back tomorrow when the sea is clear."

I headed for the proctors and curtsied to their red capes.

"Hello, proctor . . . hello, hello."

Walked the kid into the elevator, helloing like that, and we got to the twenty-seventh floor, where the tower began. We whistled to ourselves, watched the red capes go into their offices, and strolled up to the tower door, which was shut to strangers after the first Texas sniper.

I ripped the door open with that crowbar we had. Pedersen climbed down from my back and we walked up five little flights to the shelf under the clock.

I heard the damn machinery behind that clock, like wheels trying to hold an iron heart. The kid unpacked the Deerslayer. We each had a pull of water and crawled out onto the lip of the shelf.

Red roofs lay below the lip, red roofs, brown hills, and that pink baby, the capitol of Texas. I anchored the Deerslayer against a groove in the stone, and it took five minutes for Pedersen to fold himself into a crouch. He squeezed his eye to the telescope and chortled at the clock.

"Pinocchio, there's a hundred red capes in the yard. It's going to be a short Tuesday for proctors . . . have yourself a look."

I saw burly men with pink cheeks through the hairs of the scope. They could have been rabbits ready for the slaughter.

The kid got into his shooting position. He chortled and then he cried. Didn't have to ask him what that crying was about. We hated the proctors, but Pedersen couldn't hunt rabbits from a roof. He wasn't the murdering kind.

We gorged ourselves on banana bread.

The kid began to waste. He was the oldest living example of progeria, and he'd been dying a long time. He hardly talked to me and Belinda. His head would furrow as if he were listening to a secret clock.

"Pedersen, what is it?"

"The stars are crooning, Pinocchio."

I assumed he was dropping into a coma. But he didn't have the abstracted look of the near dead. He kept to the details.

"Pinocchio, it's like giant lollipops making a soft scratch."

"Is there a message in the scratch? Are they singing for us?"

Pedersen scolded me with his lips. "For themselves," he muttered.

We had a sandwich together, began a game of tic-tac-toe. Pedersen died in the middle.

Solange sent me a condolence card from *The New York Review*. She was mistress of culture now to all the United States.

> Pinocchio, come to me.
> You'll have better royalties in New York.

I wrote back. *Thanks. But I couldn't live that far from the Pecos.*

She wooed me on the phone. "My sweet imbecile, you've fallen in with a fascist country."

Ah, I was tickled by her voice. That's what an old wife can do. But I'd never have arrived at Merci-Gâteau. There was no Concorde from Texas to Manhattan.

"Idiot boy," she said. "You'll dissolve in your doghouse, Pecos Jérôme."

What was this attraction between us? I couldn't recover from her red hair. I'd shuffle across the clinic grounds in my pajamas. Pinocchio had given all his other clothes away.

I drank tequila at a beanery on Old Elm, shivering with that dread of a man who'd lost his mates to the reaper. I was in some frigging time clot. Couldn't grow old. I searched for wattles in the mirror on the wall. My throat was smooth as a Christmas duck. That was no bloody accident. Brunhilde had fixed me. I was the frozen bar mitzvah boy.

Might have gone under the table with salt on my tongue if old Belinda hadn't found me. She paid my bill out of her own slim purse, clutched my arm, and led me home to Pecos Infirmary like a cow with amnesia.

"Why are you sniffling?"

"You're my oldest friend, Belinda. We met before the fall of Charlotte Street."

She put me to bed.

She must have felt my sorrow, because Belinda climbed under the blanket that night. She had nothing on but a cotton slip.

Hadn't kissed a secondhand girl in sixty years. Our loving under the blanket was merciful and slow, like the wheels in the clock tower. That's what friendship does. She was as familiar to me as the Pedersen kid, Pedersen in a pink slip.

On the nights Belinda couldn't lie in my room, I'd clutch the blanket and mold it into a crazy ball. God didn't mean us to snore alone. I'd become a carpenter in wool, fashioning another body with that blanket.

One night, without Belinda, something dropped away from the blanket ball. My carpentering had produced a woman with blue hair. I scowled at the whore of Montegrumo.

"It's kind of you to nest in my blanket, Brunhilde, but I have a girlfriend."

"Yes, a sweetheart with more varicose veins than the Yangtze River."

"You took Pedersen away. What else do you want?"

"Took Pedersen? I kept him around as long as I could."

"What do you want?"

"To make you happy."

"Then let me age like other people."

"You had your chance to come with me, but no, no, you needed an ox like Belinda, with her forged nurse's certificate . . . Pinocchio, should I take you to the movies?"

"We don't have a projector here."

The whore laughed into her fist. "Not shadows on a screen. The real movies. Would you like to watch Salome undress? Or have a look at the jewels in Cleopatra's nipple? If you think that might bore you, what about Mozart in his father's carriage?"

"Robin Hood," I said without hesitation.

"I'm not Twentieth Century-Fox. I can't bring you myths."

"Robin Hood."

Ah, I had the lady. She could poke molecules together, hurl Bonaparte out of a bag, but she didn't have the power to invent. Old Robin Hood was beyond a witch's broom. But the whore stroked that coiffure of hers, ionized the blue hair, and I felt a sock between the eyes that could only have been history's revenge on Copernicus Charyn. I woke in a copse that had more rust and wormy bark than green leaves. This copse was bald in the middle. It had great patches of earth where nothing seemed to grow. Lord of Mozart and Mussolini, it was Sherwood Forest.

That bald wood in Nottinghamshire couldn't have hid a rabbit. But I didn't see any rabbit runs. Just two men, taller than the midget trees of Sherwood Forest. Archers by the look of them, archers in leather pants. The older one, with scars on his face, lifted a flap in the leather and pissed like a horse. The forest steamed. Little John, I suppose.

The younger lout was Robin Hood. He had a torn cheek and a milky eye, unsightly hairs in place of a moustache, and a beard that must have been cropped by his enemies, because it grew in three directions.

They were bandits, all right, rogues without a farthing in their pockets. They had no pockets. I couldn't understand their bloody yeomen's talk.

"Ropp," John said, meaning Robin Hood. I was already getting used to their diction. "We can't continue on these bloody wages. I'll sell me arse to the sheriff, I will. I'll fuck a crow. We're starving, man. Will you consider your own lads, or by the rood, I'll bash your skull, Ropp."

Robin put a black thumb into the torn cheek. "John of Lincoln, I'd love to marry you."

He must have studied advanced psychology at some teachers' school in the shire, because he got that big bugger to laugh.

"Aw Ropp, I'd sooner marry the prioress than take a fall with you. The only time I kissed a man was when we had to go in masquerade to butcher the sheriff's people. But you can't give what little treasure we have to widowers and begging friars. That's not ethical, Ropp. It's a bleeding shame."

"But it's common knowledge that when a wife dies, her man takes to hunger . . . and what a turd I would be if I couldn't contribute to the friars."

"Contribute is one thing. Making us bloody paupers is another. I've not a farthing for my old age."

Robin pissed and then closed his flap.

John pissed.

A wind blew into the low trees. A deer slapped out of the rust in Sherwood Forest. The witch plucked me home.

I felt my own sad wind under the blanket, the chill of history. What was the point of building stories, creating Pinocchios and all that, if the source was rotten? Robin Hood was a yegg in stinking leather pants. Trotsky had used him as a prototype for the Russian revolution. "The first communist," he calls him in *A History of the Snail.* "The idea of the commune began in Sherwood Forest."

Well, I was off Robin Hood. And I refused to sneak around in Napoleon's underpants. What did I care about the perfume of Proust's apartment? Or how Flaubert looked in the nude? I was homesick, brothers, homesick for the Bronx.

"Brunhilde, couldn't we go on a bus ride to heaven or hell?"

"Stop hedging, Pinocchio, and say what it is you're after."

"My uncle Lionel."

"That's easy, my dear. Should we catch him on his deathbed, or earlier?"

"Later," I told the witch. "I want uncle as he is, now."

Brunhilde had a bitter look in her eye. "I think I'll pack, Pinocchio. Having idle hours has made you naughty. Lionel Copernic is dead."

"How does that change the complexion of your molecules? The dead must have someplace to go. Where is it, Brunhilde? I'd like to meet the old uncle. I've had a laundry list of dads, but it was Lionel who really raised me."

The witch had hardened herself to Pinocchio. "You won't trap me with all that mumbo jumbo of an afterlife. Lionel's available, but not in terms you'd ever understand."

"But is there heaven and hell?"

"That's simple cosmetics for something else."

I'd learned from Little John. "By the rood," I shouted, "will you tell me where the dead go?"

"Back to the beginning."

"What beginning, witch?"

"The dead live their lives over and over again. That's your heaven and hell. Nietzsche called it the art of endless recurrence. I'm afraid it's above your head, dear Pinocchio. Philosophy and physics."

"Wait a minute. You mean Pedersen keeps getting born with progeria? Why couldn't you give him a better slot?"

"We're not talking about Gimbel's basement. We don't switch bodies and souls. All we have is the Pedersen kid. Each time you go back to the beginning, there's a vague depression, and the depression mounts. That's where the hell comes in. It gets worse and worse."

"How many times has the kid come back?"

"I told you. It's above your head. We have to talk about simultaneity, the fact that the world is everywhere at once. The centuries before and after Jesus are the same thing. Shakespeare is one insignificant cipher in the time flow. He's always forgotten and discovered again. He goes on writing his plays. He performs the girls' parts. He's a wonderful Ophelia."

"Yes, I would imagine. Old William in a tunic, binding his varicose veins. Tell me, do the stars sing? That's what the kid said."

The witch sat near me with her arms akimbo. "What do they have to sing about? They whirl towards destruction without the least bit of music. Don't you see? Biology should have ended with the giraffe. Adam and Eve come along, and it's trouble for everybody."

"For godmothers too?"

"Someone has to manage this silly business. A few of us break out of the cycle and become supervisors, sheriffs of space and time. We can swoop anywhere in the continuum, making sure that each reenactment of the world conforms to the original pattern. We only allow a swerve of ten degrees. Shakespeare might forget *Coriolanus*, but we couldn't have him go and steal Dante, or become Doris Lessing. Humans are capable of anything."

"But I don't need a godmother. Why have you come for me?"

"On account of Pinocchio. You distorted the whole landscape, reinventing that long nose. I had to tuck the creases in, or suffer a planet of Pinocchios."

"What's so terrible about that?" I said, turning wistful on the whore of Montegrumo. "I might have gotten along better with a male supervisor."

"There are none. Women evolved faster than men. Their frames are sturdier for travel. Men have rotten balance. And they don't know what it means to nurse a child."

"You shouldn't gloat about your tits," I said. "I'd like to find my uncle before all these recurrences make him so depressed, he'll think he never had a nephew . . . Brunhilde, take me to Charlotte Street."

She didn't even have to press on her hair. I turned from the witch, experienced a mild vertigo, and I was back in 1944. Lionel had his pink suit. He combed his moustache with the help of a pocket mirror. Ah, I was lonely for the ice-pick man. Wouldn't have had much of a history without my uncle Lionel. Suppose he did have enough ambiguity in him to consider murdering me later on in his career. He was still better than Robin Hood. Uncle supported us after Bruno ran away. He wouldn't scour the Bronx for rags. He skipped junior high and invented his own markets as the urchin millionaire.

Wanted to touch him on the shoulder, prove to him I'd come out of Texas, the astral boy, Pinocchio Jerome. But I might have upset his whiskers. So this was hell. Uncle would have to comb and comb until the planet popped from the heat of souls recycling themselves. I should have been Lionel's godmother. I'd have steered him from Bathsheba . . . but he's a Tatar Jew, not some golem in the attic. Bathsheba was his fire sign. He'd have orphaned himself to the pickle merchants, become a secondhand child, without her.

"Uncle, it's all right. If you forget a whisker, you can comb it straight on your next trip to Charlotte Street. That's Brunhilde's law."

But he never heard me. The whore must have figured it was dangerous for us to talk. I might have pulled Lionel out from under that fabric of endless incarnations. We'd have run away to a zone where witches couldn't grab at you: our own bald wood west of the Pecos.

Belinda found me on the floor. The witch of Montegrumo must have thrown me off the blanket after she smelled what my schemes were about. I'd never become her loyal space cadet. Only the Lord could count the number of galaxies those godmothers have filled with the molecules of movie shows, all of them going on at once. That was the singing the kid had uncovered. The stars were mute, but in his incredible old age, Pedersen could hear the galaxies bending to the noise of so many picture shows.

Whatever brittle music was grinding around me, my fortune began to leak, and I became a ward of the republic. It was curious. With molecules floating under my armpits, astral bodies everywhere, I still had to make water. I pissed like a horse.

It was as if I were challenging the godmothers with my own physicality. I turned seventy-seven at the clinic. The Super succumbed to a heart attack. Our gang fell away. The student rabbi went senile. He'd sit in the tub, pretending to swim out of Texas, and cackle at me from the soap dish. He was much more lucid with soap in his mouth.

"The guv swindled you, kid."

"Ah, Port Arthur, don't demean the dead."

"I'm not Port Arthur. The guv took me out of the slammer and taught me five holy sentences up in the chapel. I'm Willard Friendly, and I've never seen the inside of a Jewish church. I got my parole for bar mitzvahing you."

"It doesn't matter, Willard. The guv was doing what he could for Pinocchio . . ."

"You're not Pinocchio. You're an old whore, like the rest of us. But it doesn't show in your face."

Willard died. And then Belinda. And I had nothing between me and the world but my blanket. Brunhilde stopped patrolling the galaxy of Texas. She abandoned me to my boyish looks.

It was strange, living in Anno 85. Uncle Sam couldn't get out of bankruptcy. Canada started nibbling at Uncle's borders, and soon Buffalo had to exist under two flags. The quebecois formed their own republic in my seventy-ninth year, giving Buffalo a third flag.

It was becoming a century of small republics. Wales declared her independence and found her own queen. Bulgaria discovered bauxite preserves outside an old Thracian settlement and broke all ties with the Soviet Union. She was the wealthiest country in Europe. Her armies walked up Yugoslavia, entered Italy, rushed into France, stopping at Dijon long enough to offer peace, and pounced across the Seine with her computerized tanks.

Paris became a suburb of Sofia, and the war was over. The Bulgars weren't interested in the rest of France. The Turkish parliament met in secret and voted to annex itself to the Bulgarian People's Republic, but with all her bauxite, Bulgaria wouldn't have the Turks. Sofians started speaking French. It was the old story of seduction. Paris wore her prettiest skirts, and the Prix Goncourt became a Bulgarian event.

This I learned from my bed. I took nothing for granted. If Philip of Macedonia had appeared in my bathtub, I would have conversed with him as best I could. It was as if some boundary broke, and all my years of ignorance had flipped over and turned a wooden boy into a wise man. Who cared about fake rabbis in a chapel? My whole fucking life had become an invisible bar mitzvah.

Received a notice under my blanket: the Pecos Infirmary was shutting its doors. Texas was no longer interested in studying old men. All the yobs serving here would be shunted to other facilities. You couldn't imagine the weeping I encountered as I waltzed from bed to bed.

"Pinocchio, Pinocchio . . ."

"I'll help you, mateys," I muttered. But I didn't have a clue on how I could redeem the clinic. My last bit of royalties arrived. I threw it into the nurses' pot, so they wouldn't seek other jobs while we were in a state of flux.

I went up to the capitol in my blue pajamas. Austin hadn't solved its cricket plague. The little buggers nested everywhere under the dome. I felt like shipping them to Sofia. The crickets might have learned French.

I hopped around the old statehouse asking for the inspector general of hospitals and nursing homes. Had to shove past his secretary, but Inspector General Junior Harris happened to be a protégé of Briney's.

He didn't remove himself from the old men at Pecos Infirmary, but he talked about "zero return" in regard to the country's clinics.

"It's bottom line," said Junior Harris. "Texas is in the middle of a crunch."

He found me a plastic spoon and I ate from his cup of cottage cheese.

"The guv died on the premises, Junior. It's sort of a monument to him. If you shut us down, you'll lose the last trace of Briney. It'll be like he'd never been around."

"I'm on your side, Pinoke. But it will take a hundred thousand Texas dollars to keep Pecos afloat until the next fiscal year."

The republic didn't believe in greenbacks. You had to carry little silver mountains to the bank, or live with the plastic in your pocket. I'd held on to my VISA card, but I couldn't have borrowed much silver. Hadn't used the bloody card in fifteen years.

I shook Junior's hand and sang, "A hundred thou, a hundred thou," marching to the passport office. The only place I knew where I might collect some money was Paris. Where else could I go? It was curtains for the clinic if I went under the blanket again and played Rip Van Winkle.

The plastic I had couldn't buy me a seat on the Concorde. Air France was dead. And the Bulgarian People's Republic didn't believe in the bourgeois notion of saving time on a silver bird. Her diplomats traveled on flying boxcars.

I got to Montreal and boarded a Bulgarian boxcar. I was still in my pajamas. It wasn't out of lethargy. I was hoping pajamas would dramatize the plight of the clinic.

It wasn't the season for Pinocchios. Not one person bothered with my presence. It was the People's airline. We all had a box lunch.

EIGHTEEN

SOFIA WEST

YOU couldn't notice much of a difference at Charles de Gaulle. Yes, there were Bulgarian soldiers and commissars, but they didn't bully. They seemed to operate a benign black market, selling soap and razor blades at a reasonable price. The commissars took an interest in my silver dollars and offered themselves as money changers. What did I care if the commissars scalped me a little? I gave up my silver for Bulgarian francs, which were only good in Sofia West, the Bulgarian name for Paris.

No one spoke their bloody language, not even the commissars, so it was an easy transition to Bulgarian French. I jabbered with my taxi driver and never bothered about a hotel. He took me straight to that restaurant of influence, le Palais des Cocottes, which thrived under the Bulgarian regime.

I avoided the arbor, filled with Japanese tourists, and walked into that skinny terrace where I'd had lunch with Solange in 1993. The computer consoles were gone: a bourgeois notion, bills arriving on a blue screen. I drank my Schweppes in a corner and could barely coax some bread out of the waiters, who rumpled their noses at my pajamas and called me Monsieur, like they would an anonymous clown. I'd become déclassé at the restaurant, odd man out.

I asked for a lettuce sandwich. The waiters said they couldn't serve such an uncivilized thing.

"It's the national dish of Bulgaria," I informed the waiters.

Had my lettuce sandwich with a heap of mustard. I eschewed their bloody napkins and patted my lips with a pajama sleeve, Pinocchio déclassé.

Ordered another six sandwiches, burping into my sleeve, while a yob watched me from the next table. He had a bloody business suit and adjutants all around him. He was much too dark for a Frenchman, and he didn't have the feel of a pied noir. He was a Bulgar with the burnt complexion of a Tatar Jew. Wanted to ask him if he owned a third nipple, like Lionel and Jerome.

The Bulgar dismissed his adjutants. The waiters couldn't stop kissing his arse. He ordered a lettuce sandwich and never took his eyes off me.

"Le grand Pinocchio. Incroyable!"

He handed me his card, which had the People's seal on it. He was Nikola, a young jurist assigned to Sofia West. Apart from his own stinking language, he knew English, Russian, and Bulgarian French. Nikola was the highest civil judge in the People's colonies. He'd read my *Pinocchio* as a child and couldn't recover from it.

"You socked the fascists, but it was always with funny lines. We assumed you were dead. What are you doing here?"

"I've retired to Texas, but the home where I live will evaporate if I can't raise the money to keep it."

"How do you call this home?"

"The Pecos Infirmary."

"A private clinic, run by the bourgeoisie?"

"No, Nikola. It's under the republic's wing."

"Then why is it incumbent upon yourself to save this infirmary?"

Ah, he talked like a jurist. Legal language eats up the mind like a crocodile.

"Texas has stopped caring about us," I said.

He removed the lettuce from his sandwich and clawed at it.

"Isn't there a socialist opposition in your country, a voice to pressure the government?"

"I'm the only voice at the clinic."

The yob forgot his bloody manners and took to kissing me in public. Nikola kissed my eyebrows and my ear. We could have been exchanging addresses, because the restaurant didn't object to Nikola's kissing.

"I knew," he said.

Knew what? I could see that Bulgarian judges had this habit of not finishing their sentences. It must have been how they ran their courts, with ellipses and borrowed lines.

"I knew the author of *Pinocchio* had to be a socialist in his heart."

"I've withdrawn from politics," I said. "I'm an old man."

"Don't abuse yourself . . . I'll help you, my friend."

"But why should Bulgaria worry about the Pecos?"

"We can't neglect another country's wards. Whatever opinions you have of us, Pinocchio, we're the People's republic."

He signaled to the waiters, who wouldn't take money for our lettuce sandwiches, and we strode outside to the judge's car. He had a Chrysler in Sofia West. Nikola knocked on the glass, and his driver shoved off without the slightest regard for traffic.

We landed on the rue de Varenne. Nikola got me past a sentry box and we entered a bloody palace called Matignon that belonged to the governor general of the Western Frontier. I got lost searching for a toilet on the palace's ground floor. Nikola had to rescue me.

Couldn't find a bloody computer at Matignon. We passed the telex room, with sheets of paper that curled around a desk. But we never got to the governor general. He didn't have time for an audience with pensioners like me.

Nikola plagued the little ministers of Matignon, demanded that something be done for citizen Pinocchio.

"Comrades," Nikola said in French. "He is an antifascist author."

"But Nikola, we cannot interfere in the internal politics of Texas."

"What interfere? We are providing Pinocchio with an inheritance."

"He will have to work for his inheritance, my dear Nikola. Otherwise it will stink of the bourgeoisie."

"Shall he collect the People's garbage? He is an eighty-year-old man."

The little ministers studied my pajamas. "We'll locate a suitable employment for him. But he has to work, Nikola. That is final."

"Indeed," my protector told them. "Indeed." And he thanked the little ministers, gripping their hands. Texas could have used him up at the old statehouse. He was a judge that refused to bend. Nobody could buy Nikola.

He secured a bed for me in the palace. Matignon had become my hotel. We drank wine in a room with ducks in the ceiling and angels on the wall.

"Nikola, I have people in Paris I'd like to look up . . . relatives and old friends."

"Don't move." His teeth were red with wine. He handed me a Bulgarian envelope. "Write their names on the back and I'll have them come to you, brother Pinocchio."

I asked for Antoine, Edgar, Alain San Angelo, and Marie-Pierre. He rang for a bloody servant, waved the envelope, and shouted at him in Bulgarian.

"Will it mean trouble?" I asked.

"No. I sent him to our registry office. It's my privilege. I can open any document. I'm a judge."

We sat for an hour. The ducks swam into their favorite ocean on the ceiling, while we were clumsy with our wineglasses. Each of us broke two.

The servant came in and whispered to Nikola, whispered a long time. Nikola got rid of him and leaned his chair into the palace wall.

"I'm sorry, old boy. That aunt of yours is dead."

Forgot that auntie didn't grow young like other people.

"And her lover, Antoine Montesquieu?"

"Dead of a natural cause."

"The tobacconist, Alain San Angelo?"

"This one was murdered by a rival chief. Before we entered Paris."

"And my little cousin, Edgar Copernicus?"

"We don't have his file, but we're searching, brother Pinocchio. He must be indexed somewhere else."

The servant came back. Nikola didn't smile. He only said, "Your cousin was registered with our security office. Little Copernicus is an enemy of the People."

He'd been condemned to la Santé, that Devil's Island near the rue Pascal, now the People's prison of Sofia West. It had the same red walls I remembered from my first trip to Paris. Ah, it was like the bitterest borscht to imagine that the only way I could ever get inside the red walls was as a guest of the Bulgarian People's Republic, visiting my little cousin.

Didn't matter that the People had recommended me. I was subjected to a full search. Matrons felt under my pajamas. They were pretty girls imported from Bulgaria. I stood naked in front of them, my pecker rising to their touch. They smiled at Pinocchio's nose and bade me to get back into my pajamas.

My cousin was brought to the prisoners' cage. Only a monkey could stand upright in such a closet. Edgar entered the cage from a narrow tunnel and looked out at me with his torso bent like a man with a broken neck. He was wearing the famous skullcap that marked him as a citizen of la Santé.

Ah, time has an evil smell. That could have been Lionel under the skullcap. He had my uncle's brooding look.

"I told you to come to America . . . but you had to marry your gang."

His Tatar eyes shone from the cage. His pants were too small. Lord have mercy, it was like seeing Lionel at that children's jail on Valentine Avenue. I'd come back to my own beginning, even without the witch.

"Romey, I left the lulus a long time ago."

"What got you to la Santé?"

"Antisocial activity," he said. "Beat up a few commissars . . . one of the chaps died."

"But they're simpletons, Edgar, petty traders, out for the quick buck. I met them at the airport. How could they ever have harmed you?"

"They're Bulgars, aren't they? Bulgars are like the Boche. They have no business in Paris."

"But they won the war, Edgar. Countries fight. It's always been that way. In fifty years Napoleon will come from Corsica and shove the Bulgars out."

"I can't wait fifty years . . . but you shouldn't worry. The Bulgars are good to me. I won't get the choppe."

Couldn't fool the kid from Charlotte Street. Choppe was the guillotine. I'd learned that from Alain San Angelo.

"The Bulgars aren't medieval. They wouldn't shorten your neck."

"They have a different choppe. They ship you to the bauxite mines. That's where most of the lulus are. They won't survive Bulgaria. But how are you, cousin Jerome? Preparing a new book?"

"No. I have to find money for the clinic where I live."

"Ah, you're a philanthropist . . . and you collaborate with the Bulgars in your spare time."

Jesus, he was a bloody jurist in his cage. "I've come for a visit. Is that what you call aiding the Bulgars?"

"Cousin, I'm in solitary. Killed a man. You can't visit me without special permission from the high priests."

"I happened to meet a judge."

"Fancy that . . . why the fuck are you wearing pajamas?"

"I told you. I live at a clinic. This is the clothes I have left."

"Well, do you need a touch? I have my convict's pay. Romey, you can borrow on that."

"Stop it . . . maybe the judge will help. His name is Nikola."

My cousin nickered like a mad horse. He forgot the dimensions of that cage and banged his skull against the roof. "You always had the knack of falling in with lovely people . . . Nikola, eh? He's our local butcher. Has his own tribunal. He runs the security police."

"That's absurd. Nikola's with the civil courts."

"Everything is civil in Sofia West. Criminals can't exist. We're social parasites, sick people. We get rehabilitated in the bauxite mines. The real antisocials are kept out of sight at la Santé. Nikola has to be careful. We might contaminate the rest."

"I'll talk to him, Edgar. He'll listen."

"You'll only make it worse . . . I'm happy here. We get exercise. The Bulgars bring us plenty of books. Your *Pinocchio* is on the favored list. It's become my bible. I read a paragraph every morning. It's a swinish book, perfect for prison. That little big nose always avoids involvement."

"He's a puppet," I said. "And what can you expect from literature?"

"A lot. I like my Pinocchio with more hair on his chest."

"He died with Mussolini, didn't he?"

"Any idiot can die with a dictator. Couldn't he have taken a wife?"

"Who? Some Pinocchia?"

"Why not? A lady longnose. It might have taught him to care a bit."

"He cared," I said. "But he didn't have much luck with the ladies."

"That's because he never looked them in the eye. He was too busy sawing between their legs."

That boy was as kind as *The New York Review*. "You have to saw when a nose is all you've got."

"Then he should have stuck to foreplay . . ."

Edgar stooped back into his tunnel. And I had nothing but my cousin's old molecules in the cage.

I screamed blue murder at Matignon. Woke the entire hotel. A soldier came to sock me, but left after one try.

"Bring me Nikola."

Ministers prowled near my door. "Quiet, please."

I cursed the ministers and their stinking government, told them they'd all get the choppe. "Come on, arrest me. Pinocchio's an enemy of the People."

The ministers rocked their shoulders in my doorway. "We can't arrest you without a proper magistrate."

"Then find one. I want to sleep in la Santé."

"We're not barbarians. We'd never put an eighty-year man in with such parasites."

"You'll have to," I said, weaving from minister to minister, pulling noses and ears. The whores wouldn't fight back. In my bitterness I began to eat the drapes off my window.

Soldiers arrived with automatics, but the ministers couldn't tell them to shoot the People's guest.

Nikola came down in a purple robe. The son of a bitch had his own bed at the palace. He cleared the room of servants, soldiers, and ministers with one long frown.

"How's the old Gestapo?" I asked.

Nikola smashed me in the mouth. I fell. He grabbed my pajama cuff and waltzed me into the bathroom, holding my face under the tap until I finished spitting up blood. All that running water had calmed Pinocchio.

"You're the butcher of Bulgaria. You sentence children to the bauxite mines."

"You dunce," Nikola said, eying my bloody mouth. "Be specific with your accusations."

"You got rid of the lulus, Edgar's old gang."

Nikola bowed. "You'll have to pardon a republic that arrests children who are forty years old. You're not a dunce. You're precocious for someone with senile dementia."

"But the lulus still have a one-way ticket to the mines."

"Of course. They're not meant to come back. We've broken them, and the Corsican gangsters, and the last of the pieds noirs. The incorrigibles are gone from Paris."

"You give them all the choppe."

"We didn't invent the guillotine. We only improved on it. The incorrigibles will die of breathing red dust."

"Edgar's right. You are the Boche."

"Oh yes, we're the bloody Boche. We unloosened Paris from France. But there are no slaves on the boulevard Raspail. Everyone is a citizen of Bulgaria."

"What if your new Bulgars don't admire their citizenship?"

"Then they can go to Lyon . . . Pinocchio, there hasn't been a rush to leave."

"You shouldn't have lied to me, Nikola. You sent a lackey out to scratch for Edgar's dossier when you knew all the while where he was."

"Arrogant bastard. Do you think you're so important that I memorized your entire family tree? How could I have known that this Edgar was your cousin?"

"But you are chief of security."

"We have only two circuits in Paris, military and civilian. I'm responsible for the civilian side."

"You're the circuit rider," I said. "Nikola, the hanging judge."

"Didn't hang your little cousin, did I?"

"Nikola, let him out, please. I'll do another *Pinocchio* and sign all my royalties to Bulgaria . . . or you."

He made a fist but he must have realized the work it would mean if he bloodied my mouth again. "Your little cousin murdered a commissar. He's lucky to be where he is . . . we've found employment for you. You'll exhibit your person at the People's fairs. And don't consider refusing. Because I might go deeper into your cousin's case and send him to the mines after all. If you help us, I'll see to it that your cousin is taken out of solitary and allowed to have his whores once a week. You're not to visit Edgar again . . . now you've annoyed me enough for one day. Go to bed."

Nikola left his boot in my arse. I was official puppet to the Bulgarian regime. And if I started a revolution, Edgar would have to eat red dust.

Finished a basket of croissants in the morning. Had the servants pipe in coffee and hot milk. It would cost Bulgaria a fortune to maintain the People's puppet. You can't expect Pinocchio to put out for free.

Had to wear a coonskin cap. The Bulgars paraded me in a truck. I went around the boulevards doing different parts. Daniel Boone, Davy Crockett, General Custer, Ben Franklin and his electrical kite. Sometimes I was myself, Pinocchio of Texas. Tourists took my picture. Busloads arrived from the Bulgarian hinterland every afternoon. These buses docked outside the Palais de Justice. The ministers of Matignon swore to me that the first thing Bulgars asked about, getting off the bus, was citizen Pinocchio.

The mothers listed me in their guidebooks. I'd come out of obscurity in my eightieth year. I should have rejoiced. I lived in a palace. I had all the butter a man my age was allowed to eat. Doctors listened to my heart lest Daniel Boone strain himself. But I wanted my bed at the Pecos Infirmary.

I couldn't fault the Bulgars. There wasn't a fire eater on the boulevard de la Chapelle. They'd sent the Arabs to university. And the pieds noirs were in the bauxite somewhere.

I was a sentimental bugger who preferred the old boulevard de la Chapelle. You can't have a city without a fire eater or two.

The People's troubadour took what he could get. I leaned to beggars mostly, because whores and pimps had disappeared with the old aristocratic bums of the quays. It was hard to find a bloody beggar in the street. Paris had been plucked. Undesirables were sentenced to the bauxite mines or some other conciergerie. You had cake under Nikola, cake and a coonskin hat and commissars who changed your money in a picture-book regime.

But I found me a beggar on the place d'Italie, rooting in a box of trash. My beggar had red hair cupped under a kerchief. I was doing Davy Crockett from my carnival truck when I noticed the freckles on her neck. She rooted with both her shoulders in the trash. My beggar's hands were littered with black dust. A natural garbage lady.

Black hands couldn't keep me from a freckleface. I had logic on my side, up in the truck. *The New York Review* had come to the place d'Italie. It had its French offices out on the street.

Tourists gripped my cuffs. I lost the garbage lady for a moment, behind a sea of heads. I jumped down from the truck, waltzed away from the People's fair, and landed on a little concourse that held the garbage lady.

She wouldn't finish her rooting. Help me God, a howling came up from the trash, as if a hideous dog with three heads were at the bottom, guarding the mouth to hell on the place d'Italie. Ah, it was only trash rubbing in a narrow box.

I spoke to the garbage lady.

"Solange."

She continued to root. Bottles scratched inside the box, sounding like old Cerberus again. It was a dog's life in French Bulgaria.

"Solange."

I gripped her blackened hands and brought them out of the garbage, obliging her to look at Davy Crockett.

"Solange, don't you recognize the husband you had?"

She scowled something to herself. Black dust hid the freckles around her nose.

"Can't hear you, Solange."

"Take off that ridiculous hat."

Stuffed the coonskin into my pocket and escorted Solange out from under the trash. We had tea and cupcakes at an inn on the rue de Tolbac. The cupcakes were from Tonkin. I stirred the teapot and discovered a pink froth in the leaves. I'd never had the tonkinois.

Solange ate the cupcakes like a starving child with something golden in the heel of her hand.

"How long have you been in Paris?"

"Months," she said, between her gnawing at the cupcakes.

"What happened to the old review?"

"You can't spend your life on biographies of Beethoven and next year's annotated *Alice.*"

"You gave up your seat on the editorial board?"

"Didn't have to," she said. "The seat disappeared . . . we were getting slaughtered at the newsstands."

"You should have come to Texas. I would have found you a bed."

"I'd rather not retire to your hotel for decrepits."

"So you retired to Paris and you look for vital signs in the garbage."

"I'm free," she said, devouring the last cupcake.

I settled our bill for thirteen cupcakes and a pot of pink tea, but I wasn't fast enough for the old wife. She fled from the rue de Tolbac while I was in the cellar pissing the tonkinois.

Had to beg the little ministers to look her up. There wasn't a Madame Gâteau in the files.

"Please," I said. "She might have registered under the name of Copernicus Charyn. We were married once."

They couldn't find Solange under any name, and I wondered if Brunhilde was in Paris to play my wife.

I performed in other neighborhoods and began to notice scribbles in the street with a common message: Mort à la Bulgarie!

It was curious, brothers, how those messages followed me around. I'd swear somebody was weaving a kind of celestial arc for Davy . . . or Daniel Boone. A Valentine from Mars.

Mort à la Bulgarie!

Kept going out with the truck on tours of Paris. I found the garbage lady wandering in the Champ de Mars, near a bunch of cadets playing boules in the sand. The cadets wore green blouses that marked them as colonial troops. They must have come down from the École Militaire, the official training school for the cadets of Paris, under Bulgarian rule.

They snickered at Solange, who'd trespassed into their lanes and upset the alignment of balls.

"Vache," they said. "Put a move on it, before we throw you into our conciergerie for interfering with future officers."

Solange kicked absently at the balls, and the cadets ran for billy clubs.

"We'll show the vache."

They'd have bruised her if Davy Crockett hadn't been there. "Children, let her go."

They looked up at me with tightened red eyes. "Who's a child? And what's this vache to you?"

"It's my wife you're calling a cow."

"His wife," they repeated. "The vache is his wife." They sniffed my coonskin cap. "And who are you, love?"

"Pinocchio."

"Aint it a fact." They fondled their billy clubs. "Pinocchio in the flesh. What if we should take your nose off?"

"Then I'd have to tell my biggest admirer," I said, thrusting Nikola's card into their bloody faces. Their jowls shook. They curtsied to Pinocchio and ran off the field with the billy clubs tucked under their tails.

"Solange, I'm not the zookeeper. I can't always be around to protect you from wild animals."

She was holding a stone, and I recognized what she'd carved into the sand: Mort à la Bulgarie!

"Mother of Mercy, you're the artist, then."

The Eiffel Tower was behind Solange, and I shivered up into its needle. I felt like a puppet inside a puppet inside a puppet cage, with nothing to preserve him but a judge's calling card.

"Gâteau, we have to get out of here."

I heard the sirens, and then police cars jumped onto the field. Solange abandoned that clumsy drift of hers and ran like the devil across the Champ de Mars, sirens in her wake. Six of the cars surrounded her. The seventh came for me. Nikola stepped out of his Chrysler.

"Please," I said. "She's a delirious woman. Don't harm her."

The judge had a jacket around his shoulders. I tried to get out from under the wings of his jacket and help Solange. He cradled me with one arm and socked me into the ground. Pinocchio lay waltzing with his head.

Looked up from the sand and noticed a chorus of eyes. The little ministers stood behind Nikola's wings.

"Is it wise, Nikola, to treat a foreigner like that in front of the Eiffel Tower?"

"It's more than wise. It's my will."

"But how shall we explain it in our reports?"

"I disposed of a bedbug and an exploiter of the People."

"But on the Champ de Mars?"

"I'm a circuit judge. I can hold my court anywhere in Paris."

"Without stenographers and attendance books?"

"Don't be so damn technical . . . all right, take him to Matignon. But if I see his face, comrades, I'll turn him into one long mask of skin."

I saw the wings begin to trot towards Solange. Eiffel moved an inch. The ministers shoved a briefcase under my head and Pinocchio blacked out.

Didn't enter some inferno under the Champ de Mars. I woke in my bed at Matignon. A servant brought me orange juice, and I figured I was under house arrest. I drank the o.j., dreaming of the choppe. Brunhilde must have been preparing to end me in bauxite.

I blubbered without shame. I didn't want to die with red dust in my mouth.

The ministers paddled into my room.

"Mustn't cry," they said.

"But my life has come down to zero."

"Nonsense," they said. "You'll be back on your truck in a day or two."

"I'm not under house arrest?"

"What gave you such a silly idea?"

"Comrades, I can go wherever I like?"

"Within reason," they said.

"Take me to my wife."

The little ministers held their own heads. "Citizen, you mustn't incite Nikola. He's a variable fellow . . . educated like no other man. He brought you flowers while you were asleep, but if you mention this Merci-Gâteau, he'll sink all our careers."

"One visit," I said. "I have to see her."

The ministers groaned and conferred behind the door. "Be ready in twenty minutes."

I got into my working pajamas. "Comrades, is Nikola really a civilian judge?"

"Yes, a judge . . . and also our acting governor general."

They drove me to a women's jail hidden behind a wall on the boulevard des Capucines. This little conciergerie had nuns for matrons, nuns with blue hats borrowed from some Bulgarian order, I suppose.

We passed the Cour des Femmes, where the women got their exercise. The ministers left me upstairs in an alcove. Solange appeared suddenly behind a screen, and I was right back to my roots, because even with freckles and red hair, she looked like Bathsheba in prison clothes. I was that seven-year-old boy who'd come to visit his mamma in jail.

The witch of Montegrumo had made a mistake. We didn't have to die to get born again and go through the same bloody circuit. We were lightning riders who could cover that circuit in a couple of giant steps. Dreaming and waking we produced little hells and little wars.

Her cheeks were puffed. The Bulgars must have slapped her pretty. Her eyes fastened on Pinocchio through the screen.

"How are you, coco?"

"Solange, couldn't you have told me why you were in Paris without inventing a funeral for *The New York Review*?

"I tried to avoid you, darling, but you always had a nose for me."

"You're not a garbage lady?"

"No . . . I needed a disguise."

"For some revolutionary front?"

"I'm alone," she said. "Nikola has jailed everybody else."

"But what could you accomplish with slogans in the sand?"

"The illusion that an army was building up, so the Bulgars might pee in their pants . . . and the wish that words could start a rally, and then the Bulgars would have something to pee about."

"Nikola will never let them pee. He's a bloody scientist. He'll export all of Paris if he has to."

"That would be an improvement," said the old wife.

Ah, I couldn't get cured of her freckles. I was a sinking ship in matters of Solange.

"I'll buy your way out of the conciergerie."

"Nikola's a purist. He won't barter with you . . . but you needn't worry, Jérôme. Bulgaria will tire of her foreign dominions and she'll walk away from Paris."

"Then why bother to scratch words in the sand?"

"Because I want them to leave in my lifetime."

I remembered what the high priest of hospitals and nursing homes had said to Pinocchio in the statehouse, and I repeated it to Solange. "You had zero return on your investment. The scratchings got you nowhere."

"Nowhere but a reunion with my darling dope."

I might have chewed the wires between us if a nun hadn't come to fetch me. "Solange," I said, clawing the screen. I was a monkey on maneuvers, and monkeys meant nothing at the women's jail. Solange was gone. The nuns must have taken her out for exercise in a darkened vestry of the Cour des Femmes.

I searched for Nikola at Matignon.

The soldiers didn't stop me from mucking about the palace. But I couldn't penetrate Nikola's headquarters. The assistant to his assistant secretary told me to suck a snail.

"But I'm willing to wait, comrade . . . I'll sit here until tomorrow."

"Then you'll die of sitting, because Nikola never uses this door."

"Couldn't you take a message through?"

"He's ordered us to eat your messages. There's nothing to do, comrade, but kill yourself. That's the best solution."

I clopped downstairs to my bed and discovered a bulb against my ass. The ministers had prepared a hot-water bottle for the People's guest. Ah, it was like old amenities in the Bronx. Bathsheba would fix a hot rubber bottle for uncle and me during the wildest storms. I sniffled into the blanket.

The ministers arrived with my first bloody tear.

"Stop that. We insist."

"But you're so kind to me. The best comrades I ever had."

"Gibberish. Nikola pays us to look after you."

"Comrades," I said. "My own little mates."

"Desist from this fantasy. We get special compensation for each Pinocchio in the house. We're functionaries. We have no attitude towards a guest."

That was the delight of this republic. A civil servant couldn't admit to being human. I started to cough and felt the worry in their eyes. Pinocchio and the People's Seven Dwarfs.

"I beg you, comrades. Couldn't I have one last meeting with Nikola?"

The ministers marched out.

I found a second hot-water bottle under my blanket in the morning. Ah, I had a host of godmothers now. The little ministers of Matignon.

My truck was waiting for me on the rue de Varenne. But Pinocchio decided to perform without his truck. I waltzed down to the avenue de Suffren in my pajamas and coonskin cap. It was consoling to have the Eiffel Tower in back of my neck like a big iron brother that could mark the centuries for our Bulgarian regime.

I danced behind the École Militaire.

Must have been emaciated that morning, because when I doffed my cap in the middle of the dance, children socked coins into it and said, "Pauvre Pinocchio."

Did I look like a victim of the bauxite mines? None of the victims ever came back.

I sang about the importance of the Pecos to a Texan like me. But I couldn't gather in much of a crowd. Was it a Bulgarian feast day?

A Chrysler had come to see me dance. That bloody wagon parked an inch from my toes. The door opened and I got into the car with the acting inspector general of Sofia West. I turned foxy on the son of a bitch and waited for him to bring up Merci-Gâteau. But I caught Nikola in a quiet mood. He was plump and dark as a Tatar Jew. He handed me an envelope with a check inside. A hundred thousand Texas dollars endorsed by the Panhandle Shirt Company of Amarillo and Sofia West.

"So you shouldn't lose your clinic," he said, without looking at the People's puppet.

"I don't understand. Who is Panhandle Shirts?"

"We have to launder our money, like other countries. Otherwise you'd be taxed as an agent of Bulgaria, and you'd have to take the money out a nickel at a time."

I didn't even mention Solange. I talked about that other convict, Edgar Copernicus.

"Nikola, promise me that Edgar won't meet with an accident after I'm gone."

"No harm will come to the little cousin."

He got out at the People's airport and took me through all the lines as I muttered to myself, *Merci-Gâteau.* He accompanied me aboard the People's flying boxcar and blew his nose.

"Please," I shouted. "Solange doesn't belong in a conciergerie with blue nuns. She's only the least bit antisocial . . ."

He whispered at me with his Tatar eyes. "I'll drown her like a kitten if you don't forget her name."

That's how the People said goodbye in French Bulgaria. Nikola got off the plane, and it began to swarm with Bulgars, businessmen, and blue nuns. The little sweethearts had brought me a gift. Gâteau.

Who could fathom Bulgarian justice?

She had the seat next to Pinocchio. I didn't dare clasp her hand until the boxcar bumped up off the ground. Tried not to blubber too much.

"Always crying," she said. "That's how God made men."

"But Solange, he set you free."

"You have it wrong, mon coco. He sentenced me to Texas."

Nikola had monkeyed us, all right. He'd pronounced an *interdit de séjour* upon Solange's head. She was prohibited from entering Paris again while the city was part of Bulgaria. And she was listed as an "undesirable" in the international code book police chiefs loved to pass around. Nikola had given her a print-out of the listing.

- MERCI-GATEAU, SOLANGE
- AKA MADAME PINOCCHIO
- EXACT DATE OF BIRTH UNKNOWN
- ALLIED TO CORRUPT CAUSES SINCE 1991
- EDITOR OF ANARCHIST JOURNALS IN BRUSSELS, PARIS, AND NEW YORK
- ACTED AS AGENT PROVOCATEUR ON FRENCH BULGARIAN SOIL
- HELD IN SECLUSION AT THE CONCIERGERIE OF THE CAPUCINES SINCE SEPTEMBER 6, 2017
- RELEASED IN CUSTODY OF COPERNICUS CHARYN, AKA PINOCCHIO, AND DEPORTED TO THE REPUBLIC OF TEXAS, OCTOBER 17

It was like a modern novel with its own stark form and clarity of detail, but why should I care about a print-out? Solange was with me. And the Pecos Infirmary was out of the pawnshop, thanks to Nikola and Panhandle Shirts.

Pinocchio Pecos decided to stop being a bloody child. I ran for the senate and won, with Solange heading up my campaign. She was ferocious with the opposition, called everybody a weakling and a liar.

We rented a small house on Old Pecan Street. We weren't rich, but I had a paycheck from the Republic of Texas. I'd go about the country visiting schools as a member of the education committee. Children would nod and smile from their desks.

"That's Senator Pinocchio."

I blubbered into a handkerchief. It was great being the grand old man of the republic. No senator would risk interfering with my free-lunch program. The children had boots and bananas and archery equipment.

I took Cervantes and Melville off the country's forbidden reading list. I lectured on George Mills at Lone Star U. The proctors clapped.

Had a surprise package when I got home to Pecan Street. A plucked bird stood outside on the doorstep. I'd have sworn it was Pedersen's ghost, but this kid had the Copernicus complexion. It was my cousin with a shaved skull. Edgar had come out of the gulag.

I hugged him where he stood.

"Don't look so happy," he said. "Nikola is trying to influence the Texas senate by giving me to you."

And then he smiled. I brought him into the house. Solange had never seen the kid. But she took to Edgar, prepared chicken Kiev from her recipe book. Ah, it was the land of charlotte russes wherever you go.

"Cousin," that convict said, tearing into the chicken Kiev. "Will it be all right?"

"Yes."

"Romey, are you sure we'll survive in Texas? How can you tell?"

I looked at the kid and my wife and added paprika.

Pinocchio knows.